POPULAR MUSIC

D1521147

The Popular Music Series

Popular Music, 1920-1979 is a revised cumulation of and supersedes Volumes 1 through 8 of the *Popular Music* series, all of which are still in print:

Volume 1, 2nd ed., 1950-59   Volume 5, 1920-29
Volume 2, 1940-49   Volume 6, 1965-69
Volume 3, 1960-64   Volume 7, 1970-74
Volume 4, 1930-39   Volume 8, 1975-79

Published 1986:

Volume 9, 1980-1984

Other Books by Bruce Pollock

In Their Own Words: Popular Songwriting, 1955-1974

The Face of Rock and Roll: Images of a Generation

When Rock Was Young: The Heyday of Top 40

When the Music Mattered: Rock in the 1960s

ISSN 0886-442X

VOLUME 9
1980-1984

POPULAR MUSIC

An Annotated Guide to American Popular Songs,
Including Introductory Essay, Lyricists and Composers
Index, Important Performances Index, Chronological
Index, Awards Index, and List of Publishers

BRUCE POLLOCK,
Editor

GALE RESEARCH COMPANY
BOOK TOWER ● *DETROIT, MICHIGAN 48226*

Bruce Pollock, *Editor*
Thomas M. Bachmann, *Assistant Editor*

Mary Beth Trimper, *Production Supervisor*
Dorothy Kalleberg, *Senior Production Associate*
Arthur Chartow, *Art Director*

Dennis LaBeau, *Editorial Data Systems Director*
Theresa Rocklin, *Program Design*
Doris D. Goulart, *Editorial Data Entry Supervisor*
Jean Hinman Portfolio, *Editorial Data Entry Associate*
Sue Lynch, Mildred Sherman, Joyce M. Stone,
Anna Marie Woolard, *Senior Data Entry Assistants*
Cindy Pragid, Patricia Smith, *Data Entry Assistants*

Frederick G. Ruffner, *Publisher*
Dedria Bryfonski, *Editorial Director*
Ellen T. Crowley, *Director, Indexes and Dictionaries Division*
Linda S. Hubbard, *Senior Editor, Popular Music series*

Library of Congress Cataloging-in-Publication Data

(Revised for vol. 9)

Shapiro, Nat.
    Popular music; an annotated index of American
popular songs.

    Vols. by Bruce Pollock.
    Vols. published by Gale Research Co., Detroit,
Mich.
    Includes indexes.
    Contents: v. 1. 1950-59.—v. 2. 1940-49.—[etc.]—v. 9.
1980-1984.
    1. Music, Popular (Songs, etc.)—United States—
Bibliography. I. Pollock, Bruce. II. Title.
ML120.U5S5   784.5'00973   64-23761
ISBN 0-8103-0848-7(v.9)

Computerized photocomposition by
Automatech Graphics
New York, New York

Printed in the United States of America

Contents

Acknowledgments

A book as complete and exhaustive as this volume is not put together without the aid of many hands. Indispensable once again, as they've been throughout the compilation of these works, were Nancy Rosenthal of ASCAP and Al Feilich of BMI and their respective Index Departments. Thanks are also given to Margaret Mary Missar of the Washington D.C. office of Gale Research Company and Ed Konick and the offices of Charlton Publications for their efforts to aid in my copyright searches. Peerless assistance was also provided by those listed on the copyright page of this book, most especially the entirely competent and absolutely efficient Linda Hubbard. No acknowledgment would be complete, however, without a special and heartfelt nod to my loyal and outstanding staff member, Marie A. Cruz, who faced down massive amounts of paperwork without blinking and crushed many a pencil into submission in the service of this project.

About the Book and How to Use It

This volume is the ninth of a series whose aim is to set down in permanent and practical form a selective, annotated list of the significant popular songs of our times. Other indexes of popular music have either dealt with special areas, such as jazz or theater and film music, or been concerned chiefly with songs that achieved a degree of popularity as measured by the music-business trade indicators, which vary widely in reliability.

Convenient Alphabetical Arrangement, New Chronological Index

The first eight volumes in the *Popular Music* series (identified opposite the title page in this volume) presented the song listings arranged under the year of original copyright. Users had to consult the Title Index to determine where a song could be found, since a song associated with a given year was, in many cases, written a year or more earlier. When the Gale Research Company published a revised cumulation of those original volumes under the title *Popular Music, 1920-1979,* the songs were presented in a more convenient alphabetical sequence. Volume 9 of *Popular Music* follows this new format, but also includes a Chronological Index. Thus readers can go directly to the citation for the song they want, but can follow songwriting trends by consulting the year-by-year index. The Chronological Index lists songs registered for copyright between 1980 and 1984 under the year of registration; songs with earlier copyright dates are listed under the year in which they were important.

Other New Indexes Provide Additional Access

In addition to the new Chronological Index mentioned above, three other indexes make the valuable information in the song listings even more accessible to users. The Lyricists & Composers Index shows all the songs represented in *Popular Music,* 1980-1984, that are credited to a given individual. The Important Performances Index (introduced in *Popular Music, 1920-1979)* tells at a glance what albums, musicals, films, television shows, or other media featured songs that are represented in the volume. The index is arranged by broad media

About the Book and How to Use It

category, then alphabetically by the show or album title, with the songs listed under each title. Finally, the Awards Index (also introduced in the 1920-1979 revised cumulation) provides a year-by-year list of the songs nominated for awards by the American Academy of Motion Picture Arts and Sciences (Academy Award) and the American Academy of Recording Arts and Sciences (Grammy Award). Winning songs are indicated by asterisks.

List of Publishers

The List of Publishers is an alphabetically arranged directory providing performing rights affiliation (ASCAP, BMI, or SESAC) and addresses for the publishers of the songs represented in this ninth volume of *Popular Music.*

Tracking Down Information on Songs

Unfortunately, the basic records kept by the active participants in the music business are often casual, inaccurate, and transitory. There is no single source of comprehensive information about popular songs, and those sources that do exist do not publish complete material about even the musical works with which they are directly concerned. Two of the primary proprietors of basic information about our popular music are the major performing rights societies—the American Society of Composers, Authors, and Publishers (ASCAP) and Broadcast Music, Inc. (BMI). Although each of these organizations has considerable information about the songs of its own writer and publisher members and has also issued indexes of its own songs, their files and published indexes are designed primarily for clearance identification by the commercial users of music. Their publications of annual or periodic lists of their "hits" necessarily include only a small fraction of their songs, and the facts given about these are also limited. Both ASCAP and BMI are, however, invaluable and indispensable sources of data about popular music. It is just that their data and special knowledge are not readily accessible to the researcher.

Another basic source of information about musical compositions and their creators and publishers is the *Catalog of Copyright Entries* issued by the Copyright Office of the Library of Congress. Each year, two massive volumes are published by the Copyright Office, listing each published, unpublished, republished, and renewed copyright of songs registered with the Office. While these volumes are helpful in determining the precise date of the declaration of the original ownership of musical works, they contain no other information, are unwieldy, and, lacking a unified index, difficult to use. To complicate matters further, some authors, composers, and publishers have been known to employ

10

rather makeshift methods of protecting their works legally, and there are a number of songs listed in *Popular Music* that are not to be found in the Library of Congress files.

Selection Criteria

In preparing this series, the editor was faced with a number of separate problems. The first and most important of these was that of selection. The stated aim of the project—to offer the user as comprehensive and accurate a listing of significant popular songs as possible—has been the guiding criterion. The purpose has never been to offer a judgment on the quality of any songs or to indulge a prejudice for or against any type of popular music. Rather, it is the purpose of *Popular Music* to document those musical works that (1) achieved a substantial degree of popular acceptance, (2) were exposed to the public in especially notable circumstances, or (3) were accepted and given important performances by influential musical and dramatic artists.

Another problem was whether or not to classify the songs as to type. The first half of the 1980's was characterized by a continuation of the integration of several divergent streams of creative musical activity— country songs, rhythm 'n' blues, folk music, and jazz and new permutations and combinations of styles. (These significant developments are discussed in the introductory essays covering the 1960's and 1970's in *Popular Music, 1920-1979).* Under these circumstances, it seemed arbitrary and misleading to label a given song as "rhythm 'n' blues," "country," "folk," or "jazz." Most works of music are subject to any number of interpretations and, although it is possible to describe a particular performance, it is more difficult to give a musical composition a label applicable not only to its origin but to its subsequent musical history. In fact, the most significant versions of some songs are often quite at variance with their origins. It is believed, however, that the information in *Popular Music* for such songs indicates the important facts about not only their origins but also their subsequent lives.

Research Sources

The principal sources of information for the titles, authors, composers, publishers, and dates of copyright of the songs in this volume were the Copyright Office of the Library of Congress, ASCAP, BMI, and individual writers and publishers. Data about best-selling recordings were obtained principally from two of the leading music business trade journals—*Billboard* and *Cash Box.* For the historical notes; information about foreign, folk, public domain, and classical origins; and identification of theatrical, film, and television introducers of songs, the editor relied upon his own and the New York and Bridgeport,

Connecticut, public libraries' collections of record album notes, theater programs, sheet music, newspaper and magazine articles, and other material.

Contents of a Typical Entry

The primary listing for a song includes

- Title and alternate title(s)
- Country of origin (for non-U.S. songs)
- Author(s) and composer(s)
- Current publisher, copyright date
- Annotation on the song's origins or performance history

Title: The full title and alternate title or titles are given exactly as they appear on the Library of Congress copyright card or, in some cases, the sheet music. Since even a casual perusal of the book reveals considerable variation in spelling and punctuation, it should be noted that these are neither editorial nor typographical errors but the colloquialisms of the music trade. The title of a given song as it appears in this series is, in almost all instances, the one under which it is legally registered.

Foreign Origin: If the song is of foreign origin, the primary listing indicates the country of origin after the title. Additional information may be noted, such as the original title, copyright date, writer, publisher in country of origin, or other facts about the adaptation.

Authorship: In all cases, the primary listing reports the author or authors and the composer or composers. The reader may find variations in the spelling of a songwriter's name. This results from the fact that some writers used different forms of their names at different times or in connection with different songs. These variants appear in the Lyricists & Composers Index as well. In addition to this kind of variation in the spelling of writers' names, the reader will also notice that in some cases, where the writer is also the performer, the name as a writer may differ from the form of the name used as a performer.

Publisher: The current publisher is listed. Since *Popular Music* is designed as a practical reference work rather than an academic study, and since copyrights more than occasionally change hands, the current publisher is given instead of the original holder of the copyright. If a publisher has, for some reason, copyrighted a song more than once, the years of the significant copyright subsequent to the year of the original copyright are also listed after the publisher's name.

Annotation: The primary listing mentions also the musical, film, or other production in which the song was introduced or featured and, where important, by whom it was introduced in the case of theater and film songs; any other performers identified with the song; first or best-selling recordings, indicating the performer and the record company; awards and other relevant data. The name of a performer may be listed differently in connection with different songs, especially over a period of years. The name listed is the form of the name given in connection with a particular performance or record. It should be noted that the designation "best-selling record" does not mean that the record was a "hit." It means simply that the record or records noted as "best-selling" were the best-selling record or records of that particular song, in comparison with the sales of other records of the same song. Dates are provided for important recordings and performances.

Cross-References

Any alternate titles appearing in bold type after the main title in a primary listing are also cross-referenced in the song listings.

Popular Music 1980-1984

When last considered in these pages, popular music offered indications that diversity, creativity, "a cross-cultural renaissance of form and feeling" lay just around the bend, perhaps to become evident sometime around 1986. That target date now seems but a hopeful, if not entirely unfounded, projection. The recent arrival of such joyful hybrids as the Bangles, the Hooters, R.E.M., the Three O'Clock, Cyndi Lauper, Prince, Suzanne Vega, Ferron, Claudia Schmidt, The Eurythmics, and Tears for Fears, recalls the folk/pop literacy that infused the mid-sixties to mid-seventies period with so much style and energy, briefly fueling fantasies of a new and improved sensibility of the masses—heart, soul, beat, and lyrics united in a common drive for meaning, mystery, and movement. But, as if to take the wind out of even this relatively mild heroic squall, one must take note of the overwhelming dominance (enough, in fact, virtually to define the period) of pop music's heretofore untapped visual element.

Since its advent in the summer of 1981, a cable network called MTV (Music Television), using short, filmed presentations of the latest Top 40 contenders, has changed the nature of pop music, giving it a face, legs, and dozens upon dozens of dancing feet. By removing the song from the purely aural, MTV has both enhanced and diluted the tradition. It has taken mere superstars and, with constant TV exposure and an endless variety of seductive poses, turned them into demigods (Michael Jackson, Bruce Springsteen). It has transformed successful albums into long-playing TV series, as works by Huey Lewis & The News, Z.Z. Top, Van Halen, Billy Joel, Tina Turner, and others secured renewal well beyond the usual hit song or two, producing on the average three or four singles—and videos—per LP. MTV took colorful newcomers who were gifted with the savvy and intuition to master the new rules and made them into overnight role models (Madonna, Cyndi Lauper, Boy George & Culture Club, Prince, Duran Duran).

Music videos did not exclude the many aging worthies who had performed their services to pop music song after song and yet remained unheard on radio. Unlike the Mickey Mantles and Joltin' Joe DiMaggios of yore, who could only sigh when commenting on the seven-figure contracts of today's ballplayers, pop's veterans capitalized on the new exposure to lengthen shadowy careers, in some cases exploding beyond their youthful prominence. (Examples include Tina Turner, Rod Stewart, David Bowie, John Fogerty, Olivia Newton-John, Paul McCartney, and Elton John). Black performers, however, benefitted somewhat less than their contemporaries through MTV exposure. While Lionel Richie, Michael Jackson, Prince, Donna Summer, and the Pointer Sisters made strong moves toward the mainstream (and their own variety shows someday), rhythm 'n' blues was not a priority on the videoized rock 'n' pop mix. In the movies, on network television, and on Broadway, however, the Motown sound of the Supremes, the Temptations, Smokey Robinson, and the Four Tops experienced a creative coming of age, as demonstrated with the soundtrack to *The Big Chill,* the *Motown 25th Anniversary Special,* and *Dreamgirls.*

As with the small screen, so with the large. During the 1980-1984 period there were at least forty songs from movies that occupied slots in the Top 10 of their respective years. Many movies, in fact, were little more than excuses for soundtrack albums featuring material of varying quality from big-name acts. Other movies seemed to be nothing more than elaborate and elongated soundtrack albums themselves. As in the preceding five years, rock stars, now even more primed by their experience romping through the mini-movies of the MTV realm, jumped to the silver screen much as sports stars were moving from the field to the broadcast booth, and with results that were just as erratic (Rick Springfield in *Hard to Hold,* Dolly Parton in *9 to 5,* Olivia Newton-John in *Xanadu,* Bette Midler in *The Rose,* Willie Nelson in *Honeysuckle Rose,* Debbie Harry in *Videodrome,* and Neil Diamond in *The Jazz Singer).* The songs themselves generally fared better, with tunes like "Fame," "Up Where We Belong," "Eye of the Tiger," "Chariots of Fire," "It's My Turn," "Arthur's Theme," "I Just Called to Say I Love You," and "The Rose" offering a better showcase than much of the acting on the screen. And, lest we forget, among his other accomplishments of the period, Michael Jackson made a short movie of his song "Thriller" and sold many copies of it on video cassette. Jackson's *Thriller* album, in addition to producing a record seven Top 10 singles ("Beat It," "Billie Jean," "Human Nature," "PYT," "Thriller," "The Girl Is Mine," and "Wanna Be Startin' Something"), also went on to become the largest-selling album of all time (aided and abetted, of course, by constant MTV exposure).

With such imposing media guns falling in behind the mere song, equipping it and adorning it with technical values far beyond simple words and music, it is not surprising that a discussion of the period's song output should take such a backseat to matters of image and exposure, technical expertise, and abject self-promotion. These issues all but obliterated the distinctions among singer, song, and medium. If such accoutrements as setting and scene, script and stage lighting are stripped away, to our dismay (but not quite utter shock) we find a collection of love songs as undistinguished as any produced in the preceding five-year period. Unrelentingly one-track minded, the song-writers of the era, either by professional choice or inherent creative limitations (of themselves or of the general listening populace), neither strayed too far from the norm nor caused that norm to expand in any direction. Much more creative than the songwriters of the period, for the most part, were the video directors, who had to take yet another forlorn or boasting, repentant or repulsive lyric about love and cast it, dress it up, provide it with special effects, run it through its paces, stage it, edit it, and present it to the public grossly underbudgeted and short of time. That so many of these videos were trite only reflects their source, the song. And while there may be an underground in the video realm, just as there is one in the aural realm, its work, at least through most of the period, not only failed to create an impact strong enough to ripple the status quo, but seemed, on cursory inspection, mired in traps and tricks that were in circulation back in 1961 (the Talking Heads, Laurie Anderson, and other such performance artists notwithstanding).

So, from 1980-1982, at least, stagnancy reigned. If the musical underground was fertile, few significant tendrils were pushing up through the earth for the starving fan. "Another Brick in the Wall" in 1980 offered ominous signs of impending rebellion, but the prepon-derance of airless drivel from the lips of Kenny Rogers, Christopher Cross, and Air Supply was enough to suffocate the remaining diehards. "All Out of Love," "Sailing," "Do That to Me One More Time," "Lady," "Lost in Love," and "Real Love" may have made the plight of wedding bands a bit easier, but provided no indication of the pop singer's power to revitalize a moment, if not an entire generation. "Tired of Toein' the Line" had some nifty rockabilly defiance; "Brass in Pocket" introduced Chrissie Hynde's sassy style to the world; "Whip It" brought to the masses the zany Devo program for salvation. The Clash, long an underground favorite, received partial due with "Train in Vain (Stand by Me)." John Lennon's return to recording with "Just Like Starting Over" was the year's biggest heartwarming story, even if the song itself was far outweighed by the sentiment.

1981 was a year cut from the same cloth. Not even the death of John Lennon could arouse our slumbering songwriters, although Lennon's former colleagues did manage to put something down on paper. George Harrison wrote "All Those Years Ago," Paul McCartney contributed "Here Today," and New York neighbor Paul Simon gave us "The Late Great Johnny Ace." In the meantime, one of the best novels of the post-War era, *Endless Love* by Scott Spencer, was being turned into a trivial movie, sporting a trivial pop theme, scripted by Lionel Richie, whose penchant for lush love songs made him the era's Paul McCartney.

Love was in the air, it was safe to say, for the entire year; not a disparaging or thought-provoking word was uttered in song. "Jessie's Girl" had a certain intensity; "Kiss on My List" captured a feeling that the duo of Hall and Oates would hang onto for the better part of the period. A trace of poignancy could be found in the quivering carcasses of "Same Old Lang Syne," "Hey Nineteen," "Hearts," and "Don't Stand So Close to Me." Often cited as the next Lennon and McCartney, the team of Difford and Tilbrook made their first appearance on the charts with "Tempted," a rather wordy but totally charming departure from the slickness otherwise prevailing.

The drought continued into another year, with 1982 offering a number one status to such warhorses as Chicago, Steve Miller, Paul McCartney and Stevie Wonder, the J. Geils Band, and Joe Cocker (in a duet with Jennifer Warnes). However, John Cougar's "Jack and Diane" was something of a documentary, "Always on My Mind" was genuinely moving, and "Key Largo" created pictures for the soul. Satire entered the scene for the first time in a long while with "Valley Girl," while social commentary started edging back into prominence, bolstered by the majesty of "Still in Saigon." Bruce Springsteen put Gary U.S. Bonds back to work with "Out of Work," launching his own one-man crusade as the king of the blue collar poets. "Pressure," "Under Pressure," "Spirits in the Material World," "Kids in America," and Prince's "1999" all gave indications that pop music might at least be coming to grips with a purpose higher than the elemental desires.

However, before such a great leap beyond could be taken, all the elements of the period would come together into a yearlong showcase. Thus, 1983 gave us movie music ("Flashdance . . . What a Feeling," "Maniac," "It Might Be You") and image-drenched MTV productions ("Total Eclipse of the Heart," "Beat It," "Do You Really Want to Hurt Me," "Hungry Like the Wolf," "All Night Long (All Night)," "Goody Two Shoes"). There was a bit of social commentary ("Undercover of the Night," "Allentown," "New Year's Day," "Rock the Casbah") and a number of significant comeback songs ("Let's Dance," "Say Say Say," "Sexual Healing," "Come Dancing"). The English techno sound, otherwise known as the New Wave, crested on the shores of hitsville ("I Ran," "Sweet Dreams (Are Made of These)," "One Thing Leads to Another," "She Blinded Me with Science"). American superstars-in-waiting garnered precious airtime ("Heart and Soul," "Uptown Girl," "Stand Back," "Little Red Corvette"). But perhaps the largest crack in complacency was made mid-year by a little band out of Georgia by the name of R.E.M. with a song called "Radio Free Europe." Beyond the simplicity of the group's instrumentation and their utter lack of television image, the symbolism of the song's title could not be ignored. R.E.M. was a little slash in the curtain hanging over pop radio. This slight tear would not perceptibly widen throughout 1983, although bands like Big Country ("In a Big Country"), U2 ("New Year's Day"), the Pretenders ("Back on the Chain Gang"), Tears for Fears ("Change"), Scandal ("Love's Got a Line on You"), and Talking Heads ("Burning Down the House") produced sounds that were as fresh as anything heard on the air since the mid-seventies.

In 1984 Bruce Springsteen personally ushered in several millenniums of popular music with one album, a yearlong tour, and the mandatory accompanying video performances. Songs like "Born in the U.S.A.," "Glory Days," "No Surrender," and "My Home Town" simultaneously resurrected the singer-songwriter as a viable entity (casting new, favorable light on contemporaries like Billy Joel, John Cougar, and Bryan Adams, and even on an abject imitator like John Cafferty) and presented Springsteen as the working-class poet, ushering in with patriotic zeal a year of American-made rock 'n' roll unequalled since the pre-Beatles heyday of the Brill Building. Performers included Huey Lewis from San Francisco, the Cars from Boston, Cyndi Lauper from New York, Madonna from Detroit, Georgia's R.E.M., and the Bangles from Los Angeles. Springsteen's songs once again fused rock energy to folk sensibilities and caught the ears of an underground ready to surface in the works of Los Lobos, The Replacements, Husker Du, and Suzanne Vega. As a result, 1984 ended on a reaffirmation of pop's best qualities, produced by a healthy crop of newcomers. And if the deacons of the songwriter elite, Bob Dylan, Joni Mitchell, Jackson Browne, Laura Nyro, Leonard Cohen, and Paul Simon, were relatively quiet, there were new voices to be heard in T-Bone Burnette, Chrissie Hynde, Sting, Richard Thompson, the resurgent Lou Reed, and Phil Collins.

Such optimism could be carried forward into the world of musical theater, but with certain reservations. Although the period sported its share of big winners *(Cats, Dreamgirls, La Cage au Folles, Nine, Little Shop of Horrors, Pump Boys and Dinettes, Sunday in the Park with George)*, 1984 was virtually bereft of noteworthy contenders for the longevity title of *A Chorus Line*. Some big songs emanated from these shows, among them "Memory," "I Am What I Am," "And I Am Telling You I'm Not Going." Andrew Lloyd Webber established himself as the heir apparent to Stephen Sondheim in productivity if not in talent. William Finn made strides toward greater recognition with *In Trousers* and *March of the Falsettos*. Craig Carnelia garnered solid notices for his talent, even if his *Is There Life after High School* failed to graduate into the black for its backers. Elizabeth Swados teamed with the political cartoonist Garry Trudeau for the mildly entertaining *Doonesbury,* while Kander and Ebb had much more success with *The Rink* for Liza Minnelli and *Woman of the Year* for Lauren Bacall. While Sondheim himself won a Pulitzer Prize for *Sunday in the Park with George,* perhaps the most interesting recognition was conferred upon Gary Portnoy and Judy Hart Angelo, authors of the score of the otherwise unheralded *Preppies,* who went on to compose the theme songs for two of television's more successful situation comedies, *Cheers* and *Punky Brewster.*

The 1980-1984 period was not especially revolutionary in the country or rhythm 'n' blues realms. The best of those breeds managed to mingle effortlessly with pop music—Randy Goodrum, Lionel Richie, Prince. At its best, country had its share of poignant if gin-soaked gems: "Wind Beneath My Wings," "Bottom of the Fifth," "Always on My Mind," "She Got the Goldmine (I Got the Shaft)." Rhythm 'n' blues, with the focus as usual on the rhythm, caught the street beat as ever in the form of "rap music," with Grandmaster Flash and Kurtis Blow pioneering the deejay's rhyming art and, in the case of "The Message" and "The Breaks," putting that beat into the service of some angry poetics. The re-release, then, of Gil Scott-Heron's best works on a single album took on new significance as, with the Last Poets, Scott-Heron could be termed a founder of Rap. At any rate, a listen to "The Revolution Will Not Be Televised" should be all you need to persuade you of its coiled power.

As the period ended, another significant song was released, holding much hope for 1985 as a year of idealism and purpose. Bob Geldof's "Do They Know It's Christmas" was recorded by a virtual royalty of English rock stars, the profits from the song to be donated to aid Ethiopian children. Once again, the power of the song was stepping forth, to shake the senses and move the world.

Bruce Pollock

POPULAR
MUSIC

A

Abracadabra
Words and music by Steve Miller.
Sailor Music, 1982.
Best-selling record by The Steve Miller Band (Capital, 82).

Ace in the Hole
Words and music by Paul Simon.
Paul Simon Music, 1980.
Introduced by Paul Simon on *One Trick Pony* (Warner Brothers, 80)
and in the film *One Trick Pony* (80).

Adult Education
Words and music by Daryl Hall, John Oates, and Sara Allen.
Fust Buzza Music, Inc., 1983/Hot Cha Music Co., 1983/Unichappell
Music Inc., 1983.
Best-selling record by Daryl Hall and John Oates (RCA, 84).

Affair of the Heart
Words and music by Rick Springfield, Blaise Tosti, and Danny Tate.
Vogue Music, 1983/Bibo Music Publishers, 1983.
Best-selling record by Rick Springfield (RCA, 83).

Africa
Words and music by David Paich and Jeffrey Porcaro.
Hudmar Publishing Co., Inc., 1983/Cowbella Music, 1983.
Best-selling record by Toto (Columbia, 82).

After All These Years
Words by Fred Ebb, music by John Kander.
Fiddleback Music Publishing Co., Inc., 1983/Kander & Ebb Inc.,
1983.
Introduced by Male Chorus in *The Rink* (84).

After the Fall
Words and music by Steve Perry and John Friga.

Twist & Shout Music, 1982.
Best-selling record by Journey (Columbia, 83).

Against All Odds (Take a Look at Me Now) (English)
Words and music by Phil Collins.
Golden Torch Music Corp., 1984/WB Music Corp., 1984.
Best-selling record by Phil Collins (Atlantic, 84). Introduced in *Against All Odds* (84). Nominated for an Academy Award, Best Song, 1984; a National Academy of Recording Arts and Sciences Award, Song of the Year, 1984.

Against the Wind
Words and music by Bob Seger.
Gear Publishing, 1980.
Best-selling record Bob Seger (Capitol, 80).

Ah, Men
Words and music by Will Holt.
Lemon Tree Music, Inc., 1981.
Introduced by Company of *Ah, Men* (81).

Ai No Corrida (English)
Words and music by Chaz Jankel and Kenny Young.
Lazy Lizard Music, 1980/HG Music, Inc., 1980.
Best-selling record by Quincy Jones (A&M, 81). Nominated for a National Academy of Recording Arts and Sciences Award, Rhythm 'n' Blues Song of the Year, 1981.

Ain't Even Done with the Night
Words and music by John Cougar Mellencamp.
HG Music, Inc., 1980.
Best-selling record by John Cougar (Riva, 81).

Ain't Nobody
Words and music by David Wolinski.
Overdue Music, 1983.
Best-selling record by Rufus with Chaka Khan (Warner Brothers, 83).
Nominated for a National Academy of Recording Arts and Sciences Award, Rhythm 'n' Blues Song of the Year, 1983.

All American Girls
Words and music by Narada Michael Walden, Lisa Walden, Allee Willis, and Joni Sledge.
Walden Music, Inc., 1981/Gratitude Sky Music, Inc., 1981/Irving Music Inc., 1981/Kejoc Music, 1981/Baby Shoes Music, 1981.
Best-selling record by Sister Sledge (Atlantic, 81).

All I Have to Do Is Dream
Revived by Andy Gibb and Victoria Principal (Polygram, 81).See *Popular Music, 1920-1979.*

All I Need
Words and music by Clifton Magness, Glen Ballard, and David Robert Pack.
Yellow Brick Road Music, 1984/MCA, Inc., 1984/Art Street Music, 1984.
Best-selling record by Jack Wagner (Warner Brothers, 84).

All I Need to Know (Don't Know Much)
Words by Cynthia Weil and Tom Snow, music by Tom Snow and Barry Mann.
ATV Music Corp., 1980/Mann & Weil Songs Inc., 1980/Braintree Music, 1980/Snow Music, 1980.
Introduced by Bill Medley (Liberty, 81). Best-selling record by Bette Midler (Atlantic, 83).

All I Want
Words and music by Zack Smith, Patty Smyth, and Benji King.
Blackwood Music Inc., 1984.
Introduced by Scandal on *Warrior* (Columbia, 84).

All My Rowdy Friends (Have Settled Down)
Words and music by Hank Williams, Jr.
Bocephus Music Inc., 1981.
Best-selling record by Hank Williams, Jr. (Elektra, 81).

All My Rowdy Friends Are Coming Over Tonight
Words and music by Hank Williams, Jr.
Bocephus Music Inc., 1984.
Best-selling record by Hank Williams, Jr. Nominated for a National Academy of Recording Arts and Sciences Award, Country Song of the Year, 1984.

All Night Long
Words and music by Joe Walsh.
Wow and Flutter Music Publishing, 1980.
Best-selling record by Joe Walsh (Full Moon, 80).

All Night Long (All Night)
Words and music by Lionel Richie.
Brockman Enterprises Inc., 1983.
Best-selling record by Lionel Richie (Motown, 83). Nominated for National Academy of Recording Arts and Sciences Awards, Song of the Year, 1983, and Record of the Year, 1983.

All of You (Spanish-American)
English words by Cynthia Weil, music by Tony Renis and Julio
   Iglesias.
Elettra Music, 1984/Ewald Corp., 1984/Dyad Music, Ltd., 1984/
   Braintree Music, 1984.
Best-selling record by Julio Iglesias and Diana Ross (Columbia, 84).

All out of Love (Australian)
Words and music by Graham Russell.
Arista Music, Inc., 1980.
Best-selling record by Air Supply (Arista, 80).

All over the World (English)
Words and music by Jeff Lynne.
Blackwood Music Inc., 1980.
Best-selling record by ELO (MCA, 80).

All Right
Words and music by Christopher Cross.
Another Page, 1983.
Best-selling record by Christopher Cross (Warner Brothers, 83).

All the Children in a Row
Words by Fred Ebb, music by John Kander.
Fiddleback Music Publishing Co., Inc., 1983/Kander & Ebb Inc.,
   1983.
Introduced by Liza Minnelli in *The Rink* (84).

All the Right Moves
Words and music by Tom Snow and Barry Alfonso.
WB Music Corp., 1983/Sprocket Music, Inc., 1983/Warner-
   Tamerlane Publishing Corp., 1983/Rewind Music, Inc., 1983.
Best-selling record by Jennifer Warnes and Chris Thompson (Casa-
   blanca, 83). Introduced in the film *All the Right Moves* (83).

All This Love
Words and music by Eldra DeBarge.
Jobete Music Co., Inc., 1982.
Best-selling record by DeBarge (Gordy, 83).

All Those Years Ago (English)
Words and music by George Harrison.
Zero Productions, 1981.
Best-selling record by George Harrison (Dark Horse, 81). Written as a
   tribute to John Lennon.

All Through the Night
Words and music by Jules Shear.

Juters Publishing Co., 1982.
Best-selling record by Cyndi Lauper (Portrait, 84).

All Time High (English)
Words by Tim Rice, music by John Barry.
Blackwood Music Inc., 1983/United Lion Music Inc.
Introduced by Rita Coolidge in *Octopussy* (83).

Allentown
Words and music by Billy Joel.
Joelsongs, 1981.
Best-selling record by Billy Joel (Columbia, 83).

Allergies
Words and music by Paul Simon.
Paul Simon Music, 1981.
Best-selling record by Paul Simon (Warner Brothers, 83).

Almost Paradise. . .Love Theme from *Footloose*
Words by Dean Pitchford, music by Eric Carmen.
Ensign Music Corp., 1984.
Best-selling record by Mike Reno and Ann Wilson (Columbia, 84).
  Introduced in the film *Footloose* (84).

Almost Saturday Night
Best-selling record by Dave Edmunds (Swan Song, 81). See *Popular Music, 1920-1979.*

Always on My Mind
Words and music by Johnny Christopher, Wayne Thompson, and
  Mark James.
Screen Gems-EMI Music Inc., 1971/Rose Bridge Music Inc.
Best-selling record by Willie Nelson (Columbia, 82). Nominated for a
  National Academy of Recording Arts and Sciences Award, Record of
  the Year, 1982. Won National Academy of Recording Arts and
  Sciences Awards, Song of the Year, 1982, and Country Song of the
  Year, 1982.

Always Something There to Remind Me
Revived by Naked Eyes (EMI-America, 83). See *Popular Music, 1920-79.*

America
Words and music by Neil Diamond.
Stonebridge Music, 1980.
Best-selling record by Neil Diamond (Capitol, 81). Introduced in the
  film *The Jazz Singer.*

American Heartbeat
Words and music by Frank Sullivan and Jim Peterik.
Holy Moley Music, 1982/Rude Music, 1982/WB Music Corp., 1982/
   Easy Action Music, 1982.
Best-selling record by Survivor (Scotti Brothers, 82).

American Made
Words and music by Robert Dipiero and Patrick McManus.
Music City Music Inc., 1982/Combine Music Corp., 1982.
Best-selling record by The Oak Ridge Boys (MCA, 83).

American Music
Words and music by Parker McGee.
Ensign Music Corp., 1982.
Best-selling record by The Pointer Sisters (Planet, 82).

Amnesia and Jealousy (Oh Lana)
Words and music by T-Bone Burnette and Larry Poons.
Black Tent Music, 1983.
Performed by T-Bone Burnette in *Attack of the Killer B's* (Warner
   Brothers, 83).

And I Am Telling You I'm Not Going
Words by Tom Eyen, music by Henry Krieger.
Dreamgirls Music, 1981/Dreamette's Music, 1981/Tom Eyen's
   Publishing Co., 1981.
Best-selling record by Jennifer Holliday (Geffen, 82). Introduced by
   Jennifer Holliday in *Dreamgirls* (82).

And the Beat Goes On
Words and music by Leon Sylvers, Stephen Shockley, and William
   B. Shelby.
Spectrum VII, 1980/Rosy Publishing Inc., 1980.
Best-selling record by The Whispers (Solar, 80).

And The Cradle Will Rock
Words and music by Eddie Van Halen, David Lee Roth, Alex Van
   Halen, and Michael Anthony.
Van Halen Music, 1980.
Best-selling record by Van Halen (Warner Brothers, 80).

Angel Flying Too Close to the Ground
Words and music by Willie Nelson.
Willie Nelson Music Inc., 1979.
Best-selling record by Willie Nelson (Columbia, 81).

Angel in Blue
Words and music by Seth Justman.

Center City Music, 1981/Pal-Park Music, 1981.
Best-selling record by The J. Geils Band (EMI-America, 82).

Angel in Disguise
Words and music by Earl Thomas Conley and Randy Lynn Scruggs.
April Music, Inc., 1983/Blackwood Music Inc., 1983/Full Armor
    Publishing Co., 1983.
Best-selling record by Earl Thomas Conley (RCA, 84).

Angel of the Morning
Revived by Juice Newton (Capitol, 81). See *Popular Music, 1920-79.*

Another Brick in the Wall
Best-selling record by Pink Floyd (Columbia, 80). See *Popular Music,
    1920-1979.*

Another Honky Tonk Night on Broadway
Words and music by Milton L. Brown, Stephen H. Dorff, and Snuff
    Garrett.
Peso Music, 1982/Wallet Music, 1982.
Best-selling record by David Frizzell & Shelly West (Warner/Viva, 82).

Another One Bites the Dust (English)
Words and music by John Deacon.
Queen Music Ltd., 1980.
Best-selling record by Queen (Elektra, 80).

Another Sleepless Night
Words and music by Charlie Black and Rory Bourke.
Chappell & Co., Inc., 1981.
Best-selling record by Anne Murray (Capitol, 82).

Another Tricky Day (English)
Words and music by Peter Townshend.
Towser Tunes Inc., 1981.
Introduced by The Who on *Face Dances* (Warner Brothers, 81).

Any Day Now
Revived by Ronnie Milsap (RCA, 82). See *Popular Music, 1920-79.*

Any Way You Want It
Best-selling record by Journey (Columbia, 80). See *Popular Music,
    1920-1979.*

Appalachian Memories
Words and music by Dolly Parton.
Velvet Apple Music, 1983.
Introduced by Dolly Parton on *Burlap and Satin* (RCA, 83).

Popular Music, 1980-1984

The Apple Doesn't Fall
Words and music by Fred Ebb, music by John Kander.
Fiddleback Music Publishing Co., Inc., 1983/Kander & Ebb Inc., 1983.
Introduced by Liza Minnelli and Chita Rivera in *The Rink* (84).

The Apple Stretching
Words and music by Melvin Van Peebles.
Yeah Inc., 1981.
Introduced by Melvin Van Peebles in *The Waltz of the Stork* (82).

Arc of a Diver (English)
Words and music by Steve Winwood and Vivian Stanshall.
Island Music, 1980/Alley Music, 1980.
Best-selling record by Steve Winwood (Island, 81).

Are the Good Times Really Over
Words and music by Merle Haggard.
Shade Tree Music Inc., 1980.
Best-selling record by Merle Haggard (Epic, 82).

Are We Ourselves (English)
Words and music by Cyril Curnin, James West-Oram, Dan K. Brown, and Adam Woods.
EMI Music Publishing, Ltd., London, England, 1984/Colgems-EMI Music Inc., 1984.
Best-selling record by The Fixx (MCA, 84).

Are You Happy Baby
Best-selling record by Dottie West (Liberty, 81). See *Popular Music, 1920-1979.*

Are You on the Road to Lovin' Me Again
Best-selling record by Debby Boone (Warner Brothers, 80). See *Popular Music, 1920-1979.*

Are You Single
Words and music by Stephen Washington, George Curtis Jones, Starleana Young, Philip Fields, and Jennifer Ivory.
Red Aurra Publishing, 1981/Lucky Three Music Publishing Co., 1981.
Best-selling record by Aurra (Salsoul, 81).

Arthur's Theme (The Best That You Can Do)
Words by Carole Bayer Sager, words and music by Christopher Cross and Peter Allen, music by Burt Bacharach.
WB Music Corp., 1981/Warner-Tamerlane Publishing Corp., 1981/ Pop 'N' Roll Music, 1981/New Hidden Valley Music Co., 1981.

Best-selling record by Christopher Cross (Warner Brothers, 81). Introduced in the film *Arthur* (81). Nominated for National Academy of Recording Arts and Sciences Awards, Song of the Year, 1981, and Record of the year, 1981. Won an Academy Award, Best Song, 1981.

As Long as I'm Rockin' with You
Words and music by Bruce Channel and Kieran Kane.
Old Friends Music, 1981/Cross Keys Publishing Co., Inc., 1981.
Best-selling record by John Conlee (MCA, 84).

Ashes to Ashes (English)
Words and music by David Bowie.
Fleur Music, 1980/Jones Music Co., 1980.
Introduced by David Bowie on *Scary Monsters* (RCA, 80).

Athena (English)
Words and music by Peter Townshend.
Towser Tunes Inc., 1982.
Best-selling record by The Who (Warner Brothers, 82).

Atlantic Blue
Words and music by Don Reid.
Statler Brothers Music, 1984.
Best-selling record by The Statler Brothers (Mercury, 84).

Atlantic City
Words and music by Bruce Springsteen.
Bruce Springsteen, 1982.
Introduced by Bruce Springsteen in *Nebraska* (Columbia, 82).

Atomic Dog
Words and music by George Clinton, Garry Shider, and David Spradley.
Bridgeport Music Inc., 1982.
Best-selling record by George Clinton (Capitol, 83).

The Authority Song
Words and music by John Cougar Mellencamp.
Riva Music Ltd., 1983.
Best-selling record by John Cougar Mellencamp (Riva, 84).

Automatic
Words and music by Brock Walsh and Mark Goldenberg.
Music Corp. of America, 1983/MCA, Inc., 1983.
Best-selling record by The Pointer Sisters (Planet, 84).

B

Babooshka (English)
Words and music by Kate Bush.
Kate Bush Music, Ltd., London, England, 1980/EMI Music
  Publishing, Ltd., London, England, 1980.
Introduced by by Kate Bush in *Never Forever* (EMI, 80).

Baby, Come to Me (English)
Words and music by Rod Temperton.
Almo Music Corp., 1981.
Best-selling record by Patti Austin and James Ingram (Qwest, 82).

Baby Fall Down
Words and music by T-Bone Burnette.
Arthur Buster Stahr Music, 1983.
Introduced by T-Bone Burnette on *Proof Through the Night* (Warner
  Brothers, 83).

(You're So Square) Baby, I Don't Care
Words and music by Jerry Leiber and Mike Stoller.
Gladys Music, 1957.
Best-selling record by Joni Mitchell (Geffen, 82).

Baby I Lied
Words and music by Deborah Allen, Rory Bourke, and Rafe Van
  Hoy.
Posey Publishing, 1982/Unichappell Music Inc., 1982/Van Hoy
  Music, 1982.
Best-selling record by Deborah Allen (RCA, 83). Nominated for a Na-
  tional Academy of Recording Arts and Sciences Award, Country
  Song of the Year, 1983.

Baby I'm Hooked (Right into Your Love)
Words and music by Cedric Martin and Van Ross Redding.
Carollon Music Co., 1983/Van Ross Redding Music, 1983.
Best-selling record by Con Funk Shun (Mercury, 83).

Baby Jane
Words and music by Rod Stewart and Jay Davis.
Rod Stewart, 1983/Anteater Music, 1983.
Best-selling record by Rod Stewart (Warner Brothers, 83).

Back in Black (English)
Words and music by Angus Young, Malcolm Young, and Brian
  Johnson.
E. B. Marks Music Corp., 1980.
Best-selling record by AC/DC (Atlantic, 81).

Back on the Chain Gang (English)
Words and music by Chrissie Hynde.
Virgin Music, Inc., 1982.
Best-selling record by The Pretenders (Sire, 83).

Back Where You Belong (Canadian)
Words and music by Gary O'Connor.
April Music, Inc., 1983.
Best-selling record by 38 Special (A & M, 84).

Backstrokin'
Words and music by Bill Curtis and John Flippin.
Clita Music, 1980.
Best-selling record by Fatback (Spring, 80).

Ballad for D
Words and music by Peabo Bryson, Roberta Flack, and Ira
  Williams.
Peabo Bryson Enterprises, Inc., 1981/WB Music Corp., 1981/Very
  Every Music, Inc., 1981/Budson Music, 1981.
Introduced by Peabo Bryson in the film *Bustin' Loose*, 1982. Dedicated
  to Donny Hathaway.

Bar Room Buddies
Words and music by Snuff Garrett, Clifton Crofford, Stephen Dorff,
  and Milton Brown.
Peso Music, 1980/Bar Cee Music, 1980/Warner-Tamerlane
  Publishing Corp., 1980.
Best-selling record by Clint Eastwood with Merle Haggard (Elektra, 80).
  Introduced in the film *Honky Tonk Man* (80).

Be Italian
Words and music by Maury Yeston.
Yeston Music, Ltd., 1975.
Introduced by Kathi Moss in *Nine* (musical, 82).

The Beach Boys Medley
Words and music by Brian Wilson.
Best-selling record by The Beach Boys (Capitol, 81). Consists of "Good Vibrations," "Help Me, Rhonda," "I Get Around," "Shut Down," "Surfin' Safari," "Barbara Ann," "Surfin' USA," and "Fun Fun Fun."

Beast of Burden (English)
Revived by Bette Midler (Atlantic, 84). See *Popular Music, 1920-1979.*

Beat It
Words and music by Michael Jackson.
Mijac Music, 1982/Warner-Tamerlane Publishing Corp., 1982.
Best-selling record by Michael Jackson (Epic, 83). Nominated for a National Academy of Recording Arts and Sciences Award, Song of the Year, 1983. Won a National Academy of Recording Arts and Sciences Award, Record of the Year, 1983.

The Beatles' Movie Medley
Words and music by John Lennon and Paul McCartney.
Comet Music Corp./Maclen Music Inc.
Performed by The Beatles (Capitol, 82).

Beatstreet
Words and music by Melvin Glover and Reggie Griffin.
Hargreen Music, 1984/Sugar Hill Music Publishing, Ltd., 1984.
Best-selling record by Grandmaster Melle & the Furious Five with Mr. Ness and Cowboy (Sugarhill, 84). Introduced in the film *Beatstreet* (84).

Beautiful
Words and music by Stephen Sondheim.
Revelation Music Publishing Corp., 1981/Rilting Music Inc., 1981.
Introduced by Barbara Byrne and Mandy Patinkin in *Sunday in the Park with George* (83).

Beautiful Music
Words by William Dumaresq, music by Galt MacDermott.
Samuel French, Inc., 1983.
Introduced by Debra Byrd & Co. in *The Human Comedy* (83).

Beautiful You
Best-selling record by The Oak Ridge Boys (MCA, 81). See Popular Music, 1920-79

Being with You
Words and music by William Smokey Robinson, Jr.
Bertam Music Co., 1981.
Best-selling record by Smokey Robinson (Tamla, 81).

Believe It or Not, see **The Theme from** *The Greatest American Hero.*

Beneath Still Waters
Words and music by Dallas Frazier.
Acuff-Rose Publications Inc., 1967.
Best-selling record by Emmylou Harris (Warner Brothers, 80).

The Best of Times
Words and music by Dennis DeYoung.
Almo Music Corp., 1981/Stygian Songs, 1981.
Best-selling record by Styx (A & M, 81).

The Best of Times
Words and music by Jerry Herman.
Jerryco Music Co., 1983.
Introduced by George Hearn, Elizabeth Parrish & Cast in *La Cage Au Folles* (83).

Bette Davis Eyes
Best-selling record by Kim Carnes (EMI-America, 1981). See *Popular Music, 1920-79.* Won National Academy of Recording Arts and Sciences Awards, Record of the Year, 1981, and Song of the Year, 1981.

Better Love Next Time
Words and music by Steve Pippin, Larry Keith, and Johnny Slate.
Warner House of Music, 1980.
Best-selling record by Dr. Hook (Capitol, 79).

Between the Sheets
Words and music by Christopher Jasper, Ernest Isley, Marvin Isley, Ronald Isley, Rudolph Isley, and O'Kelly Isley.
April Music, Inc., 1983/Bovina Music, Inc., 1983.
Best-selling record by The Isley Brothers (T-Neck, 83).

Between Trains
Words and music by Robbie Robertson.
Medicine Hat Music, 1983.
Introduced by Robbie Robertson in *The King of Comedy* (83).

Big City
Words and music by Dean Holloway and Merle Haggard.
Shade Tree Music Inc., 1981.
Best-selling record by Merle Haggard (Epic, 82).

Big Fun
Words and music by Ronald Bell, Curtis Williams, Clifford Adams,

James Taylor, Michael Ray, Claydes Smith, George Brown, Robert Mickens, Eumir Deodato, and Robert Bell.
Delightful Music Ltd., 1982/Double F Music, 1982.
Best-selling record by Kool & The Gang (De-Lite, 82).

Big Log (English)
Words and music by Robert Plant, Robbie Blunt, and Jezz Woodruffe.
Talk Time Music, Inc., 1982.
Best-selling record by Robert Plant (Es Paranza, 83).

Big Ole Brew
Words and music by Russell Smith.
Tintagel Music, Inc., 1980/Bad Ju Ju Music, 1980.
Best-selling record by Mel McDaniel (Capitol, 82).

(The) Biggest Part of Me
Words and music by David Pack.
Rubicon Music, 1980.
Best-selling record by Ambrosia (Warner Brothers, 80).

Billie Jean
Words and music by Michael Jackson.
Mijac Music, 1982/Warner-Tamerlane Publishing Corp., 1982.
Best-selling record by Michael Jackson (Epic, 83). Nominated for a National Academy of Recording Arts and Sciences Award, Song of the Year, 1983. Won a National Academy of Recording Arts and Sciences Award, Rhythm 'n' Blues Song of the Year, 1983.

The Birds
Words by William Dumaresq, music by Galt MacDermott.
Samuel French, Inc., 1983.
Introduced by Rex Smith and Leta Galloway in *The Human Comedy* (83).

Black Limousine (English)
Words and music by Mick Jagger, Keith Richards, and Ron Wood.
Colgems-EMI Music Inc., 1981/Screen Gems-EMI Music Inc., 1981.
Introduced by The Rolling Stones on *Tattoo You* (Rolling Stones, 81).

Black Sheep
Words and music by Daniel Darst and Robert Altman.
Al Gallico Music Corp., 1983/Algee Music Corp., 1983/John Anderson Music Co. Inc., 1983.
Best-selling record by John Anderson (Warner Brothers, 83).

Blessed Are the Believers
Words and music by Charlie Black, Rory Bourke, and Sandy

Pinkard.
Chappell & Co., Inc., 1981/Unichappell Music Inc., 1981.
Best-selling record by Anne Murray (Capitol, 81).

Blizzard of Lies
Words and music by David Frishberg and Samantha Frishberg.
Swiftwater Music, 1982.
Featured in *The David Frishberg Songbook, Volume Two* (Omnisound, 83).

Blue Eyes (English)
Words by Gary Osborne, music by Elton John.
Intersong, USA Inc., 1982.
Best-selling record by Elton John (Geffen, 82).

Blue Jean (English)
Words and music by David Bowie.
Jones Music Co., 1984.
Best-selling record by David Bowie (EMI-America, 84).

Blue Moon with Heartache
Words and music by Rosanne Cash.
Atlantic Music Corp., 1982/Hotwire Music, 1982.
Best-selling record by Rosanne Cash (Columbia, 82).

Blue Rider
Words and music by Chris Williamson.
Bird Ankles Music, 1982.
Introduced by Chris Williamson on *Blue Rider* (Olivia, 82).

The Blues
Words and music by Randy Newman.
Six Pictures Music, 1983.
Best-selling record by Randy Newman and Paul Simon (Warner Brothers, 83).

Blues Power (English-American)
Words and music by Eric Clapton and Leon Russell.
Skyhill Publishing Co., Inc., 1980.
Best-selling record by Eric Clapton (RSO, 80).

Bobbie Sue
Words and music by Wood Newton, Daniel Tyler, and Adele Tyler.
Warner House of Music, 1981/Bobby Goldsboro Music, 1981.
Best-selling record by The Oak Ridge Boys (MCA, 82).

Bobby Jean
Words and music by Bruce Springsteen.

Bruce Springsteen, 1984.
Introduced by Bruce Springsteen on *Born in the U.S.A.* (Columbia, 84).

Body Language (English)
Words and music by Freddie Mercury.
Queen Music Ltd., 1982.
Best-selling record by Queen (Elektra, 82).

Bon Bon Vie
Words and music by Sandy Linzer and Lawrence Russell Brown.
Unichappell Music Inc., 1980/Featherbed Music Inc., 1980/Lar-Bell
   Music Corp., 1980.
Best-selling record by T. S. Monk (Mirage, 81).

Boomtown Blues
Words and music by Bob Seger.
Gear Publishing, 1982.
Introduced by Bob Seger on *The Distance* (Capitol, 82).

The Border
Words and music by Russ Ballard and Dewey Bunnell.
Russell Ballard, Ltd., Middlesex, England, 1983/April Music, Inc.,
   1983/Poison Oak Music, 1983.
Best-selling record by America (Capitol, 83).

Borderline
Words and music by Reginald Lucas.
Likasa Music, 1983.
Best-selling record by Madonna (Warner Brothers, 84).

Born in the U.S.A.
Words and music by Bruce Springsteen.
Bruce Springsteen, 1984.
Best-selling record by Bruce Springsteen (Columbia, 84).

Born to Run
Words and music by Paul Kennerley.
Irving Music Inc., 1981.
Best-selling record by Emmylou Harris (Warner Brothers, 82).

The Bottle
Words and music by Gil Scott-Heron.
Brouhaha Music, 1976.
Revived by Gil Scott-Heron in *The Best of Gil Scott-Heron* (Arista, 84).

Bottom of the Fifth
Words and music by Porter Wagoner and Michael Pearson.

Popular Music, 1980-1984

Senor Music, 1982/Cibie Music, 1982/Broadcast Music Inc., 1982.
Introduced on *Viva* by Porter Wagoner (Warner Brothers, 83).

Boulevard
Words and music by Jackson Browne.
Swallow Turn Music, 1980.
Best-selling record by Jackson Browne (Asylum, 80).

Boy from New York City
Revived by Manhattan Transfer (Atlantic, 81). See *Popular Music, 1920-1979.*

Boy with a Problem (English)
Words and music by Elvis Costello, words by Chris Difford.
Plangent Visions Music, Inc., London, England, 1982/Almo Music Corp., 1982.
Introduced by Elvis Costello in *Imperial Bedroom* (Columbia, 82).

The Boys of Summer
Words and music by Don Henley and Mike Campbell.
Cass County Music Co., 1984/Wild Gator Music, 1984.
Best-selling record by Don Henley (Geffen, 84).

Brand New Lover
Words and music by Marshall Crenshaw.
Belwin-Mills Publishing Corp., 1980/MHC Music, 1980.
Performed by Marshall Crenshaw on *Marshall Crenshaw* (Warner Brothers, 82).

Brass in Pocket (I'm Special) (English)
Words and music by Chrissie Hynde and James Honeyman Scott.
Virgin Music, Inc., 1979.
Best-selling record by The Pretenders (Sire, 80).

Break It to Me Gently
Revived by Juice Newton (Capitol, 82). See *Popular Music, 1920-1979.*

Break My Stride
Words and music by Matthew Wilder and Greg Prestopino.
Streetwise Music, 1983/Buchu Music, 1983/No Ears Music, 1983.
Best-selling record by Matthew Wilder (Private, 83).

Breakdance (American-West German)
English words by Irene Cara and Bunny Hull, music by Giorgio Moroder.
Giorgio Moroder Pub/April Music, 1983/Carub Music, 1983/Alcor Music, 1983/Brass Heart, 1983.

Best-selling record by Irene Cara (Network/Geffen, 84). Introduced in the film *Breakdance* (84).

Breakdown Dead Ahead
Words and music by Boz Scaggs and David Foster.
Boz Scaggs Music, 1980/Foster Frees Music Inc., 1980/Irving Music Inc., 1980.
Best-selling record by Boz Scaggs (Columbia, 80).

Breakin' Away
Words and music by Al Jarreau, Thomas Canning, and Jay Graydon.
Al Jarreau Music, 1981/Desperate Music, 1981/Garden Rake Music, Inc., 1981.
Best-selling record by Al Jarreau (Warner Brothers, 82).

Breaking Us in Two (English)
Words and music by Joe Jackson.
Almo Music Corp., 1982.
Best-selling record by Joe Jackson (A & M, 83).

Breakin'...There's No Stopping Us
Words and music by Ollie E. Brown and Jerry Knight.
Ollie Brown Sugar Music, Inc., 1984/Almo Music Corp., 1984/Crimsco Music, 1984.
Best-selling record by Ollie and Jerry (Polydor, 84). Introduced in the film *Breakin'* (84).

The Breaks
Words and music by James Moore, Lawrence Smith, Kurt Walker, Robert Ford, and Russell Simmons.
Neutral Gray Music, 1980/Funk Groove Music Publisher Co., 1980.
Best-selling record by Kurtis Blow (Mercury, 80).

The Breakup Song (They Don't Write 'Em)
Words and music by Greg Kihn, Steve Wright, and Gary Philips.
Rye-Boy Music, 1981.
Best-selling record by The Greg Kihn Band (Beserkley, 81).

Breathless
Revived by X on *Under the Big Black Sun* (Elektra, 82). Performed in the film *Breathless* (82). See *Popular Music, 1920-1979.*

Bring on the Loot
Words and music by Gary Portnoy and Judy Hart Angelo.
Koppelman Family Music, 1983/Bandier Family Music, 1983/Yontrop Music, 1983/Judy Hart Angelo Music, 1983/R. L.

August Music Co., 1983.
Introduced by Dennis Bailey in *Preppies* (83).

Bringin' on the Heartbreak (English)
Words and music by Steve Clark, Pete Willis, and Joe Elliott.
Zomba Enterprises, Inc., 1981.
Best-selling record by Def Leppard (Mercury, 81 and 84).

Broken Glass
Words and music by Claudia Schmidt.
Pragmavision Music, 1982.
Introduced by Claudia Schmidt on *Midwestern Heart* (Flying Fish, 82).

Bruce
Words and music by Rick Springfield.
Vogue Music, 1981.
Best-selling record by Rick Springfield (Mercury, 84).

Burn Rubber on Me
Words and music by Lonnie Simmons, Charley Wilson, and Rudolph
   Taylor.
Temp Co., 1980.
Best-selling record by Gap Band (Mercury, 81).

Burnin' for You
Words and music by Donald Roeser and Richard Meltzer.
B. O'Cult Songs, Inc., 1981.
Best-selling record by Blue Oyster Cult (Columbia, 81).

Burning Down the House
Words and music by David Byrne, Chris Frantz, Jerry Harrison, and
   Tina Weymouth.
Index Music/Bleu Disque Music Co., Inc., 1983.
Best-selling record by Talking Heads (Sire, 83).

Busted
Words and music by Harlan Howard.
Tree Publishing Co., Inc., 1982.
Best-selling record by John Conlee (MCA, 82).

But You Know I Love You
Best-selling record by Dolly Parton (RCA, 81). See *Popular Music,
   1920-1979.*

By Now

Words and music by Donald Pfrimmer, Charles Quillen, and Dean
    Dillon.
Hall-Clement Publications, 1981/Chess Music Inc., 1981.
Best-selling record by Steve Wariner (RCA, 81).

C

Cadillac Car
Words by Tom Eyen, music by Henry Krieger.
Dreamgirls Music, 1981/Dreamette's Music, 1981/Tom Eyen's
    Publishing Co., 1981.
Introduced by Ben Harney, Cleavant Derricks, and Obba Babatunde in
    Dreamgirls (81).

Cadillac Ranch
Words and music by Bruce Springsteen.
Bruce Springsteen, 1980.
Introduced by Bruce Springsteen in *The River* (Columbia, 80).

Call Me (West German)
English words and music by Giorgio Moroder and Debbie Harry.
Ensign Music Corp., 1980/Cookaway Music Inc., 1980.
Best-selling record by Blondie (Chrysalis, 80). Introduced by Blondie in
    the film *American Gigolo* (80).

Call Me
Words and music by Randy Muller.
One To One Music Publishing Co., 1981.
Best-selling record by Skyy (Salsoul, 82).

Candy Girl
Words and music by Maurice Starr (pseudonym for Larry Johnson)
    and Michael Jonzun.
Boston International Music, 1982/Streetwise Music, 1982.
Best-selling record by New Edition (Streetwise, 83).

Can't Even Get the Blues
Words and music by Rick Carnes and Thomas William Damphier.
Refuge Music, Inc., 1982/Coal Miner's Music Inc.
Best-selling record by Reba McEntire (Mercury, 82).

Careless Whisper
Words and music by George Michael and Andrew Ridgeley.
Chappell & Co., Inc., 1984.
Best-selling record by Wham, featuring George Michael (Columbia, 84).

Caribbean Queen (No More Love on the Run)
Words and music by Keith Diamond and Billy Ocean.
Willesden Music, Inc., 1984/Zomba Enterprises, Inc., 1984.
Best-selling record by Billy Ocean (Jive/Arista, 84). Nominated for a
    National Academy of Recording Arts and Sciences Award, Rhythm
    'n' Blues Song of the Year, 1984.

Cars (English)
Best-selling record by Gary Numan (Atco, 80). See *Popular Music,
    1920-1979.*

Cat People (Putting out Fire) (English-West German)
English words and music by David Bowie and Giorgio Moroder.
MCA, Inc., 1982/Music Corp. of America, 1982.
Best-selling record by David Bowie (Backstreet/MCA, 82). Introduced
    in the film *Cat People* (82).

Caught Up in You
Words and music by Jeff Carlisi, Jim Peterik, Richard Barnes, and
    Frankie Sullivan.
Rocknocker Music Co., 1982/Easy Action Music, 1982/Holy Moley
    Music, 1982.
Best-selling record by 38 Special (A & M, 82).

Celebration
Words and music by Ronald Bell, Claydes Smith, George Brown,
    Robert Bell, James Taylor, Eumir Deodato, Robert Mickens, Earl
    Toon, and Dennis Thomas.
Delightful Music Ltd., 1980/Double F Music, 1980/Second Decade
    Music, 1980.
Best-selling record by Kool & The Gang (De-Lite, 80).

Centerfold
Words and music by Seth Justman.
Center City Music, 1982/Pal-Park Music, 1982.
Best-selling record by J. Geils Band (EMI-America, 82).

Centipede
Words and music by Michael Jackson.
Mijac Music, 1984.
Best-selling record by Rebbie Jackson (Columbia, 84).

Chariots of Fire (Race to the End)
Music by Vangelis, words by Jon Anderson.
WB Music Corp., 1981.
Best-selling records by Melissa Manchester (Arista, 81) and Vangelis (Polydor, 82). Introduced in the film *Chariots of Fire* (81). Nominated for a National Academy of Recording Arts and Sciences Award, Record of the Year, 1982.

Charlie's Medicine
Words and music by Warren Zevon.
Zevon Music, 1982.
Introduced by Warren Zevon in *The Envoy* (Asylum, 82).

Cheating in the Next Room
Words and music by George Henry Jackson and Robert Alton Miller.
Muscle Shoals Sound Publishing Co., Inc., 1982.
Best-selling record by Z.Z. Hill (Malaco, 82).

Chicago, Illinois
Words by Leslie Bricusse, music by Henry Mancini.
CBS Affiliated Catalog Inc., 1981/Stage & Screen Music Inc., 1981/ CBS Variety Catalog, Inc., 1981/Henry Mancini Enterprises, 1981.
Introduced by Lesley Ann Warren in the film *Victor, Victoria* (82).

Children and Art
Words and music by Stephen Sondheim.
Revelation Music Publishing Corp., 1981/Rilting Music Inc., 1981.
Introduced by Bernadette Peters in *Sunday in the Park with George* (83).

China Girl (English-American)
Words and music by Iggy Pop and David Bowie.
Bug Music, 1977/James Osterberg Music, 1977/Jones Music Co., 1977/Fleur Music, 1977.
Featured on *Let's Dance* by David Bowie (EMI-America, 83).

Christie Lee
Words and music by Billy Joel.
Joelsongs, 1983.
Introduced by Billy Joel on *An Innocent Man* (Columbia, 83).

Church of the Poison Mind (English)
Words and music by Roy Hay, John Moss, Michael Craig, and George O'Dowd.
Virgin Music, Inc., 1983.
Best-selling record by Culture Club (Virgin/Epic, 83).

Circles
Words and music by Wayne Lewis and David Lewis.
Almo Music Corp., 1982/Jodaway Music, 1982.
Best-selling record by Atlantic Starr (A & M, 82).

City Drops (into the Night)
Words and music by Jim Carroll, Steve Linsley, and Brian Linsley.
Earl McGrath Music, 1980.
Introduced by Jim Carroll in *Catholic Boy* (Atlantic, 80).

City of New Orleans
Revived by Willie Nelson (Columbia, 84). See Popular Music, 1920-79
Won a National Academy of Recording Arts and Sciences Award,
  Country Song of the Year, 1984.

The Clown
Words and music by Brenda Barnett, Charles Chalmers, Sandra
  Rhodes, and Wayne Carson Thompson.
Mammoth Spring Music, 1981/Rose Bridge Music Inc., 1981.
Best-selling record by Conway Twitty (Elektra, 82).

Cold Blooded
Words and music by Rick James.
Stone City Music, 1983.
Best-selling record by Rick James (Gordy, 83).

Colored Lights
Words and music by Fred Ebb and John Kander.
Fiddleback Music Publishing Co., Inc., 1983/Kander & Ebb Inc.,
  1983.
Introduced by Liza Minnelli in *The Rink* (84).

The Colors of My Life
Words by Michael Stewart, music by Cy Coleman.
Notable Music Co., Inc., 1980.
Introduced by Jim Dale and Glenn Close in *Barnum* (80).

Come Back to Me
Words by John Doe and Exene Cervenka.
Eight/Twelve Music, 1982.
Introduced by X in *Under the Big Black Sun* (Elektra, 82).

Come Dancing (English)
Words and music by Ray Davies.
Davray Music, Ltd., London, England, 1983.
Best-selling record by The Kinks (Arista, 83).

Come Go with Me
Revived by The Beach Boys (Warner Brothers, 82). See *Popular Music, 1920-1979.*

Come on Eileen (English)
Words and music by Kevin Rowland, Jim Paterson, and Kevin Adams.
Colgems-EMI Music Inc., 1982/April Music, Inc., 1982.
Best-selling record by Dexy's Midnight Runners (Mercury, 83).

Comin' in and out of Your Life
Words and music by Richard Parker and Bobby Whiteside.
Emanuel Music, 1981/Koppelman Family Music, 1981/Jay Landers Music, 1981/Bandier Family Music, 1981/Bobby Whiteside Ltd., 1981/R. L. August Music Co., 1981.
Best-selling record by Barbra Streisand (Columbia, 81).

Coming Up (English)
Words and music by Paul McCartney.
MPL Communications Inc., 1980/Welbeck Music Corp., 1980.
Best-selling record by Paul McCartney (Columbia, 80).

Common Man
Words and music by Sammy Johns.
Lowery Music Co., Inc., 1981/Legibus Music Co., 1981/Captain Crystal Music, 1981.
Best-selling record by John Conlee (MCA, 83).

Controversy
Words and music by Prince Rogers Nelson.
Controversy Music, 1981.
Best-selling record by Prince (Warner Brothers, 82).

Cool It Now
Words and music by Vincent Brantley and Rick Timas.
New Generation Music, 1984.
Best-selling record by New Edition (MCA, 84).

Cool Love
Words and music by Cory Lerios, David Jenkins, and John Pierce.
Irving Music Inc., 1981/Pablo Cruise Music, 1981/Almo Music Corp., 1981.
Best-selling record by Pablo Cruise (A & M, 81).

Cool Night
Words and music by Paul Davis.
Web 4 Music Inc., 1981.
Best-selling record by Paul Davis (Arista, 81).

Cool Part 1
Words by Dez Dickerson, music by Prince Rogers Nelson.
Tionna Music, 1981.
Best-selling record by The Time (Warner Brothers, 82).

Cool Places
Words and music by Ron Mael and Russel Mael.
April Music, Inc., 1983.
Best-selling record by Sparks and Jane Wiedlin (Atlantic, 83).

Could I Have This Dance
Words and music by Wayland Holyfield and Bob House.
Tree Publishing Co., Inc., 1980/Bibo Music Publishers, 1980.
Introduced in *Urban Cowboy* (80). Best-selling record by Anne Murray
  (Capitol, 80).

A Country Boy Can Survive
Words and music by Hank Williams, Jr.
Bocephus Music Inc., 1981.
Best-selling record by Hank Williams, Jr. (Elektra/Curb, 82).

Cover Me
Words and music by Bruce Springsteen.
Bruce Springsteen, 1984.
Best-selling record by Bruce Springsteen (Columbia, 84).

Coward of the County
Best-selling record by Kenny Rogers (United Artists, 80). See *Popular
  Music, 1920-1979.*

Cowboys and Clowns
Words and music by Stephen Dorff, Snuff Garrett, Larry Herbstritt,
  and Gary Harju.
Peso Music, 1980/Bar Cee Music, 1980/Warner-Tamerlane
  Publishing Corp., 1980/WB Music Corp., 1980/Senor Music,
  1980/Billy Music, 1980.
Best-selling record by Ronnie Milsap (RCA, 80).

Crazy World
Words by Leslie Bricusse, music by Henry Mancini.
CBS Affiliated Catalog Inc., 1981/Stage & Screen Music Inc., 1981/
  CBS Variety Catalog, Inc., 1981/Henry Mancini Enterprises, 1981.
Introduced by Julie Andrews in *Victor, Victoria* (81).

Crimson and Clover
Revived by Joan Jett & The Blackhearts (Boardwalk, 82). See *Popular
  Music, 1920-1979.*

Cruel Summer (English)
Words and music by Tony Swain and Steve Jolley.
In A Bunch Music, London, England, 1983/Red Bus Music Ltd.,
    London, England, 1983/MCA, Inc., 1983.
Best-selling record by Bananarama (London, 84).

Crumblin' Down
Words and music by John Cougar Mellencamp and George Michael
    Green.
Riva Music Ltd., 1983.
Best-selling record by John Cougar Mellencamp (Riva, 83).

Crying
Revived by Don McLean (Millennium, 81). See *Popular Music, 1920-79.*

Crying My Heart out over You
Words and music by Jerry Organ, Louise Certain, Carl Butler, and
    Gladys Stacey.
Cedarwood Publishing Co., Inc., 1959.
Best-selling record by Ricky Scaggs (Epic, 82).

Cuban Slide (English)
Words and music by Chrissie Hynde and James Honeyman Scott.
Virgin Music Ltd., 1980.
Introduced by The Pretenders on *The Pretenders* (Sire, 81).

Cum on Feel the Noize (English)
Words and music by Noddy Holder and Jim Lea.
Barn Music, London, England, 1972.
Revived by Quiet Riot (Pasha, 83).

Cupid
Revived by The Spinners (Atlantic, 80). See *Popular Music, 1920-1979.*

The Curly Shuffle
Words and music by Peter Quinn.
Swing Tet Publishing, 1983.
Best-selling record by Jump 'n' The Saddle (Atlantic, 83). Song is based
    on the antics of The Three Stooges.

Cutie Pie
Words and music by Albert Hudson, Theodore Dudley, Dave
    Roberson, Gregory Green, Jonathan Meadows, Terry Morgan, and
    Glenda Hudson.
Duchess Music Corp., 1982/Perk's Music, Inc., 1982.
Best-selling record by One Way (MCA, 82).

Cynical Girl
Words and music by Marshall Crenshaw.
Belwin-Mills Publishing Corp., 1982/MHC Music, 1982.
Introduced by Marshall Crenshaw in *Field Day* (Warner Brothers, 83).

D

Daddy's Come Home
Words and music by Steve Van Zandt.
Blue Midnight Music, 1980.
Featured on *Dedication* by Gary U.S. Bonds (EMI-America, 83).

Dance Floor
Words and music by Roger Troutman and Larry Troutman.
Troutman's Music, 1982.
Best-selling record by Zapp (Warner Brothers, 82).

Dance Hall Days
Words and music by Jack Hues.
Warner-Tamerlane Publishing Corp., 1983.
Best-selling record by Wang Chung (Geffen, 84).

Dance Wit' Me
Words and music by Rick James.
Stone City Music, 1982.
Best-selling record by Rick James (Gordy, 82).

Dancin' Cowboys
Words and music by David Bellamy.
Bellamy Brothers Music, 1980/Famous Music Co., 1980.
Best-selling record by The Bellamy Brothers (Warner Brothers, 80).

Dancin' Your Memory Away
Words and music by Eddie Burton and Thomas Grant.
Barnwood Music, 1981.
Best-selling record by Charly McClain (Epic, 82).

Dancing in the Dark
Words and music by Bruce Springsteen.
Bruce Springsteen, 1984.
Best-selling record by Bruce Springsteen (Columbia, 84). Nominated for

a National Academy of Recording Arts and Sciences Award, Best
Record of the Year, 1984.

Dancing in the Sheets
Words by Dean Pitchford, music by Bill Wolfer.
Famous Music Co., 1984/Ensign Music Corp., 1984.
Best-selling record by Shalamar (Columbia, 84). Introduced in the film
Footloose (84). Nominated for a National Academy of Recording Arts
and Sciences Award, Rhythm 'n' Blues Record of the Year, 1984.

Dancing with Myself (English)
Words and music by Billy Idol and Tony James.
Rare Blue Music, Inc., 1980.
Best-selling record by Billy Idol and Generation X (Chrysalis, 81).
Revived by Billy Idol (Chrysalis, 84).

Daydream Believer
Revived by Anne Murray (Capitol, 80). See *Popular Music, 1920-1979.*

D.C. Cab
Words and music by Richard Feldman, Rich Kelly, and Larry John
McNally.
Unicity Music, Inc., 1983/Broadcast Music Inc., 1983.
Best-selling record by Peabo Bryson (MCA, 84). Introduced in the film
D.C. Cab (84).

De Do Do Do, De Da Da Da (English)
Words and music by Sting (pseudonym for Gordon Sumner).
Virgin Music Ltd., 1980.
Best-selling record by The Police (A & M, 80).

Dead Giveaway
Words and music by Joey Gallo, Marquis Dair, and Leon F Sylvers,
III.
Spectrum VII, 1983/LFS III Music, 1983.
Best-selling record by Shalamar (Solar, 83).

Dedicated to the One I Love
Revived by Bernadette Peters (MCA, 81). See *Popular Music, 1920-79.*

Deep Inside My Heart
Words and music by Randy Meisner and Eric Kaz.
Nebraska Music, 1980/CBS Unart Catalog Inc., 1980/Glasco Music,
Co., 1980.
Best-selling record by Randy Meisner (Epic, 80).

Deja Vu
Best-selling record by Dionne Warwick (Arista, 80). See *Popular Music, 1920-1979.*

Delirious
Words and music by Prince Rogers Nelson.
Controversy Music, 1982.
Best-selling record by Prince (Warner Brothers, 83).

Der Kommissar (West German)
German words by Falco, English words by Andrew Piercy, music by Robert Ponger.
Chappell & Co., Inc., 1983.
Best-selling record by After the Fire (Epic, 83).

Desert Moon
Words and music by Dennis De Young.
Grand Illusion Music, 1984.
Best-selling record by Dennis De Young (A & M, 84).

Desire
Best-selling record by Andy Gibb (RSO, 80). See *Popular Music, 1920-1979.*

Did It in a Minute
Words and music by Daryl Hall, Sara Allen, and Janna Allen.
Hot Cha Music Co., 1981/Fust Buzza Music, Inc., 1981/Unichappell Music Inc., 1981.
Best-selling record by Daryl Hall and John Oates (RCA, 82).

Dirty Laundry
Words and music by Don Henley and Danny Kortchmar.
Cass County Music Co., 1982.
Best-selling record by Don Henley (Asylum, 82).

Dirty Movies
Words and music by Eddie Van Halen, Alex Van Halen, David Lee Roth, and Michael Anthony.
Van Halen Music, 1981.
Introduced by Van Halen on *Fair Warning* (Warner Brothers, 81).

Dixieland Delight
Words and music by Ronnie Rogers.
Sister John Music, Inc., 1982/Maypop Music, 1982.
Best-selling record by Alabama (RCA, 83).

Do I Do
Words and music by Stevie Wonder.

Jobete Music Co., Inc., 1981/Black Bull Music, 1981.
Best-selling record by Stevie Wonder (Tamla, 82). Nominated for a
National Academy of Recording Arts and Sciences Award, Rhythm
'n' Blues Song of the Year, 1982.

Do They Know It's Christmas (Irish)
Words and music by Bob Geldof and Midge Ure.
Chappell & Co., Inc., 1984.
Best-selling record by Band-Aid (Columbia, 84). Proceeds were donated
to aid Ethiopian children. Group was composed of British rock all-
stars.

Do What You Do, also known as **Why Do You (Do What You Do)**
Words and music by Ralph Dino and Larry DiTomaso.
Unicity Music, Inc., 1980.
Best-selling record by Jermaine Jackson (Arista, 84).

Do You Believe in Love (English)
Words and music by Robert John Lange.
Zomba Enterprises, Inc., 1982.
Best-selling record by Huey Lewis & The News (Chrysalis, 82).

Do You Really Want to Hurt Me (English)
Words and music by Roy Hay, John Moss, Michael Craig, and
George O'Dowd.
Virgin Music, Inc., 1982.
Best-selling record by Culture Club (Virgin/Epic, 83).

Do You Remember
Words and music by Gary William Friedman and Will Holt.
Bussy Music, 1983/Devon Music, 1983/Hampshire House Publishing
Corp., 1983/Lemon Tree Music, Inc., 1983.
Introduced by Ted Thurston and Company of *Taking My Turn* (83).

Do You Remember Rock and Roll Radio
Introduced by The Ramones on *End of the Century* (Sire, 79). See
Popular Music, 1920-1979.

Do You Wanna Go to Heaven
Words and music by Curly Putman and Bucky Jones.
Tree Publishing Co., Inc., 1980/Cross Keys Publishing Co., Inc.,
1980.
Best-selling record by T. G. Sheppard (Warner Brothers, 80).

Do You Wanna Touch Me (English)
Words and music by Gary Glitter and Mike Leander.

Music Corp. of America, 1973.
Best-selling record by Joan Jett & The Blackhearts (Boardwalk, 82).

Doctor! Doctor! (English)
Words and music by Thomas Bailey, Alanah Currie, and Joe
  Leeway.
Zomba Enterprises, Inc., 1984.
Best-selling record by The Thompson Twins (Arista, 84).

Doggin' Around, see **Stop Doggin' Me Around.**

Donna
Words and music by David Johansen.
Buster Poindexter, Inc., 1978.
Introduced by David Johansen on *Live It Up* (Blue Sky, 82).

Don't Ask Me Why
Words and music by Billy Joel.
Impulsive Music, 1980/April Music, Inc., 1980.
Best-selling record by Billy Joel (Columbia, 80).

Don't Cry (English)
Words and music by John Wetten and Geoffrey Downes.
WB Music Corp., 1983/Island Music, 1983.
Best-selling record by Asia (Geffen, 83).

Don't Cry for Me Argentina
Best-selling record by Festival (RSO, 80). See *Popular Music, 1920-79.*

Don't Do Me Like That
Best-selling record by Tom Petty (Backstreet, 80). See *Popular Music,
  1920-1979.*

Don't Fall Apart on Me Tonight
Words and music by Bob Dylan.
Special Rider Music, 1983.
Introduced by Bob Dylan on *Infidels* (Columbia, 83).

Don't Fall in Love with a Dreamer
Words and music by Kim Carnes and Dave Ellingson.
Appian Music Co., 1980/Almo Music Corp., 1980/Quixotic Music
  Corp., 1980.
Best-selling record by Kim Carnes and Kenny Rogers (United Artists,
  80).

Don't Fight It
Words and music by Kenny Loggins and Steve Perry, words by
  Dean Pitchford.

Milk Money Music, 1982/Lacy Boulevard Music, 1982/Warner-
Tamerlane Publishing Corp., 1982/Body Electric Music, 1982.
Best-selling record by Kenny Loggins with Steve Perry (Columbia, 82).

Don't It Make You Wanna Dance
Words and music by Rusty Weir.
Prophecy Publishing, Inc., 1980.
Introduced by Bonnie Raitt in *Urban Cowboy* (80).

Don't Let Go
Best-selling record by Isaac Hayes (Polydor, 80). See *Popular Music,
1920-1979.*

Don't Let Go the Coat (English)
Words and music by Peter Townshend.
Towser Tunes Inc., 1981.
Best-selling record by The Who (Warner Brothers, 81).

Don't Let It End
Words and music by Dennis De Young.
Stygian Songs, 1983/Almo Music Corp., 1983.
Best-selling record by Styx (A & M, 83).

Don't Look Any Further
Words and music by Franne Golde, Dennis Lambert, and Duane
Hitchings.
Hitchings Music, 1984/Franne Golde Music, 1984/Vandorf Songs
Co., 1984/Rightsong Music Inc., 1984.
Best-selling record by Dennis Edwards (Gordy, 84).

Don't Make It Easy for Me
Words and music by Earl Thomas Conley and Randy Scruggs.
April Music, Inc., 1983/Blackwood Music Inc., 1983/Full Armor
Publishing Co., 1983.
Best-selling record by Earl Thomas Conley (RCA, 84).

Don't Pay the Ferryman (English)
Words and music by Chris DeBurgh.
Irving Music Inc., 1982.
Best-selling record by Chris DeBurgh (A & M, 83).

Don't Push It Don't Force It
Words and music by Leon Haywood.
Jim-Edd Music, 1979.
Best-selling record by Leon Haywood (20th Century, 80).

Don't Say Goodnight (It's Time for Love) - Parts 1 & 2
Words and music by Ernest Isley, Ronald Isley, Marvin Isley,

Rudolph Isley, Casper Jasper, and O'Kelly Isley.
Bovina Music, Inc., 1980/April Music, Inc., 1980.
Best-selling record by The Isley Brothers (T-Neck, 80).

Don't Stand So Close to Me (English)
Words and music by Sting (pseudonym for Gordon Sumner).
Virgin Music Ltd., 1980.
Best-selling record by The Police (A & M, 81).

Don't Stop Believin'
Words and music by Steve Perry, Neal Schon, and Jonathan Cain.
Twist & Shout Music, 1981.
Best-selling record by Journey (Columbia, 81).

Don't Stop the Music
Words and music by Lonnie Simmons, Alisa Peoples, and Jonah
    Ellis.
Total X Publishing Co., 1980/Blackwell Publishing, 1980.
Best-selling record by Yarbrough and Peoples (Mercury, 81).

Don't Talk to Strangers
Words and music by Rick Springfield.
Vogue Music, 1982.
Best-selling record by Rick Springfield (RCA, 82).

Don't Wait on Me
Words and music by Harold Reid and Don Reid.
American Cowboy Music Co., 1980.
Best-selling record by The Statler Brothers (Mercury, 81).

Don't Wanna Be Like That
Words and music by Joe Jackson.
Almo Music Corp., 1979.
Introduced by Joe Jackson on *I'm the Man* (A & M, 79).

Don't Waste Your Time
Words and music by Jonah Ellis.
Temp Co., 1984.
Best-selling record by Yarbrough and Peoples (Total Experience, 84).

Don't Worry 'bout Me Baby
Words and music by Deborah Allen, Bruce Channel, and Kieran
    Kane.
Music Corp. of America, 1981/Old Friends Music, 1981/Posey
    Publishing, 1981/Cross Keys Publishing Co., Inc., 1981.
Best-selling record by Janie Fricke (Columbia, 82).

Don't You Get So Mad
Words and music by Jeffrey Osborne, Michael Sembello, and Donald
    Freeman.
Almo Music Corp., 1980/March 9 Music, 1980/Gravity Raincoat
    Music, 1980/Haymaker Music, 1980/Warner-Tamerlane
    Publishing Corp., 1980.
Best-selling record by Jeffrey Osborne (A & M, 83).

Don't You Want Me (English)
Words and music by Jo Callis, Phil Oakey, and Adrian Wright.
Virgin Music, Inc., 1981/WB Music Corp., 1981.
Best-selling record by Human League (A & M/Virgin, 82).

Double Dutch Bus
Words and music by Frankie Smith and William Bloom.
Frashon Music Co., 1980/Front Wheel Music, Inc., 1980/Wimot
    Music Publishing, 1980.
Best-selling record by Frankie Smith (WMOT, 81).

Down to My Last Broken Heart
Words and music by Chick Rains.
Tree Publishing Co., Inc., 1980/Chick Rains Music, 1980.
Best-selling record by Janie Fricke (Columbia, 81).

Down Under (Australian)
Words and music by Colin Hay and Roy Strykert.
Blackwood Music Inc., 1982.
Best-selling record by Men at Work (Columbia, 82).

Dreamer (English)
Words and music by Roger Davies and Roger Hodgson.
Almo Music Corp., 1974/Delicate Music, 1980.
Best-selling record by Supertramp (A & M, 80).

Dreaming (English)
Words and music by Alan Tarney and Leo Sayer.
ATV Music Corp., 1980/Rare Blue Music, Inc., 1980.
Best-selling record by Cliff Richard (EMI-America, 80).

Drifter
Words and music by Don Pfrimmer and Archie Jordan.
Pi-Gem Music Publishing Co, Inc., 1980/Jack & Bill Music Co.,
    1980.
Best-selling record by Sylvia (RCA, 81).

Drive
Words and music by Ric Ocasek.

Lido Music Inc., 1984.
Best-selling record by The Cars (Electra, 84).

Drivin' My Life Away
Words and music by Eddie Rabbitt, Even Stevens, and David Malloy.
Debdave Music Inc., 1980/Briarpatch Music, 1980.
Best-selling record by Eddie Rabbitt (Elektra, 80). Nominated for a National Academy of Recording Arts and Sciences Award, Country Song of the Year, 1980.

Dynamite
Words and music by Andy Goldmark and Bruce Roberts.
Nonpariel Music, 1984/Broozertoones, Inc., 1984.
Best-selling record by Jermaine Jackson (Arista, 84).

E

Early in the Morning
Words and music by Charles Wilson, Rudolph Taylor, and Lonnie
    Simmons.
Temp Co., 1982.
Best-selling record by The Gap Band (Total Experience, 82).

Easier to Love
Words by Richard Maltby, music by David Shire.
Fiddleback Music Publishing Co., Inc., 1984/Progeny Music, 1984/
    Revelation Music Publishing Corp., 1984/Long Pond Music, 1984.
Introduced by James Congdon in *Baby* (83).

Easy Lover (American-English)
Words and music by Philip Bailey, Phil Collins, and Nathan East.
Pun Music Inc., London, England, 1984/Sir & Trini Music, 1984/
    New East Music, 1984.
Best-selling record by Philip Bailey (Kalimba/Columbia, 84).

Eat It
Words and music by Michael Jackson, words by Al Yankovic.
Mijac Music, 1984, 1982/Warner-Tamerlane Publishing Corp., 1984.
Best-selling record by Weird Al Yankovic (Rock 'n' Roll, 84). Parody
    of Michael Jackson's "Beat It."

Ebony and Ivory (English)
Words and music by Paul McCartney.
MPL Communications Inc., 1982.
Best-selling record by Paul McCartney and Stevie Wonder (Columbia,
    82). Nominated for National Academy of Recording Arts and
    Sciences Awards, Song of the Year, 1982, and Record of the Year,
    1982.

Edge of Seventeen
Words and music by Stephanie Nicks.

Welsh Witch Publishing, 1981.
Best-selling record by Stevie Nicks (Modern, 82).

867-5309/Jenny
Words and music by Alex Call and James Keller.
Tutone-Keller Music, 1982/New Daddy Music, 1982.
Best-selling record by Tommy Tutone (Columbia, 82).

Electric Avenue (English)
Words and music by Eddy Grant.
Greenheart Music, Ltd., 1982.
Best-selling record by Eddy Grant (Portrait/Ice, 83). Nominated for a
    National Academy of Recording Arts and Sciences Award, Rhythm
    'n' Blues Song of the Year, 1983.

Elizabeth
Words and music by Jimmy Fortune.
American Cowboy Music Co., 1983.
Best-selling record by The Statlers (Mercury, 84).

Elvira
Words and music by Dallas Frazier.
Acuff-Rose Publications Inc., 1965.
Best-selling record by The Oak Ridge Boys (MCA, 81). Nominated for
    a National Academy of Recording Arts and Sciences Award, Country
    Song of the Year, 1981.

Emotional Rescue (English)
Words and music by Mick Jagger and Keith Richards.
Colgems-EMI Music Inc., 1980.
Best-selling record by The Rolling Stones (Rolling Stones, 80).

The Empire Strikes Back
Words and music by John T. Williams.
Warner-Tamerlane Publishing Corp., 1980/Bantha Music, 1980.
Best-selling record by Meco (RSO, 80). Introduced in the film *The
    Empire Strikes Back* (80).

Empty Garden (Hey Hey Johnny) (English)
Music by Elton John, words by Bernie Taupin.
Intersong, USA Inc., 1982.
Best-selling record by Elton John (Geffen, 82).

Encore
Words and music by Terry Lewis and James Harris, III.
Tan Division Music Publishing, 1983/Flyte Tyme Tunes, 1983.
Best-selling record by Cheryl Lynn (Columbia, 84).

Endless Love
Words and music by Lionel Richie, Jr.
Popular Music Co., 1981/Brockman Enterprises Inc., 1981.
Best-selling record by Diana Ross and Lionel Richie, Jr. (Motown, 81).
   Introduced in the movie *Endless Love* (81). Nominated for an Academy Award, Best Song, 1981; National Academy of Recording Arts and Sciences Awards, Song of the Year, 1981, and Record of the Year, 1981.

Even It Up
Words and music by Ann Wilson, Sue Ennis, and Nancy Wilson.
Strange Euphoria Music, 1980/Know Music, 1980/Sheer Music, 1980.
Best-selling record by Heart (Portrait, 80).

Even Now
Words and music by Bob Seger.
Gear Publishing, 1982.
Best-selling record by Bob Seger & The Silver Bullet Band (Capitol, 83).

Even the Nights Are Better
Words and music by J. L. Wallace, Kenneth Bell, and Terry Skinner.
Hall-Clement Publications, 1979.
Best-selling record by Air Supply (Arista, 82).

Every Breath You Take (English)
Words and music by Sting (pseudonym for Gordon Sumner).
Reggatta Music, Ltd., 1983/Illegal Songs, Inc., 1983.
Best-selling record by The Police (A & M, 83). Nominated for a National Academy of Recording Arts and Sciences Award, Record of the Year, 1983. Won a National Academy of Recording Arts and Sciences Award, Song of the Year, 1983.

Every Day
Words and music by Dave Loggins and J.D. Martin.
Leeds Music Corp., 1984/Patchwork Music, 1984/Music Corp. of America, 1984.
Best-selling record by The Oak Ridge Boys (MCA, 84).

Every Day I Write the Book (English)
Words and music by Elvis Costello.
Plangent Visions Music, Inc., London, England, 1983.
Best-selling record by Elvis Costello (Columbia, 83).

Every Grain of Sand
Words and music by Bob Dylan.
Special Rider Music, 1981.
Introduced by Bob Dylan on *Shot of Love* (Columbia, 81).

Every Little Thing She Does Is Magic (English)
Words and music by Sting (pseudonym for Gordon Sumner).
Virgin Music, Inc., 1981.
Best-selling record by The Police (A & M, 81).

Every Time I Turn Around
Words and music by Jody Hart Angelo and Gary Portnoy.
Addax Music Co., Inc., 1984.
Introduced by Gary Portnoy on *Punky Brewster* (84).

Every Woman in the World
Words and music by Dominic Bugatti and Frank Musker.
Unichappell Music Inc., 1980.
Best-selling record by Air Supply (Arista, 80).

Everybody Wants You
Words and music by Billy Squier.
Songs of the Knight, 1982.
Best-selling record by Billy Squier (Capitol, 82).

Everybody's Got to Learn Sometime (English)
Words and music by James Warren.
WB Music Corp., 1980.
Best-selling record by The Korgis (Asylum, 80).

Everything That Touches You
Words and music by Michael Kamen.
Mother Fortune Inc., 1980.
Introduced by by Sheryl Lee Ralph in *Reggae* (Musical, 80).

Everything Works If You Let It
Words and music by Richard Nielsen.
Screen Gems-EMI Music Inc., 1980.
Best-selling record by Cheap Trick (Epic, 80). Introduced in the film
    Roadie (80).

Eye in the Sky (English)
Words and music by Eric Woolfson and Alan Parsons.
Careers Music Inc., 1982.
Best-selling record by The Alan Parsons Project (Arista, 82).

Eye of the Tiger (The Theme from *Rocky III*)
Words and music by Frank Sullivan and Jim Peterik.
Holy Moley Music, 1982/Rude Music, 1982/WB Music Corp., 1982/
    Easy Action Music, 1982.
Best-selling record by Survivor (Scotti Brothers, 82). Introduced in the
    film *Rocky III* (82). Nominated for an Academy Award, Best Song,

1982; a National Academy of Recording Arts and Sciences Award, Song of the Year, 1982.

Eyes Without a Face (English-American)
Words and music by Billy Idol and Steve Stevens.
Boneidol Music, 1983/Rare Blue Music, Inc., 1983/Rock Steady Inc., 1983.
Best-selling record by Billy Idol (Chrysalis, 84).

F

The Facts of Life
Words and music by Alan Thicke, Gloria Loring, and Al Burton.
Norbud, 1981/Bramalea Music, 1981/Thickouit Music, 1981.
Introduced on the TV series *The Facts of Life* (81).

Fade Away
Words and music by Bruce Springsteen.
Bruce Springsteen, 1980.
Best-selling record by Bruce Springsteen (Columbia, 81).

Faithfully
Words and music by Jonathan Cain.
Twist & Shout Music, 1982.
Best-selling record by Journey (Columbia, 83).

Faithless Love
Words and music by John David Souther.
WB Music Corp., 1974/Golden Spread Music.
Best-selling record by Glen Campbell (Atlantic America, 84). Nominated for a National Academy of Recording Arts and Sciences Award, Country Song of the Year, 1984.

Faking Love
Words and music by Bobby Braddock and Matraca Berg.
Tree Publishing Co., Inc., 1982.
Best-selling record by T. G. Sheppard and Karen Brooks (Warner Brothers, 82).

Fall in Love with Me
Words and music by Maurice White, D. Vaughn, and Wayne Vaughn.
Saggifire Music, 1983/Yougoulei Music, 1983/Wenkewa Music, 1983.
Best-selling record by Earth, Wind and Fire (Columbia, 83).

Popular Music, 1980-1984

Falling Again
Words and music by Bob McDill.
Hall-Clement Publications, 1980.
Best-selling record by Don Williams (MCA, 81).

Fame
Words by Dean Pitchford, music by Michael Gore.
CBS Affiliated Catalog Inc., 1980.
Best-selling record by Irene Cara (RSO, 80). Introduced in the film *Fame* (80). Nominated for an Academy Award, Best Song, 1980; a National Academy of Recording Arts and Sciences Award, Song of the Year, 1980.

Family Man (English)
Words and music by Mike Oldfield, Morris Pert, Tim Cross, Rick Fenn, Mike Frye, and Maggie Reilly.
Josef Weinberger, Frankfurt, Federal Republic of Germany, 1982/ Chappell & Co., Inc., 1982/April Music, Inc., 1982.
Best-selling record by Daryl Hall and John Oates (RCA, 83).

Fantastic Voyage
Words and music by F. Alexander, O. Stokes, N. Beavers, M. Wood, M. Craig, F. Lewis, T. McCain, S. Shockley, and T. Shelby.
Spectrum VII, 1980/Circle L Publishing, 1980.
Best-selling record by Lakeside (Solar, 81).

Fantasy
Words and music by Aldo Nova.
ATV Music Corp., 1982.
Best-selling record by Aldo Nova (Portrait, 82).

Far from Over
Words and music by Frank Stallone and Vince DiCola.
Famous Music Co., 1983.
Best-selling record by Frank Stallone (RSO, 83). Introduced in the film *Staying Alive* (83).

The Farm Yard Connection (English)
Words and music by Fun Boy Three.
Plangent Visions Music, Inc., London, England, 1982.
Introduced by Fun Boy Three in *Waiting* (Chrysalis, 83).

(Keep Feeling) Fascination (English)
Words and music by Phil Oakey and Jo Callis.
Virgin Music, Inc., 1983/WB Music Corp., 1983.
Best-selling record by The Human League (A & M, 83).

Fatherhood Blues
Words by Richard Maltby, music by David Shire.
Fiddleback Music Publishing Co., Inc., 1984/Progeny Music, 1984/
  Revelation Music Publishing Corp., 1984/Long Pond Music, 1984.
Introduced by James Congdon, Martin Vidnovic and Todd Graff in
  Baby (83).

Favorite Waste of Time
Words and music by Marshall Crenshaw.
MHC Music, 1983.
Best-selling record by Bette Midler (Atlantic, 83).

Feed Me
Words by Howard Ashman, music by Alan Menken.
Samuel French, Inc., 1982.
Introduced by Ron Taylor as the voice of Audrey II in *Little Shop of
  Horrors* (82).

Feels So Real (Won't Let Go)
Words and music by Patrice Rushen and Fred Washington.
Baby Fingers Music, 1984/Mumbi Music, 1984.
Best-selling record by Patrice Rushen (Elektra, 84).

Feels So Right
Words and music by Randy Owen.
Maypop Music, 1980.
Best-selling record by Alabama (RCA, 81).

Fidelity
Words and music by Garland Jeffreys.
April Music, Inc., 1982/Garland Jeffreys Music/April Music, Inc.,
  1982.
Introduced by Garland Jeffreys on *Guts for Love* (Epic, 82).

Fields of Fire (Scottish)
Words and music by Big Country.
Virgin Music, Inc., 1983.
Best-selling record by Big Country (Mercury, 84).

Find Another Fool
Words and music by Marv Ross.
Bonnie Bee Good Music, 1981/Geffen/Kaye Music, 1981.
Best-selling record by Quarterflash (Geffen, 82).

Find Your Way Back
Words and music by Craig Chaquico and Thomas Borsdorf.
Lunatunes Music, 1981.
Best-selling record by Jefferson Starship (Grunt, 81).

Finder of Lost Loves
Words by Carol Bayer Sager, music by Burt Bacharach.
SVO Music, 1984/New Hidden Valley Music Co., 1984/Carole
 Bayer Sager Music, 1984/Spelling Venture Music, 1984.
Introduced by Dionne Warwick and Glenn Jones on *Finder of Lost
 Loves* (84). Featured on the LP *Finder of Lost Loves* (Arista, 85).

A Fine Fine Day (English)
Words and music by Tony Carey.
Warner-Tamerlane Publishing Corp., 1984.
Best-selling record by Tony Carey (MCA, 84).

Finishing the Hat
Words and music by Stephen Sondheim.
Revelation Music Publishing Corp., 1981/Rilting Music Inc., 1981.
Introduced by Mandy Patinkin in *Sunday in the Park with George* (83).

Fire and Ice
Words and music by Tom Kelly, Scott Sheets, and Pat Benatar.
Rare Blue Music, Inc., 1981/Big Tooth Music Corp., 1981/Discott
 Music, 1981/Denise Barry Music, 1981.
Best-selling record by Pat Benatar (Chrysalis, 81).

Fire and Smoke
Words and music by Earl Thomas Conley.
April Music, Inc., 1981.
Best-selling record by Earl Thomas Conley (Sunbird, 81).

A Fire I Can't Put Out
Words and music by Darrell Staedtler.
Music City Music Inc., 1982.
Best-selling record by George Strait (MCA, 83).

Fire Lake
Words and music by Bob Seger.
Gear Publishing, 1980.
Best-selling record by Bob Seger (Capitol, 80).

The First Time It Happens
Words and music by Joe Raposo.
ATV Music Corp., 1981.
Introduced in the film *The Great Muppet Caper* (81). Nominated for an
 Academy Award, 1981.

Flashdance...What a Feeling
English words by Keith Forsey and Irene Cara, music by Giorgio
 Moroder.
Intersong, USA Inc., 1983/Famous Music Co., 1983.

Best-selling record by Irene Cara (Casablanca, 83). Introduced in the film *Flashdance* (83). Nominated for a National Academy of Recording Arts and Sciences Award, Record of the Year, 1983. Won an Academy Award, Best Song, 1983.

Flirtin' with Disaster
Words and music by David Lawrence Hludeck, Danny Joe Brown, and Banner Harvey Thomas.
Mister Sunshine Music, Inc., 1979.
Best-selling record by Molly Hatchet (Epic, 80).

Flo's Yellow Rose
Words and music by Fred Werner and Suzie Glickman.
WB Music Corp., 1981.
Best-selling record by Hoyt Axton (Elektra, 81). Introduced on *Flo* (81).

Flying High Again (English-American)
Words and music by Ozzy Osbourne, Randy Rhoads, Bob Daisley, and Lee Gary Kerslake.
Blizzard Music, London, England, 1981.
Best-selling record by Ozzy Osbourne (Jet, 81).

Folies Bergeres
Words and music by Maury Yeston.
Yeston Music, Ltd., 1975.
Introduced by Lilian Montevecchi in *Nine* (musical, 82).

Fool for Your Love
Words and music by Don Singleton.
Tree Publishing Co., Inc., 1983/Black Sheep Music Inc., 1983.
Best-selling record by Mickey Gilley (Epic, 83).

Fool Hearted Memory
Words and music by Alan R. Mevis and Byron Hill.
Welbeck Music Corp., 1982/Make Believus Music, 1982.
Best-selling record by George Strait (MCA, 82).

Fool in the Rain (English)
Words and music by John Paul Jones, Jimmy Page, and Robert Plant.
Flames Of Albion Music, Inc., 1979.
Best-selling record by Led Zeppelin (Swan Song, 80).

Foolin'
Words and music by Steve Clark, Robert John Lange, and Joe Elliott.

73

Zomba Enterprises, Inc., 1980.
Best-selling record by Def Leppard (Mercury, 83).

Footloose
Words by Dean Pitchford, music by Kenny Loggins.
Famous Music Co., 1984/Ensign Music Corp., 1984/Milk Money
   Music, 1984.
Best-selling record by Kenny Loggins (Columbia, 84). Introduced in the
   film *Footloose* (84). Nominated for an Academy Award, Best Song,
   1984.

For a Rocker
Words and music by Jackson Browne.
Night Kitchen Music, 1983.
Best-selling record by Jackson Browne (Asylum, 84).

For All the Wrong Reasons
Words and music by David Bellamy.
Famous Music Co., 1982/Bellamy Brothers Music, 1982.
Best-selling record by The Bellamy Brothers (Elektra/Curb, 82).

For You
Revived by Manfred Mann's Earth Band (Warner Brothers, 81). See
   Popular Music, 1920-1979.

For Your Eyes Only
Words and music by Bill Conti and M Leeson.
CBS U Catalog, Inc., 1981/CBS Unart Catalog Inc., 1981.
Best-selling record by Sheena Easton (Liberty, 81). Introduced in the
   film *For Your Eyes Only* (81). Nominated for an Academy Award,
   Best Song, 1981.

Forget Me Nots
Words and music by Patrice Rushen, Fred Washington, and Terry
   McFadden.
Baby Fingers Music, 1981/Freddie Dee Music, 1981/Yanina Music,
   1981.
Best-selling record by Patrice Rushen (Elektra, 82).

Fourteen Carat Mind
Words and music by Dallas Frazier and Larry Lee.
Acuff-Rose Publications Inc., 1981.
Best-selling record by Gene Watson (MCA, 81).

Fran and Janie
Words and music by Craig Carnelia.
Samuel French, Inc., 1982.

Introduced by Sandy Faison and Maureen Silliman in *Is There Life After High School* (82).

Franklin Shepard, Inc.
Words and music by Stephen Sondheim.
Revelation Music Publishing Corp., 1981/Rilting Music Inc., 1981.
Introduced by Lonny Price in *Merrily We Roll Along* (81).

Freak-a-Zoid
Words and music by Vincent Calloway, Reginald Calloway, and William Simmons.
Hip-Trip Music Co., 1983/Midstar Music, Inc., 1983.
Best-selling record by Midnight Star (Solar, 83).

Freakshow on the Dancefloor
Words and music by James Alexander, Michael Beard, Mark Bynum, Larry Dodson, Harvey Henderson, Lloyd Smith, Winston Stewart, Frank Thompson, and Allen A. Jones.
Warner-Tamerlane Publishing Corp., 1984/Bar-Kay Music, 1984.
Best-selling record by The Bar-Kays (Mercury, 84).

Freaky Dancin'
Words and music by Larry Blackmon and Tomi Jenkins.
Better Days Music, 1981/Better Night Music, 1981.
Best-selling record by Cameo (Chocolate City, 81).

Freeze-Frame
Words and music by Peter Wolf and Seth Justman.
Center City Music, 1981/Pal-Park Music, 1981.
Best-selling record by J. Geils Band (EMI-America, 82).

Friday Night Blues
Words and music by Sonny Throckmorton and Rafe Van Hoy.
Tree Publishing Co., Inc., 1979/Cross Keys Publishing Co., Inc., 1980.
Best-selling record by John Conlee (MCA, 80).

Friends
Words and music by Johnny Slate and Dan Morrison.
Warner House of Music, 1980.
Best-selling record by Razzy Bailey (RCA, 81).

From Small Things (Big Things One Day Come)
Words and music by Bruce Springsteen.
Bruce Springsteen, 1979.
Featured on *D.E. 7th* by Dave Edmunds (Columbia, 82).

Funkin' for Jamaica (N.Y.)
Words and music by Tom Browne.
Thomas Browne Publishing, 1980/Roaring Fork Music, 1980.
Best-selling record by Tom Browne (GRP, 80).

Funky Town
Best-selling record by Lipps, Inc. (Casablanca, 80). See *Popular Music, 1920-1979.*

G

The Games I Play
Words and music by William Finn.
Samuel French, Inc., 1981.
Introduced by Stephen Bogardus in *March of the Falsettos* (81).

Games People Play (English)
Words and music by Eric Woolfson and Alan Parsons.
Irving Music Inc., 1979.
Best-selling record by The Alan Parsons Project (Arista, 80).

Games Without Frontiers (East German)
English words and music by Peter Gabriel.
Hidden Music, 1980.
Introduced by Peter Gabriel on *Peter Gabriel* (Mercury, 80).

General Hospi-tale
Words and music by Harry King and L. Tedesco.
Solid Smash Music Publishing Co, Inc., 1981/American Broadcasting
   Music, Inc., 1981.
Best-selling record by The Afternoon Delights (MCA, 81).

Genius of Love
Words and music by Tom Tom Club.
Metered Music, Inc., 1981.
Best-selling record by Tom Tom Club (Sire, 82).

Get Closer
Words and music by Jonathan Carroll.
Cherry Lane Music Co., Inc., 1981.
Best-selling record by Linda Ronstadt (Asylum, 82).

Get Down on It
Words and music by Ronald Bell, Eumir Deodato, Robert Mickens,
   James Taylor, Charles Smith, Robert Bell, and George Brown.

Delightful Music Ltd., 1981/Double F Music, 1981.
Best-selling record by Kool & The Gang (De-Lite, 82).

Get It Right
Words and music by Luther Vandross and Marcus Miller.
Uncle Ronnie's Music Co., Inc., 1983/April Music, Inc., 1983/
    Thriller Miller Music, 1983.
Best-selling record by Aretha Franklin (Arista, 83).

Ghost Town (English)
Words and music by Jerry Dammers.
Plangent Visions Music, Inc., London, England, 1981.
Introduced by The Specials on an import LP in 1981. Written about the
    1981 riots in England.

Ghostbusters
Words and music by Ray Parker, Jr.
Golden Torch Music Corp., 1984/Raydiola Music, 1984.
Best-selling record by Ray Parker, Jr. (Arista, 84). Introduced in the film
    Ghostbusters (84). Nominated for an Academy Award, Best Song,
    1984.

The Gigolo
Words and music by O'Bryan Burnette and Don Cornelius.
Big Train Music Co., 1981.
Best-selling record by O'Bryan (Capitol, 82).

Gimme All Your Lovin'
Words and music by Billy Gibbons, Dusty Hill, and Frank Beard.
Hamstein Music, 1983.
Best-selling record by Z.Z. Top (Warner Brothers, 83).

Gimme Some Lovin'
Revived by The Blues Brothers (Atlantic, 80). See *Popular Music,
    1920-1979.*

Girl, Don't Let It Get You Down
Words and music by Kenny Gamble and Leon Huff.
Mighty Three Music, 1979.
Best-selling record by The O'Jays (TSOP, 80).

A Girl in Trouble (Is a Temporary Thing)
Words and music by Debora Iyall, Peter Woods, Frank Zincavage,
    and David Kahne.
Talk Dirty Music, 1984/Seesquared Music, 1984.
Best-selling record by Romeo Void (Columbia/415, 84).

The Girl Is Mine
Words and music by Michael Jackson.
Mijac Music, 1982/Warner-Tamerlane Publishing Corp., 1982.
Best-selling record by Michael Jackson and Paul McCartney (Epic, 82).

Girl Talk (English)
Featured in *Mad Love* (Asylum, 80) by Linda Ronstadt. See *Popular Music, 1920-1979.*

Girls
Words and music by Dwight Twilley.
Dionio Music, 1984.
Best-selling record by Dwight Twilley (EMI-America, 84).

Girls Just Want to Have Fun
Words and music by Robert Hazard.
Heroic Music, 1979.
Best-selling record by Cyndi Lauper (Portrait, 84). Nominated for a National Academy of Recording Arts and Sciences Award, Record of the Year, 1984.

The Girls of Summer
Words and music by Stephen Sondheim.
Revelation Music Publishing Corp., 1982/Rilting Music Inc., 1982.
Introduced by Craig Lucas in *Marry Me a Little* (81).

Girls on Film (English)
Words and music by Andy Taylor, John Taylor, Roger Taylor, Simon Le Bon, and Nick Rhodes.
Chappell & Co., Inc., 1981.
Best-selling record by Duran Duran (Harvest, 81).

Give It All You Got
Music by Chuck Mangione.
Gates Music Inc., 1980.
Best-selling record by Chuck Mangione (A & M, 80).

Give It to Me Baby
English words and music by Rick James.
Jobete Music Co., Inc., 1981.
Best-selling record by Rick James (Gordy, 81).

Give It Up
Words and music by Harry Casey and Deborah Carter.
Harrick Music Inc., 1982.
Best-selling record by K. C. (Mecca/Alpha Distributors, 84).

Popular Music, 1980-1984

Give Me One More Chance
Words and music by James Pennington and Sonny LeMaire.
Careers Music Inc., 1984/Tree Publishing Co., Inc., 1984.
Best-selling record by Exile (Epic, 84).

Give Me the Night (English)
Words and music by Rod Temperton.
Almo Music Corp., 1980.
Best-selling record by George Benson (Warner Brothers, 80). Nominated
    for a National Academy of Recording Arts and Sciences Award,
    Rhythm 'n' Blues Song of the Year, 1980.

Giving It Up for Your Love
Words and music by Jerry Williams.
Blackwood Music Inc., 1979/Urge Music, 1979.
Best-selling record by Delbert McClinton (MMS/Capitol, 80).

Giving Up Easy
Words and music by Jerry Foster and Bill Rice.
April Music, Inc., 1979.
Best-selling record by Leon Everette (RCA, 81).

The Glamorous Life
Words and music by Prince Rogers Nelson.
Girlsongs, 1984.
Best-selling record by Sheila E. (Warner Brothers, 84). Nominated for
    a National Academy of Recording Arts and Sciences Award, Rhythm
    'n' Blues Song of the Year, 1984.

Gloria (Italian-American)
English words by Trevor Veitch, Italian words and music by
    Giancarlo Bigazzi and Umberto Tozzi.
Sugar Song Publications, 1980/Music Corp. of America, 1980.
Best-selling record by Laura Branigan (Atlantic, 82).

Glory Days
Words and music by Bruce Springsteen.
Bruce Springsteen, 1984.
Introduced by Bruce Springsteen on *Born in the U.S.A.* (Columbia, 84).

God Bless the U.S.A.
Words and music by Lee Greenwood.
Music Corp. of America, 1984/Sycamore Valley Music Inc., 1984.
Best-selling record by Lee Greenwood (MCA, 84). Nominated for a
    National Academy of Recording Arts and Sciences Award, Country
    Song of the Year, 1984.

Goin' Down
Words and music by Greg Guidry and D. Martin.
World Song Publishing, Inc., 1980.
Best-selling record by Greg Guidry (Columbia/Badlands, 82).

Going, Going, Gone
Words and music by Jan Crutchfield.
Jan Crutchfield Music, 1983.
Best-selling record by Lee Greenwood (MCA, 84).

Going Where the Lonely Go
Words and music by Merle Haggard and Dean Holloway.
Shade Tree Music Inc., 1982.
Best-selling record by Merle Haggard (Epic, 83).

Gone Too Far
Words and music by Even Stevens, Eddie Rabbitt, and David
    Malloy.
Debdave Music Inc., 1979/Briarpatch Music.
Best-selling record by Eddie Rabbitt (Elektra, 80).

Good News
Words and music by Shirley Eikhard.
Visa Music, 1983.
Featured on *White Shoes* by Emmylou Harris (Warner Brothers, 83).

Good Ole Boys Like Me
Words and music by Bob McDill.
Hall-Clement Publications, 1979.
Best-selling record by Don Williams (MCA, 80).

Good Thing Going (Going Gone)
Words and music by Stephen Sondheim.
Revelation Music Publishing Corp., 1981/Rilting Music Inc., 1981.
Introduced by Lonny Price in *Merrily We Roll Along* (81).

Goodbye to You
Words and music by Zack Smith.
Blackwood Music Inc., 1981.
Best-selling record by Scandal (Columbia, 83).

Goodnight Saigon
Words and music by Billy Joel.
Joelsongs, 1981.
Best-selling record by Billy Joel (Columbia, 83).

Goody Two Shoes (English)
Words and music by Adam Ant and Marco Pirroni.

EMI Music Publishing, Ltd., London, England, 1982/Colgems-EMI
   Music Inc., 1982.
Best-selling record by Adam Ant (Epic, 82).

Got a Hold on Me (English)
Words and music by Christine McVie and Todd Sharp.
Alimony Music, 1984/Cement Chicken Music, 1984.
Best-selling record by Christine McVie (Warner Brothers, 84).

The Grammy Song
Words and music by Loudon Wainwright.
Snowden Music, 1980.
Introduced on *Fame and Wealth* by Loudon Wainwright (Rounder, 83).

Grandma Got Run Over by a Reindeer
Words and music by Randy Brooks.
Kris Publishing, 1979.
Best-selling record by Elmo 'n' Patsy (Soundwaves, 84).

The Grass Is Always Greener
Words by Fred Ebb, music by John Kander.
Fiddleback Music Publishing Co., Inc., 1981/Kander & Ebb Inc.,
   1981.
Introduced by Marilyn Cooper and Lauren Bacall in *Woman of the Year*
   (81).

Gravity's Angel
Words and music by Laurie Anderson.
Difficult Music, 1984.
Introduced by Laurie Anderson on *Mr. Heartbreak* (Warner Brothers,
   84).

Growing Up in Public
Words and music by Lou Reed and Michael Fonfara.
Metal Machine Music, 1980.
Introduced by Lou Reed in *Growing Up in Public* (RCA, 80).

Guilty (English)
Words and music by Barry Gibb, Robin Gibb, and Maurice Gibb.
Gibb Brothers Music, 1980.
Best-selling record by Barbra Streisand and Andy Gibb (Columbia, 80).

Gus the Theatre Cat (English)
Words by T. S. Eliot, words and music by Andrew Lloyd Webber.
Deco Music, 1982/Charles Koppelman Music, 1982/Jonathan Three

Music Co., 1982/Martin Bandier Music, 1982.
Introduced by Stephen Hanan in *Cats* (82). Adapted from the poetry of
T. S. Eliot.

H

Hand of Kindness (English)
Words and music by Richard Thompson.
Island Music, 1983.
Introduced by Richard Thompson on *Hand of Kindness* (Hannibal, 83).

Hand to Hold Onto
Words and music by John Cougar Mellencamp.
Riva Music Ltd., 1983.
Best-selling record by John Cougar (Riva, 83).

Hang Fire (English)
Words and music by Mick Jagger and Keith Richards.
Colgems-EMI Music Inc., 1981.
Best-selling record by The Rolling Stones (Rolling Stones, 82).

Happy Birthday Dear Heartache
Words and music by Mack David and Archie Jordan.
Collins Court Music, Inc., 1984.
Best-selling record by Barbara Mandrell (MCA, 84).

Happy Man
Words and music by Greg Kihn and Steve Wright.
Rye-Boy Music, 1982/Well Received Music, 1982.
Best-selling record by The Greg Kihn Band (Beserkley, 82).

Hard Habit to Break
Words and music by Steve Kipner and John Parker.
April Music, Inc., 1984/Stephen A. Kipner Music, 1984/Parker
  Music, 1984.
Best-selling record by Chicago (Full Moon/Warner Brothers, 84).
  Nominated for a National Academy of Recording Arts and Sciences
  Award, Record of the Year, 1984.

Hard Love
Words and music by Bob Franke.

Telephone Pole Music Publishing Co., 1982.
Featured in *New Goodbyes, Old Helloes* by Claudia Schmidt (Flying Fish, 83).

Hard Times
Words and music by James Taylor.
Country Road Music Inc., 1981.
Best-selling record by James Taylor (Columbia, 81).

Hard to Say I'm Sorry
Words and music by Peter Cetera and David Foster.
Double Virgo Music, 1982/Foster Frees Music Inc., 1982.
Best-selling record by Chicago (Full Moon/Warner Brothers, 82). Introduced in the film *The Summer Lovers* (82).

Harden My Heart
Words and music by Marv Ross.
Bonnie Bee Good Music, 1980/WB Music Corp., 1980.
Best-selling record by Quarter Flash (Geffen, 81).

He Reminds Me
Words and music by Russell Stone and Mike McNaught.
Dejamus Inc., 1982.
Featured on *Windsong* by Randy Crawford (Warner Brothers, 82).

He Stopped Loving Her Today
Best-selling record by George Jones (Epic, 80). See Popular Music, 1920-79 Nominated for a National Academy of Recording Arts and Sciences Award, Country Song of the Year, 1980.

Head Over Heels
Words and music by Charlotte Caffey and Kathy Valentine.
Daddy Oh Music, 1984/Some Other Music, 1984.
Best-selling record by The Go-Go's (I.R.S., 84).

A Headache Tomorrow (or a Heartache Tonight)
Words and music by Chick Rains.
Blue Lake Music, 1980/Chick Rains Music, 1980.
Best-selling record by Mickey Gilley (Epic, 81).

Heart and Soul
Words and music by Mike Chapman and Nicky Chinn.
Arista Music, Inc., 1981.
Best-selling record by Huey Lewis & The News (Chrysalis, 83).

Heart Hotels
Best-selling record by Dan Fogelberg (Full Moon, 80). See *Popular Music, 1920-1979.*

A Heart in New York (English)
Words and music by Benny Gallagher and Graham Lyle.
Irving Music Inc., 1981.
Best-selling record by Art Garfunkel (Columbia, 81).

Heart of Mine
Words and music by Bob Dylan.
Special Rider Music, 1981.
Best-selling record by Bob Dylan (Columbia, 81).

The Heart of Rock and Roll
Words and music by Johnny Colla and Huey Lewis.
Hulex Music, 1983/Red Admiral Music Inc., 1983.
Best-selling record by Huey Lewis & The News (Chrysalis, 84). Nominated for a National Academy of Recording Arts and Sciences Award, Record of the Year, 1984.

Heart to Heart
Words and music by Kenny Loggins, Michael McDonald, and David Foster.
Milk Money Music, 1982/Genevieve Music, 1982/Foster Frees Music Inc., 1982.
Best-selling record by Kenny Loggins (Columbia, 82).

Heartbreak Hotel
Words and music by Michael Jackson.
Warner-Tamerlane Publishing Corp., 1981.
Best-selling record by The Jacksons (Epic, 80).

Heartbreaker (English)
Words and music by Geoff Gill and Cliff Wade.
Dick James Music Inc., 1979.
Best-selling record by Pat Benatar (Chrysalis, 80).

Heartbreaker (English)
Words and music by Barry Gibb, Robin Gibb, and Maurice Gibb.
Gibb Brothers Music, 1982.
Best-selling record by Dionne Warwick (Arista, 82).

Hearts
Words and music by Jeff Barish.
Mercury Shoes Music, 1980/Great Pyramid Music, 1980.
Best-selling record by Marty Balin (EMI-America, 81).

Popular Music, 1980-1984

Hearts on Fire
Words and music by Randy Meisner and Eric Kaz.
Nebraska Music, 1980/CBS U Catalog, Inc., 1980/Glasco Music,
  Co., 1980.
Best-selling record by Randy Meisner (Epic, 81).

Heat of the Moment (English)
Words and music by John Wetton and Geoffrey Downes.
WB Music Corp., 1982/Ackee Music Inc., 1982.
Best-selling record by Asia (Geffen, 82).

Heaven (Canadian)
Words and music by Bryan Adams and Jim Vallance.
Irving Music Inc., 1984/Adams Communications, Inc., 1984/Calypso
  Toonz, 1984.
Introduced in the film *A Night in Heaven* (84). Best-selling record by
  Bryan Adams (A&M, 85).

Heavy Metal (Takin' a Ride)
Words and music by Don Felder.
Fingers Music, 1981.
Best-selling record by Don Felder (Full Moon/Asylum, 81). Introduced
  in the film *Heavy Metal* (81).

Hello
Words and music by Lionel Richie, Jr.
Brockman Enterprises Inc., 1983.
Best-selling record by Lionel Richie (Motown, 84). Nominated for a
  National Academy of Recording Arts and Sciences Award, Song of
  the Year, 1984.

Hello Again
Words and music by Neil Diamond and Alan Lindgren.
Stonebridge Music, 1980.
Best-selling record by Neil Diamond (Capitol, 80). Introduced in the
  film *The Jazz Singer* (80).

Hello Again
Words and music by R. C. Ocasek.
Lido Music Inc., 1984.
Best-selling record by The Cars (Elektra, 84).

Her Town Too
Words and music by James Taylor, John David Souther, and Waddy
  Wachtel.
Country Road Music Inc., 1981/Lead Sheetland Music, 1981/Ice
  Age Music, 1981.
Best-selling record by James Taylor and J. D. Souther (Columbia, 81).

Here Comes My Girl
Words and music by Tom Petty and Mike Campbell.
Skyhill Publishing Co., Inc., 1979/Tarka Music Co.
Best-selling record by Tom Petty & The Heartbreakers (Backstreet, 80).

Here Comes the Rain Again (English)
Words and music by Annie Lennox and David Stewart.
Blue Network Music, 1983.
Best-selling record by Eurythmics (RCA, 84).

Here I Am
Words and music by Norman Sallitt.
Al Gallico Music Corp., 1980/Turtle Music, 1980.
Best-selling record by Air Supply (Arista, 81).

Here Today (English)
Words and music by Paul McCartney.
MPL Communications Inc., 1982.
Introduced by Paul McCartney in *Tug of War* (Columbia, 82). Song was
    dedicated to John Lennon.

Hero, see **Wind Beneath My Wings.**

He's a Heartache (Looking for a Place to Happen)
Words and music by Jeff Silbar and Larry Henley.
WB Gold Music Corp., 1982/Warner House of Music, 1982.
Best-selling record by Janie Fricke (Columbia, 83).

He's So Shy
Words by Cynthia Weil, music by Tom Snow.
Mann & Weil Songs Inc., 1980/Braintree Music, 1980/Snow Music,
    1980/ATV Music Corp., 1980.
Best-selling record by The Pointer Sisters (Planet, 80).

Hey Nineteen
Words and music by Walter Becker and Donald Fagen.
Zeitgeist Music Co., 1980/Freejunket Music, 1980.
Best-selling record by Steely Dan (MCA, 80).

High on Emotion (English)
Words and music by Chris DeBurgh.
Irving Music Inc., 1984.
Best-selling record by Chris DeBurgh (S&M, 84).

Highway 40 Blues
Words and music by Larry Cordle.
Amanda-Lin Music, 1979/Jack & Bill Music Co.
Best-selling record by Ricky Scaggs (Epic, 83).

Highway Patrolman
Words and music by Bruce Springsteen.
Bruce Springsteen, 1982.
Featured on *Johnny 99* by Johnny Cash (Columbia, 83). Introduced by
  Bruce Springsteen in *Nebraska* (Columbia, 82).

The Hills of Tomorrow
Words and music by Stephen Sondheim.
Revelation Music Publishing Corp., 1981/Rilting Music Inc., 1981.
Introduced by Company of *Merrily We Roll Along* (81).

Him
Words and music by Rupert Holmes.
Best-selling record by Rupert Holmes (MCA, 80).

Hit and Run
Words and music by Lloyd Smith, A. A. Jones, Michael Beard,
  Larry Dudson, Sherman Guy, Mark Bynum, Harvey Henderson,
  Charles Allen, Winston Stewart, Frank Thompson, and James
  Alexander.
Bar-Kay Music, 1982/Warner-Tamerlane Publishing Corp., 1982.
Best-selling record by The Bar-Kays (Mercury, 82).

Hit Me with Your Best Shot (Canadian)
Words and music by Eddie Schwartz.
ATV Music Corp., 1980.
Best-selling record by Pat Benatar (Chrysalis, 80).

Hold Me (English)
Words and music by Christine McVie and Robbie Patton.
Fleetwood Mac Music Ltd., 1982/Red Snapper, 1982.
Best-selling record by Fleetwood Mac (Warner Brothers, 82).

Hold Me Now (English)
Words and music by Thomas Bailey, Alannah Currie, and Joe
  Leeway.
Zomba Enterprises, Inc., 1983.
Best-selling record by The Thompson Twins (Arista, 84).

Hold On (Canadian)
Words and music by Ian Thomas.
Over The Rainbow Music Co., 1982.
Best-selling record by Santana (Columbia, 82).

Hold on Tight (English)
Words and music by Jeff Lynne.
April Music, Inc., 1981.
Best-selling record by ELO (Jet, 81).

Hold on to My Love (English-American)
Words and music by Robin Gibb and Blue Weaver.
Gibb Brothers Music, 1980/Pentagon Music Co., 1980.
Best-selling record by Jimmy Ruffin (RSO, 80).

Holding out for a Hero
Words and music by Jim Steinman and Dean Pitchford.
Ensign Music Corp., 1984.
Best-selling record by Bonnie Tyler (Columbia, 84). Introduced in the
    film *Footloose* (84).

Honey (Open That Door)
Words and music by Mel Tillis.
Cedarwood Publishing Co., Inc., 1962.
Best-selling record by Ricky Scaggs (Epic, 84).

Honky Tonkin'
Revived by Hank Williams, Jr. (Elektra/Curb, 82). See *Popular Music,
    1920-1979.*

Hooked on Classics
Chappell & Co., Inc., 1981.
Best-selling record by The Royal Philharmonic Orchestra, conducted by
    Louis Clark (RCA, 81). Medley of classical tunes.

Hooked on Music
Words and music by Mac Davis.
Song Painter Music, 1980.
Best-selling record by Mac Davis (Casablanca, 81).

Hot Girls in Love (Canadian)
Words and music by Paul Dean and Bruce Fairbarn.
Blackwood Music Inc., 1983.
Best-selling record by Loverboy (Columbia, 83).

Hot in the City (English)
Words and music by Billy Idol.
Rare Blue Music, Inc., 1982.
Best-selling record by Billy Idol (Chrysalis, 82).

Hot Rod Hearts
Words and music by Bill LaBounty and Stephen Geyer.
Captain Crystal Music, 1980/Blackwood Music Inc., 1980/Darjen
    Music, 1980.
Best-selling record by Robbie Dupree (Elektra, 80).

How Am I Supposed to Live Without You
Words and music by Michael Bolton and Doug James.

April Music, Inc., 1983/Is Hot Music, Ltd., 1983/Blackwood Music Inc., 1983.
Best-selling record by Laura Branigan (Atlantic, 83).

How 'bout Us
Words and music by Dana Walden.
Walkin Music, 1981.
Best-selling record by Champaign (Columbia, 81).

How Do I Make You
Best-selling record by Linda Ronstadt (Asylum, 80). See *Popular Music, 1920-1979.*

How Do I Survive
Words and music by Paul Bliss.
April Music, Inc., 1979.
Best-selling record by Amy Holland (Capitol, 80).

How Do You Keep the Music Playing
Words by Marilyn Bergman and Alan Bergman, music by Michel Legrand.
WB Music Corp., 1982.
Introduced in the film *Best Friends* (82). Best-selling record by Patti Austin and James Ingram (Qwest, 82). Nominated for an Academy Award, Best Song, 1982.

How Many Times Can We Say Goodbye
Words and music by Steve Goldman.
Goldrian Music, 1983.
Best-selling record by Dionne Warwick and Luther Vandross (Arista, 83).

How the Heart Approaches What It Yearns
Words and music by Paul Simon.
Paul Simon Music, 1978.
Introduced by Paul Simon in the album and the film *One Trick Pony* (80).

Human Nature
Words by John Bettis, music by Jeff Porcaro.
John Bettis Music, 1982/Porcara Music, 1982.
Best-selling record by Michael Jackson (Epic, 83).

Human Touch
Words and music by Rick Springfield.
Vogue Music, 1983.
Best-selling record by Rick Springfield (RCA, 83).

Hundreds of Hats
Words and music by Jonathan Sheffer and Howard Ashman.
Samuel French, Inc., 1984.
Introduced by Dick Latessa & Cast of *Diamonds* (84).

Hungry Heart
Words and music by Bruce Springsteen.
Bruce Springsteen, 1980.
Best-selling record by Bruce Springsteen (Columbia, 80).

Hungry Like the Wolf (English)
Words and music by Duran Duran.
Chappell & Co., Inc., 1983.
Best-selling record by Duran Duran (Capitol, 83).

The Hungry Wolf
Words and music by John Doe and Exene Cervenka, music by X.
Eight/Twelve Music, 1982.
Introduced by X in *More Fun in the New World* (Elektra, 82).

Hurricane
Words and music by Keith Stegall, Tom Schuyler, and Stewart
   Harris.
Blackwood Music Inc., 1980.
Best-selling record by Leon Everette (RCA, 81).

Hurt So Bad
Revived by Linda Ronstadt (Asylum, 80). See *Popular Music, 1920-79.*

Hurt So Good
Words and music by John Cougar Mellencamp and George Michael
   Green.
Riva Music Ltd., 1982.
Best-selling record by John Cougar (Rival/Mercury, 82).

I

I Ain't Gonna Stand for It
Words and music by Stevie Wonder.
Jobete Music Co., Inc., 1980/Black Bull Music, 1980.
Best-selling record by Stevie Wonder (Tamla, 80).

I Ain't Living Long Like This
Best-selling record by Waylon Jennings (RCA, 80). See *Popular Music, 1920-1979.*

I Always Get Lucky with You
Words and music by Tex Whitson, Freddy Powers, and Gary Church.
Shade Tree Music Inc., 1981.
Best-selling record by George Jones (Epic, 83).

I Am Love
Words and music by Maurice White, David Foster, and Allee Willis.
Saggifire Music, 1983/Off Backstreet Music, 1983/Foster Frees Music Inc., 1983.
Best-selling record by Jennifer Holliday (Geffen, 83).

I Am What I Am
Words and music by Jerry Herman.
Jerryco Music Co., 1983.
Introduced by George Hearn in *La Cage Au Folles* (83).

I and I
Words and music by Bob Dylan.
Special Rider Music, 1983.
Introduced on *Infidels* by Bob Dylan (Columbia, 83).

I Believe in You (English)
Words and music by Roger Cook and Sam Hogin.
Cookhouse Music, 1980/Roger Cook Music, 1980.
Best-selling record by Don Williams (MCA, 80). Nominated for a Na-

tional Academy of Recording Arts and Sciences Award, Country Song of the Year, 1980.

I Can Dream About You
Words and music by Dan Hartman.
Blackwood Music Inc., 1983.
Best-selling record by Dan Hartman (MCA, 84).

I Can Have It All
Words by Garry Trudeau, music by Elizabeth Swados.
Music Corp. of America, 1983.
Introduced by Laura Dean in *Doonesbury* (83).

I Can Tell by the Way You Dance (How You're Gonna Love Me Tonight)
Words and music by Robb Strandlund and Sandy Pinkard.
Tree Publishing Co., Inc., 1980/Jensong Music, Inc., 1980.
Best-selling record by Vern Gosdin (Compleat, 84).

I Can't Go for That (No Can Do)
Words and music by Daryl Hall, John Oates, and Sara Allen.
Fust Buzza Music, Inc., 1981/Hot Cha Music Co., 1981/Unichappell Music Inc., 1981.
Best-selling record by Daryl Hall and John Oates (RCA, 82).

I Can't Help It
Best-selling record by Andy Gibb and Olivia Newton-John (RSO, 80).
See *Popular Music, 1920-1979.*

I Can't Hold Back
Words and music by Frank Sullivan and Jim Peterik.
Rude Music, 1984/WB Music Corp., 1984/Easy Action Music, 1984.
Best-selling record by Survivor (Scotti Brothers, 84).

I Can't Stand It (English)
Words and music by Eric Clapton.
Unichappell Music Inc., 1981.
Best-selling record by Eric Clapton (RSO, 81).

I Can't Tell You Why
Best-selling record by The Eagles (Asylum, 80). See *Popular Music, 1920-1979.*

I Could Never Miss You More Than I Do (English)
Words and music by Neil Harrison.
Abesongs USA, 1978.
Best-selling record by Lulu (Alfa, 81).

I Don't Care
Revived by Ricky Scaggs (Epic, 82). See *Popular Music, 1920-1979.*

I Don't Know a Thing About Love
Words and music by Harlan Howard.
Tree Publishing Co., Inc., 1983.
Best-selling record by Conway Twitty (Warner Brothers, 84).

I Don't Know Where to Start
Words and music by Thom Schuyler.
Briarpatch Music, 1981/Debdave Music Inc., 1981.
Best-selling record by Eddie Rabbitt (Elektra, 82).

I Don't Like Mondays
Best-selling record by The Boomtown Rats (Columbia, 80). See *Popular Music, 1920-1979.*

I Don't Need You (Icelandic)
English words and music by Rick Christian.
Bootchute Music, 1978.
Best-selling record by Kenny Rogers (Liberty, 81).

I Don't Think She's in Love Anymore
Words and music by Kent Robbins.
Royalhaven Music, Inc., 1981.
Best-selling record by Charley Pride (RCA, 82).

I Don't Wanna Be a Memory
Words and music by Sonny LeMaire and James P. Pennington.
Tree Publishing Co., Inc., 1983/Careers Music Inc., 1983.
Best-selling record by Exile (Epic, 84).

I Don't Wanna Lose Your Love
Words and music by Joey Carbone.
Sixty Ninth Street Music, 1983.
Best-selling record by Crystal Gayle (Warner Brothers, 84).

I Feel for You
Words and music by Prince Rogers Nelson.
Controversy Music, 1979.
Best-selling record by Chaka Khan (Warner Brothers, 84). Won a National Academy of Recording Arts and Sciences Award, Rhythm 'n' Blues Song of the Year, 1984.

I Feel Like Loving You Again
Words and music by Bobby Braddock and Sonny Throckmorton.
Tree Publishing Co., Inc., 1978/Cross Keys Publishing Co., Inc.
Best-selling record by T. G. Sheppard (Warner Brothers, 80).

I. G. Y. (What a Beautiful World)
Words and music by Donald Fagen.
Freejunket Music, 1982.
Best-selling record by Donald Fagen (Warner Brothers, 82). Nominated
for a National Academy of Recording Arts and Sciences Award, Song
of the Year, 1982.

I Got Mexico
Words and music by Eddy Raven and Frank J. Myers.
Michael H. Goldsen, Inc., 1983/Ravensong Music, 1983.
Best-selling record by Eddy Raven (RCA, 84).

I Got You (Australian)
Words and music by Neil Finn.
Enz Music, 1980.
Featured on *True Colours* by Split Enz (A & M, 80).

I Guess It Never Hurts to Hurt Sometimes
Words and music by Randy Van Warner.
Fourth Floor Music Inc., 1980/Terraform Music, 1980.
Best-selling record by The Oak Ridge Boys (MCA, 84).

I Guess That's Why They Call It the Blues (English)
Words by Bernie Taupin, music by Elton John.
Intersong, USA Inc., 1983.
Best-selling record by Elton John (Geffen, 83).

I Have Loved You, Girl (But Not Like This Before)
Words and music by Earl Thomas Conley.
Blue Moon Music, 1975/Equestrian Music.
Best-selling record by Earl Thomas Conley (RCA, 83).

I Heard It Through the Grapevine
Revived by Roger (Warner Brothers, 82). See *Popular Music, 1920-79.*

I Just Called to Say I Love You
Words and music by Stevie Wonder.
Jobete Music Co., Inc., 1984/Black Bull Music, 1984.
Best-selling record by Stevie Wonder (Motown, 84). Introduced in the
film *The Lady in Red* (84). Won an Academy Award, Best Song, 1984;
a National Academy of Recording Arts and Sciences Award, Song of
the Year, 1984.

I Keep Coming Back
Words and music by Johnny Slate, Jim Hurt, and Larry Keith.
WB Music Corp., 1980.
Best-selling record by Razzy Bailey (RCA, 80).

I Keep Forgettin' (Every Time You're Near)
Words and music by Jerry Leiber and Mike Stoller.
Bienstock Publishing Co., 1962/Jerry Leiber Music, 1962/Mike
    Stoller Music, 1962.
Best-selling record by Michael McDonald (Warner Brothers, 82).

I Know There's Something Going On (Canadian)
Words and music by Russ Ballard.
Russell Ballard, Ltd., Middlesex, England, 1982/Island Music, 1982.
Best-selling record by Frida (Atlantic, 82).

I Know What Boys Like
Words and music by Christopher Butler.
Merovingian Music, 1980.
Best-selling record by The Waitresses (Polydor, 82).

I Lie
Words and music by Thomas William Damphier.
Coal Miner's Music Inc., 1980.
Best-selling record by Loretta Lynn (MCA, 82).

I Lobster But Never Flounder
Words and music by Bobby Braddock and Sparky Braddock
    (pseudonym for Wilma Sue Lawrence).
Tree Publishing Co., Inc., 1979.
Featured on *Writers in Disguise* by Pinkard and Bowen (Warner Broth-
    ers, 84).

I Love a Rainy Night
Words and music by Eddie Rabbitt, Even Stevens, and David
    Malloy.
Debdave Music Inc., 1980/Briarpatch Music, 1980.
Best-selling record by Eddie Rabbitt (Elektra, 80).

I Love L.A.
Words and music by Randy Newman.
Six Pictures Music, 1983.
Introduced by Randy Newman in *Trouble in Paradise* (Warner Broth-
    ers, 83).

I Love Rock and Roll
Words and music by Jake Hooker and Alan Merrill.
Finchley Music Corp., 1975.
Best-selling record by Joan Jett & The Blackhearts (Boardwalk, 82).

I Love to Dance
Words by Alan Bergman and Marilyn Bergman, music by Billy
    Goldenberg.

Izzylumoe Music, 1978/Threesome Music, 1978.
Introduced by Dorothy Loudon and Vincent Gardenia in *Ballroom* (Musical, 78). Performed by Sandy Duncan in *Five, Six, Seven, Eight. . . Dance* (Revue, 83).

I Love You
Words and music by Derek Holt.
CBB Music, Tortola, British Virgin Islands, 1980.
Best-selling record by The Climax Blues Band (Warner Brothers, 81).

I Loved 'Em Every One
Words and music by Phil Sampson.
Tree Publishing Co., Inc., 1980.
Best-selling record by T. G. Sheppard (Warner/Curb, 81).

I Made It Through the Rain
Words and music by Gerald Kenny, Drey Shepperd, Bruce Sussman, Jack Feldman, and Barry Manilow.
Unichappell Music Inc., 1979.
Best-selling record by Barry Manilow (Arista, 80).

I Never Wanted to Love You
Words and music by William Finn.
Samuel French, Inc., 1981.
Introduced by company of *March of the Falsettos* (81).

I Pledge My Love
Best-selling record by Peaches and Herb (Polydor, 80). See *Popular Music, 1920-1979.*

I Ran (English)
Words and music by Ali Score, Paul Reynolds, Mike Score, and Frank Maudley.
Zomba Enterprises, Inc., 1982.
Best-selling record by A Flock of Seagulls (Jive/Arista, 82).

I Really Don't Need No Light
Words and music by Jeffrey Osborne and David Wolinski.
Almo Music Corp., 1982/March 9 Music, 1982/WB Music Corp., 1982/Overdue Music, 1982.
Best-selling record by Jeffrey Osborne (A & M, 82).

I Still Believe in Waltzes
Words and music by Michael Hughes, Johnny Macrae, and Bob Morrison.
Southern Nights Music Co., 1980.
Best-selling record by Conway Twitty and Loretta Lynn (MCA, 81).

I Still Can't Get Over Loving You
Words and music by Ray Parker, Jr.
Raydiola Music, 1983.
Best-selling record by Ray Parker, Jr. (Arista, 84).

I Think I'll Just Stay Here and Drink
Words and music by Merle Haggard.
Shade Tree Music Inc., 1981.
Best-selling record by Merle Haggard (MCA, 81).

I Told You So
Words by Fred Ebb, music by John Kander.
Fiddleback Music Publishing Co., Inc., 1981/Kander & Ebb Inc., 1981.
Introduced by Roderick Cook and Grace Keagy in *Woman of the Year* (81).

I Wanna Be Your Lover
Words and music by Prince Rogers Nelson.
Controversy Music, 1979.
Best-selling record by Prince (Warner Brothers, 80).

I Want a New Drug
Words and music by Christopher Hayes and Huey Lewis.
Hulex Music, 1983/Red Admiral Music Inc., 1983.
Best-selling record by Huey Lewis & The News (Chrysalis, 84).

I Want Candy
Revived by Bow Wow Wow (RCA, 82). See *Popular Music, 1920-79.*

I Want It All
Words by Richard Maltby, music by David Shire.
Fiddleback Music Publishing Co., Inc., 1984/Progeny Music, 1984/
Revelation Music Publishing Corp., 1984/Long Pond Music, 1984.
Introduced by Beth Fowler, Catherine Cox and Liz Callaway in *Baby* (83).

I Want to Hold Your Hand (English)
Revived by Lakeside (Solar, 82). See *Popular Music, 1920-1979.*

I Want to Know What Love Is (English)
Words and music by Mick Jones.
Somerset Songs Publishing, Inc., 1984/E S P Management, Inc., 1984.
Best-selling record by Foreigner (Atlantic, 84).

I Was Country When Country Wasn't Cool
Words and music by Kye Fleming and Dennis Morgan.

Pi-Gem Music Publishing Co, Inc., 1981.
Best-selling record by Barbara Mandrell (MCA, 81). Nominated for a National Academy of Recording Arts and Sciences Award, Country Song of the Year, 1981.

I Will Follow (Irish)
Words and music by Larry Mullen, Dave Evans, Adam Clayton, and Paul Hewson.
Island Music, 1980.
Featured in *Boy* by U2 (Island, 82).

I Will Follow
Words and music by James Taylor.
Country Road Music Inc., 1981.
Introduced by James Taylor in *Dad Loves His Work* (Columbia, 81).

I Wish I Was Eighteen Again
Best-selling record by George Burns (Mercury, 80). See *Popular Music, 1920-1979.*

I Won't Be Home Tonight (English)
Words and music by Tony Carey.
WB Music Corp., 1982.
Best-selling record by Tony Carey (Rocshire, 83).

I Won't Hold You Back
Words and music by Steve Lukather.
Rehtakul Veets Music, 1982.
Best-selling record by Toto (Columbia, 83).

I Would Die 4 U
Words and music by Prince Rogers Nelson.
Controversy Music, 1984/WB Music Corp., 1984.
Best-selling record by Prince & The Revolution (Warner Brothers, 84).

I Wouldn't Change You If I Could
Words and music by Arthur Q. Smith and Paul H. Jones.
Peer International Corp., 1952.
Best-selling record by Ricky Scaggs (Epic, 83).

I Wouldn't Have Missed It for the World
Words and music by Kye Fleming, Dennis Morgan, and Charles Quillen.
Hall-Clement Publications, 1981/Chess Music Inc., 1981.
Best-selling record by Ronnie Milsap (RCA, 82).

I Write Your Name
Words and music by Jim Carroll and Wayne Woods.

Dr. Benway Music, 1983.
Introduced by Jim Carroll in *I Write Your Name* (Atlantic, 83).

Ice Cream for Crow
Words and music by Don Van Vliet.
Singing Ink Music, 1982.
Introduced on *Ice Cream for Crow* by Captain Beefheart (Virgin/Epic, 82).

I'd Love to Lay You Down
Best-selling record in 1980 by Conway Twitty (MCA). See *Popular Music, 1920-1979.*

If Anyone Falls
Words and music by Sandy Stewart and Stephanie Nicks.
Welsh Witch Publishing, 1982/Sweet Talk Music Co., 1982.
Best-selling record by Stevie Nicks (Modern, 83).

If Ever You're in My Arms Again
Words by Cynthia Weil, words and music by Michael Masser, music by Tom Snow.
Almo Music Corp., 1984/Prime Street Music, 1984/Snow Music, 1984/Dyad Music, Ltd., 1984.
Best-selling record by Peabo Bryson (Elektra, 84).

If Hollywood Don't Need You Honey I Still Do
Words and music by Bob McDill.
Hall-Clement Publications, 1982.
Best-selling record by Don Williams (MCA, 82).

If I'd Been the One
Words and music by Don Barnes, Jeff Carlisi, Donnie Van Zant, and Larry Steele.
Rocknocker Music Co., 1983.
Best-selling record by 38 Special (A & M, 83).

If It Ain't One Thing It's Another
Words and music by Richard "Dimples" Fields and Belinda Wilson.
On the Boardwalk Music, 1982/Dat Richfield Kat Music, 1982/Songs Can Sing, 1982.
Best-selling record by Richard "Dimples" Fields (Boardwalk, 82).

If Love Were All (English)
Revived by Barbara Cook on *It's Better with a Band* (Moss Music Group, 81). See Popular Music, 1920-79

If Only You Knew
Words and music by Kenny Gamble, Dexter Wansel, and Cynthia

Biggs.
Assorted Music, 1981.
Best-selling record by Patti LaBelle (Philadelphia International, 84).

If This Is It
Words and music by John Colla and Huey Lewis.
Hulex Music, 1983/Red Admiral Music Inc., 1983.
Best-selling record by Huey Lewis & The News (Chrysalis, 84).

If This World Were Mine
Words and music by Marvin Gaye.
Jobete Music Co., Inc., 1967.
Featured on *Instant Love* by Cheryl Lynn (Columbia, 82).

If We Were in Love
Words by Alan Bergman and Marilyn Bergman, music by John
    Williams.
CBS Variety Catalog, Inc., 1981/Threesome Music, 1981.
Introduced by Placido Domingo in *Yes Giorgio* (81). Nominated for an
    Academy Award, Best Song of the Year, 1982.

If You Ever Change Your Mind
Words and music by Parker McGee and Bob Gundry.
Dawnbreaker Music Co., 1980/Silver Nightingale Music, 1980.
Best-selling record by Crystal Gayle (Columbia, 80).

If You Think You're Lonely Now
Words and music by Bobby Womack, Patrick Moten, and Richard
    Griffin.
Ashtray Music, 1981/Moriel Music, 1981/ABKCO Music Inc., 1981.
Best-selling record by Bobby Womack (Beverly Glen, 82).

**If You're Gonna Play in Texas (You Gotta Have a Fiddle in the
    Band)**
Words and music by Dan Mitchell and Murry Kellum.
Baray Music Inc., 1984/Dale Morris Music, 1984.
Best-selling record by Alabama (RCA, 84).

**If You're Thinking You Want a Stranger (There's One Coming
    Home)**
Words and music by Blake Mevis and David Willis.
Jack & Bill Music Co., 1981.
Best-selling record by George Strait (MCA, 82).

I'll Tumble 4 Ya (English)
Words and music by Roy Hay, Jon Moss, Michael Craig, and
    George O'Dowd.

Virgin Music, Inc., 1982.
Best-selling record by Culture Club (Virgin/Epic, 83).

I'll Wait
Words and music by Eddie Van Halen, Alex Van Halen, Michael
  Anthony, David Lee Roth, and Michael H. McDonald.
Van Halen Music, 1983/Genevieve Music, 1983.
Best-selling record by Van Halen (Warner Brothers, 84).

Illusions
Words and music by Will Holt.
Lemon Tree Music, Inc., 1981.
Introduced by Jane White in *Ah, Men* (81).

I'm Alive
Words and music by Clint Ballard, Jr.
Camelback Mountain Music Corp., 1982.
Best-selling record by ELO (MCA, 80).

I'm Alright (Theme from *Caddyshack*)
Words and music by Kenny Loggins.
Milk Money Music, 1980.
Best-selling record by Kenny Loggins (Columbia, 80). Introduced in the
  film *Caddyshack* (80).

I'm Coming Out
Words and music by Bernard Edwards and Nile Rodgers.
Chic Music Inc., 1980.
Best-selling record by Diana Ross (Motown, 80).

I'm Glad You Didn't Know Me
Words and music by Craig Carnelia.
Samuel French, Inc., 1982.
Introduced by Philip Hoffman and Cynthia Carle in *Is There Life After
  High School* (82).

I'm Gonna Hire a Wino to Decorate Our Home
Words and music by DeWayne Blackwell.
Peso Music, 1982/Wallet Music, 1982.
Best-selling record by David Frizzell (Warner/Viva, 82). Nominated for
  a National Academy of Recording Arts and Sciences Award, Country
  Song of the Year, 1982.

I'm Gonna Love Her for the Both of Us
Words and music by Jim Steinman.
E. B. Marks Music Corp., 1981/Peg Music Co., 1981.
Best-selling record by Meat Loaf (Cleveland International, 81).

I'm in Love
Words and music by Kashif (pseudonym for Michael Jones).
Music Corp. of America, 1981.
Best-selling record by Evelyn King (RCA, 81).

I'm Just an Old Chunk of Coal (But I'm Gonna Be a Diamond Someday)
Words and music by Billy Jo Shaver.
ATV Music Corp., 1981.
Best-selling record by John Anderson (Warner Brothers, 81).

I'm Not That Lonely Yet
Words and music by Bill Rice and Mary S. Rice.
Swallowfork Music, Inc., 1981.
Best-selling record by Reba McEntire (Mercury, 82).

I'm So Excited
Words and music by Anita Pointer, June Pointer, Trevor Lawrence, and Ruth Pointer.
Braintree Music, 1982/Ruth Pointer Publishing, 1982/Blackwood Music Inc., 1982/Anita Pointer Publishing, 1982/Leggs Four Publishing, 1982.
Best-selling record by The Pointer Sisters (Planet, 82).

I'm So Glad I'm Standing Here Today
Words and music by Joe Sample and Will Jennings.
Irving Music Inc., 1981/Blue Sky Rider Songs, 1981/Four Knights Music Co., 1981.
Best-selling record by The Crusaders (MCA, 81).

I'm Still Standing (English)
Words by Bernie Taupin, music by Elton John.
Intersong, USA Inc., 1983.
Best-selling record by Elton John (Geffen, 83).

Impossible
Words and music by Peabo Bryson.
Peabo Bryson Enterprises, Inc., 1984/WB Music Corp., 1984.
Introduced by Peabo Bryson in *I Am Love* (Capitol, 82).

In a Big Country (Scottish)
Words and music by Big Country.
Virgin Music, Inc., 1983.
Best-selling record by Big Country (Mercury, 83).

In America
Words and music by Charles Hayward, James Marshall, Joel DiGregorio, Charlie Daniels, Tom Crain, and Fred Edwards.

Hat Band Music, 1980.
Best-selling record by The Charlie Daniels Band (Epic, 80).

In Cars
Words and music by Jimmy Webb.
White Oak Songs, 1981.
Featured in *Angel Heart* (Columbia/Lorimar, 82).

In My Eyes
Words and music by Barbara Wyrick.
Intersong, USA Inc., 1983.
Best-selling record by John Conlee (MCA, 84).

In the Air Tonight (English)
Words and music by Phil Collins.
Pun Music Inc., London, England, 1981.
Best-selling record by Phil Collins (Atlantic, 81). Featured on *Miami Vice* (84).

In the Cards
Words by David Zippel, music by Alan Menken.
Menken Music, 1984/Trunksong Music, 1984.
Introduced by Wade Raley in *Diamonds* (84).

In the Dark
Words and music by Billy Squier.
Songs of the Knight, 1981.
Best-selling record by Billy Squier (Capitol, 81).

(Pride) In the Name of Love (Irish)
Words and music by Paul Henson, Dave Evans, Adam Clayton, and Larry Mullen.
Island Music, 1984.
Best-selling record by U2 (Island, 84).

In Your Letter
Words and music by Gary Ricrath.
Slam Dunk Music, 1980.
Best-selling record by REO Speedwagon (Epic, 81).

Independence Day
Introduced by Bruce Springsteen *The River* (Columbia, 80). See *Popular Music, 1920-1979*.

Infatuation
Words and music by Rod Stewart, Duane Hitchings, and Michael Omartian.
Rod Stewart, 1984/Hitchings Music, 1984/Roland Robinson Music,

107

1984.
Best-selling record by Rod Stewart (Warner Brothers, 84).

An Innocent Man
Words and music by Billy Joel.
Joelsongs, 1983.
Best-selling record by Billy Joel (Columbia, 84).

Inside Love (So Personal)
Words and music by Kashif (pseudonym for Michael Jones).
Music Corp. of America, 1983.
Best-selling record by George Benson (Warner Brothers, 83).

Into the Heart (Irish)
Words and music by Paul Hewson, Larry Mullen, Adam Clayton, and Dave Evans.
Island Music, 1980.
Introduced by U2 in *Boy* (Island, 80).

Into the Night
Words and music by Benny Mardones and Robert Tepper.
Conus Music, 1980.
Best-selling record by Benny Mardones (Polydor, 80).

I.O.U.
Words and music by Kerry Chater and Austin Roberts.
Vogue Music, 1983/MCA, Inc., 1983.
Best-selling record by Lee Greenwood (MCA, 83). Nominated for a National Academy of Recording Arts and Sciences Award, Country Song of the Year, 1983.

Ireland (English)
Words and music by Marianne Faithfull and Barry Reynolds.
Island Music, 1983.
Introduced by Marianne Faithfull on *A Child's Adventure* (Island, 83).

Is It You
Words and music by Lee Ritenour, Eric Tagg, and Bill Champlin.
Rit of Habeas, 1981.
Best-selling record by Lee Ritenour (Elektra, 81).

Is There Something I Should Know (English)
Words and music by Duran Duran.
Chappell & Co., Inc., 1983.
Best-selling record by Duran Duran (Capitol, 83).

Islands in the Stream (English)
Words and music by Barry Gibb, Robin Gibb, and Maurice Gibb.

Gibb Brothers Music, 1983.
Best-selling record by Kenny Rogers and Dolly Parton (RCA, 83).

It Ain't Enough (Canadian)
Words and music by Corey Hart.
Liesse Publishing, 1982.
Best-selling record by Corey Hart (EMI-America, 84).

It Didn't Take Long
Words and music by Holly Knight.
Jiru Music, 1980/Arista Music, Inc., 1980/Land of Dreams Music, 1980.
Best-selling record by Spider (Dreamland, 81).

It Don't Hurt Me Half as Bad
Words and music by Joe Allen, Deoin Lay, and Bucky Lindsey.
Combine Music Corp., 1977.
Best-selling record by Ray Price (Dimension, 81).

It Might Be You
Words by Alan Bergman and Marilyn Bergman, music by Dave Grusin.
Gold Horizon Music Corp., 1982/Threesome Music, 1982/Golden Torch Music Corp., 1982.
Best-selling record by Stephen Bishop (Warner Brothers, 83). Introduced in the film *Tootsie* (83). Nominated for an Academy Award, Best Song, 1982.

It's a Love Thing
Words and music by William Shelby and Dana Griffey.
Spectrum VII, 1980.
Best-selling record by The Whispers (Solar, 81).

It's a Lovely, Lovely World
Best-selling record by Gail Davies (Warner Brothers, 81). See *Popular Music, 1920-1979.*

It's a Miracle (English)
Words and music by George O'Dowd, Jon Moss, Roy Hay, Mickey Craig, and Phil Pickett.
Virgin Music, Inc., 1983/Warner-Tamerlane Publishing Corp., 1983.
Best-selling record by Culture Club (Virgin/Epic, 84).

It's a Mistake (Australian)
Words and music by Colin Hay.
April Music, Inc., 1983.
Best-selling record by Men at Work (Columbia, 83).

It's Better with a Band
Words by David Zippel, music by Wally Harper.
Notable Music Co., Inc., 1981.
Performed by Sandy Duncan in *Five-Six-Seven-Eight. . .Dance* (83).

It's Gonna Take a Miracle
Revived by Deniece Williams (Arc/Columbia, 82). See Popular Music,
1920-79 Nominated for a National Academy of Recording Arts and
Sciences Award, Rhythm 'n' Blues Song of the Year, 1982.

It's Like We Never Said Goodbye (English)
Words and music by Roger Greenaway and Geoff Stephens.
Dejamus Inc., 1978.
Best-selling record by Crystal Gayle (Columbia, 80).

It's My Turn
Words by Carole Bayer Sager, music by Michael Masser.
Colgems-EMI Music Inc., 1980/Unichappell Music Inc., 1980/
Begonia Melodies, Inc., 1980.
Best-selling record by Diana Ross (Motown, 80). Introduced in the film
It's My Turn (80).

It's Now or Never
Revived by John Schneider (Scotti Brothers, 81). See *Popular Music,
1920-1979.*

It's Raining Again (English)
Words and music by Rick Davies and Roger Hodgson.
Delicate Music, 1982.
Best-selling record by Supertramp (A & M, 82).

It's Raining Men
Words and music by Paul Jabarra and Paul Shaffer.
Songs of Manhattan Island Music Co., 1981/Olga Music, 1981/
Postvalda Music, 1981.
Best-selling record by The Weather Girls (Columbia, 83).

It's Still Rock and Roll to Me
Words and music by Billy Joel.
Impulsive Music, 1980/April Music, Inc., 1980.
Best-selling record by Billy Joel (Columbia, 80).

I've Been Around Enough to Know
Words and music by Bob McDill and Dickey Lee.
Hall-Clement Publications, 1975.
Best-selling record by John Schneider (MCA, 84).

I've Got a Rock and Roll Heart
Words and music by Troy Seals, Eddie Setser, and Steve Diamond.
WB Music Corp., 1981/Warner-Tamerlane Publishing Corp., 1981/
    Diamond Mine Music, 1981/Face the Music, 1981.
Best-selling record by Eric Clapton (Warner Brothers/Duck, 83).

I've Never Been to Me
Revived by Charlene (Motown, 82). See *Popular Music, 1920-1979.*

I've Still Got My Bite
Words and music by Micki Grant.
Samuel French, Inc., 1980.
Introduced by Mabel King in *It's So Nice to Be Civilized* (80).

J

Jack and Diane
Words and music by John Cougar Mellencamp.
Riva Music Ltd., 1982.
Best-selling record by John Cougar (Riva/Mercury, 82).

Jam on It
Words and music by Maurice Cenac.
Wicked Stepmother Music Publishing Corp., 1984/Wedot Music, 1984.
Best-selling record by Newcleus (Sunnyview, 84).

James
Words and music by Vicki Peterson.
Illegal Songs, Inc., 1984/Bangaphile Music, 1984.
Introduced by The Bangles on *All Over the Place* (Columbia, 84).

Jamie
Words and music by Ray Parker, Jr.
Raydiola Music, 1984.
Best-selling record by Ray Parker, Jr. (Arista, 84).

Jane
Words and music by David Friedberg, Jim McPherson, Craig Chaquico, and Paul Kantner.
Pods Publishing, 1979/Lunatunes Music, 1979/Little Dragon Music, 1979/Kosher Dill Music, 1979.
Best-selling record by The Jefferson Starship (Grunt, 80).

Jeopardy
Words and music by Greg Kihn and Steven Wright.
Rye-Boy Music, 1983/Well Received Music, 1983.
Best-selling record by The Greg Kihn Band (Beserkley, 83).

Jersey Girl
Words and music by Tom Waits.

Fifth Floor Music Inc., 1980.
Introduced by Tom Waits on *Heartattack and Vine* (Asylum, 80).
  Recorded by Bruce Springsteen (Columbia, 84).

Jesse
Words and music by Carly Simon and Mike Mainieri.
Quackenbush Music, Ltd., 1980/Redeye Music Publishing Co., 1980.
Best-selling record by Carly Simon (Warner Brothers, 80).

Jessie's Girl
Words and music by Rick Springfield.
Vogue Music, 1981.
Best-selling record by Rick Springfield (RCA, 81).

Joan Crawford
Words and music by Albert Bouchard, David R. Ruter, and John
  Lennert Rigg.
B. O'Cult Songs, Inc., 1981.
Introduced by Blue Oyster Cult on *Fire of Unknown Origin* (Columbia,
  81).

Joanna
Words and music by Charles Smith, James Taylor, James Bonneford,
  Ronald Bell, Curtis Williams, Robert Bell, George Brown, and
  Clifford Adams.
Delightful Music Ltd., 1983.
Best-selling record by Kool & The Gang (De-Lite, 83).

Johannesburg
Revived by Gil Scott-Heron on *The Best of Gil Scott-Heron* (Arista, 84).
  See *Popular Music, 1920-1979.*

Johnny 99
Words and music by Bruce Springsteen.
Bruce Springsteen, 1982.
Featured on *Johnny 99* by Johnny Cash (Columbia, 83). Introduced by
  Bruce Springsteen on *Nebraska* (Columbia, 82).

JoJo
Words and music by David Foster and Boz Scaggs.
Boz Scaggs Music, 1980/Foster Frees Music Inc., 1980/Almo Music
  Corp., 1980/Irving Music Inc., 1980.
Best-selling record by Boz Scaggs (Columbia, 80).

Jokerman
Words and music by Bob Dylan.
Special Rider Music, 1983.
Introduced by Bob Dylan on *Infidels* (Columbia, 83).

Jose Cuervo
Words and music by Cathy Jordan.
Easy Listening Music Corp., 1981/Galleon Music, Inc., 1981.
Best-selling record by Shelly West (Warner/Viva, 83).

Joystick
Words and music by Bobby Harris and Eric Fearman.
Jobete Music Co., Inc., 1983.
Best-selling record by Dazz Band (Motown, 84).

Juicy Fruit
Words and music by James Mtume.
Mtume Music Publishing, 1983.
Best-selling record by Mtume (Epic, 83).

Juke Box Hero (English-American)
Words and music by Lou Gramm and Mick Jones.
Somerset Songs Publishing, Inc., 1981/ESP Management Inc., 1981.
Best-selling record by Foreigner (Atlantic, 82).

Jump
Words and music by Eddie Van Halen, Alex Van Halen, Michael
  Anthony, and David Lee Roth.
Van Halen Music, 1983.
Best-selling record by Van Halen (Warner Brothers, 84).

Jump (for My Love)
Words and music by Marti Sharron, Steve Mitchell, and Gary
  Skardina.
Welbeck Music, 1983/Stephen Mitchell Music, 1983/Anidraks
  Music/Porchester Music, Inc., 1983.
Best-selling record by The Pointer Sisters (Planet, 84).

Jump to It
Words and music by Luther Vandross and Marcus Miller.
April Music, Inc., 1982/Uncle Ronnie's Music Co., Inc., 1982/
  Sunset Burgundy Music, Inc., 1982.
Best-selling record by Aretha Franklin (Arista, 82).

Junior's Bar
Words and music by Joe Grushecky, Gil Snyder, and Eddie Britt.
Cleveland International, 1980/Brick Alley, 1980.
Introduced by by The Iron City Rockers on *Have a Good Time (But Get
  Out Alive)* (MCA, 80).

Just Another Woman in Love
Words and music by Patti Ryan and Wanda Mallette.

Southern Nights Music Co., 1982.
Best-selling record by Anne Murray (Capitol, 84).

Just Be Good to Me
Words and music by Terry Lewis and James Harris, III.
Flyte Tyme Tunes, 1983/Avant Garde Music Publishing, Inc., 1983.
Best-selling record by The S.O.S. Band (Tabu, 83).

Just Be Yourself
Words and music by Charles Singleton, Larry Blackmon, and Toni
   Jenkins.
All Seeing Eye Music, 1981/Cameo Five Music.
Best-selling record by Cameo (Chocolate City, 82).

Just My Daydream
Words and music by William Smokey Robinson, Jr.
Jobete Music Co., Inc., 1982.
Featured on *Jump to It* by Aretha Franklin (Arista, 82).

Just the Motion (English)
Words and music by Linda Thompson.
Island Music, 1982.
Introduced by Richard and Linda Thompson on *Shoot out the Lights*
   (Hannbal, 82).

Just the Two of Us
Words and music by Bill Withers, William Salter, and Ralph
   MacDonald.
Antisia Music Inc., 1981/Bleunig Music, 1981.
Best-selling record by Grover Washington, Jr. and Bill Withers (Elektra,
   81). Nominated for National Academy of Recording Arts and
   Sciences Awards, Song of the Year, 1981, and Record of the Year,
   1981. Won a National Academy of Recording Arts and Sciences
   Award, Rhythm 'n' Blues Song of the Year, 1981.

Just the Way You Like It
Words and music by Terry Lewis and James Harris, III.
Flyte Tyme Tunes, 1984/Avant Garde Music Publishing, Inc., 1984.
Best-selling record by The S.O.S. Band (Tabu, 84).

Just to Satisfy You
Words and music by Don Bowman and Waylon Jennings.
Irving Music Inc., 1964/Parody Publishing.
Best-selling record by Waylon and Willie (RCA, 82).

K

Karma Chameleon (English)
Words and music by George O'Dowd, Jon Moss, Roy Hay, Mickey Craig, and Phil Pickett.
Virgin Music, Inc., 1983/Warner-Tamerlane Publishing Corp., 1983.
Best-selling record by Culture Club (Virgin/Epic, 83).

Keep on Loving You
Words and music by Kevin Cronin.
Fate Music, 1980.
Best-selling record by REO Speedwagon (Epic, 80).

Keep the Fire Burnin'
Words and music by Kevin Cronin.
Fate Music, 1982.
Best-selling record by REO Speedwagon (Epic, 82).

Key Largo
Words and music by Sonny Limbo and Bertie Higgins.
Jen-Lee Music Co., 1981/Chappell & Co., Inc., 1981/Lowery Music Co., Inc., 1981/Brother Bill's Music, 1981.
Best-selling record by Bertie Higgins (Kat Family, 82).

Kid (English)
Words and music by Chrissie Hynde.
Virgin Music, Inc., 1980.
Introduced by The Pretenders in *Pretenders* (Sire, 80).

Kids in America
Words and music by Ricky Wilde and Marty Wilde.
Finchley Music Corp., 1981.
Best-selling record by Kim Wilde (EMI-America, 82).

King of Pain (English)
Words and music by Sting (pseudonym for Gordon Sumner).

117

Illegal Songs, Inc., 1983/Reggatta Music, Ltd., 1983.
Best-selling record by The Police (A & M, 83).

King's Call (English)
Words and music by Phil Lynott.
Chappell & Co., Inc., 1980.
Introduced by Phil Lynott on *Solo in Soho* (Warner Brothers, 80).

Kiss on My List
Words and music by Janna Allen and Daryl Hall.
Hot Cha Music Co., 1980/Unichappell Music Inc., 1980/Fust Buzza
    Music, Inc., 1980.
Best-selling record by Daryl Hall and John Oates (RCA, 81).

Kiss the Bride (English)
Words by Bernie Taupin, music by Elton John.
Intersong, USA Inc., 1983.
Best-selling record by Elton John (Geffen, 83).

Kokoku
Words and music by Laurie Anderson.
Difficult Music, 1984.
Introduced by Laurie Anderson on *Mr. Heartbreak* (Warner Brothers,
    84).

L

Labeled with Love (English)
Words by Christopher Difford, music by Glenn Tilbrook.
Illegal Songs, Inc., 1980.
Introduced by Squeeze on *Argybargy* (A & M, 80).

Lady
Words and music by Lionel Richie, Jr.
Brockman Enterprises Inc., 1980.
Best-selling record by Kenny Rogers (Liberty, 80). Nominated for National Academy of Recording Arts and Sciences Awards, Song of the Year, 1980, and Record of the Year, 1980.

Lady (You Bring Me Up) (Icelandic)
English words and music by William King, Howard Hudson, and S. King.
Jobete Music Co., Inc., 1981/Hanna Music, 1981/Commodores Entertainment Publishing Corp, 1981.
Best-selling record by The Commodores (Motown, 81). Nominated for a National Academy of Recording Arts and Sciences Award, Rhythm 'n' Blues Song of the Year, 1981.

Lady Down on Love
Words and music by Randy Owen.
Maypop Music, 1981/Buzzherb Music, 1981.
Best-selling record by Alabama (RCA, 83). Nominated for a National Academy of Recording Arts and Sciences Award, Country Song of the Year, 1983.

The Lady Takes the Cowboy Every Time
Words and music by Larry Gatlin.
Larry Gatlin Music, 1984.
Best-selling record by Larry Gatlin and the Gatlin Brothers Band (Columbia, 84).

Lady You Are
Words and music by Kevin McCord, Dave Roberson, and Al
  Hudson.
Duchess Music Corp., 1984/Park's Music, 1984.
Best-selling record by One Way (MCA, 84).

Landlord
Words and music by Nick Ashford and Valerie Simpson.
Nick-O-Val Music, 1980.
Best-selling record by Gladys Knight & The Pips (Columbia, 80).

The Language of Love
Words and music by Dan Fogelberg.
Hickory Grove Music, 1984/April Music, Inc., 1984.
Best-selling record by Dan Fogelberg (Full Moon/Epic, 84).

Last Date, see **(Lost His Love) On Our Last Date.**

The Late Great Johnny Ace
Words and music by Paul Simon.
Paul Simon Music, 1981.
Introduced by Simon and Garfunkel on *The Concert in Central Park*
  (Warner Brothers, 82).

Late in the Evening
Words and music by Paul Simon.
Paul Simon Music, 1978.
Best-selling record by Paul Simon (Warner Brothers, 80). Introduced in
  the film *One Trick Pony* (80).

Lawyers in Love
Words and music by Jackson Browne.
Night Kitchen Music, 1983.
Best-selling record by Jackson Browne (Asylum, 83).

Leader of the Band
Words and music by Dan Fogelberg.
Hickory Grove Music, 1981/April Music, Inc., 1981.
Best-selling record by Dan Fogelberg (Full Moon/Epic, 81).

Learn How to Live
Words and music by Billy Squier.
Songs of the Knight, 1982.
Introduced by Billy Squier on *Emotions in Motion* (Capitol, 82).

Leather and Lace
Words and music by Stephanie Nicks.

Welsh Witch Publishing, 1975.
Best-selling record by Stevie Nicks with Don Henley (Modern, 81).

Left in the Dark
Words and music by Jim Steinman.
Lost Boys Music, 1980/Charles Family Music, 1980/Alibee Music,
 1980/Dela Music, 1980.
Best-selling record by Barbra Streisand (Columbia, 84).

Legendary Hearts
Words and music by Lou Reed.
Metal Machine Music, 1982.
Introduced on *Legendary Hearts* by Lou Reed (RCA, 83).

Legs
Words and music by Billy Gibbons, Dusty Hill, and Frank Beard.
Hamstein Music, 1983.
Best-selling record by Z.Z. Top (Warner Brothers, 84).

Lenny Bruce
Words and music by Bob Dylan.
Special Rider Music, 1981.
Introduced by Bob Dylan *Shot of Love* (Columbia, 82).

A Lesson in Leavin'
Words and music by Randy Goodrum and Brent Maher.
Chappell & Co., Inc., 1979/Sailmaker Music, 1979/Welbeck Music,
 1979/Blue Quill Music, 1979.
Best-selling record by Dottie West (United Artists, 80).

Let It Whip
Words and music by Reginald Andrews and Leon Chancler.
Ujima Music, 1981/Mac Vac Alac Music Co., 1981.
Best-selling record by The Dazz Band (Mowtown, 82). Nominated for
 a National Academy of Recording Arts and Sciences Award, Rhythm
 'n' Blues Song of the Year, 1982.

Let Me Be the Clock
Words and music by William Smokey Robinson, Jr.
Bertam Music Co., 1980.
Best-selling record by Smokey Robinson (Tamla, 80).

Let Me Be Your Angel
Words and music by Narada Michael Walden and Bunny Hill.
Walden Music, Inc., 1980/Cotillion Music Inc., 1980/Brass Heart,
 1980.
Best-selling record by Stacy Lattisaw (Cotillion, 80).

Let Me Go
Words and music by Ray Parker, Jr.
Raydiola Music, 1982.
Best-selling record by Ray Parker, Jr. (Arista, 82).

Let Me Love You Tonight
Words and music by Jeff Wilson, Dan Greer, and Steve Woodard.
Kentucky Wonder Music, 1980/Pure Prairie League Music, 1980.
Best-selling record by Pure Prairie League (Casablanca, 80).

Let Me Tickle Your Fancy
Words and music by Jermaine Jackson, Paul M. Jackson, Jr., Pamela
    Sawyer, and Marilyn McLeod.
Fat Jack the Second Music Publishing Co., 1982/Jobete Music Co.,
    Inc., 1982/Stone Diamond Music Corp., 1982.
Best-selling record by Jermaine Jackson (Motown, 82).

Let My Love Open the Door (English)
Words and music by Peter Townshend.
Towser Tunes Inc., 1980.
Best-selling record by Pete Townshend (Atco, 80).

Let the Feeling Flow
Words and music by Peabo Bryson.
WB Music Corp., 1981/Peabo Bryson Enterprises, Inc., 1981.
Best-selling record by Peabo Bryson (Capitol, 82).

Let the Music Play
Words and music by Chris Barbosa and Ed Chisolm.
Shapiro, Bernstein & Co., Inc., 1983/Emergency Music Inc., 1983.
Best-selling record by Shannon (Mirage, 84).

Let's Dance (English)
Words and music by David Bowie.
Jones Music Co., 1983.
Best-selling record by David Bowie (RCA, 83).

Let's Fall to Pieces Together
Words and music by Dickey Lee, Tommy Rocco, and Johnny
    Russell.
Hall-Clement Publications, 1983/Sunflower County Songs, 1983.
Best-selling record by George Strait (MCA, 84).

Let's Get Serious
Words and music by Stevie Wonder and Lee Garrett.
Black Bull Music, 1980/Jobete Music Co., Inc., 1980/Broadcast
    Music Inc., 1980.
Best-selling record by Jermaine Jackson (Motown, 80). Nominated for

a National Academy of Recording Arts and Sciences Award, Rhythm 'n'Blues, 1980.

Let's Go Crazy
Words and music by Prince Rogers Nelson.
Controversy Music, 1984/WB Music Corp., 1984.
Best-selling record by Prince & the Revolution (Warner Brothers, 84). Introduced in the film *Purple Rain* (84).

Let's Groove
Words and music by Maurice White, Wayne Vaughn, and W. Vaughn.
Saggifire Music, 1981/Yougoulei Music, 1981.
Best-selling record by Earth, Wind & Fire (Arc/Columbia, 81).

Let's Hear It for the Boy
Words by Dean Pitchford, music by Tom Snow.
Ensign Music Corp., 1984.
Best-selling record by Deniece Williams (Columbia, 84). Introduced in the film *Footloose* (84). Nominated for an Academy Award, Best Song, 1984.

Let's Stay Together
Revived by Tina Turner (Capitol, 84). See *Popular Music, 1920-1979.*

Let's Stop Talkin' About It
Words and music by Rory Bourke, Rafe Van Hoy, and Deborah Allen.
Unichappell Music Inc., 1983/Van Hoy Music, 1983/Chappell & Co., Inc., 1982/Duchess Music Corp., 1983.
Best-selling record by Janie Fricke (Columbia, 84).

Lick It Up
Words and music by Paul Stanley and Vinnie Vincent.
Kiss, 1983/Kissway Music, Inc., 1983.
Best-selling record by Kiss (Mercury, 83).

Life Gets Better (English)
Words and music by Graham Parker.
Participation Music, Inc., 1983.
Introduced on The Real Macaw by Graham Parker (Arista, 83).

Lights Out
Words and music by Peter Wolf and Don Covay.
Pal-Park Music, 1984/Ze'ev Music, 1984.
Best-selling record by Peter Wolf (EMI-America, 84).

Like a Virgin
Words and music by Billy Steinberg and Tom Kelly.
Billy Steinberg Music, 1984/Denise Barry Music, 1984.
Best-selling record by Madonna (Warner Brothers, 84).

Like an Inca
Words and music by Neil Young.
Silver Fiddle, 1982.
Featured in *Trans* by Neil Young (Reprise, 83).

Limelight (Canadian)
Words by Neil Peart, music by Alex Lifeson and Geddy Lee.
Core Music Publishing, 1981.
Best-selling record by Rush (Mercury, 81).

A Little Good News
Words and music by Charlie Black, Rory Bourke, and Thomas
   Rocco.
Chappell & Co., Inc., 1983/Bibo Music Publishers, 1983.
Best-selling record by Anne Murray (Capitol, 83). Nominated for a
   National Academy of Recording Arts and Sciences Award, Country
   Song of the Year, 1983.

Little H and Little G
Words and music by Ronald Melrose.
Rabbit Rabbit Music Co., 1982.
Introduced by Ensemble of *Upstairs at O'Neals* (82).

A Little in Love (English)
Words and music by Alan Tarney.
ATV Music Corp., 1980.
Best-selling record by Cliff Richard (EMI-America, 80).

A Little Is Enough (English)
Words and music by Peter Townshend.
Towser Tunes Inc., 1980.
Best-selling record by Pete Townshend (Atco, 80).

Little Jeannie (English)
Words by Gary Osborne, music by Elton John.
Intersong, USA Inc., 1980.
Best-selling record by Elton John (MCA, 80).

Little Red Corvette
Words and music by Prince Rogers Nelson.
Controversy Music, 1982.
Best-selling record by Prince (Warner Brothers, 83).

Little Too Late
Words and music by Alex Call.
Unichappell Music Inc., 1981/Roseynotes Music, 1981.
Best-selling record by Pat Benatar (Chrysalis, 83).

Live
Words and music by Emmit Rhodes.
La Brea Music, 1984/Thirty-Four Music, 1984.
Featured on *All Over the Place* by The Bangles (Columbia, 84).

Living a Lie
Words and music by Chris Stamey and Peter Holsapple.
Misery Loves Co., 1982.
Introduced on *Repercussion* by The DBs (Albion, 82).

Living Inside Myself
Words and music by Gino Vanelli.
Black Keys, 1981.
Best-selling record by Gino Vanelli (Arista, 81).

Living It Up
Words and music by Rickie Lee Jones.
Easy Money Music, 1981.
Introduced by Rickie Lee Jones on *Pirates* (Warner Brothers, 82).

Living Through Another Cuba (English)
Words and music by Andy Partridge.
Nymph Music, 1980.
Performed by XTC in *Life in the European Theatre* (Sire, 82).

Lonely Nights
Words and music by Harris Stewart and Keith Stegall.
Blackwood Music Inc., 1981.
Best-selling record by Mickey Gilley (Epic, 81).

Long Gone Dead
Words and music by Chip Kinman and Tony Kinman.
Black Impala Music, 1984.
Introduced by Rank and File on *Long Gone Dead* (Slash, 84).

Long Hard Road (the Sharecropper's Dream)
Words and music by Rodney Crowell.
Coolwell Music, 1984/Granite Music Corp., 1984.
Best-selling record by The Nitty Gritty Dirt Band (Warner Brothers, 84).

A Long Night
Music by Alec Wilder, words by Loonis Reeves McGlohon.

Ludlow Music Inc., 1982/Saloon Songs, Inc., 1982.
Introduced by Frank Sinatra on *She Shot Me Down* (Reprise, 81).

The Longest Time
Words and music by Billy Joel.
Joelsongs, 1983/Blackwood Music Inc., 1983.
Best-selling record by Billy Joel (Columbia, 84).

The Look of Love (English)
Words and music by Martin Fry, Mark Lickley, Stephen Singleton,
    and David Palmer.
Virgin Music, Inc., 1982.
Best-selling record by ABC (Mercury, 82).

Look Over There
Words and music by Jerry Herman.
Jerryco Music Co., 1983.
Introduced by Gene Barry in *La Cage Au Folles* (83).

Look What You Done to Me
Words and music by Boz Scaggs and David Foster.
Boz Scaggs Music, 1980/Foster Frees Music Inc., 1980/Irving Music
    Inc., 1980.
Best-selling record by Boz Scaggs (Columbia, 80). Featured in the film
    Urban Cowboy (80).

Lookin' for Love
Words and music by Wanda Mallette, Patti Ryan, and Bob
    Morrison.
Southern Nights Music Co., 1979.
Best-selling record by Johnny Lee (Asylum, 80). Nominated for a Na-
    tional Academy of Recording Arts and Sciences Award, Country
    Song of the Year, 1980.

Looking for the Next Best Thing
Words and music by Kenny Edwards, Leroy P. Marinell, and
    Warren Zevon.
Tiny Tunes, 1982/Valgovino Music, 1982/Zevon Music, 1982.
Introduced by Warren Zevon in *The Envoy* (Asylum, 82).

Lord, I Hope This Day Is Good
Words and music by Dave Hanner.
Sabal Music, Inc., 1981.
Best-selling record by Don Williams (MCA, 82).

Lost in Love (Australian)
Words and music by Graham Russell.

126

Careers Music Inc., 1980.
Best-selling record by Air Supply (Arista, 80).

Love Come Down
Words and music by Kashif (pseudonym for Michael Jones).
MCA, Inc., 1982/Kashif Music, 1982.
Best-selling record by Evelyn King (RCA, 82).

Love Has Finally Come at Last
Words and music by Bobby Womack.
ABKCO Music Inc., 1983/Ashtray Music, 1983/Spaced Hands
  Music, 1983/Beverly Glen Publishing, 1983.
Best-selling record by Bobby Womack and Patti La Belle (Beverly Glen,
  84).

Love in the First Degree
Words and music by Jim Hurt and James Dubois.
Warner House of Music, 1980.
Best-selling record by Alabama (RCA, 82).

Love Is a Battlefield
Words and music by Mike Chapman and Holly Knight.
Makiki Publishing Co., Ltd., 1983/Arista Music, Inc., 1983.
Best-selling record by Pat Benatar (Chrysalis, 83).

Love Is a Stranger (English)
Words and music by Annie Lennox and David Stewart.
Red Network Music, 1982/Carbert Music Inc., 1982.
Best-selling record by Eurythmics (RCA, 83).

Love Is Alright Tonite
Words and music by Rick Springfield.
Portal Music, 1981/Muscleman Music, 1981.
Best-selling record by Rick Springfield (RCA, 82).

Love Is for Lovers
Words and music by Peter Holsapple and Darby Hall.
Misery Loves Co., 1984.
Introduced by The DB's on *Like This* (Bearsville, 84).

Love Is in Control (Finger on the Trigger) (American-English)
Words and music by Quincy Jones, Merria Ross, and Rod
  Temperton.
Yellow Brick Road Music, 1982/Almo Music Corp., 1982/Grager
  Music, 1982.
Best-selling record by Donna Summer (Geffen, 82).

Love Is on a Roll (American-English)
Words and music by Roger Cook and John Prine.
Roger Cook Music, 1983/Big Ears Music Inc., 1983/Bruised
    Oranges, 1983.
Best-selling record by Don Williams (MCA, 83).

Love Makes Such Fools of Us All
Words by Michael Stewart, music by Cy Coleman.
Notable Music Co., Inc., 1980.
Introduced by Marianne Tatum in *Barnum* (80).

Love Me Tomorrow
Words and music by Peter Cetera and David Foster.
Double Virgo Music, 1982/Foster Frees Music Inc., 1982/Irving
    Music Inc., 1982.
Best-selling record by Chicago (Full Moon/Warner Brothers, 82).

Love My Way (English)
Words and music by John Ashton, Timothy Butler, Richard Butler,
    and Vincent Ely.
Blackwood Music Inc., 1982.
Best-selling record by The Psychedelic Furs (Columbia, 83).

Love Never Goes Away
Words and music by Al Kasha and Joel Hirschhorn.
Morning Pictures Music, 1978/Fire and Water Songs.
Introduced by Debby Boone in *Seven Brides for Seven Brothers* (82).

Love on a Two Way Street
Revived by Stacy Lattisaw (Atlantic, 81). See *Popular Music, 1920-79.*

Love on the Rocks (American-French)
English words and music by Neil Diamond, English words and
    music by Gilbert Becaud.
Artistique Editions Music, France, 1980/Stonebridge Music, 1980.
Best-selling record by Neil Diamond (Capitol, 81). Introduced in the
    film *The Jazz Singer* (80).

Love on Your Side (English)
Words and music by Tom Bailey, Alannah Currie, and Joe Leeway.
Zomba Enterprises, Inc., 1982.
Best-selling record by The Thompson Twins (Arista, 83).

Love Over and Over Again
Words and music by Bobby DeBarge and Bunny DeBarge
    (pseudonym for Etterlene Jordan).
Jobete Music Co., Inc., 1980.
Best-selling record by Switch (Gordy, 80).

Love Plus One (English)
Words and music by Nick Heyward.
Bryan Morrison Music, Ltd., London, England, 1982/Bryan
    Morrison Music, Inc., 1982.
Best-selling record by Haircut One Hundred (Arista, 82).

Love Somebody
Words and music by Rick Springfield.
Vogue Music, 1984.
Best-selling record by Rick Springfield (RCA, 84).

Love Stinks
Words and music by Peter Wolf and Seth Justman.
Center City Music, 1979/Pal-Park Music, 1979.
Best-selling record by The J. Geils Band (EMI-America, 80).

Love the World Away
Words and music by Bob Morrison and Johnny Wilson.
Southern Nights Music Co., 1980.
Best-selling record by Kenny Rogers (United Artists, 80).

Love Theme from *Shogun* (Mariko's Theme)
Music by Maurice Jarre.
Addax Music Co., Inc., 1980.
Best-selling record by Meco (RSO, 80). Introduced on the TV mini-series
    Shogun.

Love T.K.O.
Words and music by Cecil Womack and Gib Nobel.
Assorted Music, 1980.
Best-selling record by Teddy Pendergrass (Philadelphia International,
    80).

Love Will Turn You Around
Words and music by Kenny Rogers, Even Stevens, Thom Schuyler,
    and David Malloy.
Lionsmate Music, 1982/Debdave Music Inc., 1982/Briarpatch Music,
    1982/Lionscub Music, 1982.
Best-selling record by Kenny Rogers (Liberty, 82).

Lovelight
Words and music by O'Bryan Burnette and Don Cornelius.
Big Train Music Co., 1984.
Best-selling record by O'Bryan (Capitol, 84).

Lovely One
Words and music by Michael Jackson and Randy Jackson.

Renjack Music, 1980/Mijac Music, 1980.
Best-selling record by The Jacksons (Epic, 80).

Lover Boy
Words and music by Billy Alessi and Bobby Alessi.
Alessi Music, 1979.
Best-selling record by Billy Ocean (Jive/Arista, 84).

Love's Been a Little Bit Hard on Me
Words and music by Gary Burr.
WB Gold Music Corp., 1982.
Best-selling record by Juice Newton (Capitol, 82).

Love's Got a Line on You
Words and music by Zack Smith and Kathe Green.
KJG Music, 1981/Blackwood Music Inc., 1981.
Best-selling record by Scandal (Columbia, 83).

Love's on the Line
Words and music by Bruce Springsteen.
Bruce Springsteen, 1982.
Featured in *On the Line* by Gary U.S. Bonds (EMI-America, 82).

Lovin' Her Was Easier
Revived by Tompall & The Glaser Brothers (Elektra, 81). See *Popular Music, 1920-1979.*

Loving Up a Storm
Words and music by Dan Morrison and Johnny Slate.
Warner House of Music, 1979.
Best-selling record by Razzy Bailey (RCA, 80).

Lucky Star
Words and music by Madonna Ciccone.
WB Music Corp., 1983/Bleu Disque Music, 1983/Webo Girl Music/
    WB Music Corp., 1983.
Best-selling record by Madonna (Sire, 84).

Lyin' in a Bed of Fire
Words and music by Steve Van Zandt.
Blue Midnight Music, 1982.
Introduced by Little Steven & The Disciples of Soul on *Men Without Women* (EMI, 82).

M

Magic
Words and music by John Farrar.
John Farrar Music, 1980.
Best-selling record by Olivia Newton-John (MCA, 80).

Magic
Words and music by Ric Ocasek.
Lido Music Inc., 1984.
Best-selling record by The Cars (Elektra, 84).

Magic Man
Words and music by Herb Alpert, Michael Stokes, and Melvin
  Ragin.
Almo Music Corp., 1981/Irving Music Inc., 1981.
Best-selling record by Herb Alpert (A & M, 81).

Major Tom (Coming Home) (East German)
English words and music by Peter Shilling and David Lodge.
Southern Music Publishing Co., Inc., 1982.
Best-selling record by Peter Shilling (Elektra, 83).

Make a Move on Me
Words and music by John Farrar and Tom Snow.
John Farrar Music, 1981/Snow Music, 1981.
Best-selling record by Olivia Newton-John (MCA, 82).

Make Love Stay
Words and music by Dan Fogelberg.
Hickory Grove Music, 1982/April Music, Inc., 1982.
Best-selling record by Dan Fogelberg (Full Moon/Epic, 83).

Make My Day
Words and music by Dewayne Blackwell.
Peso Music, 1984/Wallet Music, 1984.

Best-selling record by T. G. Sheppard with Clint Eastwood (Warner/ Curb, 84).

Make That Move
Words and music by William Shelby, Ricky Smith, and Kevin Spencer.
Spectrum VII, 1980.
Best-selling record by Shalamar (Solar, 81).

Make Up Your Mind
Words and music by George Jones, Starleana Young, and Stephen Washington.
Lucky Three Music Publishing Co., 1982/Red Aurra Publishing, 1982.
Best-selling record by Aurra (Salsoul, 82).

Makin' Thunderbirds
Words and music by Bob Seger.
Gear Publishing, 1983.
Introduced by Bob Seger on *The Distance* (Capitol, 83).

Making Love
Words and music by Carole Bayer Sager, Burt Bacharach, and Bruce Roberts.
Twentieth Century Music Corp., 1982/New Hidden Valley Music Co., 1982/Carole Bayer Sager Music, 1982/Fox Fanfare Music Inc., 1982.
Best-selling record by Roberta Flack (Atlanta, 82). Introduced in the film *Making Love* (82).

Making Love out of Nothing at All
Words and music by Jim Steinman.
E. B. Marks Music Corp., 1983/Lost Boys Music, 1983.
Best-selling record by Air Supply (Arista, 83).

Making Plans
Words and music by Dolly Parton.
Velvet Apple Music, 1980.
Best-selling record by Dolly Parton with Porter Wagoner (RCA, 80).

Mama He's Crazy
Words and music by Kenny O'Dell.
Kenny O'Dell Music, 1983.
Best-selling record by The Judds (RCA, 84). Nominated for a National Academy of Recording Arts and Sciences Award, Country Song of the Year, 1983.

Mama Used to Say
Words and music by Junior Gisombe and Bob Carter.
Colgems-EMI Music Inc., 1981/Junior Music, Ltd., 1981.
Best-selling record by Junior (Mercury, 82).

Maman
Words and music by Jim Wann.
Shapiro, Bernstein & Co., Inc., 1981.
Introduced by Jim Wann in *Pump Boys and Dinettes* (81).

A Man in Need (English)
Words and music by Richard Thompson.
Island Music, 1981.
Introduced by Richard Thompson in *Shoot out the Lights* (Hannibal, 82).

Man on the Corner (English)
Words and music by Phil Collins.
Pun Music Inc., London, England, 1981.
Best-selling record by Genesis (Atlantic, 82).

Man on Your Mind (Australian)
Words and music by Glenn Shorrock and Kerryn Tolhurst.
Little River Band Music, Victoria, Australia, 1981.
Best-selling record by Little River Band (Capitol, 82).

Maneater
Words and music by Daryl Hall, John Oates, and Sara Allen.
Fust Buzza Music, Inc., 1982/Hot Cha Music Co., 1982/Unichappell Music Inc., 1982.
Best-selling record by Hall and Oates (RCA, 82).

Maniac
Words and music by Michael Sembello and Dennis Matkosky.
Intersong, USA Inc., 1983/Famous Music Co., 1983.
Best-selling record by Michael Sembello (Casablanca, 83). Introduced in the film *Flashdance* (83). Nominated for an Academy Award, Best Song, 1983; National Academy of Recording Arts and Sciences Awards, Record of the Year, 1983, and Song of the Year, 1983.

Marilyn Monroe
Words and music by David Frishberg.
Swiftwater Music, 1981.
Introduced by David Frishberg in *The David Frishberg Songbook* (Omnisound, 83).

Marty Feldman Eyes
Words and music by Bruce Baum and Dick Bright.

Hollywood Boulevard Music, 1981.
Best-selling record by Bruce "Baby Man" Baum (Horn 11, 81).

Master Blaster (Jammin')
Words and music by Stevie Wonder.
Jobete Music Co., Inc., 1980/Black Bull Music, 1981.
Best-selling record by Stevie Wonder (Tamla, 80).

Maybe We Went Too Far
Words and music by Zack Smith, Patty Smyth, and Keith Mack.
Blackwood Music Inc., 1984.
Introduced by Scandal on *Warrior* (Columbia, 84).

Memory (English)
Words by Trevor Nunn and T. S. Eliot, music by Andrew Lloyd
    Webber.
Deco Music, 1982/Charles Koppelman Music, 1982/Jonathan Three
    Music Co., 1982/Martin Bandier Music, 1982.
Introduced by Betty Buckley in the musical *Cats* (82). Best-selling
    records by Barbra Streisand (Columbia) and Barry Manilow (Arista,
    82). Adapted from T. S. Eliot's poetry, primarily "Rhapsody on a
    Windy Night," written in 1917.

Menemsha
Words and music by Carly Simon, music by Peter Wood.
C'est Music, 1983/Hythefield Music, 1983.
Introduced by Carly Simon on *Hello Big Man* (Warner Brothers, 83).

The Message
Words and music by Melvin Glover, Sylvia Robinson, E. Fletcher,
    and Clifton Chase.
Sugar Hill Music Publishing, Ltd., 1982.
Best-selling record by Grand Master Flash & The Furious Five (Sugar-
    hill, 82).

The Metro
Words and music by John Crawford.
Safespace Music, 1982.
Best-selling record by Berlin (Geffen, 83).

Mexican Radio
Words and music by Stanard Funsten, Charles Gray, Oliver Nanini,
    and Marc Moreland.
Big Talk Music, 1982.
Best-selling record by Wall of Voodoo (I.R.S., 83).

Mickey
Words and music by Nicky Chinn and Mike Chapman.

Arista Music, Inc., 1979.
Best-selling record by Toni Basil (Chrysalis, 82).

Middle of the Road
Words and music by Chrissie Hynde.
Virgin Music Ltd., 1984.
Best-selling record by The Pretenders (Warner Brothers, 84).

Midnight Flight (Canadian)
Words and music by Kate McGarrigle.
Garden Court Music Co., 1983.
Introduced by Kate and Anna McGarrigle in *Love Over and Over* (Polydor, 83).

Midnight Hauler
Words and music by James DuBois and Wood Newton.
Warner House of Music, 1981.
Best-selling record by Razzy Bailey (RCA, 81).

Minimum Love
Words and music by Mac McAnnally and Gerry Wexler.
I've Got The Music Co., 1982/Song Tailors Music Co., 1982.
Best-selling record by Mac McAnnally (Warner Brothers, 83).

Mirror Mirror
Words and music by Michael Sembello and Dennis Natkosky.
Koppelman Family Music, 1981/Bandier Family Music, 1981/ Foghorn Music, 1981/Rosstown Music, 1981/R. L. August Music Co., 1981.
Best-selling record by Diana Ross (RCA, 82).

Miss Me Blind (English)
Words and music by George O'Dowd, Jon Moss, Roy Hay, and Michael Craig.
Virgin Music, Inc., 1983.
Best-selling record by Culture Club (Virgin/Epic, 84).

Miss Sun
Words and music by David Paich and Boz Scaggs.
Hudmar Publishing Co., Inc., 1980.
Best-selling record by Boz Scaggs (Columbia, 80).

Missing You
Words and music by Dan Fogelberg.
Hickory Grove Music, 1982/April Music, Inc., 1982.
Best-selling record by Dan Fogelberg (Full Moon/Epic, 82).

Popular Music, 1980-1984

Missing You
Words and music by John Waite, Chas Sanford, and Mark Leonard.
Hudson Bay Music Co., 1984/Paperwaite Music, 1984/Fallwater
    Music, 1984/Markmeem Music, 1984.
Best-selling record by John Waite (EMI-America, 84).

Mr. Roboto
Words and music by Dennis DeYoung.
Stygian Songs, 1983.
Best-selling record by Styx (A & M, 83).

Mister Sandman
Revived by Emmylou Harris with Linda Ronstadt and Dolly Parton
    (Warner Brothers, 81). See *Popular Music, 1920-1979.*

Misunderstanding (English)
Words and music by Phil Collins.
Pun Music Inc., London, England, 1980.
Best-selling record by Genesis (Atlantic, 80).

Modern Girl
Words and music by Dominic Bugatti and Frank Musker.
Unichappell Music Inc., 1980.
Best-selling record by Sheena Easton (EMI, 81).

Modern Love (English)
Words and music by David Bowie.
Jones Music Co., 1983.
Best-selling record by David Bowie (EMI-America, 83).

Mona Lisa's Lost Her Smile
Words and music by Johnny Cunningham.
Rocksmith Music, 1984/Lockhill-Selma Music, 1984.
Best-selling record by David Allan Coe (Columbia, 84).

Money Changes Everything
Words and music by Thomas Gray.
ATV Music Corp., 1978.
Introduced by The Brains on *The Brains* (Mercury, 80). Featured on
    She's So Unusual by Cyndi Lauper (Portrait, 83).

Moon at the Window
Words and music by Joni Mitchell.
Crazy Crow Music, 1982.
Introduced by Joni Mitchell in *Wild Things Run Fast* (Asylum, 82).

The Moon Is a Harsh Mistress
Revived by Linda Ronstadt in *Get Closer* (Asylum, 82). See *Popular Music, 1920-1979.*

More Bounce to the Ounce - Part 1
Words and music by Roger Troutman.
Rubber Band Music, Inc., 1980.
Best-selling record by Zapp (Warner Brothers, 80).

More Love
Words and music by William Smokey Robinson, Jr.
Jobete Music Co., Inc., 1980.
Best-selling record by Kim Carnes (EMI-America, 80).

More Than I Can Say
Words and music by Sonny Curtis and Jerry Allison.
Warner-Tamerlane Publishing Corp., 1960.
Best-selling record by Leo Sayer (Warner Brothers, 80).

More Than Just the Two of Us
Words and music by Michael Carey Schneider and Mitch Crane.
Shel Sounds Music, 1980/Sneaker Songs, 1980.
Best-selling record by Sneaker (Handshake, 81).

Mornin'
Words and music by Al Jarreau, Jay Graydon, and David Foster.
Al Jarreau Music, 1983/Garden Rake Music, Inc., 1983/Foster Frees
   Music Inc., 1983.
Best-selling record by Al Jarreau (Warner Brothers, 83).

Morning Train
Words and music by Florrie Palmer.
Unichappell Music Inc., 1981.
Best-selling record by Sheena Easton (EMI America, 81).

Motel Matches (English)
Words and music by Elvis Costello.
Plangent Visions Music, Inc., London, England, 1980.
Introduced by Elvis Costello on *Get Happy* (Columbia, 80).

Mountain Music
Words and music by Randy Owen.
Maypop Music, 1980.
Best-selling record by Alabama (RCA, 82).

Mountain of Love
Revived by Charley Pride (RCA, 82). See *Popular Music, 1920-1979.*

Move On
Words and music by Stephen Sondheim.
Revelation Music Publishing Corp., 1981/Rilting Music Inc., 1981.
Introduced by Mandy Patinkin and Bernadette Peters in *Sunday in the Park with George* (83).

Murphy's Law (Canadian)
Words and music by Geraldine Hunt and Daniel Joseph.
Hygroton, 1981/Lo Pressor, 1981.
Best-selling record by Cheri (Venture, 82).

Muscles
Words and music by Michael Jackson.
Mijac Music, 1982.
Best-selling record by Diana Ross (RCA, 82).

My Attorney, Bernie
Words and music by David Frishberg.
Swiftwater Music, 1982.
Featured in *The Dave Frishberg Songbook, Volume Two* (Omnisound, 83).

My City Was Gone (English)
Words and music by Chrissie Hynde.
Virgin Music, Inc., 1982.
Introduced by The Pretenders as the A-Side of "Back on the Chain Gang" (Sire, 82). Featured on *Learning to Crawl* (Sire, 83).

My Edge of the Razor
Words and music by John Hiatt.
Lillybilly, 1982.
Introduced on *All of a Sudden* by John Hiatt (Geffen, 82).

My Ever Changing Moods (English)
Words and music by Paul Weller.
Colgems-EMI Music Inc., 1984.
Best-selling record by The Style Council (Geffen, 84).

My Girl (Canadian)
Words and music by Bill Henderson and Brian MacLeod.
ATV Music Corp., 1980.
Best-selling record by Chilliwack (Millennium, 81).

My Heart
Best-selling record by Ronnie Milsap (RCA, 80). See *Popular Music, 1920-1979.*

My Heroes Have Always Been Cowboys
Best-selling record by Willie Nelson (Columbia, 80). See *Popular Music, 1920-1979.*

My Hometown
Words and music by Bruce Springsteen.
Bruce Springsteen, 1984.
Introduced by Bruce Springsteen in *Born in the U.S.A.* (Columbia, 84).

My House
Words and music by Lou Reed.
Metal Machine Music, 1981.
Introduced by Lou Reed on *The Blue Mask* (RCA, 82).

My Life Is Good
Words and music by Randy Newman.
Six Pictures Music, 1983.
Introduced by Randy Newman in *Trouble in Paradise* (Warner Brothers, 83).

My Love
Words and music by Lionel Richie, Jr.
Brockman Enterprises Inc., 1982.
Best-selling record by Lionel Richie (Motown, 83).

My, Oh My
Words and music by Noddy Holder and Jim Lea.
Whild John, London, England, 1984/Barn Music, London, England, 1984.
Best-selling record by Slade (CBS Associated, 84).

My Old Yellow Car
Words and music by Thom Schuyler.
Featured on *Dream Baby* by Lacy J. Dalton (Columbia, 83).

Mystery Achievement (English)
Words and music by Chrissie Hynde.
Virgin Music, Inc., 1979.
Introduced by The Pretenders on *Pretenders* (Sire, 80).

N

Nataasha (English)
Words by Dick Vosberg, music by Frank Lazarus.
Regent Music, 1978.
Introduced by David Garrison in *A Day in Hollywood/A Night in the Ukraine* (Musical, 80).

The Natural
Music by Randy Newman.
TSP Music, Inc., 1984/Randy Newman Music, 1984.
Introduced in the film *The Natural* (84).

Nelson
Words and music by Jerry Herman.
Jerryco Music Co., 1979.
Introduced by by Peggy Hewett in *A Day in Hollywood/A Night in the Ukraine* (Musical, 80).

Never Be the Same
Best-selling record by Christopher Cross (Warner Brothers, 80). See *Popular Music, 1920-1979.*

Never Gonna Let You Go
Words by Cynthia Weil, music by Barry Mann.
ATV Music Corp., 1981/Mann & Weil Songs Inc., 1981.
Best-selling record by Sergio Mendes (A & M, 83).

Never Knew Love Like This Before
Words and music by James Mtume and Reginald Lucas.
Frozen Butterfly Music Publishing, 1979.
Best-selling record by Stephanie Mills (20th Century, 80). Won a National Academy of Recording Arts and Sciences Award, Rhythm 'n' Blues Song of the Year, 1980.

New Age
Words and music by Lou Reed.

Popular Music, 1980-1984

Oakfield Avenue Music Ltd., 1980/Unichappell Music Inc., 1980.
Featured on *Protect the Innocent* by Rachel Sweet (Columbia, 80).

New Moon on Monday (English)
Words and music by Duran Duran.
Chappell & Co., Inc., 1983.
Best-selling record by Duran Duran (Capitol, 84).

The New World
Words and music by John Doe and Exene Cervenka, music by X.
Eight/Twelve Music, 1983.
Introduced by X on *More Fun in the New World* (Electra, 83).

New World Man (Canadian)
Words by Neil Peart, music by Alex Lifeson and Geddy Lee.
Core Music Publishing, 1982.
Best-selling record by Rush (Mercury, 82).

New Year's Day (Irish)
Words and music by Paul Hewson, Larry Mullen, Adam Clayton, and Dave Evans.
Island Music, 1983.
Best-selling record by U2 (Island, 83).

New York, New York
Words and music by Melvin Glover, Sylvia Robinson, Edward Fletcher, and Reginald Griffin.
Sugar Hill Music Publishing, Ltd., 1983.
Best-selling record by Grand Master Flash & The Furious Five (Sugar Hill, 83).

Night (Feel Like Getting Down)
Words and music by Billy Ocean and Nigel Martinez.
Blackwood Music Inc., 1981/World Song Publishing, Inc., 1981.
Best-selling record by Billy Ocean (Epic, 81).

The Night Dolly Parton Was Almost Mine
Words and music by Jim Wann.
Shapiro, Bernstein & Co., Inc., 1981.
Introduced by Mark Hardwick in *Pump Boys and Dinettes* (81).

A Night in Tunisia
Revived by Chaka Khan on *What Cha Gonna Do for Me* (Warner Brothers, 81). See *Popular Music, 1920-1979.*

The Night Owls (Australian)
Words and music by Graham Goble.

142

Colgems-EMI Music Inc., 1981.
Best-selling record by Little River Band (Capitol, 81).

9 to 5
Words and music by Dolly Parton.
Velvet Apple Music, 1980/Warner-Tamerlane Publishing Corp.,
   1980.
Best-selling record by Dolly Parton (RCA, 81). Introduced in the film
   9 to 5 (81). Nominated for a National Academy of Recording Arts and
   Sciences Award, Song of the Year, 1981. Won an Academy Award,
   Best Song, 1980; a National Academy of Recording Arts and Sciences
   Award, Country Song, 1981.

No Gettin' Over Me
Words and music by Tom Brasfield and Walt Aldridge.
Rick Hall Music, 1981.
Best-selling record by Ronnie Milsap (RCA, 81).

No More Lonely Nights (English)
Words and music by Paul McCartney.
MPL Communications Inc., 1984.
Best-selling record by Paul McCartney (Columbia, 84). Introduced in
   the film *Give My Regards to Broad Street* (84).

No Night So Long (English)
Words by Will Jennings, music by Richard Kerr.
Irving Music Inc., 1980.
Best-selling record by Dionne Warwick (Arista, 80).

No Reply at All (English)
Words and music by Tony Banks, Phil Collins, and Mike
   Rutherford.
Pun Music Inc., London, England, 1981.
Best-selling record by Genesis (Atlantic, 81).

No Surrender
Words and music by Bruce Springsteen.
Bruce Springsteen, 1984.
Introduced by Bruce Springsteen in *Born in the U.S.A.* (Columbia, 84).

No Way Out
Words and music by Peter Wolf and Ina Wolf.
Petwolf Music, 1984/Jobete Music Co., Inc., 1984/Stone Diamond
   Music Corp., 1984/Kikiko Music Corp., 1984.
Best-selling record by The Jefferson Starship (Grunt, 84).

Nobody
Words and music by Kye Fleming and Dennis W. Morgan.

143

Tom Collins Music Corp., 1982.
Best-selling record by Sylvia (RCA, 82). Nominated for a National Academy of Recording Arts and Sciences Award, Country Song of the Year, 1982.

Nobody Said It Was Easy
Words and music by Tony Haseldon.
Screen Gems-EMI Music Inc., 1982.
Best-selling record by Le Roux (RCA, 82).

Nobody Told Me
Words and music by John Lennon.
Ono Music, 1982.
Best-selling record by John Lennon (Polydor, 84).

Not a Day Goes By
Words and music by Stephen Sondheim.
Revelation Music Publishing Corp., 1981/Rilting Music Inc., 1981.
Introduced by Jim Walton in *Merrily We Roll Along* (81).

Nothing Really Happened
Words and music by Craig Carnelia.
Samuel French, Inc., 1982.
Introduced by Alma Cuervo in *Is There Life After High School* (82).

Now
Words by David Rogers, music by Charles Strouse.
Four Kids Music, 1978.
Introduced by P. J. Benjamin and Sandy Falson in *Charlie and Algernon* (musical, 80).

O

O Superman
Words and music by Laurie Anderson.
Difficult Music, 1981.
Introduced by Laurie Anderson on *Big Science* (Warner Brothers, 82).

Off the Wall
Best-selling record by Michael Jackson (Epic, 80). See *Popular Music, 1920-1979.*

Oh No
Words and music by Lionel Richie, Jr.
Jobete Music Co., Inc., 1981/Brockman Enterprises Inc., 1981.
Best-selling record by The Commodores (Motown, 81).

Oh, Sherrie
Words and music by Steve Perry, Randy Goodrum, Bill Cuomo, and
Craig Krampf.
Street Talk Tunes, 1984/April Music, Inc., 1984/Pants Down Music,
1984/Random Notes, 1984/Phosphene Music, 1984.
Best-selling record by Steve Perry (Columbia, 84).

Oklahoma Nights
Words and music by Jimmy Webb.
White Oak Songs, 1981.
Introduced by Arlo Guthrie in *Power of Love* (Warner Brothers, 81).

Old-Fashion Love
Words and music by Milan Williams.
Jobete Music Co., Inc., 1980/Old Fashion Music, 1980.
Best-selling record by The Commondores (Motown, 80).

Old Flame (Icelandic)
English words and music by Donny Lowery and Mac McAnnally.
I've Got The Music Co., 1981.
Best-selling record by Alabama (RCA, 81).

Old Flames Can't Hold a Candle to You
Words and music by Hugh Moffatt and Pebe Sebert.
Rightsong Music Inc., 1978.
Best-selling record by Dolly Parton (RCA, 80).

Old Friends
Words and music by Stephen Sondheim.
Revelation Music Publishing Corp., 1981/Rilting Music Inc., 1981.
Introduced by Ann Morrison in *Merrily We Roll Along* (81).

Old Men Sleeping on the Bowery
Words and music by Willie Nile.
Lake Victoria Music, 1979.
Introduced by Willie Nile on *Willie Nile* (Arista, 80).

The Old Songs
Words and music by David Pomeranz and Buddy Kaye.
WB Music Corp., 1979/Upward Spiral Music, 1979.
Best-selling record by Barry Manilow (Arista, 81). Introduced by David
    Pomeranz on *The Truth of Us* (Pacific Records, 80).

Old Time Rock and Roll
Words and music by George Jackson and Tom Jones, III.
Muscle Shoals Sound Publishing Co., Inc., 1977.
Best-selling record by Bob Seger and The Silver Bullet Band (Capitol,
    83). Featured in the film *Risky Business* (83).

Older Women
Words and music by James O'Hara.
Tree Publishing Co., Inc., 1981.
Best-selling record by Ronnie McDowell (Epic, 81).

(Lost His Love) On Our Last Date, also known as **Last Date**
Revived by Emmylou Harris (Warner Brothers, 82). See *Popular Music,
    1920-1979.*

On the Dark Side
Words and music by John Cafferty.
Warner-Tamerlane Publishing Corp., 1982/John Cafferty Music,
    1982.
Best-selling record by John Cafferty & The Beaver Brown Band (Scotti
    Brothers, 84). Introduced in the film *Eddie and the Cruisers* (82).

On the Nickel
Words and music by Tom Waits.
Fifth Floor Music Inc., 1980.
Featured in *Heartattack and Vine* by Tom Waits (Asylum, 80). Used in
    the film *On the Nickel* (80).

146

On the Radio
Best-selling record by Donna Summer (Casablanca, 80). See *Popular Music, 1920-1979.*

On the Road Again
Words and music by Willie Nelson.
Willie Nelson Music Inc., 1979.
Best-selling record by Willie Nelson (Columbia, 80). Introduced in the film *Honeysuckle Rose* (80). Nominated for an Academy Award, 1980. Won a National Academy of Recording Arts and Sciences Award, Country Song of the Year, 1980.

On the Wings of a Nightingale (English)
Words and music by Paul McCartney.
MPL Communications Inc., 1984.
Best-selling record by The Everly Brothers (Mercury, 84).

On the Wings of Love
Words and music by Peter Schless and Jeffrey Osborne.
Lincoln Pond Music, 1982/Almo Music Corp., 1982/March 9 Music, 1982.
Best-selling record by Jeffrey Osborne (A & M, 82).

On Third Street
Words and music by David Lasley.
Almo Music Corp., 1981.
Introduced by David Lasley on *Missin' Twenty Grand* (EMI, 82).

Once in a Lifetime (American-English)
Words and music by David Byrne, Chris Franz, Jerry Harrison, Tina Weymouth, and Brian Eno.
Bleu Disque Music, 1980/E.G. Music, Inc., 1980.
Best-selling record by Talking Heads (Sire, 81).

One Day at a Time
Words and music by Marijohn Wilkin and Kris Kristofferson.
Buckhorn Music Publishing Co., Inc., 1973.
Best-selling record by Cristy Lane (United Artists, 80).

One Fine Day
Revived by Carole King (Capitol, 80). See Popular Music, 1920-79

One Hello
Words by Carole Bayer Sager, music by Marvin Hamlisch.
Chappell & Co., Inc., 1982/Red Bullet Music, 1982/Twentieth Century-Fox Music Corp., 1982/Carole Bayer Sager Music, 1982/Fox Fanfare Music Inc., 1982.
Introduced in the film *I Oughta Be in Pictures* (82) by Dinah Manoff.

Popular Music, 1980-1984

One Hundred Ways
Words and music by Kathy Wakefield, Benjamin Wright, and Tony Coleman.
State of the Arts Music, 1981/Kidada Music Inc., 1981.
Best-selling record by Quincy Jones featuring James Ingram (A & M, 82).

One in a Million You
Words and music by Sam Dees.
Irving Music Inc., 1980.
Best-selling records in 1980 by Larry Graham (Warner Brothers) and by Johnny Lee (Asylum).

One More Hour
Words and music by Randy Newman.
Wide Music, 1981.
Introduced by Jennifer Warnes in the film *Ragtime* (81). Nominated for an Academy Award, Best Song, 1981.

One Night Only
Words by Tom Eyen, music by Henry Krieger.
Dreamgirls Music, 1981/Dreamette's Music, 1981/August Dream Music Ltd., 1981.
Introduced by Jennifer Holliday and Vondee Curtis Hall in *Dreamgirls* (81). Featured in *Call Me* by Sylvester (Megatone, 83).

One of the Boys
Words by Fred Ebb, music by John Kander.
Fiddleback Music Publishing Co., Inc., 1981/Kander & Ebb Inc., 1981.
Introduced by Lauren Bacall in *Woman of the Year* (81).

One on One
Words and music by Daryl Hall.
Hot Cha Music Co., 1982/Unichappell Music Inc., 1982.
Best-selling record by Daryl Hall and John Oates (RCA, 83).

The One That You Love (Australian)
Words and music by Graham Russell.
Careers Music Inc., 1981/Nottsongs, 1981.
Best-selling record by Air Supply (Arista, 81).

One Thing Leads to Another (English)
Words and music by Cy Curnin, Adam Woods, Jamie West-Oram, Rupert Greenall, and Alfred Agius.
Colgems-EMI Music Inc., 1982.
Best-selling record by The Fixx (MCA, 83).

148

1999
Words and music by Prince Rogers Nelson.
Controversy Music, 1982.
Best-selling record by Prince (Warner Brothers, 83).

One Time for Old Times (Canadian)
Words and music by Gary O'Connor.
April Music, Inc., 1983.
Introduced by 38 Special on *Tour de Force* (A & M, 83).

One Trick Pony
Words and music by Paul Simon.
Paul Simon Music, 1979.
Best-selling record by Paul Simon (Warner Brothers, 80). Introduced in
the film *One Trick Pony* (80).

1-2-3 Go (This Town's a Fairground)
Words and music by Joe Jackson.
Almo Music Corp., 1983.
Introduced in *Mike's Murder* by Joe Jackson (A & M, 83).

The One You Love
Words and music by Glenn Frey and Jack Tempchin.
Red Cloud Music Co., 1982/Night River Publishing, 1982.
Best-selling record by Glenn Frey (Asylum, 82).

Only a Lonely Heart Knows
Words and music by Dennis W. Morgan and Steve Davis.
Tom Collins Music Corp., 1983/Dick James Music Inc., 1983.
Best-selling record by Barbara Mandrell (MCA, 83).

The Only Flame in Town (English)
Words and music by Elvis Costello.
Plangent Visions Music, Inc., London, England, 1984.
Introduced by Elvis Costello in *Goodbye Cruel World* (Columbia, 84).

Only One You
Words and music by Michael Garvin and Bucky Jones.
Tree Publishing Co., Inc., 1981/Cross Keys Publishing Co., Inc.,
1981.
Best-selling record by T. G. Sheppard (Warner/Curb, 82).

Only the Lonely
Words and music by Martha Davis.
Clean Sheets Music, 1981.
Best-selling record by The Motels (Capitol, 82).

Only the Young
Words and music by Steve Perry, Jonathan Cain, and Neal Schon.
Weed High Nightmare Music, 1983.
Introduced by Scandal on *The Warrior* (Columbia, 84). Featured in the
film *Vision Quest* (85). Best-selling record by Journey (Columbia, 85).

Only Time Will Tell (English)
Words and music by John Wetton and Geoffrey Downes.
WB Music Corp., 1982/Ackee Music Inc., 1982.
Best-selling record by Asia (Geffen, 82).

Only with You
Words and music by Maury Yeston.
Yeston Music, Ltd., 1975.
Introduced by Raul Julia in *Nine* (Musical, 82).

Open Arms
Words and music by Steve Perry and Jonathan Cain.
Weed High Nightmare Music, 1981.
Best-selling record by Journey (Columbia, 82).

Opportunity to Cry
Words and music by Willie Nelson.
Tree Publishing Co., Inc., 1982.
Featured in *Poncho and Lefty* (Epic, 83) by Willie (Nelson) and Waylon
(Jennings).

The Other Guy (Australian)
Words and music by Graham Goble.
Screen Gems-EMI Music Inc., 1983.
Best-selling record by Little River Band (Capitol, 83).

The Other Woman
Words and music by Ray Parker, Jr.
Raydiola Music, 1982.
Best-selling record by Ray Parker, Jr. (Arista, 82).

Our House (English)
Words and music by Charles Smyth and Christopher Foreman.
WB Music Corp., 1982.
Best-selling record by Madness (Warner Brothers, 83).

Our Lips Are Sealed
Words and music by Jane Weidlin and Terry Hill.
Plangent Visions Music, Inc., London, England, 1981/Lipsync
Music, 1981.
Best-selling record by The Go-Go's (I.R.S., 81).

Our Love Is on the Fault Line (English)
Words and music by Reece Kirk.
Irving Music Inc., 1981.
Best-selling record by Crystal Gayle (Warner Brothers, 83).

Our Night
Words and music by Gary Portnoy and Judy Hart Angelo.
Koppelman Family Music, 1983/R. L. August Music Co., 1983/
Bandier Family Music, 1983/Yontrop Music, 1983/Judy Hart
Angelo Music, 1983.
Introduced by Bob Walton and Kathleen Rowe McAllen in *Preppies*
(83).

Our Time
Words and music by Stephen Sondheim.
Revelation Music Publishing Corp., 1981/Rilting Music Inc., 1981.
Introduced by Jim Walton, Lonny Price, and Ann Morrison in *Merrily
We Roll Along* (81).

Out Here on My Own
Words and music by Michael Gore and Leslie Gore.
MGM Affiliated Music, Inc., 1979/CBS Variety Catalog, Inc.
Best-selling record by Irene Cara (RSO, 80). Introduced in the film *Fame*
(80). Nominated for an Academy Award, 1980.

Out of Touch
Words and music by Daryl Hall and John Oates.
Hot Cha Music Co., 1984/Unichappell Music Inc., 1984.
Best-selling record by Daryl Hall and John Oates (RCA, 84).

Out of Work
Words and music by Bruce Springsteen.
Bruce Springsteen, 1982.
Best-selling record by Gary U.S. Bonds (EMI-America, 82).

Over You
Words and music by Austin Roberts and Bobby Hart.
Colgems-EMI Music Inc., 1981/Father Music, 1981.
Introduced in the film *Tender Mercies* (81). Best-selling record by Lane
Brody (Liberty, 81). Nominated for an Academy Award, Best Song,
1983.

Overkill (Australian)
Words and music by Colin Hay.
April Music, Inc., 1983.
Best-selling record by Men at Work (Columbia, 83).

Owner of a Lonely Heart (English)

Words and music by Trevor Rabin, Jon Anderson, Chris Squire, and
Trevor Horn.

WB Music Corp., 1983/Unforgettable Songs, 1983.

Best-selling record by Yes (Atco, 83).

P

P. Y. T. (Pretty Young Thing)
Words and music by James Ingram and Quincy Jones.
Eiseman Music Co., Inc., 1982/Hen-Al Publishing Co., 1982/Kings
    Road Music, 1982/Yellow Brick Road Music, 1982.
Best-selling record by Michael Jackson (Epic, 83). Nominated for a
    National Academy of Recording Arts and Sciences Award, Rhythm
    'n' Blues Song of the Year, 1983.

Pac-Man Fever
Words and music by Jerry Buckner and Gary Garcia.
BGO Music, 1981.
Best-selling record by Buckner and Garcia (Columbia, 82).

Panama
Words and music by Eddie Van Halen, Alex Van Halen, Michael
    Anthony, and David Lee Roth.
Van Halen Music, 1983.
Best-selling record by Van Halen (Warner Brothers, 84).

Pancho and Lefty
Best-selling record by Willie Nelson and Merle Haggard (Epic, 83). See
    Popular Music, 1920-1979.

Papa Can You Hear Me
Words by Alan Bergman and Marilyn Bergman, music by Michel
    Legrand.
Emanuel Music, 1983/Threesome Music, 1983/Ennes Productions,
    Ltd., 1983.
Introduced by Barbra Streisand in *Yentl* (83). Nominated for an Acad-
    emy Award, Best Song, 1983.

Paradise
Music by David Romani and Mauro Malavasi, words by Tanyayette
    Willoughby.

WB Music Corp., 1981.
Best-selling record by Change (Atlantic, 81).

Paradise Tonight
Words and music by Mark Wright and Bill Kenner.
Receive Music, 1982/CBS Unart Catalog Inc., 1982.
Best-selling record by Charly McClain and Mickey Gilley (Epic, 83).

Party Time
Words and music by Bruce Channel.
Tree Publishing Co., Inc., 1980.
Best-selling record by T. G. Sheppard (Warner/Curb, 81).

Party Train
Words and music by Lonnie Simmons, Ronnie Wilson, Charles
    Wilson, and Rudy Taylor.
Temp Co., 1983.
Best-selling record by The Gap Band (Total Experience, 83).

Partyup
Words and music by Prince Rogers Nelson.
Controversy Music, 1980.
Introduced by Prince in *Dirty Mind* (Warner Brothers, 80).

Pass the Dutchie
Words and music by Jackie Mitoo, Lloyd Ferguson, and Fitzroy
    Simpson.
Ellipsis Music Corp., 1981/Hal Shaper Inc., 1981.
Best-selling record by Musical Youth (MCA, 83).

Passion
Words and music by Rod Stewart, Phil Chen, Jim Cregan, Gary
    Grainger, and Kevin Stuart Savigar.
Riva Music Ltd., 1980/WB Music Corp., 1980/Rod Stewart, 1980.
Best-selling record by Rod Stewart (Warner Brothers, 80).

Peace in Our Time (English)
Words and music by Elvis Costello.
Plangent Visions Music, Inc., London, England, 1983.
Introduced by Elvis Costello on *Goodbye Cruel World* (Columbia, 83).

Penny Lover
Words and music by Lionel Richie, Jr. and Brenda Harvey-Richie.
Brockman Enterprises Inc., 1983.
Best-selling record by Lionel Richie (Motown, 84).

People Alone
Words by Will Jennings, music by Lalo Shifrin.

Gold Horizon Music Corp., 1980/Irving Music Inc., 1980.
Introduced in the film *The Competition* (80). Nominated for an Academy Award, 1980.

People Like Us
Words and music by Gary Portnoy and Judy Hart Angelo.
Koppelman Family Music, 1983/R. L. August Music Co., 1983/
   Bandier Family Music, 1983/Yontrop Music, 1983/Judy Hart
   Angelo Music, 1983.
Introduced by Company of *Preppies* (83).

People Who Died
Words and music by Jim Carroll.
Earl McGrath Music, 1980.
Introduced by Jim Carroll in *Catholic Boy* (Atco, 80).

Perhaps Love
Words and music by John Denver.
Cherry Lane Music Co., Inc., 1980.
Best-selling record by Placido Domingo and John Denver (Columbia,
   82).

Personally
Words and music by Paul Kelly.
Tree Publishing Co., Inc., 1978/Five of a Kind, Inc.
Best-selling record by Karla Bonoff (Columbia, 82).

Peter Pan
Words and music by Chris Williamson.
Bird Ankles Music, 1980.
Introduced by Chris Williamson on *Blue Rider* (Olivia, 80).

Photograph (English)
Words and music by Steve Clark, John Savage, Robert John Lange,
   Pete Willis, and Joe Elliott.
Zomba Enterprises, Inc., 1983.
Best-selling record by Def Leppard (Mercury, 83).

Physical
Words and music by Stephen Kipner and Terry Shaddick.
Stephen A. Kipner Music, 1981/April Music, Inc., 1981/Terry
   Shaddick Music, 1981.
Best-selling record by Olivia Newton-John (MCA, 81).

Pickin' Up Strangers
Words and music by Byron Hill.
Welbeck Music Corp., 1980.
Best-selling record by Johnny Lee (Full Moon/Asylum, 81).

Pilot of the Airwaves
Best-selling record by Charlie Dore (Island, 80). See *Popular Music, 1920-1979.*

Pink Cadillac
Words and music by Bruce Springsteen.
Bruce Springsteen, 1983.
Introduced by Bruce Springsteen on the flipside of the single "Dancing in the Dark" (Columbia, 83).

Pink Houses
Words and music by John Cougar Mellencamp.
Riva Music Ltd., 1983.
Best-selling record by John Cougar Mellencamp (Warner Brothers, 83).

Planet Rock
Words by Ellis Williams, words and music by Arthur Henry Baker, John Miller, Bhambatta Aasim, and Robert Allen, music by John Robie.
Shakin Baker Music, Inc., 1982.
Best-selling record by Afrika Bambaataa & The Soul Sonic Force (Tammy Boy, 82).

Play the Game Tonight
Words and music by Kerry Livgren, Phil Ehart, Richard Williams, Robert Frazier, and Danny Flower.
Don Kirshner Music Inc., 1982/Blackwood Music Inc., 1982/Fifty Grand Music, Inc., 1982.
Best-selling record by Kansas (Kirshner, 82).

Please Don't Go
Best-selling record by Teri DeSario with K.C. (Casablanca, 80). See *Popular Music, 1920-1979.*

Power of Love
Words and music by T-Bone Burnette.
Black Tent Music, 1983.
Featured on *Power of Love* by Arlo Guthrie (Warner Brothers, 81).

Precious (English)
Words and music by Chrissie Hynde.
Virgin Music, Inc., 1980.
Introduced by The Pretenders in *Pretenders* (Sire, 80).

Pressure
Words and music by Billy Joel.
Joelsongs, 1981.
Best-selling record by Billy Joel (Columbia, 82).

156

Pretty in Pink (English)
Words and music by Richard Butler, Timothy Butler, Vincent Ely,
    Duncan Kilburn, John Ashton, and Roger Morris.
Blackwood Music Inc., 1981.
Introduced by The Psychedelic Furs on *Talk, Talk, Talk* (Columbia, 81).

(Oh) Pretty Woman
Revived by Van Halen (Warner Brothers, 82). See *Popular Music,
    1920-1979.*

Princess of Little Italy
Words and music by Steve Van Zandt.
Blue Midnight Music, 1982.
Introduced by Little Steven & The Disciples of Soul on *Men Without
    Women* (EMI-America, 82).

Prisoner of Hope
Words and music by Sterling Whipple and Gerald Metcalf.
Elektra/Asylum Music Inc., 1981.
Best-selling record by Johnny Lee (Asylum, 81).

Private Eyes
Words and music by Warren Pash, Sara Allen, Janna Allen, and
    Daryl Hall.
Fust Buzza Music, Inc., 1981/Hot Cha Music Co., 1981/Wong
    Music, 1981/Unichappell Music Inc., 1981.
Best-selling record by Daryl Hall and John Oates (RCA, 81).

Private Idaho
Words and music by Frederick Schneider, J. Keith Strickland, Ricky
    Wilson, Cynthia Wilson, and Kate Pierson.
Island Music, 1980.
Best-selling record by The B-52's (Warner Brothers, 80).

Promises, Promises (Australian)
Words and music by Pete Bryne and Rob Fisher.
Almo Music Corp., 1983.
Revived by Naked Eyes (EMI-America, 83).

Pulling Mussels (from the Shell)
Words by Christopher Difford, music by Glenn Tilbrook.
Illegal Songs, Inc., 1980.
Introduced by Squeeze on *Argybargy* (A & M, 80).

Purple Rain
Words and music by Prince Rogers Nelson.
Controversy Music, 1984/WB Music Corp., 1984.

Best-selling record by Prince (Warner Brothers, 84). Introduced in the film *Purple Rain* (84).

Put Your Hands on the Screen
Words and music by Martin Briley.
Miserable Melodies, 1983/Rare Blue Music, Inc., 1983.
Featured on *One Night with a Stranger* by Martin Briley (Mercury, 83)

Puttin' on the Ritz
Revived by Taco (RCA, 83). See *Popular Music, 1920-1979.*

Q

Queen of Hearts
Words and music by Hank DeVito.
Drunk Monkey Music, 1979.
Best-selling record by Juice Newton (Capitol, 81).

R

Radio Free Europe
Words and music by William Berry, Peter Buck, Michael Mills, and
  John Stipe.
Night Garden Music, 1981.
Best-selling record by R.E.M. (I.R.S., 83).

Radio Ga-Ga (English)
Words and music by Roger Taylor.
Beechwood Music Corp., 1983.
Best-selling record by Queen (Capitol, 84).

Rappin' Rodney
Words and music by Rodney Dangerfield, Dennis Blair, Scott Henry,
  Douglas Hoyt, J.B. Moore, and R. Ford, Jr.
Best-selling record by Rodney Dangerfield (RCA, 83).

Rapture
Words by Debbie Harry, music by Chris Stein.
Rare Blue Music, Inc., 1980.
Best-selling record by Blondie (Chrysalis, 81).

Read 'em and Weep
Words and music by Jim Steinman.
E. B. Marks Music Corp., 1981/Peg Music Co., 1981.
Best-selling records by Meat Loaf (Cleveland International, 81) and
  Barry Manilow (Arista, 83).

The Real End
Words and music by Rickie Lee Jones.
Easy Money Music, 1984.
Best-selling record by Rickie Lee Jones (Warner Brothers, 84).

Real Love
Words and music by Michael McDonald and Patrick Henderson.
Tauripin Tunes, 1980/Monosteri Music, 1980/April Music, Inc.,

1980.
Best-selling record by The Doobie Brothers (Warner Brothers, 80).

Real Men (English)
Words and music by Joe Jackson.
Almo Music Corp., 1982.
Introduced by Joe Jackson on *Night and Day* (A & M, 82).

Really Wanna Know You (Canadian-English)
Words and music by Gary Wright, music by Ali Thomson.
Almo Music Corp., 1981/High Wave Music, Inc., 1981.
Best-selling record by Gary Wright (Warner Brothers, 81).

Rebel Yell (American-English)
Words and music by Billy Idol and Steve Stevens.
Boneidol Music, 1983/Rock Steady Inc., 1983/Rare Blue Music,
    Inc., 1983.
Best-selling record by Billy Idol (Chrysalis, 84).

Red Neckin' Love Makin' Night
Words and music by Max Barnes and Troy Seals.
Blue Lake Music, 1981/Warner-Tamerlane Publishing Corp., 1981.
Best-selling record by Conway Twitty (MCA, 81).

The Reflex
Words and music by Duran Duran.
Chappell & Co., Inc., 1983.
Best-selling record by Duran Duran (Capitol, 84).

Refugee
Words and music by Tom Petty and Mike Campbell.
Skyhill Publishing Co., Inc., 1979/Tarka Music Co.
Best-selling record by Tom Petty & The Heartbreakers (Backstreet, 80).

Relax (English)
Words and music by Peter Gill, William Johnson, and Mark
    O'Toole.
Island Music, 1984.
Best-selling record by Frankie Goes to Hollywood (Island, 84). Intro-
    duced in the film *Body Double* (84).

Rene and Georgette Magritte with Their Dog After the War
Words and music by Paul Simon.
Paul Simon Music, 1982.
Introduced by Paul Simon on *Heart and Bones* (Warner Brothers, 83).

Rest Your Love on Me (English)
Words and music by Barry Gibb.

Unichappell Music Inc., 1976.
Best-selling record by Conway Twitty (MCA, 81).

Restless
Words by Vicki Peterson, music by Susanna Hoffs.
Bangaphile Music, 1984/Illegal Songs, Inc., 1984.
Introduced by The Bangles on *All Over the Place* (Columbia, 84).

The Revolution Will Not Be Televised
Words and music by Gil Scott-Heron.
Bob Thiele Music, Ltd., 1974.
Featured on *The Best of Gil Scott-Heron* (Arista, 84).

Ricky
Words and music by Nicky Chinn, Mike Chapman, Al Yankovic, H.
  Adamson, and E. Daniel.
Arista Music, Inc., 1981.
Best-selling record by Weird Al Yankovic (Rock 'n' Roll, 83), parody
  of "Mickey" and "I Love Lucy Theme Song."

Ride Like the Wind
Best-selling record by Christopher Cross (Warner Brothers, 80). See
  Popular Music, 1920-79

Riding with the King
Words and music by John Haitt.
Lillybilly, 1983.
Introduced on *Riding with the King* by John Hiatt (84).

Right or Wrong
Words and music by Arthur Sizemore and Paul Biese.
Edwin H. Morris Co., 1921.
Best-selling record by George Strait (MCA, 84).

Ring on Her Finger, Time on Her Hands
Words and music by Don Goodman, Mary Ann Kennedy, and Pam
  Rose.
Tree Publishing Co., Inc., 1981/Love Wheel Music, 1981/Southern
  Soul Music, 1981.
Best-selling record by Lee Greenwood (MCA, 82). Nominated for a
  National Academy of Recording Arts and Sciences Award, Country
  Song of the Year, 1982.

Rio (English)
Words and music by Duran Duran.
Chappell & Co., Inc., 1982.
Best-selling record by Duran Duran (Capitol, 83).

Rise and Stand Again
Words by Peter Udell, music by Garry Sherman.
Music Theatre International, 1983.
Introduced by Rhetta Hughes in *Amen Corner* (83).

The River
Words and music by Bruce Springsteen.
Bruce Springsteen, 1980.
Introduced by Bruce Springsteen on *The River* (Columbia, 80).

Rock Lobster
Words and music by Fred Schneider and Ricky Wilson.
Boo-Fant Tunes, Inc., 1978.
Best-selling record by The B-52s (Warner Brothers, 80).

Rock Me Tonite
Words and music by Billy Squier.
Songs of the Knight, 1984.
Best-selling record by Billy Squier (Capitol, 84).

Rock 'n' Roll Is King (English)
Words and music by Jeff Lynne.
April Music, Inc., 1983.
Best-selling record by ELO (A & M, 83).

Rock of Ages (English)
Words and music by Steve Clark, Robert John Lange, and Joe
  Elliott.
Zomba Enterprises, Inc., 1983.
Best-selling record by Def Leppard (Mercury, 83).

Rock the Casbah (English)
Words and music by Paul Simonon, Topper Headon, Joe Strummer
  (pseudonym for John Mellor), and Mick Jones.
Nineden, Ltd., London, England, 1982.
Best-selling record by The Clash (Epic, 82).

Rock This Town
Words and music by Brian Setzer.
Zomba Enterprises, Inc., 1981.
Best-selling record by The Stray Cats (EMI-America, 82).

Rock You Like a Hurricane (East German)
English words and music by Rudolf Schenker, Klaus Meine, and
  Herman Rarebell.
WB Music Corp., 1984.
Best-selling record by The Scorpions (Mercury, 84).

Rockit
Words and music by Herbie Hancock, Bill Laswell, and Michael
    Beinhorn.
Hancock Music Co., 1983/Dad Music, 1983.
Best-selling record by Herbie Hancock (Columbia, 83).

Romancing the Stone (English)
Words and music by Eddy Grant.
Greenheart Music, Ltd., 1984.
Best-selling record by Eddy Grant (Portrait, 84).

Romeo and Juliet (English)
Words and music by Mark Knopfler.
Almo Music Corp., 1980.
Introduced by Dire Straits on *Making Movies* (Warner Brothers, 80).

Romeo's Tune
Best-selling record by Steve Forbert (Nemperor, 80). See *Popular Music,
    1920-1979.*

Rosanna
Words and music by David Paich.
Hudmar Publishing Co., Inc., 1982.
Best-selling record by Toto (Columbia, 82). The song is dedicated to the
    actress Rosanna Arquette. Nominated for a National Academy of
    Recording Arts and Sciences Award, Song of the Year, 1982. Won a
    National Academy of Recording Arts and Sciences Award, Record of
    the Year, 1982.

The Rose
Best-selling record by Bette Midler (Atlantic, 80). See Popular Music,
    1920-79 Nominated for National Academy of Recording Arts and
    Sciences Awards, Song of the Year, 1980, and Record of the Year,
    1980.

Rough Boys (English)
Words and music by Peter Townshend.
Towser Tunes Inc., 1980.
Introduced by Pete Townshend on *Empty Glass* (Atco, 80).

Round and Round
Words and music by Warren DeMartini, Stephen Pearcy, and
    Robbin Crosby.
Time Coast Music, 1984/Rightsong Music Inc., 1984/Ratt Music,
    1984.
Best-selling record by Ratt (Elektra, 84).

Run for the Roses
Words and music by Dan Fogelberg.
Hickory Grove Music, 1980/April Music, Inc., 1980.
Best-selling record by Dan Fogelberg (Full Moon/Epic, 82). Used as
theme for the Kentucky Derby.

Run, Runaway (English)
Words and music by Noddy Holder and Jim Lea.
Whild John, London, England, 1984/Barn Music, London, England,
1984.
Best-selling record by Slade (CBS Associated, 84).

Run to You (Canadian)
Words and music by Bryan Adams and Jim Vallance.
Adams Communications, Inc., 1984/Calypso Toonz, 1984/Irving
Music Inc., 1984.
Best-selling record by Bryan Adams. (A & M, 84).

Runaway
Words and music by Jon Bon Jovi and George Karak.
Famous Music Co., 1983/George Karakoglou, 1983/Simile Music,
Inc., 1983.
Best-selling record by Bon Jovi (Mercury, 84).

The Runner (Canadian)
Words and music by Ian Thomas.
Intersong, USA Inc., 1981.
Best-selling record by Manfred Mann's Earth Band (Arista, 84).

Running Away
Words and music by Frankie Beverly.
Amazement Music, 1981.
Best-selling record by Maze featuring Frankie Beverly (Capitol, 81).

Running With the Night
Music by Lionel Richie, Jr., words by Cynthia Weil.
Brockman Enterprises Inc., 1983/Dyad Music, Ltd., 1983.
Best-selling record by Lionel Richie (Motown, 83).

S

Sad Songs (Say So Much) (English)
Words by Bernie Taupin, music by Elton John.
Intersong, USA Inc., 1984.
Best-selling record by Elton John (Warner Brothers, 84).

The Safety Dance (Canadian)
Words and music by Ivan Doroschuk.
Off Backstreet Music, 1981.
Best-selling record by Men Without Hats (Backstreet, 83).

Sailing
Words and music by Christopher Cross.
Pop 'N' Roll Music, 1979.
Best-selling record by Christopher Cross (Warner Brothers, 80). Won
    National Academy of Recording Arts and Sciences Awards, Song of
    the Year, 1980, and Record of the Year, 1980.

The Salt in My Tears
Words and music by Martin Briley.
Rare Blue Music, Inc., 1982/Miserable Melodies, 1982.
Best-selling record by Martin Briley (Mercury, 83).

Same Old Lang Syne
Words and music by Dan Fogelberg.
Hickory Grove Music, 1979/April Music, Inc.
Best-selling record by Dan Fogelberg (Full Moon, 80).

Same Ole Me
Words and music by Paul Overstreet.
Silverline Music, Inc., 1981.
Best-selling record by George Jones (Epic, 82).

San Diego Serenade
Words and music by Tom Waits.

167

Fifth Floor Music Inc., 1979.
Featured on *Take Heart* by Juice Newton (Capitol, 80).

Sat in Your Lap (English)
Words and music by Kate Bush.
Kate Bush Music, Ltd., London, England, 1981.
Introduced by Kate Bush in *The Dreaming* (EMI-America, 82).

Sausalito Summernight (Netherlands)
Dutch words and music by Marc Boon Lucian and Robert
    Vundernik.
Southern Music Publishing Co., Inc., 1980/Holland Music, 1980.
Best-selling record by Diesel (Regency, 81).

Save the Overtime for Me
Words by Bubba Knight, Gladys Knight, and Sam Dees, music by
    Rickey Smith and Joey Gallo.
Richer Music, 1983/Chappell & Co., Inc., 1983/Bubba Knight
    Enterprises Ltd., 1983/Irving Music Inc., 1983/Shakeji Music,
    1983/Lijesrika Music Pub., 1983.
Best-selling record by Gladys Knight & The Pips (Columbia, 83).

Say Goodbye to Hollywood
Revived by Billy Joel (Columbia, 81). See *Popular Music, 1920-1979*.

Say Hello
Words by Sammy Cahn, music by Richard Evan Behrke.
Sergeant Music Co., 1981/Elliot Music Co., Inc., 1981.
Best-selling record by Frank Sinatra (Reprise, 81).

Say It Isn't So
Words and music by Daryl Hall.
Hot Cha Music Co., 1983/Unichappell Music Inc., 1983.
Best-selling record by Daryl Hall and John Oates (RCA, 83).

Say It Isn't True
Words and music by Jackson Browne.
Night Kitchen Music, 1983.
Introduced by Jackson Browne in *Lawyers in Love* (Asylum, 83).

Say Say Say (English)
Words and music by Paul McCartney and Michael Jackson.
MPL Communications Inc., 1983/Mijac Music, 1983.
Best-selling record by Paul McCartney and Michael Jackson (Columbia,
    83).

Say You'll Be Mine
Words and music by Christopher Cross.

Pop 'N' Roll Music, 1979.
Best-selling record by Christopher Cross (Warner Brothers, 81).

Scatterlings of Africa (South African)
Afrikaans words and music by Johnny Clegg.
WB Music Corp., 1982.
Introduced by Juluka on *Scatterlings of Africa* (Warner Brothers, 82).

Scissor Cut
Words and music by Jimmy Webb.
White Oak Songs, 1981.
Featured in *Angel Heart* (Columbia/Lorimar, 82).

Scratch My Back (and Whisper in My Ear)
Words and music by Marcell Strong, Raymond Moore, and Earl
    Cage, Jr.
Fame Publishing Co., Inc., 1970.
Best-selling record by Razzy Bailey (RCA, 82).

Sea of Love
Revived by The Honeydrippers (Esparanza, 84). See *Popular Music,
    1920-1979.*

Second Thoughts
Words and music by Craig Carnelia.
Samuel French, Inc., 1982.
Introduced by Company of *Is There Life After High School* (82).

The Seduction (Love Theme from *American Gigolo*) (West
    German)
German words and music by Giorgio Moroder.
Ensign Music Corp., 1980.
Best-selling record by The James Last Band (Polydor, 80). Introduced
    in the film *American Gigolo* (80).

Seeing's Believing
Words and music by Rodney Crowell.
Jolly Cheeks Music, 1980.
Featured in *Right or Wrong* by Rosanne Cash (Columbia, 80).

Self Control (English)
English words by Steve Piccolo, Italian words and music by Raffaele
    Riefoli and Giancarlo Bigazzi.
Edition Sunrise Publishing, Inc., 1984.
Best-selling record by Laura Branigan (Atlantic, 84).

Send Her My Love
Words and music by Steve Perry and Jonathan Cain.

Twist & Shout Music, 1982.
Best-selling record by Journey (Columbia, 83).

Separate Ways (World's Apart)
Words and music by Steve Perry and Jonathan Cain.
Twist & Shout Music, 1982.
Best-selling record by Journey (Columbia, 83).

Sequel
Words and music by Harry Chapin.
Chapin Music, 1980.
Best-selling record by Harry Chapin (Boardwalk, 80).

Set Me Free
Best-selling record by Utopia (Bearsville, 80). See *Popular Music, 1920-1979.*

Set the House Ablaze (English)
Words and music by Paul Weller.
Colgems-EMI Music Inc., 1981.
Introduced by Paul Weller on *Sound Affects* (Polydor, 81).

Seven Year Ache
Words and music by Rosanne Cash.
Hotwire Music, 1979/Atlantic Music Corp.
Best-selling record by Rosanne Cash (Columbia, 81).

17
Words and music by Rick James.
Stone City Music, 1984.
Best-selling record by Rick James (Gordy, 84).

Sex (I'm A)
Words and music by John Crawford, David Diamond, and Terri Nunn.
Safespace Music, 1982.
Best-selling record by Berlin (Warner Brothers, 83).

Sexual Healing
Words and music by Marvin Gaye.
April Music, Inc., 1982/Blackwood Music Inc., 1982.
Best-selling record by Marvin Gaye (Columbia, 82). Nominated for a National Academy of Recording Arts and Sciences Award, Rhythm 'n' Blues Song of the Year, 1982.

(She's) Sexy & 17
Words and music by Brian Setzer.

Willesden Music, Inc., 1983.
Best-selling record by The Stray Cats (EMI-America, 83).

Sexy Eyes
Best-selling record by Dr. Hook (Capitol, 80). See *Popular Music, 1920-1979.*

Sexy Girl
Words and music by Jack Tempchin and Glenn Frey.
Night River Publishing, 1984/Red Cloud Music Co., 1984.
Best-selling record by Glenn Frey (MCA, 84).

Shackles
Words and music by Ralph Rice.
Arrival Music, 1983/Alva Music, 1983.
Best-selling record by R.J.'s Latest Arrival (Golden Boy/Quality, 84).

Shaddup Your Face
Words and music by Joe Dolce.
April Music, Inc., 1980.
Best-selling record by Joe Dolce (MCA, 81).

Shadows of the Night
Words and music by David Leigh Byron.
Inner Sanctum, 1980.
Best-selling record by Pat Benatar (Chrysalis, 82).

Shake It Up
Words and music by Ric Ocasek.
Lido Music Inc., 1981.
Best-selling record by The Cars (Elektra, 82).

Shake It Up Tonight
Words and music by Michael Sutton and Brenda Sutton.
April Music, Inc., 1981.
Best-selling record by Cheryl Lynn (Columbia, 81).

Shame on the Moon
Words and music by Rodney Crowell.
Coolwell Music, 1981/Granite Music Corp., 1981.
Best-selling record by Bob Seger & The Silver Bullet Band (Capitol, 82).

Shanghai Breezes
Words and music by John Denver.
Cherry Lane Music Co., Inc., 1981.
Best-selling record by John Denver (RCA, 82).

Share Your Love with Me
Words and music by Al Bragg and Deadric Malone.
Duchess Music Corp., 1963.
Best-selling record by Kenny Rogers (Liberty, 81).

Sharkey's Day
Words and music by Laurie Anderson.
Difficult Music, 1984.
Introduced by Laurie Anderson in *Mr. Heartbreak* (Warner Brothers, 84).

Sharkey's Night
Words and music by Laurie Anderson.
Difficult Music, 1984.
Introduced by Laurie Anderson in *Mr. Heartbreak* (Warner Brothers, 84).

Sharp Dressed Man
Words and music by Billy Gibbons, Dusty Hill, and Frank Beard.
Hamstein Music, 1983.
Best-selling record by Z.Z. Top (Warner Brothers, 83).

She Blinded Me with Science (English)
Words and music by Thomas Dolby and Joe Kerr.
Participation Music, Inc., 1982.
Best-selling record Thomas Dolby (Capitol, 83).

She Bop
Words and music by Cyndi Lauper, Stephen Lunt, Gary Corbett, and Richard Chertoff.
Reilla Music Corp., 1983/Noyb Music, 1983/Perfect Pinch Music, 1983/Hobbler Music, 1983.
Best-selling record by Cyndi Lauper (Portrait, 84).

She Can't Say That Anymore
Words and music by John Conlee.
WB Gold Music Corp., 1980.
Best-selling record by John Conlee (MCA, 80).

She Got the Goldmine (I Got the Shaft)
Words and music by Tim DuBois.
Warner House of Music, 1981.
Best-selling record by Jerry Reed (MCA, 82).

She Left Love All over Me
Words and music by Chester Lester.
Warner House of Music, 1981.
Best-selling record by Razzy Bailey (RCA, 82).

She Sure Got Away with My Heart
Words and music by James Aldridge and Howard Brasfield.
Rick Hall Music, 1982.
Best-selling record by John Anderson (Warner Brothers, 84).

She Was Hot (English)
Words and music by Mick Jagger and Keith Richards.
Colgems-EMI Music Inc., 1983.
Best-selling record by The Rolling Stones (Rolling Stones, 84).

She Works Hard for the Money
Words and music by Donna Summer and Michael Omartian.
Sweet Summer Night Music, 1983/See This House Music, 1983.
Best-selling record by Donna Summer (Mercury, 83).

She's a Bad Mama Jama
Words and music by Leon Haywood.
Jim-Edd Music, 1981.
Best-selling record by Carl Carlton (20th Century-Fox, 81). Nominated
  for a National Academy of Recording Arts and Sciences Award,
  Rhythm 'n' Blues Song of the Year, 1981.

She's a Beauty
Words and music by Steve Lukather, David Foster, and Fee Waybill.
Foster Frees Music Inc., 1983/Rehtakul Veets Music, 1983/Screen
  Gems-EMI Music Inc., 1983/Boone's Tunes, 1983.
Best-selling record by The Tubes (Capitol, 83).

She's Got a Way
Best-selling record by Billy Joel (Columbia, 81). See *Popular Music,
  1920-1979.*

She's Not Really Cheatin' (She's Just Gettin' Even)
Words and music by Randy Shaffer.
Baray Music Inc., 1982/Wood Hall Publishing Co., 1982.
Best-selling record by Moe Bandy (Columbia, 82).

She's Out of My Life
Best-selling record by Michael Jackson (Epic, 80). See *Popular Music,
  1920-1979.*

She's So Cold (English)
Words and music by Mick Jagger and Keith Richards.
Colgems-EMI Music Inc., 1980.
Best-selling record by The Rolling Stones (Rolling Stones, 80).

She's Strange
Words and music by Larry Blackmon, Charlie Singleton, Nathan

Leftenant, and Tomi Jenkins.
All Seeing Eye Music, 1984/Cameo Five Music, 1984.
Best-selling record by Cameo (Atlanta Artists, 84).

Shining Star
Words and music by Leo Graham, Jr. and Paul Richmond.
Content Music, Inc., 1980.
Best-selling record by The Manhattans (Columbia, 80). Nominated for
a National Academy of Recording Arts and Sciences Award, Rhythm
'n' Blues Song of the Year, 1980.

Shipbuilding (English)
Words and music by Elvis Costello and Clive Langer.
Plangent Visions Music, Inc., London, England, 1982/Warner
Brothers, Inc., 1982.
Introduced by Elvis Costello in *Punch the Clock* (Columbia, 83).

Shock the Monkey (East German)
German words and music by Peter Gabriel.
Hidden Music, 1982.
Best-selling record by Peter Gabriel (Geffen, 82).

Shoo-Rah Shoo-Rah
Words and music by Allen Toussaint.
Marsaint Music Inc., 1981/Warner-Tamerlane Publishing Corp.,
1981.
Featured on *Rock Away* by Phoebe Snow (Mirage, 81).

Should I Do It
Words and music by Layng Martine, Jr.
Unichappell Music Inc., 1981/Watch Hill Music, 1981.
Best-selling record by The Pointer Sisters (Planet, 82).

Should've Never Let You Go
Words and music by Neil Sedaka and Phil Cody.
Kirshner/April Music Publishing, 1978/Kiddio Music Co., 1978.
Neil and Dara Sedaka (Elektra, 80).

Show Her
Words and music by Mike Reid.
Lodge Hall Music, Inc., 1982.
Best-selling record by Ronnie Milsap (RCA, 84).

Show Me (English)
Words and music by Chrissie Hynde.
Virgin Music, Inc., 1984.
Best-selling record by The Pretenders (Sire, 84).

Silent Treatment
Words and music by Earl Thomas Conley.
April Music, Inc., 1983.
Best-selling record by Earl Thomas Conley (Sunbird, 81).

Silly People
Words and music by Stephen Sondheim.
Revelation Music Publishing Corp., 1982/Rilting Music Inc., 1982.
Introduced by Suzanne Henry and Craig Lucas in *Marry Me a Little*
   (82).

Simple
Words and music by Maury Yeston.
Yeston Music, Ltd., 1975.
Introduced by Anita Morris in *Nine* (Musical, 82).

Since I Don't Have You
Revived by Don McLean (Millennium, 81). See *Popular Music, 1920-79.*

Since You're Gone
Words and music by Ric Ocasek.
Lido Music Inc., 1981.
Best-selling record by The Cars (Elektra, 82).

Sister Christian
Words and music by Kelly Keagy.
Kid Bird Music, 1983.
Best-selling record by Night Ranger (Camel/MCA, 84).

Sisters (English)
Words and music by Richard Thompson.
Island Music, 1980.
Introduced on *Sunnyvista* by Richard Thompson (Hannibal, 83).

Sisters
Words and music by Jim Wann.
Shapiro, Bernstein & Co., Inc., 1981.
Introduced by Cass Morgan and Debra Monk in *Pump Boys and Di-
   nettes* (81).

'65 Love Affair
Words and music by Paul Davis.
Web 4 Music Inc., 1981.
Best-selling record by Paul Davis (Arista, 82).

Skateaway (English)
Words and music by Mark Knopfler.

Almo Music Corp., 1980.
Best-selling record by Dire Straits (Warner Brothers, 81).

Slow Burn
Words and music by Tommy Rocco and Charlie Black.
Bibo Music Publishers, 1983.
Best-selling record by T.G. Sheppard (Warner/Curb, 84).

Slow Hand
Music by Michael Clark, words by John Bettis.
Warner-Tamerlane Publishing Corp., 1980/Flying Dutchman, 1980/
    WB Music Corp., 1980.
Best-selling record by The Pointer Sisters (Planet, 81).

Small Paradise
Words and music by John Cougar Mellencamp.
HG Music, Inc., 1979.
Best-selling record by John Cougar (Riva, 80).

Smokey Mountain Rain
Words and music by Kye Fleming and Dennis Morgan.
Hall-Clement Publications, 1980.
Best-selling record by Ronnie Milsap (RCA, 80).

So Alone
Words and music by Lou Reed and Michael Fontara.
Metal Machine Music, 1980.
Introduced by Lou Reed in *Growing Up in Public* (RCA, 80).

So Bad (English)
Words and music by Paul McCartney.
MPL Communications Inc., 1983.
Best-selling record by Paul McCartney (Columbia, 84).

So Fine
Revived by Howard Johnson (A & M, 82). See *Popular Music, 1920-79.*

Solid
Words and music by Nicholas Ashford and Valerie Simpson.
Nick-O-Val Music, 1984.
Best-selling record by Ashford and Simpson (Capitol, 84).

Solisbury Hill (East German)
English words and music by Peter Gabriel.
Hidden Music, 1977.
Best-selling record by Peter Gabriel (Geffen, 83).

Solitaire (French-English)
English words by Diane Warren, French words and music by
  Martine Clemenceau.
Arista Music, Inc., 1982.
Best-selling record by Laura Branigan (Atlantic, 83).

Some Guys Have All the Luck
Words and music by Jeff Fortgang.
Kirshner/April Music Publishing, 1973.
Best-selling record by Rod Stewart (Warner Brothers, 84).

Some Kind of Friend
Words by Adrienne Anderson, music by Barry Manilow.
Townsway Music, 1982/Angela Music, 1982.
Best-selling record by Barry Manilow (Arista, 83).

Somebody Else's Guy
Words and music by Jocelyn Brown and Annette Brown.
Jocelyn Brown's Music, 1980.
Best-selling record by Jocelyn Brown (Vinyl Dreams, 84).

Somebody's Baby
Words and music by Jackson Browne and Danny Kortchmar.
Night Kitchen Music, 1982/Kortchmar Music, 1982.
Best-selling record by Jackson Browne (Asylum, 82). Introduced in the
  film *Fast Times at Ridgemont High* (82).

Somebody's Gonna Love You
Words and music by Don Cook and Rafe Van Hoy.
Cross Keys Publishing Co., Inc., 1982/Unichappell Music Inc.,
  1982/Van Hoy Music, 1982.
Best-selling record by Lee Greenwood (MCA, 83).

Somebody's Knockin'
Words and music by Ed Penny and Jerry Gillespie.
Chiplin Music Co., 1980/Tri-Chappell Music Inc., 1980.
Best-selling record by Terri Gibbs (MCA, 81). Nominated for a National
  Academy of Recording Arts and Sciences Award, Country Song of the
  Year, 1981.

Somebody's Needin' Somebody
Words and music by Len Chera.
Intersong, USA Inc., 1984/Ja-Len Music Co/Intersong USA, Inc.,
  1984.
Best-selling record by Conway Twitty (Warner Brothers, 84).

Somebody's Watching Me
Words and music by Rockwell.

177

Jobete Music Co., Inc., 1983.
Best-selling record by Rockwell (Motown, 84).

Someday, Someway
Words and music by Marshall Crenshaw.
Belwin-Mills Publishing Corp., 1980/MHC Music, 1980.
Best-selling record by Robert Gordon (RCA, 81).

Someday When Things Are Good
Words and music by Merle Haggard and Leona Williams.
Shade Tree Music Inc., 1984.
Best-selling record by Merle Haggard (Epic, 84).

Someone Could Lose a Heart Tonight
Words and music by David Malloy, Eddie Rabbitt, and Even
    Stevens.
Briarpatch Music, 1981/Debdave Music Inc., 1981.
Best-selling record by Eddie Rabbitt (Elektra, 82).

Someone That I Used to Love
Words by Gerry Goffin, music by Michael Masser.
Screen Gems-EMI Music Inc., 1978/Prince Street Music/Arista
    Music, Inc.
Best-selling record by Natalie Cole (Capitol, 80).

Something to Grab For
Words and music by Ric Ocasek.
Lido Music Inc., 1982.
Best-selling record by Ric Ocasek (Warner Brothers, 83).

Something's on Your Mind
Words and music by Hubert Eaves, III and James Williams.
Trumar Music, 1983/Huemar Music, 1983/Diesel Music, 1983.
Best-selling record by D Train (Prelude, 84).

Somewhere Down the Line
Words and music by Lewis Anderson and Casey Kelly.
Old Friends Music, 1983/Golden Bridge Music, 1983.
Best-selling record by T.G. Sheppard (Warner/Curb, 84).

Somewhere Down the Road
Words and music by Cynthia Weil, music by Tom Snow.
ATV Music Corp., 1981/Mann & Weil Songs Inc., 1981/Snow
    Music, 1981.
Best-selling record by Barry Manilow (Arista, 81).

Somewhere That's Green
Words by Howard Ashman, music by Alan Menken.

Samuel French, Inc., 1982.
Introduced by Ellen Greene in *Little Shop of Horrors* (82).

Song for a Future Generation
Words and music by Fred Schneider, Cynthia Wilson, Ricky Wilson,
    Catherine Pierson, and Julie Strickland.
Island Music, 1983.
Introduced on *Whammy* by The B52's (Warner Brothers, 83).

Song on the Sand
Words and music by Jerry Herman.
Jerryco Music Co., 1983.
Introduced by Gene Barry in *La Cage Au Folles* (83).

Souls
Words and music by Rick Springfield.
Vogue Music, 1983.
Best-selling record by Rick Springfield (RCA, 83).

The Sound of Goodbye
Words and music by Hugh Prestwood.
Parquet Music, 1983/Lawyer's Daughter, 1983.
Best-selling record by Crystal Gayle (Warner Brothers, 84).

Soup for One
Words and music by Bernard Edwards and Nile Rodgers.
Warner-Tamerlane Publishing Corp., 1982.
Best-selling record by Chic (Mirage, 82). Introduced in the film *Soup for
    One* (82).

South Central Rain (I'm Sorry)
Words and music by Mike Mills, Bill Berry, Peter Buck, and
    Michael Stipe.
Unichappell Music Inc., 1984.
Best-selling record by R.E.M. (I.R.S., 84).

South to a Warmer Place
Words by Loonis McGlohon, music by Alec Wilder.
Ludlow Music Inc., 1980/Saloon Songs, Inc., 1980.
Introduced by by Frank Sinatra on *She Shot Me Down* (Reprise, 81).

Southern Cross
Words and music by Steve Stills, Richard Curtis, and Michael
    Curtis.
Kenwon Music, 1974/Catpatch Music/Gold Hill Music, Inc.
Best-selling record by Crosby, Stills and Nash (Atlantic, 82).

179

Southern Rains
Words and music by Roger Murrah.
Magic Castle Music, Inc., 1980/Blackwood Music Inc., 1980.
Best-selling record by Mel Tillis (Elektra, 81).

Spanish Johnny
Words and music by Paul Siebel.
Sweet Jelly Roll Music, Inc., 1978.
Featured on *Evangeline* by Emmylou Harris (Warner Brothers, 81).

Special Lady
Best-selling record by Ray, Goodman, and Brown (Polydor, 80). See
  Popular Music, 1920-1979.

The Spirit of Radio (Canadian)
Words by Neil Peart, music by Geddy Lee and Alex Lifeson.
Core Music Publishing, 1980.
Best-selling record by Rush (Mercury, 80).

Spirits in the Material World (English)
Words and music by Sting (pseudonym for Gordon Sumner).
Virgin Music, Inc., 1981.
Best-selling record by The Police (A & M, 82).

Square Biz
Words and music by Teena Marie Brockert and Allen McGrier.
Jobete Music Co., Inc., 1981/McNella Music, 1981.
Best-selling record Teena Marie (Gordy, 81).

Square Pegs
Words and music by Christopher Butler, Daniel Klayman, Marc
  Williams, Tracy Wormworth, Patty Donahue, and William Ficca.
Belfast Music, 1982.
Featured in *I Could Rule the World If I Could Only Get the Parts* by
  The Waitresses (Polydor, 83). Introduced on the TV series *Square
  Pegs* (83).

Stand Back
Words and music by Stephanie Nicks and Prince Rogers Nelson.
Welsh Witch Publishing, 1983/Controversy Music, 1983.
Best-selling record by Stevie Nicks (Modern, 83).

Stand by Me
Revived by Mickey Gilley (Full Moon, 80). See *Popular Music, 1920-79.*

Stand or Fall (English)
Words and music by Peter Greenall, Adam Woods, Cy Curnin,
  Charls Barrett, and Jamie West-Oram.

Colgems-EMI Music Inc., 1981.
Best-selling record by The Fixx (MCA, 82).

Standing on the Top
Words and music by Rick James.
Stone City Music, 1982.
Best-selling record by The Temptations Featuring Rick James (Gordy, 82).

Stars on 45
Best-selling record by Stars on 45 (Radio Records, 81). Record is a medley of "Venus," "Sugar Sugar," "No Reply," "I'll Be Back," "Drive My Car," "Do You Want to Know a Secret," "We Can Work It Out," "I Should Have Known Better," "Nowhere Man," and "You're Gonna Lose That Girl."

Start Me Up (English)
Words and music by Mick Jagger and Keith Richards.
Screen Gems-EMI Music Inc., 1981.
Best-selling record by The Rolling Stones (Rolling Stones, 81).

(Just Like) Starting Over
Words and music by John Lennon.
Lenono Music, 1980.
Best-selling record by John Lennon (Geffen, 80).

Starting Over Again
Best-selling record by Dolly Parton (RCA, 80). See *Popular Music, 1920-1979.*

State of Shock
Words and music by Michael Jackson and Randy Hansen.
Mijac Music, 1984/Warner-Tamerlane Publishing Corp., 1984.
Best-selling record by Michael Jackson and Mick Jagger (Epic, 84).

Stay the Night
Words and music by Peter Cetera and David Foster.
Double Virgo Music, 1984/Foster Frees Music Inc., 1984.
Best-selling record by Chicago (Full Moon/Warner Brothers, 84).

Stay with Me Tonight
Words and music by Raymond Jones.
Zubaida Music, 1983/Arista Music, Inc., 1983.
Best-selling record by Jeffrey Osborne (A & M, 83).

Stay Young (English)
Words and music by Benny Gallagher and Graham Lyle.

Irving Music Inc., 1976.
Best-selling record by Don Williams (MCA, 84).

Steal Away
Best-selling record by Robbie Dupree (Elektra, 80). See *Popular Music, 1920-1979.*

Step by Step
Words and music by Eddie Rabbitt, Even Stevens, and David Malloy.
Briarpatch Music, 1981/Debdave Music Inc., 1981.
Best-selling record by Eddie Rabbitt (Elektra, 81).

Steppin' Out (English)
Words and music by Joe Jackson.
Almo Music Corp., 1982.
Best-selling record by Joe Jackson (A & M, 82). Nominated for a National Academy of Recording Arts and Sciences Award, Record of the Year, 1982.

Still in Saigon
Words and music by Dan Daley.
Dreena Music, 1981/Dan Daley Music, 1981.
Best-selling record by The Charlie Daniels Band (Epic, 82).

Still Losing You
Words and music by Mike Reid.
Lodge Hall Music, Inc., 1984.
Best-selling record by Ronnie Milsap (RCA, 84).

Still Such a Thing
Words and music by Nick Ashford and Valerie Simpson.
Nick-O-Val Music, 1980.
Introduced on *High-Rise* by Ashford and Simpson (Capitol, 83).

Still Taking Chances
Words and music by Michael Murphy.
Timberwolf Music, 1982.
Best-selling record by Michael Murphy (Liberty, 83).

Still They Ride
Words and music by Steve Perry, Neal Schon, and Jonathan Cain.
Weed High Nightmare Music, 1981.
Best-selling record by Journey (Columbia, 82).

Stomp (American-English)
Words and music by Louis Johnson, George Johnson, Valerie Johnson, and Rod Temperton.

State of the Arts Music, 1980/Brojay Music, 1980/Kidada Music
   Inc., 1980.
Best-selling record by The Brothers Johnson (A & M, 80).

Stone Cold (English)
Words and music by Ritchie Blackmore, Roger Glover, and Joe
   Lynn Turner.
Thames Talent Publishing, Ltd., 1981/Lyon Farm Music Ltd., 1981.
Best-selling record by Rainbow (Mercury, 82).

Stop Doggin' Me Around, also known as **Doggin' Around**
Words and music by Lena Agree.
Lena Music, Inc., 1960.
Revived by Klique (MCA, 83).

Stop Draggin' My Heart Around
Words and music by Tom Petty and Mike Campbell.
Gone Gator Music, 1981/Wild Gator Music, 1981.
Best-selling record by Stevie Nicks with Tom Petty & The Heartbreakers
   (Modern, 81).

Stop Your Sobbing (English)
Words and music by Ray Davies.
Jay-Boy Music Corp., 1964.
Best-selling record by The Pretenders (Sire, 80).

The Story Goes On
Words by Richard Maltby, music by David Shire.
Fiddleback Music Publishing Co., Inc., 1984/Progeny Music, 1984/
   Revelation Music Publishing Corp., 1984/Long Pond Music, 1984.
Introduced by Liz Callaway in *Baby* (83).

Straight from the Heart (Canadian)
Words and music by Bryan Adams and Eric Kagna.
Irving Music Inc., 1980/Adams Communications, Inc., 1980.
Best-selling record by Bryan Adams (A & M, 83).

Stranger in My House
Words and music by Mike Reid.
Lodge Hall Music, Inc., 1983.
Best-selling record by Ronnie Milsap (RCA, 83). Won a National Acad-
   emy of Recording Arts and Sciences Award, Country Song of the
   Year, 1983.

Stranger in the House (English)
Words and music by Elvis Costello.
Plangent Visions Music, Inc., London, England, 1980.
Introduced by Elvis Costello in *Get Happy* (Columbia, 80).

Stray Cat Strut
Words and music by Brian Setzer.
Zomba Enterprises, Inc., 1981.
Best-selling record The Stray Cats (EMI-America, 83).

Street Corner
Words and music by Nick Ashford and Valerie Simpson.
Nick-O-Val Music, 1982.
Best-selling record by Ashford and Simpson (Capitol, 82).

The Stroke
Words and music by Billy Squier.
Songs of the Knight, 1981.
Best-selling record by Billy Squier (Capital, 81).

Stroker's Theme
Words and music by Charlie Daniels.
Music Corp. of America, 1983.
Best-selling record by The Charlie Daniels Band (Epic, 83). Introduced
in the film *Stroker Ace* (83).

Strut (English)
Words and music by Charlene Dore and J. Littman.
Ackee Music Inc., 1983.
Best-selling record by Sheena Easton (EMI-America, 84).

Stuck on You
Words and music by Lionel Richie, Jr.
Brockman Enterprises Inc., 1983.
Best-selling record by Lionel Richie (Motown, 84).

Suddenly
Words and music by John Farrar.
John Farrar Music, 1980.
Best-selling record by Olivia Newton-John (MCA, 80).

Suddenly Last Summer
Words and music by Martha Davis.
Clean Sheets Music, 1983.
Best-selling record by The Motels (Capitol, 83).

Suddenly Seymour
Words by Howard Ashman, music by Alan Menken.
Samuel French, Inc., 1982.
Introduced by Ellen Greene and Lee Wilkof in *Little Shop of Horrors*
(82).

Sugar Daddy
Words and music by David Bellamy.
Famous Music Co., 1980/Bellamy Brothers Music, 1980.
Best-selling record by The Bellamy Brothers (Warner Brothers, 80).

Sukiyaki
Revived by A Taste of Honey (Capitol, 81). See *Popular Music, 1920-79.*

Sunday
Words and music by Stephen Sondheim.
Revelation Music Publishing Corp., 1981/Rilting Music Inc., 1981.
Introduced by Company of *Sunday in the Park with George* (84).

Sunglasses at Night (Canadian)
Words and music by Corey Hart.
Liesse Publishing, 1983.
Best-selling record by Corey Hart (EMI-America, 84).

Surround Me with Love
Words and music by Wayland Hollyfield and Norris Wilson.
Bibo Music Publishers, 1981/Al Gallico Music Corp., 1981.
Best-selling record by Charly McClain (Epic, 81).

Sweet Baby
Words and music by George Duke.
Mycenae Music Publishing Co., 1981.
Best-selling record by Stanley Clarke and George Duke (Epic, 81).

Sweet Dreams (Australian)
Words and music by Graham Russell.
Careers Music Inc., 1981/Nottsongs, 1981.
Best-selling record by Air Supply (Arista, 82).

Sweet Dreams (English)
Words and music by Annie Lennox and Dave Stewart.
Blue Network Music, 1983.
Best-selling record by Eurhythmics (RCA, 83).

Sweet Sensation
Words and music by James Mtume and Reggie Lucas.
Frozen Butterfly Music Publishing, 1979.
Best-selling record by Stephanie Mills (20th Century, 80).

The Sweetest Thing (I've Ever Known)
Words and music by Otha Young.
Sterling Music Co., 1976/Addison Street Music, 1976.
Best-selling record by Juice Newton (Capitol, 81).

Sweetheart

Words and music by Frankie Previte and W. Elworthy.

Lyon Farm Music Ltd., 1981/Bright Smile Music, 1981/ELMusic, 1981.

Best-selling record by Franke & The Knockouts (Millennium, 81).

Sweetheart Like You

Words and music by Bob Dylan.

Special Rider Music, 1983.

Introduced by Bob Dylan on *Infidels* (Columbia, 83).

Swept Away

Words and music by Daryl Hall and Sara Allen.

Fust Buzza Music, Inc., 1984/Unichappell Music Inc., 1984.

Best-selling record by Diana Ross (RCA, 84).

Swingin'

Words and music by John D. Anderson and Lionel Delmore.

John Anderson Music Co. Inc., 1982/Hall-Clement Publications, 1982.

Best-selling record by John Anderson (Warner Brothers, 83).

Synchronicity II (English)

Words and music by Sting (pseudonym for Gordon Sumner).

Reggatta Music, Ltd., 1983/Illegal Songs, Inc., 1983.

Best-selling record by The Police (A & M, 83).

T

Tainted Love (English)
Words and music by Ed Cobb.
Equinox Music, 1976.
Best-selling record by Tainted Love (Sire, 82).

Take a Little Rhythm (Canadian)
Words and music by Ali Thompson.
Almo Music Corp., 1980.
Best-selling record by Ali Thompson (A & M, 80).

Take It Away (English)
Words and music by Paul McCartney.
MPL Communications Inc., 1982.
Best-selling record by Paul McCartney (Columbia, 82).

Take It Easy on Me (Australian)
Words and music by Graham Goble.
Little River Band Music, Victoria, Australia, 1981.
Best-selling record by Little River Band (Capitol, 82).

Take It on the Run
Words and music by Gary Richrath.
Slam Dunk Music, 1980.
Best-selling record by REO Speedwagon (Epic, 81).

Take Me Down
Words and music by Mark Gray and James Pennington.
Irving Music Inc., 1980/Careers Music Inc., 1980.
Best-selling record by Alabama (RCA, 82).

Take Me to Heart
Words and music by Marv Ross.
Narrow Dude Music, 1983/Bonnie Bee Good Music, 1983/WB
  Music Corp., 1983.
Best-selling record by Quarterflash (Geffen, 83).

Take My Heart
Words and music by Charles Smith, James Taylor, George Brown, and Eumir Deodato.
Delightful Music Ltd., 1981/Double F Music, 1981.
Best-selling record by Kool & The Gang (De-Lite, 81).

Take Off (Canadian)
Words and music by Kerry Crawford, Jonathan Goldsmith, Mark Giacommelli, Rick Moranis, and Dave Thomas.
McKenzie Brothers, 1981.
Best-selling record by Bob & Doug McKenzie (Mercury, 82).

Take Your Time (Do It Right) Part 1
Words and music by Harold Clayton and Sigidi.
Avant Garde Music Publishing, Inc., 1980/Interior Music, 1980.
Best-selling record by S.O.S. Band (Tabu, 80).

Takin' It Easy
Words and music by Lacy Dalton, Mark Sherrill, and Billy Sherrill.
Algee Music Corp., 1981.
Best-selling record by Lacy J. Dalton (Columbia, 81).

Talk of the Town (English)
Words and music by Chrissie Hynde.
Virgin Music, Inc., 1980.
Introduced by The Pretenders on *Pretenders II* (Sire, 82).

Talk Talk
Words and music by Edwin Hollis and Mark Hollis.
Lexicon Music Inc., 1982.
Best-selling record by Talk Talk (EMI-America, 82).

Talk to Me of Mendocino
Words and music by Kate McGarrigle.
Garden Court Music Co., 1975.
Revived by Linda Ronstadt on *Get Closer* (Asylum, 82).

Talk to Ya Later
Words and music by David Foster and Steve Lukather, music by Tubes.
Pseudo Songs, 1981/Irving Music Inc., 1981/Foster Frees Music Inc., 1981/Rehtakul Veets Music, 1981.
Best-selling record by The Tubes (Capitol, 81).

Talking in the Dark (English)
Words and music by Elvis Costello.
Plangent Visions Music, Inc., London, England, 1979.
Featured in *Mad Love* by Linda Ronstadt (Asylum, 80).

Talking in Your Sleep
Words and music by Jimmy Marinos, Wally Palmar, Mike Skill, Coz Canler, and Pete Solley.
Foreverendeavor Music, Inc., 1983.
Best-selling record by The Romantics (Nemperor, 83).

Taxi
Words and music by Homer Banks and Charles Brooks.
Backlog Music, 1983.
Best-selling record by J. Blackfoot (Soundtown, 84).

Teacher Teacher (Canadian)
Words and music by Bryan Adams and James Vallance.
Irving Music Inc., 1984/Adams Communications, Inc., 1984/Calypso Toonz, 1984.
Best-selling record by 38 Special (Capitol, 84).

Tears of the Lonely
Words and music by Wayland Holyfield.
Bibo Music Publishers, 1978.
Best-selling record by Mickey Gilley (Epic, 82).

Telefone (Long Distance Love Affair)
Words and music by Gregory Mathieson and Trevor Veitch.
Mighty Mathieson Music, 1983/Slapshot Music, 1983.
Best-selling record by Sheena Easton (EMI-America, 83).

Tell Her About It
Words and music by Billy Joel.
Joelsongs, 1983.
Best-selling record by Billy Joel (Columbia, 83).

Tell It Like It Is
Revived by Heart (Epic, 80). See *Popular Music, 1920-1979.*

Tell Me a Lie
Words and music by Barbara Wyrick and Mickey Buckins.
Rick Hall Music, 1973/Fame Publishing Co., Inc.
Best-selling record by Janie Fricke (Columbia, 83).

Tell Me Tomorrow
Words and music by Gary Goetzman and Mike Piccirillo.
Chardax Music, 1981.
Best-selling record by Smokey Robinson (Tamla, 82).

Tell That Girl to Shut Up
Words and music by Christopher Butler.

Island Music, 1980.
Featured in *The Right to Be Italian* by Holly & The Italians (Virgin, 81).

Temporary Beauty (English)
Words and music by Graham Parker.
Participation Music, Inc., 1982.
Introduced by Graham Parker on *Another Grey Area* (Arista, 82).

Temptation (English)
Words and music by Glenn Gregory, Ian Craig Marsh, and Martyn Ware.
WB Music Corp., 1982/Virgin Music, Inc., 1982.
Introduced by Heaven 17 on *The Luxury Gap* (Sire, 82).

Tempted (English)
Words and music by Christopher Difford and Glenn Tilbrook.
Illegal Songs, Inc., 1981.
Best-selling record by Squeeze (A & M, 81).

Tender Is the Night
Words and music by Russ Kunkel, Danny Kortchmar, and Jackson Browne.
Night Kitchen Music, 1983.
Best-selling record by Jackson Browne (Asylum, 83).

Tennessee Homesick Blues
Words and music by Dolly Parton.
Velvet Apple Music, 1984/Warner-Tamerlane Publishing Corp., 1984.
Best-selling record by Dolly Parton (RCA, 84).

Tennessee River
Words and music by Randy Owen.
Buzzherb Music, 1980.
Best-selling record by Alabama (RCA, 80).

Thank God for the Radio
Words and music by Max D. Barnes and Robert John Jones.
Blue Lake Music, 1982.
Best-selling record by The Kendalls (Mercury, 84).

That Girl
Words and music by Stevie Wonder.
Jobete Music Co., Inc., 1981/Black Bull Music, 1981.
Best-selling record by Stevie Wonder (Tamla, 82). Nominated for a National Academy of Recording Arts and Sciences Award, Rhythm 'n' Blues Song of the Year, 1982.

That Girl Could Sing
Words and music by Jackson Browne.
Swallow Turn Music, 1980.
Best-selling record by Jackson Browne (Asylum, 80).

That's All (English)
Words and music by Tony Banks, Phil Collins, and Mike
   Rutherford.
Pun Music Inc., London, England, 1983.
Best-selling record by Genesis (Atlantic, 83).

That's All That Matters
Best-selling record by Mickey Gilley (Epic, 80). See *Popular Music,
   1920-1979.*

That's the Thing About Love
Words and music by Gary Nicholson and Richard Leigh.
Cross Keys Publishing Co., Inc., 1983/April Music, Inc., 1983.
Best-selling record by Don Williams (MCA, 84).

That's the Way Love Goes
Best-selling record by Merle Haggard (Epic, 84). See Popular Music,
   1920-79

Theme from *Continental Divide* (Never Say Goodbye)
Music by Michael Small, words by Carole Bayer Sager.
Duchess Music Corp., 1981.
Best-selling record by Helen Reddy (MCA, 81). Introduced in the film
   Continental Divide (81).

Theme from *Doctor Detroit*
Words and music by Gerald Casale and Mark Mothersbaugh.
Devo Music, 1983.
Best-selling record by Devo (Backstreet, 83). Introduced in the film *Dr.
   Detroit* (83).

Theme from *Dynasty*
Words and music by Bill Conti.
Glamour Music, 1981.
Best-selling record by Bill Conti (Arista, 82).

Theme from *E.T.*
Music by John Williams.
Music Corp. of America, 1982.
Best-selling record by The Walter Murphy Band (MCA, 82).

The Theme from *Hill Street Blues*
Music by Mike Post.

MTM Enterprises Inc., 1980.
Best-selling record by Mike Post (Elektra, 81). Introduced on the TV
series *Hill Street Blues* (80).

Theme from *Magnum P.I.*
Music by Mike Post and Pete Carpenter.
Leeds Music Corp., 1981.
Best-selling record by Mike Post (Elektra, 82). Introduced on the TV
series *Magnum P. I.* (82).

Theme from *New York, New York*
Revived by Frank Sinatra (Reprise, 80). Chosen as the official song of
New York City. See *Popular Music, 1920-79.* Nominated for National
Academy of Recording Arts and Sciences Awards, Song of the Year,
1980, and Record of the Year, 1980.

Theme from *Raging Bull*
Words and music by Harold Wheeler and Joel Diamond.
CBS U Catalog, Inc., 1981.
Best-selling record by Joel Diamond (Motown, 81). Introduced in the
film *Raging Bull* (81).

Theme from *The Black Hole*
Words and music by William Collins, George Clinton, and J. S.
Theracon, music by Jim Vitti.
Rick's Music Inc., 1980/Malbiz Publishing, 1980/Rubber Band
Music, Inc., 1980.
Best-selling record by Parliament (Casablanca, 80). Introduced in the
film *The Black Hole* (80).

Theme from *The Dukes of Hazzard* (Good Ol' Boys)
Words and music by Waylon Jennings.
Warner-Tamerlane Publishing Corp., 1979/Rich Way Music, Inc.
Best-selling record by Waylon Jennings (RCA, 80). Introduced on the
TV series *The Dukes of Hazzard* (79).

**The Theme from *The Greatest American Hero*, also known as
Believe It or Not**
Words by Stephen Geyer, music by Mike Post.
April Music, Inc., 1981/Blackwood Music Inc., 1981/Mike Post
Productions, Inc., 1981/Darjen Music, 1981/S J C Music, 1981.
Best-selling record by Joey Scarbury (Elektra, 81). Introduced on the TV
series *The Greatest American Hero* (81).

Then Came You
Words by Madeline Sunshine, music by Steve Nelson.
Addax Music Co., Inc., 1983.
Introduced on the TV Show *Webster* (83).

They Don't Know (English)
Words and music by Kirsty MacColl.
MCA, Inc., 1983.
Best-selling record by Tracey Ullman (MCA, 84).

They Say
Words and music by Skip Scarborough and Terri McFadden.
Unichappell Music Inc., 1983/Little Birdie Music, 1983.
Introduced on *I'm So Proud* by Deniece Williams (Columbia, 83).

Thighs High I Wanna (Grip Your Hips and Move)
Words by Dave Grusin, Sekou Bunch, and Thomasina Smith, music
    by Thomas Browne.
Best-selling record by Tom Browne (GRP, 81).

Thin Line Between Love and Hate
Revived by The Pretenders on *Learning to Crawl* (Sire, 84). See *Popular Music, 1920-1979.*

A Thing about You
Words and music by Tom Petty.
Gone Gator Music, 1981.
Introduced by Tom Petty on *Hard Promises* (Backstreet, 81).

Think About Me (English)
Best-selling record by Fleetwood Mac (Warner Brothers, 80). See *Popular Music, 1920-1979.*

Think I'm in Love
Words and music by Eddie Money and Randy Oda.
Soft Music, 1982.
Best-selling record by Eddie Money (Columbia, 82).

This Day
Words and music by Edwin Hawkins.
Edwin R. Hawkins Music Co., 1983.
Introduced on *Feel My Soul* by Jennifer Holliday (Geffen, 83).

This Is My Song
Words and music by Gary William Friedman and Will Holt.
Bussy Music, 1983/Devon Music, 1983/Hampshire House Publishing
    Corp., 1983/Lemon Tree Music, Inc., 1983.
Introduced by Company in *Taking My Turn* (83).

This Little Girl
Words and music by Bruce Springsteen.
Bruce Springsteen, 1980.
Best-selling record by Gary U.S. Bonds (EMI-America, 81).

Popular Music, 1980-1984

This Time (Canadian)
Words and music by Bryan Adams and Jim Vallance.
Irving Music Inc., 1983/Adams Communications, Inc., 1983.
Best-selling record by Bryan Adams (A & M, 83).

This Woman (English)
Words and music by Barry Gibb and Albhy Galuten.
Gibb Brothers Music, 1983.
Best-selling record by Kenny Rogers (RCA, 84).

Three Times in Love
Best-selling record by Tommy James (Millennium, 80). See *Popular Music, 1920-1979.*

Thriller (English)
Words and music by Rod Temperton.
Almo Music Corp., 1982.
Best-selling record by Michael Jackson (Epic, 84).

Through the Years
Words and music by Steve Dorff and Marty Panzer.
Peso Music, 1980/Swanee Bravo Music, 1980.
Best-selling record by Kenny Rogers (Liberty, 82).

The Tide Is High (English)
Words and music by John Holt.
Gemrod Music, Inc., 1968.
Best-selling record by Blondie (Chrysalis, 80).

Tight Fittin Jeans
Words and music by Mike Huggman.
Prater Music, Inc., 1980.
Best-selling record by Conway Twitty (MCA, 81).

A Tight Knit Family
Words and music by William Finn.
Samuel French, Inc., 1981.
Introduced by Michael Rupert in *March of the Falsettos* (81).

'Til I Gain Control Again
Words and music by Rodney Crowell.
Jolly Cheeks Music, 1976.
Best-selling record by Crystal Gayle (Elektra, 82).

Till You're Gone
Words and music by James Aldridge and Tom Brasfield.
Rick Hall Music, 1982.
Best-selling record by Barbara Mandrell (MCA, 82).

Time (English)
Words and music by Eric Woolfson and Alan Parsons.
CBS Unart Catalog Inc., 1980.
Best-selling record by The Alan Parsons Project (Arista, 81).

Time (English)
Words and music by Roy Hay, Jon Moss, and Michael Craig.
Virgin Music, Inc., 1982.
Best-selling record by Culture Club (Virgin/Epic, 83).

Time After Time
Words and music by Cyndi Lauper and Rob Hyman.
Reilla Music Corp., 1983/Dub Notes/WB Music Corp., 1983.
Best-selling record by Cyndi Lauper (Portrait, 84). Nominated for a
   National Academy of Recording Arts and Sciences Award, Best Song
   of the Year, 1984.

Time Is Time
Words and music by Andy Gibb and Barry Gibb.
Stigwood Music Inc., 1980/Joy U.S.A. Music Co., 1980/Hugh &
   Barbara Gibb Music, 1980/Andy Gibb Music, 1980/Gibb Brothers
   Music, 1980.
Best-selling record by Andy Gibb (RSO, 80).

Time Like Your Wire Wheels
Words and music by Wendy Waldman.
Cotillion Music Inc., 1980.
Introduced by Wendy Waldman on *Which Way to Main Street* (Epic,
   82).

Time the Avenger (English)
Words and music by Chrissie Hynde.
Virgin Music, Inc., 1984.
Introduced by The Pretenders on *Learning to Crawl* (Sire, 84).

Time Will Reveal
Words and music by Bunny DeBarge and Eldra DeBarge.
Jobete Music Co., Inc., 1983.
Best-selling record by DeBarge (Gordy, 83).

Tired of Toein' the Line
Words and music by Rocky Burnette and Ron Coleman.
Cheshire Music Inc., 1979.
Best-selling record by Rocky Burnette (EMI-America, 80).

To All the Girls I've Loved Before
Words by Hal David, music by Albert Hammond.

April Music, Inc., 1975/Casa David, 1975.
Best-selling record by Julio Iglesias and Willie Nelson (Columbia, 84).

To Me
Words and music by Mack David and Mike Reid.
Collins Court Music, Inc., 1983/Lodge Hall Music, Inc., 1983.
Best-selling record by Barbara Mandell and Lee Greenwood (MCA, 84).

Together
Best-selling record by Tierra (Boardwalk, 80). See *Popular Music, 1920-1979.*

Together
Words and music by Rob Wirth and Rik Howard.
Embassy TV, 1982.
Introduced on the TV series *Silver Spoons* (82).

Tom Sawyer (Canadian)
Words by Neil Peart and Pye Dubois, music by Geddy Lee and Alex Lifeson.
Core Music Publishing, 1981.
Best-selling record by Rush (Mercury, 81).

Tonight
Words and music by James Taylor, Curtis Williams, Ronald Bell, George Brown, Robert Bell, Michael Ray, Clifford Adams, Charles Smith, and James Bonnefond.
Delightful Music Ltd., 1983.
Best-selling record by Kool & The Gang (De-Lite, 84).

Tonight I Celebrate My Love
Music by Michael Masser, words by Gerry Goffin.
Almo Music Corp., 1983/Prince Street Music, 1983/Screen Gems-EMI Music Inc., 1983.
Best-selling record by Peabo Bryson and Roberta Flack (Capitol, 83).

Tonight I'm Yours (Don't Hurt Me)
Words by Rod Stewart, music by Jim Cregan and Kevin Savigar.
Riva Music Ltd., 1981/WB Music Corp., 1981/Rod Stewart, 1981.
Best-selling record by Rod Stewart (Warner Brothers, 82).

Tonight Is What It Means to Be Young
Words and music by Jim Steinman.
Lost Boys Music, 1984/Off Backstreet Music, 1984.
Best-selling record by Fire Inc. (MCA, 84). Introduced in the film *Streets of Fire* (84).

Too Hot
Best-selling record by Kool & The Gang (De-Lite, 80). See *Popular Music, 1920-1979.*

Too Many Lovers
Words and music by Mark True, Ted Lindsay, and Sam Hogin.
Cookhouse Music, 1980/Mother Tongue Music, 1980.
Best-selling record by Crystal Gayle (Columbia, 81).

Too Much Time on My Hands
Words and music by Tommy Shaw.
Stygian Songs, 1981/Almo Music Corp., 1981.
Best-selling record by Styx (A & M, 81).

Too Shy (English)
Words and music by Limahl and Nick Beggs.
Chappell & Co., Inc., 1983.
Best-selling record by Kajagoogoo (Capitol, 83).

Too Tight
Words and music by Michael Cooper.
Val-ie Joe Music, 1980.
Best-selling record by Con Funk Shun (Mercury, 81).

Total Eclipse of the Heart
Words and music by Jim Steinman.
E. B. Marks Music Corp., 1982.
Best-selling record by Bonnie Tyler (Columbia, 83).

Touch a Four Leaf Clover
Words and music by David Lewis and Wayne Lewis.
Almo Music Corp., 1983/Jodaway Music, 1983.
Best-selling record by Atlantic Starr (A & M, 83).

Touch Me When We're Dancing
Words and music by Terry Skinner, J. L. Wallace, and Kenneth Bell.
Welk Music Group, 1979.
Best-selling record by The Carpenters (A & M, 81).

Train in Vain (Stand by Me) (English)
Best-selling record by The Clash (Epic, 80). See *Popular Music, 1920-79.*

Treat Me Right
Words and music by Doug Lubahn.
Blackwood Music Inc., 1980.
Best-selling record by Pat Benatar (Chrysalis, 81).

Popular Music, 1980-1984

Trouble
Words and music by Lindsay Buckingham.
Now Sounds Music, 1981.
Best-selling record by Lindsay Buckingham (Asylum, 82).

True (English)
Words and music by Gary Kemp.
Reformation Publishing USA, 1983.
Best-selling record by Spandau Ballet (Chrysalis, 83).

True Love Ways
Revived by Mickey Gilley (Epic, 80). See *Popular Music, 1920-1979.*

Truly
Words and music by Lionel Richie, Jr.
Brockman Enterprises Inc., 1982.
Best-selling record by Lionel Richie (Motown, 82).

Try Again
Words and music by Dana Walden, Michael Day, and Rocky Maffit.
Walkin Music, 1983.
Best-selling record by Champaign (Columbia, 83).

Trying to Live My Life Without You
Words and music by Eugene Williams.
Happy Hooker Music Inc., 1977.
Best-selling record by Bob Seger (Capitol, 81). Introduced by The J.
Geils Band on the Flipside of "I Do."

Trying to Love Two Women
Best-selling record by The Oak Ridge Boys (MCA, 80). See *Popular Music, 1920-1979.*

Tunnel of Love (English)
Words and music by Mark Knopfler.
Almo Music Corp., 1980.
Introduced by Dire Straits on *Making Movies* (Warner Brothers, 80).

Turn Your Love Around
Words and music by Jay Graydon, Steve Lukather, and Bill
Champlin.
Garden Rake Music, Inc., 1981/Rehtakul Veets Music, 1981/J S H
Music, 1981.
Best-selling record by George Benson (Warner Brothers, 81). Won a
National Academy of Recording Arts and Sciences Award, Rhythm
'n' Blues Song of the Year, 1982.

Turning Away
Words and music by Tim Krekel.
Combine Music Corp., 1983.
Best-selling record by Crystal Gayle (Warner Brothers, 84).

Turning Japanese (English)
Words and music by David Fenton.
Glenwood Music Corp., 1979.
Best-selling record by The Vapors (United Artists, 81).

Twilight Zone (Netherlands)
English words and music by George Kooymans.
Fever Music, Inc., 1982.
Best-selling record by Golden Earring (21 Records, 83).

Twist of Fate
Words and music by Steven Kipner and Peter Beckett.
Stephen A. Kipner Music, 1983/April Music, Inc., 1983/Big Stick
  Music, 1983/Careers Music Inc., 1983.
Best-selling record by Olivia Newton-John (MCA, 83). Introduced in the
  film *Two of a Kind* (83).

Two Hearts Beat as One (Irish)
Words and music by Bono Hewson, Larry Mullen, Adam Clayton,
  and Dave Evans.
Island Music, 1983.
Introduced on *War* by U2 (Island, 83).

Two Story House
Words and music by Glen Tubb, David Lindsey, and Tammy
  Wynette.
ATV Music Corp., 1980/First Lady Songs, Inc., 1980.
Best-selling record by George Jones with Tammy Wynette (Epic, 80).

2000 Miles (English)
Words and music by Chrissie Hynde.
Virgin Music, Inc., 1983.
Introduced by The Pretenders in *Learning to Crawl* (Sire, 84).

Two Tribes (English)
Words and music by Peter Gill, William Johnson, and Mark
  O'Toole.
Island Music, 1984.
Best-selling record Frankie Goes to Hollywood (Island, 84).

U

Uncle Pen
Best-selling record by Ricky Scaggs (Sugar Hill/Epic, 84). See *Popular Music, 1920-1979.*

Under One Banner
Words and music by Billy Nicholls.
HG Music, Inc., 1981.
Featured on *Modern Dreams* by Carolyn Mas (Mercury, 81).

Under Pressure
Words and music by David Bowie, music by Queen.
Queen Music Ltd., 1981/Jones Music Co., 1981.
Best-selling record by Queen and David Bowie (Elektra, 82).

Under the Big Black Sun
Words and music by John Doe and Exene Cervenka, music by X.
Eight/Twelve Music, 1982.
Introduced by X on *Under the Big Black Sun* (Elektra, 82).

Under the Cover
Words and music by Janis Ian.
Mine Music, Ltd., 1981.
Best-selling record by Janis Ian (Columbia, 81).

Undercover of the Night (English)
Words and music by Mick Jagger and Keith Richards.
Colgems-EMI Music Inc., 1983.
Best-selling record by The Rolling Stones (Rolling Stones, 83).

Understanding
Words and music by Bob Seger.
Gear Publishing, 1984.
Best-selling record by Bob Seger & The Silver Bullet Band (Capitol, 84).
  Introduced in the film *Teachers* (84).

Union of the Snake (English)
Words and music by Duran Duran.
Chappell & Co., Inc., 1983.
Best-selling record by Duran Duran (Capitol, 83).

United Together
Words and music by Chuck Jackson and Phil Perry.
Jay's Enterprises, Inc., 1980/Baby Love Music, Inc., 1980/Chappell
    & Co., Inc., 1980/Phivin International Enterprises, 1980.
Best-selling record by Aretha Franklin (Arista, 80).

Until the Good Is Gone
Words and music by Steve Van Zandt.
Blue Midnight Music, 1982.
Introduced by Little Steven & The Disciples of Soul on *Men Without
    Women* (EMI, 82).

Up Where We Belong
Words and music by Jack Nitzsche, Will Jennings, and Buffy Sainte-
    Marie.
Famous Music Co., 1982/Ensign Music Corp., 1982.
Best-selling record by Joe Cocker and Jennifer Warnes (Island, 82).
    Introduced in the film *An Officer and a Gentleman* (82). Won an
    Academy Award, Best Song, 1982.

Upside Down
Words and music by Bernard Edwards and Nile Rodgers.
Chic Music Inc., 1980.
Best-selling record by Diana Ross (Motown, 80).

Uptown Girl
Words and music by Billy Joel.
Joelsongs, 1983.
Best-selling record by Billy Joel (Columbia, 83).

Urgent (English)
Words and music by Mick Jones.
Somerset Songs Publishing, Inc., 1981/E S P Management, Inc.,
    1981.
Best-selling record by Foreigner (Atlantic, 81).

Useless Waltz
Words by David Frishberg, music by Bob Brookmeyer.
Swiftwater Music, 1979.
Performed by David Frishberg on *The David Frishberg Songbook, Vol.
    II* (Omnisound, 83).

V

Vacation
Words and music by Kathy Valentine, words by Charlotte Caffey
and Jane Wiedlin.
Some Other Music, 1980/Daddy Oh Music, 1980/Lipsync Music,
1980.
Best-selling record by The Go Gos (I.R.S., 82).

Valley Girl
Words and music by Frank Zappa and Moon Zappa.
Munchkin Music, 1982.
Best-selling record by Frank and Moon Unit Zappa (Barking Pumpkin,
82).

Valotte (English)
Words and music by Julian Lennon, Justin Clayton, and Carlton
Morales.
Chappell & Co., Inc., 1984.
Best-selling record by Julian Lennon (Atlantic, 84).

Very Special
Words and music by William Jeffery and Lisa Peters.
At Home Music, 1981/Jeffix Music Co., 1981.
Best-selling record by Debra Laws (Elektra, 81).

The Voice (English)
Words and music by Justin Hayward.
WB Music Corp., 1981.
Best-selling record by The Moody Blues (Threshold, 81).

W

Wait for Me
Best-selling record by Hall and Oates (RCA, 80). See *Popular Music, 1920-1979.*

The Waiting
Words and music by Tom Petty.
Gone Gator Music, 1981.
Best-selling record by Tom Petty & The Heartbreakers (Backstreet, 81).

Waiting for a Girl Like You (English-American)
Words and music by Mick Jones and Lou Gramm.
Somerset Songs Publishing, Inc., 1981/E S P Management, Inc., 1981.
Best-selling record by Foreigner (Atlantic, 81).

Waiting for the Weekend (English)
Words and music by David Fenton.
EMI Music Publishing, Ltd., London, England, 1980.
Introduced by The Vapors in *New Clear Days* (Liberty, 80).

Waiting on a Friend (English)
Words and music by Mick Jagger and Keith Richards.
Colgems-EMI Music Inc., 1981.
Best-selling record by The Rolling Stones (Rolling Stones, 81).

Wake Me Up Before You Go-Go (English)
Words and music by George Michael.
Chappell & Co., Inc., 1984.
Best-selling record by Wham (Columbia, 84).

Wake Up and Live (Jamaican)
Words and music by Bob Marley and Horace Anthony Davis.
Bob Marley Music, Ltd., 1979.
Featured on *Uprising* by Bob Marley (Island, 80).

Walking on a Thin Line
Words and music by Andre Pessis and Kevin Wells.
Endless Frogs Music, 1983/Bug/Slimey Limey Music, 1983/
   McNoodle Music, 1983.
Best-selling record by Huey Lewis and The News (Chrysalis, 84).

Walking on Thin Ice
Words and music by Yoko Ono.
Lenono Music, 1981/Warner-Tamerlane Publishing Corp., 1981.
Best-selling record by Yoko One (Geffen, 81).

Wall of Death (English)
Words and music by Richard Thompson.
Island Music, 1982.
Introduced by Richard and Linda Thompson on *Shoot out the Lights*
   (Hannibal, 82).

The Wanderer (American-West German)
English words by Donna Summer, music by Giorgio Moroder.
Giorgio Moroder Pub/April Music, 1980/Sweet Summer Night
   Music, 1980.
Best-selling record by Donna Summer (Geffen, 80).

Wango Tango
Words and music by Ted Nugent.
Magicland Music, 1980.
Best-selling record by Ted Nugent (Epic, 80).

Wanna Be Startin' Something
Words and music by Michael Jackson.
Mijac Music, 1982/Warner-Tamerlane Publishing Corp., 1982.
Best-selling record by Michael Jackson (Epic, 83). Nominated for a
   National Academy of Recording Arts and Sciences Award, Rhythm
   'n' Blues Song of the Year, 1983.

War Is Hell (on the Homefront Too)
Words and music by Curly Putman, Dan Wilson, and Bucky Jones.
Tree Publishing Co., Inc., 1982/Cross Keys Publishing Co., Inc.,
   1982.
Best-selling record by T. G. Sheppard (Warner/Curb, 83).

The Warrior (English)
Words and music by Holly Knight and Nick Gilder.
Makiki Publishing Co., Ltd., 1984/Arista Music, Inc., 1984/Red
   Admiral Music Inc., 1984.
Best-selling record by Scandal (Columbia, 84).

Wasted on the Way
Words and music by Graham Nash.
Putzy-Putzy Music, 1982.
Best-selling record by Crosby, Stills & Nash (Atlantic, 82).

Watching the Wheels
Words and music by John Lennon.
Lenono Music, 1980.
Best-selling record by John Lennon (Geffen, 81).

Watching You
Words and music by Mark Adams, Raye Turner, Daniel Webster,
    Stephen Washington, and Steve Arrington.
Cotillion Music Inc., 1980.
Best-selling record by Slave (Warner Brothers, 81).

The Way He Makes Me Feel
Words by Alan Bergman and Marilyn Bergman, music by Michel
    Legrand.
Ennes Productions, Ltd., 1983/Emanuel Music/April Music, Inc.,
    1983/Threesome Music, 1983.
Best-selling record by Barbra Streisand (Columbia, 83). Introduced in
    the film *Yentl* (83). Nominated for an Academy Award, Best Song,
    1983.

The Way I Am
Words and music by Sonny Throckmorton.
Cross Keys Publishing Co., Inc., 1979.
Best-selling record by Merle Haggard (MCA, 80).

We Belong
Words and music by David Lowen and Daniel Navarro.
Screen Gems-EMI Music Inc., 1984.
Best-selling record by Pat Benatar (Chrysalis, 84).

We Belong Together
Words and music by Rickie Lee Jones.
Easy Money Music, 1980.
Best-selling record by Rickie Lee Jones (Warner Brothers, 81).

We Can Make It
Words by John Ebb, music by Fred Kander.
Fiddleback Music Publishing Co., Inc., 1983/Kander & Ebb Inc.,
    1983.
Introduced by Chita Rivera in *The Rink* (84).

Popular Music, 1980-1984

We Don't Talk Anymore
Best-selling record by Rick Springfield (RCA, 80). See *Popular Music, 1920-1979.*

We Go a Long Way Back
Words and music by Charles Love.
Blackwood Music Inc., 1980.
Best-selling record by Bloodstone (T-Neck, 82).

We Got the Beat
Words and music by Charlotte Caffey.
Daddy Oh Music, 1981.
Best-selling record by The Go-Gos (I. R. S., 82).

We Live for Love
Words and music by Neil Geraldo.
Rare Blue Music, Inc., 1979/Neil Geraldo Music Co.
Best-selling record by Pat Benatar (Chrysalis, 80).

We Live So Fast (English)
Words and music by Glenn Gregory, Ian Craig Marsh, and Martyn Ware.
Virgin Music, Inc., 1982/WB Music Corp., 1982.
Introduced by Heaven 17 in *The Luxury Gap* (Sire, 82).

We're Going All the Way
Words by Cynthia Weil, music by Barry Mann.
Dyad Music, Ltd., 1983.
Best-selling record by Jeffrey Osbourne (A & M, 84).

We're in This Love Together
Words and music by Roger Murrah and Keith Stegall.
Blackwood Music Inc., 1980/Magic Castle Music, Inc., 1980.
Best-selling record by Al Jarreau (Warner Brothers, 81).

We've Got Each Other
Words and music by Gary Portnoy and Judy Hart Angelo.
Koppelman Family Music, 1983/Bandier Family Music, 1983/R. L. August Music Co., 1983/Yontrop Music, 1983/Judy Hart Angelo Music, 1983.
Introduced by Michael Ingram and Beth Fowler in *Preppies* (83).

We've Got Tonight
Revived by Kenny Rogers and Dolly Parton (Liberty, 83). See *Popular Music, 1920-1979.*

What Are We Doin' in Love
Words and music by Randy Goodrum.

Chappell & Co., Inc., 1981/Sailmaker Music, 1981.
Best-selling record by Dottie West (Liberty, 81).

What Cha' Gonna Do for Me
Words and music by James Stuart and Ned Doheny.
Average Music, 1981/Longdog Music, 1981.
Best-selling record by Chaka Khan (Warner Brothers, 81).

What Kind of Fool (English)
Words and music by Barry Gibb and Albhy Galuten.
Gibb Brothers Music, 1980/Unichappell Music Inc., 1980.
Best-selling record by Barbra Streisand and Barry Gibb (Columbia, 81).
    See *Popular Music, 1920-1979.*

What You'd Call a Dream
Words and music by Craig Carnelia.
Samuel French, Inc., 1984.
Introduced by Scott Holmes in *Diamonds* (84).

Whatever Happened to Old Fashioned Love
Words and music by Lewis Anderson.
Old Friends Music, 1983.
Best-selling record by B.J. Thomas (Cleveland International/Epic, 83).

What's Forever For
Words and music by Rafe Van Hoy.
Tree Publishing Co., Inc., 1978.
Best-selling record by Michael Murphy (Liberty, 82).

What's Love Got to Do with It (English)
Words and music by Terry Britten and Graham Lyle.
Chappell & Co., Inc., 1984/Irving Music Inc., 1984.
Best-selling record by Tina Turner (Capitol, 84). Nominated for a National Academy of Recording Arts and Sciences Award, Best Song of the Year, 1984. Won a National Academy of Recording Arts and Sciences Award, Best Record of the Year, 1984.

What's New
Revived by Linda Ronstadt (Asylum, 83). See *Popular Music, 1920-1979.*

When a Man Loves a Woman
Revived by Bette Midler in the film *The Rose* (79). Best-selling record by Bette Midler (Atlantic, 80). See *Popular Music, 1920-1979.*

When Doves Cry
Words and music by Prince Rogers Nelson.
Controversy Music, 1984/WB Music Corp., 1984.

Best-selling record by Prince (Warner Brothers, 84). Introduced in the film *Purple Rain* (84).

When I Wanted You
Best-selling record by Barry Manilow (Arista, 79-80). See *Popular Music, 1920-1979.*

When I'm Away from You
Words and music by Frankie Miller.
Rare Blue Music, Inc., 1979.
Best-selling record by The Bellamy Brothers (Elektra/Curb, 83).

When Love Calls
Music by David Lewis, words by Wayne Lewis.
Almo Music Corp., 1980.
Best-selling record by Atlantic Starr (A & M, 81).

When She Was My Girl
Words and music by Marc Blatte and Larry Gottlieb.
MCA, Inc., 1980.
Best-selling record by The Four Tops (Casablanca, 81). Nominated for a National Academy of Recording Arts and Sciences Award, Rhythm 'n' Blues Song of the Year, 1981.

When the Night Falls
Words and music by T-Bone Burnette.
Black Tent Music, 1983.
Introduced by T-Bone Burnette on *Proof Through the Night* (Warner Brothers, 83).

When We Make Love
Words and music by Troy Seals and Mentor Williams.
Two-Sons Music, 1983/WB Music Corp., 1983/Welbeck Music Corp., 1983/Cavesson Music Enterprises Co., 1983.
Best-selling record by Alabama (RCA, 84).

When You Close Your Eyes
Words and music by Jack Blades, Alan Fitzgerald, and Brad Gillis.
Kid Bird Music, 1983.
Best-selling record by Night Ranger (Camel/MCA, 84).

When You Were Mine
Words and music by Prince Rogers Nelson.
Controversy Music, 1980.
Introduced by Prince on *Dirty Mind* (Warner Brothers, 80). Featured on *She's So Unusual* by Cyndi Lauper (Portrait, 83).

Whenever You're on My Mind
Words and music by Marshall Crenshaw and Bill Teeley.
MHC Music, 1982.
Introduced by Marshall Crenshaw in *Field Day* (Warner Brothers, 83).

Where Everybody Knows Your Name
Words and music by Gary Portnoy and Judy Hart Angelo.
Addax Music Co., Inc., 1982.
Best-selling record by Gary Portnoy (Applause, 83). Introduced on TV
  series *Cheers* (82).

While You See a Chance (English)
Words by Will Jennings, music by Steve Winwood.
Island Music, 1980/Irving Music Inc., 1980/Blue Sky Rider Songs,
  1980.
Best-selling record by Steve Winwood (Island, 81).

Whip It
Words and music by Mark Mothersbaugh and Gerry V. Casale.
Devo Music, 1980/Nymph Music, 1980.
Best-selling record by Devo (Warner Brothers, 80).

White Horse
Words and music by Tim Stahl and John Goldberg.
Sing a Song Publishing Co., 1984/Bleu Disque Music, 1984.
Best-selling record by Laid Back (Sire, 84).

White Shoes
Words and music by Jack Tempchin.
Night River Publishing, 1980.
Featured on *White Shoes* by Emmylou Harris (Warner Brothers, 83).

White Wedding
Words and music by Billy Idol.
Rare Blue Music, Inc., 1982.
Best-selling record by Billy Idol (Chrysalis, 83).

Who Can It Be Now (Australian)
Words and music by Colin Hay.
Blackwood Music Inc., 1982.
Best-selling record by Men at Work (Columbia, 82).

Who Wears These Shoes (English)
Words by Bernie Taupin, music by Elton John.
Intersong, USA Inc., 1984.
Best-selling record by Elton John (Geffen, 84).

Who's Cheating Who
Words and music by Jerry Hayes.
Partner Music, 1980/Algee Music Corp., 1980/Vogue Music, 1980.
Best-selling record by Charlie McClain (Epic, 81).

Who's Crying Now
Words and music by Steve Perry and Jonathan Cain.
Weed High Nightmare Music, 1981.
Best-selling record by Journey (Columbia, 81).

Who's That Girl (English)
Words and music by Annie Lennox and Dave Stewart.
Blue Network Music, 1983.
Best-selling record by Eurythmics (RCA, 84).

Why Do Fools Fall in Love
Revived by Diana Ross (RCA, 82). See *Popular Music, 1920-1979.*

Why Do You (Do What You Do), see **Do What You Do.**

Why Don't You Spend the Night
Best-selling record by Ronnie Milsap (RCA, 80). See *Popular Music, 1920-1979.*

Why Lady Why
Words and music by Randy Owen.
Maypop Music, 1980.
Best-selling record by Alabama (RCA, 80).

Why Me? (English)
Words and music by Tony Carey.
Safespace Music, 1983.
Best-selling record by Irene Cara (Geffen/Network, 83).

Why Not Me
Words and music by Fred Knoblock and Carson Whitsett.
CBS U Catalog, Inc., 1980/Flowering Stone Music, 1980/Whitsett
   Churchill Music, 1980/Holy Moley Music, 1980.
Best-selling record by Fred Knoblock (Scotti Brothers, 80).

The Wild Boys (English)
Words and music by Duran Duran.
Chappell & Co., Inc., 1984.
Best-selling record by Duran Duran (Capitol, 84).

Wind Beneath My Wings, also known as **Hero**
Words and music by Jeff Silber and Larry Henley.
Warner House of Music, 1981/WB Gold Music Corp., 1981.

Best-selling records by Lou Rawls (Epic, 83), Gary Morris (Warner Brothers, 83), and Gladys Knight & The Pips (Columbia, 83).

Wine, Women and Song
Words and music by William Smokey Robinson, Jr.
Bertam Music Co., 1980.
Introduced by Smokey Robinson on *Being with You* (Tamla, 80).

The Winner Takes It All (Swedish)
English words and music by Benny Anderson and Bjorn Ulvaeus.
Artwork Music Co., Inc., 1980.
Best-selling record by Abba (Atlantic, 80).

Winning
Words and music by Russ Ballard.
Island Music, 1977.
Best-selling record by Santana (Columbia, 81).

With You on My Arm
Words and music by Jerry Herman.
Jerryco Music Co., 1983.
Introduced by Gene Barry and George Hearn in *La Cage Au Folles* (83).

Without Us
Words by Jeff Barry, music by Tom Scott.
Bruin Music Co., 1982.
Introduced by Johnny Mathis and Deniece Williams on *Family Ties* (82).

Without Your Love
Words and music by Billy Nicholls.
HG Music, Inc., 1977.
Best-selling record by Roger Daltrey (Polydor, 80).

WKRP in Cincinnati
Best-selling record by Steve Carlisle (MCA/Sweet City, 81). Introduced on the TV show *WKRP in Cincinnati* (78). See *Popular Music, 1920-1979.*

Woke Up in Love
Words and music by James P. Pennington.
Careers Music Inc., 1983.
Best-selling record by Exile (Epic, 84).

Woman
Words and music by John Lennon.
Lenono Music, 1981.
Best-selling record by John Lennon (Geffen, 81).

Popular Music, 1980-1984

Woman in Love (English)
Words and music by Barry Gibb and Robin Gibb.
Gibb Brothers Music, 1980.
Best-selling record by Barbra Streisand (Columbia, 80). Nominated for
   National Academy of Recording Arts and Sciences Awards, Song of
   the Year, 1980, and Record of the Year, 1980.

The Woman in You (English)
Words and music by Barry Gibb, Robin Gibb, and Maurice Gibb.
Gibb Brothers Music, 1982.
Best-selling record by The Bee Gees (RSO, 83).

A Woman Needs Love
Words and music by Ray Parker, Jr.
Raydiola Music, 1981.
Best-selling record by Ray Parker Jr. & Raydio (Arista, 81).

Woman's World (English)
Words by Christopher Difford, music by Glenn Tilbrook.
Illegal Songs, Inc., 1981.
Introduced by Squeeze on *East Side Story* (A & M, 81).

Women I've Never Had
Best-selling record by Hank Williams (Elektra, 80). See *Popular Music,
   1920-1979.*

Wondering Where the Lions Are (Canadian)
Best-selling record by Bruce Cockburn (Millennium, 80). See *Popular
   Music, 1920-1979.*

Working for the Weekend (Canadian)
Words and music by Paul Dean, Mike Reno, and Matthew Frenette.
Blackwood Music Inc., 1981/April Music, Inc., 1981.
Best-selling record by Loverboy (Columbia, 82).

Working in the Coal Mine
Revived by Devo (Elektra, 81). Featured in the film *Heavy Metal* (81).
   See *Popular Music, 1920-1979.*

A World Without Heroes
Words and music by Paul Stanley, Bob Ezrin, Lou Reed, and Gene
   Simmons.
Kiss, 1981/Under Cut Music Publishing Co., Inc., 1981/Metal
   Machine Music, 1981.
Best-selling record by Kiss (Casablanca, 82).

Would You Catch a Falling Star
Words and music by Bobby Braddock.
Tree Publishing Co., Inc., 1981.
Best-selling record by John Anderson (Warner Brothers, 82).

Wrapped Around Your Finger (English)
Words and music by Sting (pseudonym for Gordon Sumner).
Reggatta Music, Ltd., 1983/Illegal Songs, Inc., 1983.
Best-selling record by The Police (A & M, 84).

Wrong 'Em Boyo (English)
Words and music by Joe Strummer and Mick Jones.
WB Music Corp., 1979.
Introduced by The Clash on *London Calling* (Epic, 80).

X

Xanadu (English)
Words and music by Jeff Lynne.
Blackwood Music Inc., 1980.
Best-selling record by ELO with Olivia Newton-John (MCA, 80). Introduced in the film *Xanadu* (80).

Y

Yah Mo B There (English)
Words and music by James Ingram, Michael McDonald, Rod
    Temperton, and Quincy Jones.
Eiseman Music Co., Inc., 1983/Yellow Brick Road Music, 1983/
    Almo Music Corp., 1983/Genevieve Music, 1983.
Best-selling record by James Ingram with Michael McDonald (Quest,
    83). Nominated for a National Academy of Recording Arts and
    Sciences Award, Best Rhythm 'n' Blues Song of the Year, 1984.

Yearning for Your Love
Words and music by Ronnie Wilson and Oliver Scott.
Temp Co., 1980/Total X Publishing Co., 1980.
Best-selling record by Gap Band (Mercury, 81).

Years
Revived by Wayne Newton (Aries II, 80). See *Popular Music, 1920-1979.*

The Yellow Rose
Words and music by John Wilder.
WB Music Corp., 1984.
Best-selling record by Johnny Lee with Lane Brody (Warner Brothers,
    84).

Yes, I'm Ready
Best-selling record by Teri DeSario with K.C. (TK, 80). See *Popular
    Music, 1920-1979.*

Yesterday's Songs
Words and music by Neil Diamond.
Stonebridge Music, 1981.
Best-selling record by Neil Diamond (Columbia, 81).

You and I
Words and music by Frank Myers.

Popular Music, 1980-1984

Cottonpatch Music, 1980/Mallven Music, 1980.
Best-selling record by Eddie Rabbitt and Crystal Gayle (Elektra, 82).

You Are
Words and music by Lionel Richie, Jr. and Brenda Richie.
Brockman Enterprises Inc., 1982.
Best-selling record by Lionel Richie (Motown, 83).

You Better You Bet (English)
Words and music by Peter Townshend.
Towser Tunes Inc., 1981.
Best-selling record by The Who (Warner Brothers, 81).

You Can Do Magic (Canadian)
Words and music by Russ Ballard.
Russell Ballard, Ltd., Middlesex, England, 1982/April Music, Inc.,
    1982.
Best-selling record by America (Capitol, 82).

You Can't Get What You Want (English)
Words and music by Joe Jackson.
Pokazuka, 1984/Almo Music Corp., 1984.
Best-selling record by Joe Jackson (A & M, 84).

You Can't Hurry Love
Revived by Phil Collins (Atlantic, 83). See *Popular Music, 1920-1979.*

You Could Have Been with Me
Words and music by Lea Maalfried.
ATV Music Corp., 1981.
Best-selling record by Sheena Easton (EMI-America, 81).

You Don't Know Me
Revived by Mickey Gilley (Epic, 81). See *Popular Music, 1920-1979.*

You Don't Want Me Anymore
Words and music by Kenneth Goorabian.
Toneman Music Inc., 1982/Wood Street Music, Inc., 1982/Al
    Gallico Music Corp., 1982.
Best-selling record by Steel Breeze (RCA, 82).

You Dream Flat Tires
Words and music by Joni Mitchell.
Crazy Crow Music, 1982.
Introduced by Joni Mitchell on *Wild Things Run Fast* (Geffen, 82).

You Get the Best from Me
Words and music by Kevin McCord and Albert Hudson.

Duchess Music Corp., 1984.
Best-selling record by Alicia Myers (MCA, 84).

You Got Lucky
Words and music by Tom Petty and Mike Campbell.
Gone Gator Music, 1982/Wild Gator Music, 1982.
Best-selling record by Tom Petty & The Heartbreakers (Backstreet, 83).

You Look So Good in Love
Words and music by Kerry Chater, Rory Bourke, and Glen Ballard.
Vogue Music, 1983/Chappell & Co., Inc., 1983/MCA, Inc., 1983.
Best-selling record by George Strait (MCA, 84).

You Make My Dreams
Words and music by Daryl Hall, words by John Oates and Sara Allen.
Hot Cha Music Co., 1980/Unichappell Music Inc., 1980/Fust Buzza Music, Inc., 1980.
Best-selling record by Daryl Hall and John Oates (RCA, 81).

You May Be Right
Best-selling record by Billy Joel (Columbia, 80). See *Popular Music, 1920-1979.*

You, Me and He
Words and music by James Mtume.
Mtume Music Publishing, 1984.
Best-selling record by Mtume (Epic, 84).

You Might Think
Words and music by Ric Ocasek.
Lido Music Inc., 1984.
Best-selling record by The Cars (Elektra, 84).

You Never Gave Up on Me
Words and music by Leslie Pearl.
Michael O'Connor Music, 1980.
Best-selling record by Crystal Gayle (Columbia, 82).

You Shook Me All Night Long (English)
Words and music by Angus Young, Malcolm Young, and Brian Johnson.
E. B. Marks Music Corp., 1980.
Best-selling record by AC/DC (Atlanta, 80).

You Should Hear How She Talks About You
Words and music by Tom Snow and Dean Pitchford.

Snow Music, 1981/Warner-Tamerlane Publishing Corp., 1981.
Best-selling record by Melissa Manchester (Arista, 82).

You Take Me for Granted
Words and music by Leona Williams.
Shade Tree Music Inc., 1981.
Best-selling record by Merle Haggard (Epic, 83).

You Win Again
Words and music by Hank Williams.
Fred Rose Music, Inc., 1952.
Revived by Charley Pride (RCA, 80).

You'll Accompany Me
Words and music by Bob Seger.
Gear Publishing, 1979.
Best-selling record by Bob Seger (Capitol, 80).

You'll Be Back Every Night in My Dreams
Words and music by Johnny Russell and Wayland Holyfield.
Sunflower County Songs, 1978/Bibo Music Publishers.
Best-selling record by The Statler Brothers (Mercury, 82).

Young Turks
Words by Rod Stewart, music by Carmine Appice, Kevin Savigar, and Duane Hitchings.
Riva Music Ltd., 1981/Hitchings Music, 1981/Rod Stewart, 1981.
Best-selling record by Rod Stewart (Warner Brothers, 81).

Your Love Is Driving Me Crazy
Words and music by Sammy Hagar.
WB Music Corp., 1983.
Best-selling record by Sammy Hagar (Geffen, 83).

Your Love's on the Line
Words and music by Earl Thomas Conley and Randy Scruggs.
Blackwood Music Inc., 1983/April Music, Inc., 1983/Full Armor Publishing Co., 1983.
Best-selling record by Earl Thomas Conley (RCA, 83).

You're Gettin' to Me Again
Words and music by Pat McManus and Woody Bomar.
Music City Music Inc., 1983.
Best-selling record by Jim Glaser (Noble Vision, 84).

You're My Favorite Waste of Time
Words and music by Marshall Crenshaw.
MHC Music, 1982.

Introduced by Marshall Crenshaw & the Handsome, Ruthless and Stu-
pid Band (Warner Brothers, 82).

You're My Latest, My Greatest Inspiration
Words and music by Kenny Gamble and Leon Huff.
Assorted Music, 1981.
Best-selling record by Teddy Pendergrass (Philadelphia International,
82).

You're the Best Break This Old Heart Ever Had
Words and music by Robert Hatch and Wayland Hollyfield.
Vogue Music, 1980/Bibo Music Publishers, 1980.
Best-selling record by Ed Bruce (MCA, 82).

You're the First Time I've Thought About Leaving
Words and music by Dickey Betts and Kerry Chater.
Maplehill Music, 1982/Hall-Clement Publications, 1982.
Best-selling record by Reba McEntire (Mercury, 83).

You're the Inspiration
Words and music by Pete Cetera and David Foster.
Double Virgo Music, 1984/Foster Frees Music Inc., 1984.
Best-selling record by Chicago (Full Moon/Warner Brothers, 84).

You're the Only Woman (You and I)
Words and music by David Pack.
Rubicon Music, 1980.
Best-selling record by Ambrosia (Warner Brothers, 80).

You're the Reason God Made Oklahoma
Words and music by Larry Collins and Sandy Pinkard.
House of Bryant Publications, 1980.
Best-selling record by David Frizzell and Shelly West (Warner Brothers,
80). Introduced in the film *Any Which Way You Can* (80). Nomi-
nated for a National Academy of Recording Arts and Sciences Award,
Country Song of the Year, 1981.

You've Got Another Thing Comin'
Words and music by Rob Halford, Kenneth Downing, and Glenn
Tipton.
April Music, Inc., 1981.
Best-selling record by Judas Priest (Columbia, 81).

You've Lost That Lovin' Feeling
Revived by Daryl Hall and John Oates (RCA, 80). See *Popular Music,
1920-1979.*

You've Still Got a Place in My Heart
Words and music by Leon Payne.
Fred Rose Music, Inc., 1978.
Best-selling record by George Jones (Epic, 84).

Z

ZaZ Turned Blue
Words by David Was (pseudonym for David Weiss), music by Don
   Was (pseudonym for Donald Faganson).
Los Was Cosmipolitanos, 1983/State of the Artless, 1983/Ackee
   Music Inc., 1983.
Introduced by Was Not Was on *Born to Laugh at Tornadoes* (Warner
   Brothers, 1983).

Indexes and List of Publishers

Lyricists & Composers Index

Lyricists & Composers Index

Allen, Peter
  Arthur's Theme (The Best That You
    Can Do)
Allen, Robert
  Planet Rock
Allen, Sara
  Adult Education
  Did It in a Minute
  I Can't Go for That (No Can Do)
  Maneater
  Private Eyes
  Swept Away
  You Make My Dreams
Allison, Jerry
  More Than I Can Say
Alpert, Herb
  Magic Man
Altman, Robert
  Black Sheep
Anderson, Adrienne
  Some Kind of Friend
Anderson, Benny
  The Winner Takes It All
Anderson, John D.
  Swingin'
Anderson, Jon
  Chariots of Fire (Race to the End)
  Owner of a Lonely Heart
Anderson, Laurie
  Gravity's Angel
  Kokoku
  O Superman
  Sharkey's Day
  Sharkey's Night
Anderson, Lewis
  Somewhere Down the Line
  Whatever Happened to Old
    Fashioned Love
Andrews, Reginald
  Let It Whip
Angelo, Judy Hart
  Bring on the Loot
  Every Time I Turn Around
  Our Night
  People Like Us
  We've Got Each Other
  Where Everybody Knows Your
    Name

Ant, Adam
  Goody Two Shoes
Anthony, Michael
  And The Cradle Will Rock
  Dirty Movies
  I'll Wait
  Jump
  Panama
Appice, Carmine
  Young Turks
Arrington, Steve
  Watching You
Ashford, Nicholas
  Solid
Ashford, Nick
  Landlord
  Still Such a Thing
  Street Corner
Ashman, Howard
  Feed Me
  Hundreds of Hats
  Somewhere That's Green
  Suddenly Seymour
Ashton, John
  Love My Way
  Pretty in Pink
Bacharach, Burt
  Arthur's Theme (The Best That You
    Can Do)
  Finder of Lost Loves
  Making Love
Bailey, Philip
  Easy Lover
Bailey, Thomas
  Doctor! Doctor!
  Hold Me Now
Bailey, Tom
  Love on Your Side
Baker, Arthur Henry
  Planet Rock
Ballard, Clint, Jr.
  I'm Alive
Ballard, Glen
  All I Need
  You Look So Good in Love
Ballard, Russ
  The Border
  I Know There's Something Going On
  Winning
  You Can Do Magic

Lyricists & Composers Index

Lyricists & Composers Index

Lyricists & Composers Index

Lyricists & Composers Index

Dees, Sam
  One in a Million You
  Save the Overtime for Me
Delmore, Lionel
  Swingin'
DeMartini, Warren
  Round and Round
Denver, John
  Perhaps Love
  Shanghai Breezes
Deodato, Eumir
  Big Fun
  Celebration
  Get Down on It
  Take My Heart
DeVito, Hank
  Queen of Hearts
DeYoung, Dennis
  The Best of Times
  Desert Moon
  Don't Let It End
  Mr. Roboto
Diamond, David
  Sex (I'm A)
Diamond, Joel
  Theme from *Raging Bull*
Diamond, Keith
  Caribbean Queen (No More Love on
    the Run)
Diamond, Neil
  America
  Hello Again
  Love on the Rocks
  Yesterday's Songs
Diamond, Steve
  I've Got a Rock and Roll Heart
Dickerson, Dez
  Cool Part 1
DiCola, Vince
  Far from Over
Difford, Chris
  Boy with a Problem
Difford, Christopher
  Labeled with Love
  Pulling Mussels (from the Shell)
  Tempted
  Woman's World
DiGregorio, Joel
  In America

Dillon, Dean
  By Now
Dino, Ralph
  Do What You Do
Dipiero, Robert
  American Made
DiTomaso, Larry
  Do What You Do
Dodson, Larry
  Freakshow on the Dancefloor
Doe, John
  Come Back to Me
  The Hungry Wolf
  The New World
  Under the Big Black Sun
Doheny, Ned
  What Cha' Gonna Do for Me
Dolby, Thomas
  She Blinded Me with Science
Dolce, Joe
  Shaddup Your Face
Donahue, Patty
  Square Pegs
Dore, Charlene
  Strut
Dorff, Stephen
  Bar Room Buddies
  Cowboys and Clowns
Dorff, Stephen H.
  Another Honky Tonk Night on
    Broadway
Dorff, Steve
  Through the Years
Doroschuk, Ivan
  The Safety Dance
Downes, Geoffrey
  Don't Cry
  Heat of the Moment
  Only Time Will Tell
Downing, Kenneth
  You've Got Another Thing Comin'
Dubois, James
  Love in the First Degree
  Midnight Hauler
Dubois, Pye
  Tom Sawyer
DuBois, Tim
  She Got the Goldmine (I Got the
    Shaft)

Suddenly
Fearman, Eric
  Joystick
Felder, Don
  Heavy Metal (Takin' a Ride)
Feldman, Jack
  I Made It Through the Rain
Feldman, Richard
  D.C. Cab
Fenn, Rick
  Family Man
Fenton, David
  Turning Japanese
  Waiting for the Weekend
Ferguson, Lloyd
  Pass the Dutchie
Ficca, William
  Square Pegs
Fields, Philip
  Are You Single
Fields, Richard "Dimples"
  If It Ain't One Thing It's Another
Finn, Neil
  I Got You
Finn, William
  The Games I Play
  I Never Wanted to Love You
  A Tight Knit Family
Fisher, Rob
  Promises, Promises
Fitzgerald, Alan
  When You Close Your Eyes
Flack, Roberta
  Ballad for D
Fleming, Kye
  I Was Country When Country
    Wasn't Cool
  I Wouldn't Have Missed It for the
    World
  Nobody
  Smokey Mountain Rain
Fletcher, E.
  The Message
Fletcher, Edward
  New York, New York
Flippin, John
  Backstrokin'
Flower, Danny
  Play the Game Tonight

Fogelberg, Dan
  The Language of Love
  Leader of the Band
  Make Love Stay
  Missing You
  Run for the Roses
  Same Old Lang Syne
Fonfara, Michael
  Growing Up in Public
Fontara, Michael
  So Alone
Ford, R., Jr.
  Rappin' Rodney
Ford, Robert
  The Breaks
Foreman, Christopher
  Our House
Forsey, Keith
  Flashdance...What a Feeling
Fortgang, Jeff
  Some Guys Have All the Luck
Fortune, Jimmy
  Elizabeth
Foster, David
  Breakdown Dead Ahead
  Hard to Say I'm Sorry
  Heart to Heart
  I Am Love
  JoJo
  Look What You Done to Me
  Love Me Tomorrow
  Mornin'
  She's a Beauty
  Stay the Night
  Talk to Ya Later
  You're the Inspiration
Foster, Jerry
  Giving Up Easy
Franke, Bob
  Hard Love
Frantz, Chris
  Burning Down the House
Franz, Chris
  Once in a Lifetime
Frazier, Dallas
  Beneath Still Waters
  Elvira
  Fourteen Carat Mind
Frazier, Robert
  Play the Game Tonight

Lyricists & Composers Index

Lyricists & Composers Index

Jasper, Christopher
  Between the Sheets
Jeffery, William
  Very Special
Jeffreys, Garland
  Fidelity
Jenkins, David
  Cool Love
Jenkins, Tomi
  Freaky Dancin'
  She's Strange
Jenkins, Toni
  Just Be Yourself
Jennings, Waylon
  Just to Satisfy You
  Theme from *The Dukes of Hazzard*
    (Good Ol' Boys)
Jennings, Will
  I'm So Glad I'm Standing Here
    Today
  No Night So Long
  People Alone
  Up Where We Belong
  While You See a Chance
Joel, Billy
  Allentown
  Christie Lee
  Don't Ask Me Why
  Goodnight Saigon
  An Innocent Man
  It's Still Rock and Roll to Me
  The Longest Time
  Pressure
  Tell Her About It
  Uptown Girl
Johansen, David
  Donna
John, Elton
  Blue Eyes
  Empty Garden (Hey Hey Johnny)
  I Guess That's Why They Call It the
    Blues
  I'm Still Standing
  Kiss the Bride
  Little Jeannie
  Sad Songs (Say So Much)
  Who Wears These Shoes
Johns, Sammy
  Common Man

Johnson, Brian
  Back in Black
  You Shook Me All Night Long
Johnson, George
  Stomp
Johnson, Larry, *see* Starr, Maurice
Johnson, Louis
  Stomp
Johnson, Valerie
  Stomp
Johnson, William
  Relax
  Two Tribes
Jolley, Steve
  Cruel Summer
Jones, A. A.
  Hit and Run
Jones, Allen A.
  Freakshow on the Dancefloor
Jones, Bucky
  Do You Wanna Go to Heaven
  Only One You
  War Is Hell (on the Homefront Too)
Jones, George
  Make Up Your Mind
Jones, George Curtis
  Are You Single
Jones, John Paul
  Fool in the Rain
Jones, Michael, *see* Kashif
Jones, Mick
  I Want to Know What Love Is
  Juke Box Hero
  Rock the Casbah
  Urgent
  Waiting for a Girl Like You
  Wrong 'Em Boyo
Jones, Paul H.
  I Wouldn't Change You If I Could
Jones, Quincy
  Love Is in Control (Finger on the
    Trigger)
  P. Y. T. (Pretty Young Thing)
  Yah Mo B There
Jones, Raymond
  Stay with Me Tonight
Jones, Rickie Lee
  Living It Up
  The Real End
  We Belong Together

Lyricists & Composers Index

Lyricists & Composers Index

250

Lyricists & Composers Index

Lyricists & Composers Index

Lyricists & Composers Index

Spradley, David
  Atomic Dog
Springfield, Rick
  Affair of the Heart
  Bruce
  Don't Talk to Strangers
  Human Touch
  Jessie's Girl
  Love Is Alright Tonite
  Love Somebody
  Souls
Springsteen, Bruce
  Atlantic City
  Bobby Jean
  Born in the U.S.A.
  Cadillac Ranch
  Cover Me
  Dancing in the Dark
  Fade Away
  From Small Things (Big Things One Day Come)
  Glory Days
  Highway Patrolman
  Hungry Heart
  Johnny 99
  Love's on the Line
  My Hometown
  No Surrender
  Out of Work
  Pink Cadillac
  The River
  This Little Girl
Squier, Billy
  Everybody Wants You
  In the Dark
  Learn How to Live
  Rock Me Tonite
  The Stroke
Squire, Chris
  Owner of a Lonely Heart
Stacey, Gladys
  Crying My Heart out over You
Staedtler, Darrell
  A Fire I Can't Put Out
Stahl, Tim
  White Horse
Stallone, Frank
  Far from Over
Stamey, Chris
  Living a Lie

Stanley, Paul
  Lick It Up
  A World Without Heroes
Stanshall, Vivian
  Arc of a Diver
Starr, Maurice
  Candy Girl
Steele, Larry
  If I'd Been the One
Stegall, Keith
  Hurricane
  Lonely Nights
  We're in This Love Together
Stein, Chris
  Rapture
Steinberg, Billy
  Like a Virgin
Steinman, Jim
  Holding out for a Hero
  I'm Gonna Love Her for the Both of Us
  Left in the Dark
  Making Love out of Nothing at All
  Read 'em and Weep
  Tonight Is What It Means to Be Young
  Total Eclipse of the Heart
Stephens, Geoff
  It's Like We Never Said Goodbye
Stevens, Even
  Drivin' My Life Away
  Gone Too Far
  I Love a Rainy Night
  Love Will Turn You Around
  Someone Could Lose a Heart Tonight
  Step by Step
Stevens, Steve
  Eyes Without a Face
  Rebel Yell
Stewart, Dave
  Sweet Dreams
  Who's That Girl
Stewart, David
  Here Comes the Rain Again
  Love Is a Stranger
Stewart, Harris
  Lonely Nights
Stewart, Michael
  The Colors of My Life

Lyricists & Composers Index

265

Lyricists & Composers Index

Important Performances Index

Songs are listed under the works in which they were introduced or given significant renditions. The index is organized into major sections by performance medium: Album, Movie, Musical, Revue, Television Show.

Album
All of a Sudden
  My Edge of the Razor
All Over the Place
  James
  Live
  Restless
Angel Heart
  In Cars
  Scissor Cut
Another Grey Area
  Temporary Beauty
Argybargy
  Labeled with Love
Attack of the Killer B's
  Amnesia and Jealousy (Oh Lana)
Being with You
  Wine, Women and Song
The Best of Gil Scott-Heron
  The Bottle
  Johannesburg
  The Revolution Will Not Be
    Televised
Big Science
  O Superman

The Blue Mask
  My House
Blue Rider
  Blue Rider
  Peter Pan
Born in the U.S.A.
  Bobby Jean
  Glory Days
  My Hometown
  No Surrender
Born to Laugh at Tornadoes
  ZaZ Turned Blue
Boy
  I Will Follow
  Into the Heart
The Brains
  Money Changes Everything
Burlap and Satin
  Appalachian Memories
Call Me
  One Night Only
Catholic Boy
  City Drops (into the Night)
  People Who Died

271

Important Performances Index - Album

White Shoes
  Good News
  White Shoes
Wild Things Run Fast
  Moon at the Window
  You Dream Flat Tires
Willie Nile
  Old Men Sleeping on the Bowery
Windsong
  He Reminds Me
Writers in Disguise
  I Lobster But Never Flounder

Movie

Against All Odds
  Against All Odds (Take a Look at
  Me Now)
All the Right Moves
  All the Right Moves
American Gigolo
  Call Me
  The Seduction (Love Theme from
  American Gigolo)
Any Which Way You Can
  You're the Reason God Made
  Oklahoma
Arthur
  Arthur's Theme (The Best That You
  Can Do)
Beatstreet
  Beatstreet
Best Friends
  How Do You Keep the Music
  Playing
The Black Hole
  Theme from *The Black Hole*
Body Double
  Relax
Breakdance
  Breakdance
Breakin'
  Breakin'. . .There's No Stopping Us
Breathless
  Breathless
Bustin Loose
  Ballad for D
Caddyshack
  I'm Alright (Theme from
  Caddyshack)

Cat People
  Cat People (Putting out Fire)
Chariots of Fire
  Chariots of Fire (Race to the End)
The Competition
  People Alone
Continental Divide
  Theme from *Continental Divide*
  (Never Say Goodbye)
D.C. Cab
  D.C. Cab
Dr. Detroit
  Theme from *Doctor Detroit*
Eddie and the Cruisers
  On the Dark Side
The Empire Strikes Back
  The Empire Strikes Back
Endless Love
  Endless Love
Fame
  Fame
  Out Here on My Own
Fast Times at Ridgemont High
  Somebody's Baby
Flashdance
  Flashdance. . .What a Feeling
  Maniac
Footloose
  Almost Paradise. . .Love Theme from
  Footloose
  Dancing in the Sheets
  Footloose
  Let's Hear It for the Boy
For Your Eyes Only
  For Your Eyes Only
Ghostbusters
  Ghostbusters
Give My Regards to Broad Street
  No More Lonely Nights
The Great Muppet Caper
  The First Time It Happens
Heavy Metal
  Heavy Metal (Takin' a Ride)
  Working in the Coal Mine
Honeysuckle Rose
  On the Road Again
Honky Tonk Man
  Bar Room Buddies
I Oughta Be in Pictures
  One Hello

Musical

Revue

It's Better with a Band
Upstairs at O'Neals
  Little H and Little G

Television Show
Cheers
  Where Everybody Knows Your
    Name
The Dukes of Hazzard
  Theme from *The Dukes of Hazzard*
    (Good Ol' Boys)
Dynasty
  Theme from *Dynasty*
The Facts of Life
  The Facts of Life
Family Ties
  Without Us
Finder of Lost Loves
  Finder of Lost Loves
Flo
  Flo's Yellow Rose
The Greatest American Hero
  The Theme from *The Greatest
    American Hero*
Hill Street Blues
  The Theme from *Hill Street Blues*
Magnum P. I.
  Theme from *Magnum P.I.*
Miami Vice
  In the Air Tonight
Punky Brewster
  Every Time I Turn Around
Shogun
  Love Theme from *Shogun* (Mariko's
    Theme)
Silver Spoons
  Together
Square Pegs
  Square Pegs
Webster
  Then Came You
WKRP in Cincinnati
  WKRP in Cincinnati

Chronological Index

Songs registered for copyright protection between 1980 and 1984 are listed under the year of registration. Songs with a copyright date before 1980 are listed under the year covered by this volume in which they were important.

1980

Ace in the Hole
Against the Wind
Ai No Corrida
Ain't Even Done with the Night
All I Need to Know (Don't Know Much)
All Night Long
All out of Love
All over the World
America
And the Beat Goes On
And the Cradle Will Rock
Another Brick in the Wall
Another One Bites the Dust
Any Way You Want It
Arc of a Diver
Are the Good Times Really Over
Are You on the Road to Lovin' Me Again
Ashes to Ashes
Babooshka
Back in Black
Backstrokin'

Bar Room Buddies
Beneath Still Waters
Better Love Next Time
Big Ole Brew
(The) Biggest Part of Me
Blues Power
Bon Bon Vie
Boulevard
Brand New Lover
Brass in Pocket (I'm Special)
Breakdown Dead Ahead
The Breaks
Burn Rubber on Me
Cadillac Ranch
Call Me
Cars
Celebration
City Drops (into the Night)
The Colors of My Life
Coming Up
Could I Have This Dance
Coward of the County
Cowboys and Clowns
Cuban Slide
Cupid

Three Times in Love
Through the Years
The Tide Is High
Tight Fittin Jeans
Time
Time Is Time
Time Like Your Wire Wheels
Tired of Toein' the Line
Together
Too Hot
Too Many Lovers
Too Tight
Train in Vain (Stand by Me)
Treat Me Right
True Love Ways
Trying to Love Two Women
Tunnel of Love
Two Story House
United Together
Upside Down
Wait for Me
Waiting for the Weekend
Wake Up and Live
The Wanderer
Wango Tango
Watching the Wheels
Watching You
The Way I Am
We Belong Together
We Don't Talk Anymore
We Go a Long Way Back
We Live for Love
We're in This Love Together
What Kind of Fool
When a Man Loves a Women
When I Wanted You
When Love Calls
When She Was My Girl
When You Were Mine
While You See a Chance
Whip It
White Shoes
Who's Cheating Who
Why Do You (Do What You Do), see
 Do What You Do
Why Don't You Spend the Night
Why Lady Why
Why Not Me
Wine, Women and Song
The Winner Takes It All

Without Your Love
Woman in Love
Women I've Never Had
Wondering Where the Lions Are
Wrong 'Em Boyo
Xanadu
Yearning for Your Love
Years
Yes, I'm Ready
You and I
You Make My Dreams
You May Be Right
You Never Gave Up on Me
You Shook Me All Night Long
You Win Again
You'll Accompany Me
You're the Best Break This Old Heart
 Ever Had
You're the Only Woman (You and I)
You're the Reason God Made
 Oklahoma
You've Lost That Lovin' Feeling

1981

Ah, Men
All American Girls
All I Have to Do Is Dream
All My Rowdy Friends (Have Settled
 Down)
All Those Years Ago
Allentown
Allergies
Almost Saturday Night
And I Am Telling You I'm Not Going
Angel Flying Too Close to the Ground
Angel in Blue
Angel of the Morning
Another Sleepless Night
Another Tricky Day
The Apple Stretching
Are You Happy Baby
Are You Single
Arthur's Theme (The Best That You
 Can Do)
As Long as I'm Rockin' with You
Baby, Come to Me
Ballad for D
The Beach Boys Medley

1982

1983

1984

Awards Index

A year-by-year list of songs nominated for Academy Awards by the Academy of Motion Picture Arts and Sciences and Grammy Awards from the National Academy of Recording Arts and Sciences. Asterisks indicate the winners.

1980

Academy Award
Fame
9 to 5*
On the Road Again
Out Here on My Own
People Alone

National Academy of Recording Arts and Sciences Award
Drivin' My Life Away
Fame
Give Me the Night
He Stopped Loving Her Today
I Believe in You
Lady
Let's Get Serious
Lookin' for Love
Never Knew Love Like This Before*
On the Road Again*
The Rose
Sailing*
Shining Star
Theme from *New York, New York*
Woman in Love

1981

Academy Award
Arthur's Theme (The Best That You Can Do)*
Endless Love
The First Time It Happens
For Your Eyes Only
One More Hour

National Academy of Recording Arts and Sciences Award
Ai No Corrida
Arthur's Theme (The Best That You Can Do)
Bette Davis Eyes*
Elvira
Endless Love
I Was Country When Country Wasn't Cool
Just the Two of Us
Just the Two of Us*
Lady (You Bring Me Up)
9 to 5
9 to 5*
She's a Bad Mama Jama

297

Somebody's Knockin'
When She Was My Girl
You're the Reason God Made
Oklahoma

1982
Academy Award
Eye of the Tiger (The Theme from
  Rocky III)
How Do You Keep the Music
  Playing
If We Were in Love
It Might Be You
Up Where We Belong*

National Academy of Recording Arts
  and Sciences Award
Always on My Mind
Always on My Mind*
Chariots of Fire (Race to the End)
Do I Do
Ebony and Ivory
Eye of the Tiger (The Theme from
  Rocky III)
I. G. Y. (What a Beautiful World)
I'm Gonna Hire a Wino to Decorate
  Our Home
It's Gonna Take a Miracle
Let It Whip
Nobody
Ring on Her Finger, Time on Her
  Hands
Rosanna*
Rosanna
Sexual Healing
Steppin' Out
That Girl
Turn Your Love Around*

1983
Academy Award
Flashdance. . .What a Feeling*
Maniac
Over You
Papa Can You Hear Me
The Way He Makes Me Feel

National Academy of Recording Arts
  and Sciences Award
Ain't Nobody
All Night Long (All Night)
Baby I Lied

Beat It*
Beat It
Billie Jean
Billie Jean*
Electric Avenue
Every Breath You Take
Every Breath You Take*
Flashdance. . .What a Feeling
I.O.U.
Lady Down on Love
A Little Good News
Mama He's Crazy
Maniac
P. Y. T. (Pretty Young Thing)
Stranger in My House*
Wanna Be Startin' Something

1984
Academy Award
Against All Odds (Take a Look at
  Me Now)
Footloose
Ghostbusters
I Just Called to Say I Love You*
Let's Hear It for the Boy

National Academy of Recording Arts
  and Sciences Award
Against All Odds (Take a Look at
  Me Now)
All My Rowdy Friends Are Coming
  Over Tonight
Caribbean Queen (No More Love on
  the Run)
City of New Orleans*
Dancing in the Dark
Dancing in the Sheets
Faithless Love
Girls Just Want to Have Fun
The Glamorous Life
God Bless the U.S.A.
Hard Habit to Break
The Heart of Rock and Roll
Hello
I Feel for You*
I Just Called to Say I Love You*
Time After Time
What's Love Got to Do with It
What's Love Got to Do with It*
Yah Mo B There

List of Publishers

A directory to publishers of the songs included in *Popular Music* 1980-1984. Publishers that are members of the American Society of Composers, Authors, and Publishers or whose catalogs are available under ASCAP license are indicated by the designation (ASCAP). Publishers that have granted performing rights to Broadcast Music, Inc., are designated by the notation (BMI). Publishers whose catalogs are represented by SESAC, Inc., are indicated by the designation (SESAC).

The addresses were gleaned from a variety of sources, including ASCAP, BMI, SESAC, The Harry Fox Agency, *Billboard* magazine, and the National Music Publishers' Association. As in any volatile industry, many of the addresses may become quickly outdated. In the interim between the book's completion and its subsequent publication, some publishers may have been consolidated into others or changed hands. This is a fact of life long endured by the music business and its constituents. The data collected here, and throughout the book, are as accurate as such circumstances allow.

A

Abesongs USA (BMI)
see Almo Music Corp.

ABKCO Music Inc. (BMI)
1700 Broadway
New York, New York 10019

Ackee Music Inc. (ASCAP)
see Island Music

Acuff-Rose Publications Inc. (BMI)
2510 Franklin Road
Nashville, Tennessee 37204

Adams Communications, Inc. (BMI)
see Almo Music Corp.

Addax Music Co., Inc. (ASCAP)
c/o Famous Music Corp.
Attention: Sidney Herman
1 Gulf & Western Plaza
New York, New York 10023

List of Publishers

Addison Street Music (ASCAP)
c/o Sterling Music Co.
8150 Beverly Boulevard
Suite 202
Los Angeles, California 90048

Alamo Music, Inc. (ASCAP)
11th Floor
1619 Broadway
New York, New York 10019

Alcor Music (BMI)
see April Music, Inc.

Alessi Music
528 Cedar Swamp Road
Glen Head, New York 11545

Algee Music Corp. (BMI)
see Notable Music Co., Inc.

Alibee Music (BMI)
The Entertainment Music Co.
1700 Broadway
New York, New York 10019

Alimony Music (BMI)
c/o Shapiro and Steinberg
315 South Beverly Drive
Suite 210
Beverly Hills, California 90212

All Seeing Eye Music (ASCAP)
Suite 816
1422 West Peachtreet Street
Northwest
Atlanta, Georgia 30309

Alley Music (BMI)
1619 Broadway
11th Floor
New York, New York 10019

Almo Music Corp. (ASCAP)
1416 North La Brea Avenue
Hollywood, California 90028

Alva Music (BMI)
3929 Kentucky Drive
Los Angeles, California 90068

Amanda-Lin Music (ASCAP)
Post Office Box 15871
Nashville, Tennessee 37215

Amazement Music (BMI)
805 Moraga
Lafayette, California 94549

American Broadcasting Music, Inc.
(ASCAP)
Attention: Georgett Studnicka
4151 Prospect Avenue
Hollywood, California 90027

American Cowboy Music Co. (BMI)
14 Music Circle East
Nashville, Tennessee 37203

John Anderson Music Co. Inc. (BMI)
c/o Al Gallico Music Corporation
Suite 1A B
344 East 49th Street
New York, New York 10017

Angela Music (ASCAP)
c/o Peter C. Bennett, Esq.
9060 Santa Monica Boulevard
Suite 300
Los Angeles, California 90069

Judy Hart Angelo Music
see Entertainment Co. Music Group

Anidraks Music/Porchester Music, Inc.
(ASCAP)
Mitchell, Silberberg & Knupp
Attention: Richard I. Leher, Esq.
11377 West Olympic Boulevard
Los Angeles, California 90064

Another Page (ASCAP)
c/o First South-West Associates
Suite 717
114 West 7th Street
Austin, Texas 78701

Anteater Music (ASCAP)
c/o Bradshaw & Thomas
8607 Sherwood Drive
Los Angeles, California 90069

Antisia Music Inc. (ASCAP)
c/o Ralph MacDonald
1674 Broadway
Suite 200
New York, New York 10019

Appian Music Co. (ASCAP)
c/o Mitchell, Silberberg & Knupp
1800 Century Park East
Los Angeles, California 90067

April Music, Inc. (ASCAP)
49 East 52nd Street
New York, New York 10022

Arista Music, Inc.
8370 Wilshire Boulevard
Beverly Hills, California 90211

Arrival Music (BMI)
c/o Mietus Copyright Management
2351 Laurana Road
Post Office Box 432
Union, New Jersey 07083

Art Street Music (BMI)
c/o Fitzgerald Hartley Co.
7250 Beverly Boulevard
Suite 200
Los Angeles, California 90036

Artwork Music Co., Inc. (ASCAP)
c/o Ivan Mogull Music Corp.
625 Madison Avenue
New York, New York 10022

Ashtray Music (BMI)
c/o Bobby Womack
2841 Firenze Place
Los Angeles, California 90046

Assorted Music (BMI)
Attention: Earl Shelton
309 South Broad Street
Philadelphia, Pennsylvania 19107

At Home Music (ASCAP)
Attention: Wayne Henderson
Post Office Box 2682
Hollywood, California 90028

Atlantic Music Corp. (BMI)
6124 Selma Avenue
Hollywood, California 90028

ATV Music Corp. (BMI)
c/o ATV Group
6255 Sunset Boulevard
Hollywood, California 90028

August Dream Music Ltd. (BMI)
c/o Tom Eyen
41 Fifth Avenue
New York, New York 10003

R. L. August Music Co.
Attention: Bonnie Blumenthal
40 West 57th Street
Suite 1510
New York, New York 10019

Avant Garde Music Publishing, Inc.
(ASCAP)
Attention: Clarence Avant
No. 331
9229 Sunset Boulevard
Los Angeles, California 90069

Average Music (ASCAP)
47 Brookmere Drive
Fairfield, Connecticut 06430

B

B. O'Cult Songs, Inc. (ASCAP)
c/o Robbins Speilman
Attention: Bruce Slayton
1700 Broadway
New York, New York 10019

Baby Fingers Music (ASCAP)
Post Office Box 6278
Altadena, California 91001

Baby Love Music, Inc. (ASCAP)
c/o Fischbach & Fischbach, PC
No. 1260
1925 Century Park East
Los Angeles, California 90067

Baby Shoes Music (BMI)
1358 North La Brea
Los Angeles, California 90028

Backlog Music (BMI)
c/o Edward Pollack
Post Office Box 9711
Memphis, Tennessee 38109

Bad Ju Ju Music (ASCAP)
Attention: Howard Russell Smith
Post Office Box 58
College Grove, Tennessee 37046

Bandier Family Music (ASCAP)
c/o The Entertainment Music Co.
1700 Broadway
41st Floor
New York, New York 10019

Martin Bandier Music
see Entertainment Co. Music Group

Bangaphile Music (BMI)
8033 Sunset Boulevard
No. 853
Los Angeles, California 90046

Bantha Music (ASCAP)
c/o Lucasfilm Ltd.
Post Office Box 2009
San Rafael, California 94912

Bar Cee Music (BMI)
see Peso Music

Bar-Kay Music (BMI)
see WB Music Corp.

Baray Music Inc. (BMI)
49 Music Square East
Nashville, Tennessee 37203

Barnwood Music (BMI)
see Singletree Music Co., Inc.

Denise Barry Music (ASCAP)
c/o Peter T. Paterno, Esq.
Manatt-Phelps-Rothenberg & Tunne
11355 West Olympic Boulevard
Los Angeles, California 90064

Beechwood Music Corp. (BMI)
6255 Sunset Boulevard
Hollywood, California 90028

Begonia Melodies, Inc. (BMI)
c/o Unichappell Music Inc.
810 7th Avenue
New York, New York 10019

Belfast Music (BMI)
c/o Embassy Television
1901 Avenue of the Stars
Suite 666
Los Angeles, California 90067

Bellamy Brothers Music (ASCAP)
Route 2
Post Office Box 294
Dade City, Florida 33525

Belwin-Mills Publishing Corp. (ASCAP)
1776 Broadway
11th Floor
New York, New York 10019

Bertam Music Co. (ASCAP)
see Jobete Music Co., Inc.

Better Days Music (BMI)
Moultrie Accountancy Corp.
Attention: Fred S. Moultrie, C.P.A.
Post Office Box 5270
Beverly Hills, California 90210

Better Night Music (ASCAP)
see Better Days Music

John Bettis Music (ASCAP)
c/o Harley Williams
Suite 1200
1900 Avenue of the Stars
Los Angeles, California 90067

BGO Music (ASCAP)
3864 Oakcliff Industrial Court
Doraville, Georgia 30340

Bibo Music Publishers (ASCAP)
see Welk Music Group

Bienstock Publishing Co. (ASCAP)
Attention: Freddy Bienstock
1619 Broadway
Penthouse
New York, New York 10019

Big Ears Music Inc. (ASCAP)
c/o Sy Miller
Suite 1001
565 Fifth Avenue
New York, New York 10017

Big Stick Music (BMI)
c/o Paul Palmer
1903 Midvale Avenue
Los Angeles, California 90025

Big Talk Music (BMI)
c/o Michael N. Miller, C.P.A.
9060 Santa Monica Boulevard
Suite 305
Los Angeles, California 90069

Big Tooth Music Corp. (ASCAP)
see Rare Blue Music, Inc.

Big Train Music Co. (ASCAP)
9110 Sunset Boulevard
Suite 200
Los Angeles, California 90069

Billy Music (ASCAP)
c/o Kaufman & Bernstein, Inc.
22nd Floor
1900 Avenue of the Stars
Los Angeles, California 90067

Bird Ankles Music
c/o Chris Williamson
Olivia Records
4400 Market Street
Oakland, California 94608

Black Bull Music (ASCAP)
Attention: Stevland Morris
4616 Magnolia Boulevard
Burbank, California 91505

Black Impala Music (BMI)
c/o Austin Texas Sounds
3300 Hollywood
Austin, Texas 78722

Black Keys (BMI)
Post Office Box 3633
Thousand Oaks, California 91360

Black Sheep Music Inc. (BMI)
1009 17th Avenue South
Nashville, Tennessee 37212

Black Tent Music (BMI)
c/o Bug Music
6777 Hollywood Boulevard
9th Floor
Hollywood, California 90028

Blackwell Publishing (ASCAP)
c/o C. Allen, Jr.
6914 South Honore Street
Chicago, Illinois 60636

Blackwood Music Inc. (BMI)
1350 Avenue of the Americas
23rd Floor
New York, New York 10019

Bleu Disque Music (ASCAP)
c/o Warner Brothers Music
Penthouse
9000 Sunset Boulevard
Los Angeles, California 90069

Bleunig Music (ASCAP)
Attention: Bill Withers
2600 Benedict Canyon Road
Beverly Hills, California 90210

Blue Lake Music (BMI)
c/o Ovation Inc.
Richard Schory
1249 Waukegan Road
Glenview, Illinois 60025

Blue Midnight Music (ASCAP)
c/o Bug Music
9th Floor
6777 Hollywood Boulevard
Hollywood, California 90028

Blue Moon Music (ASCAP)
1233 17th Avenue South
Nashville, Tennessee 37212

Blue Network Music
see Interworld Music Group

Blue Quill Music (ASCAP)
see Cherry Lane Music Co., Inc.

Blue Sky Rider Songs (BMI)
c/o Prager and Fenton
6363 Sunset Boulevard
Suite 706
Los Angeles, California 90028

Bocephus Music Inc. (BMI)
see Singletree Music Co., Inc.

Body Electric Music (BMI)
1701 Queens Road
Los Angeles, California 90069

Boneidol Music (ASCAP)
c/o Aucoin Management Inc.
645 Madison Avenue
New York, New York 10022

Bonnie Bee Good Music (ASCAP)
1336 Grant Street
Santa Monica, California 90405

Boo-Fant Tunes, Inc. (BMI)
c/o Zissu, Stein, Bergman,
Couture & Mosher
270 Madison Avenue
Suite 1410
New York, New York 10016

Boone's Tunes (BMI)
c/o Richard Kaye Publications
13251 Ventura Boulevard
Suite 3
Studio City, California 91604

Bootchute Music (BMI)
Post Office Box 12025
485 North Hollywood
Memphis, Tennessee 38112

Boston International Music (ASCAP)
159 West 53rd Street
Suite 11A
New York, New York 10019

List of Publishers

Bovina Music, Inc. (ASCAP)
c/o Mae Attaway
Apartment 12F
330 West 56th Street
New York, New York 10019

Braintree Music (BMI)
c/o Segel & Goldman Inc.
9348 Santa Monica Boulevard
Number 304
Beverly Hills, California 90210

Bramalea Music
see New Tandem Music Co.

Brass Heart (BMI)
c/o Jeri K. Hull, Jr.
5970 Airdrome Street
Los Angeles, California 90035

Briarpatch Music (BMI)
Box 140110
Donelson, Tennessee 37214

Brick Alley (ASCAP)
1704 8th Street
Irwin, Pennsylvania 15642

Bridgeport Music Inc. (BMI)
c/o Norman R. Kurtz
712 5th Avenue
New York, New York 10019

Bright Smile Music (ASCAP)
c/o Millennium Corp.
1619 Broadway
Suite 1209
New York, New York 10019

Broadcast Music Inc. (BMI)
10 Music Square East
Nashville, Tennessee 37203

Brockman Enterprises Inc. (ASCAP)
Leibren Music Division
c/o Jess S. Morgan & Co., Inc.
6420 Wilshire Blvd.
19th Floor
Los Angeles, California 90048

Brojay Music (ASCAP)
c/o State of the Arts Music
7250 Beverly Boulevard
Los Angeles, California 90036

Broozertoones, Inc. (ASCAP)
c/o Segel, Goldman and Macnow Inc.
9348 Santa Monica Boulevard
Beverly Hills, California 90210

Brother Bill's Music (ASCAP)
3051 Clairmont Road Northeast
Atlanta, Georgia 30329

Brouhaha Music (ASCAP)
c/o Satin Tenenbaum Eichler & Zimm
1776 Broadway
New York, New York 10019

Jocelyn Brown's Music
267 Grove Street
Jersey City, New Jersey 07302

Bruin Music Co. (BMI)
see Famous Music Co.

Bruised Oranges (ASCAP)
c/o Sy Miller
Suite 1001
565 Fifth Avenue
New York, New York 10017

Buchu Music (ASCAP)
c/o Donald B. Bachrach, Esq.
1515 North Crescent Heights
Boulevard
Los Angeles, California 90046

Buckhorn Music Publishing Co., Inc. (BMI)
Box 120547
Nashville, Tennessee 37212

Budson Music (BMI)

Bug Music (BMI)
Bug Music Group
6777 Hollywood Boulevard
9th Floor
Hollywood, California 90028

Bug/Slimey Limey Music (BMI)
6777 Hollywood Boulevard
9th Floor
Hollywood, California 90028

Bussy Music (BMI)
c/o Gary William Friedman
150 East 72nd Street
New York, New York 10021

Buzzherb Music (BMI)
c/o Scott Tutt Music
903 18th Avenue South
Second Floor
Nashville, Tennessee 37212

C

John Cafferty Music (BMI)
17 Towanda Drive
Providence, Rhode Island 02911

Calypso Toonz (BMI)
see Irving Music Inc.

Camelback Mountain Music Corp. (ASCAP)
c/o Shapiro, Bernstein & Co., Inc.
10 East 53rd Street
New York, New York 10022

Cameo Five Music (BMI)
Moultrie Accountancy Corp.
Attention: Fred S. Moultrie, C.P.A.
Post Office Box 5270
Beverly Hills, California 90210

Canopy Music Inc. (ASCAP)
c/o Bruce V. Grakal
1427 7th Street
Santa Monica, California 90401

Captain Crystal Music (BMI)
7505 Jerez Court
Number E
Rancho La Costa, California 92008

Carbert Music Inc. (BMI)
1619 Broadway
Room 609
New York, New York 10019

Careers Music Inc. (ASCAP)
see Arista Music, Inc.

Carollon Music Co.
Attention: Jay Warner
6351 Drexel Avenue
Los Angeles, California 90048

Carub Music (ASCAP)
c/o Daniel Rosenbloom
150 Broadway
New York, New York 10038

Casa David (ASCAP)
see Jac Music Co., Inc.

Cass County Music Co. (ASCAP)
c/o Breslauer, Jacobson & Rutman
Suite 2110
10880 Wilshire Boulevard
Los Angeles, California 90024

Catpatch Music (BMI)
c/o Ken Weiss
5032 Lankershim Boulevard
Suite 2
North Hollywood, California 91601

Cavesson Music Enterprises Co. (ASCAP)
Joiner Music Division
Lariat Music Co. Division
815 18th Avenue South
Nashville, Tennessee 37203

CBS Affiliated Catalog Inc. (BMI)
49 East 52nd Street
New York, New York 10022

CBS U Catalog, Inc. (ASCAP)
49 East 52nd Street
New York, New York 10022

CBS Unart Catalog Inc. (BMI)
49 East 52nd Street
New York, New York 10022

CBS Variety Catalog, Inc. (ASCAP)
49 East 52nd Street
New York, New York 10022

Cedarwood Publishing Co., Inc. (BMI)
39 Music Square East
Nashville, Tennessee 37203

Cement Chicken Music (ASCAP)
13504 Contour Drive
Sherman Oaks, California 91423

Center City Music (ASCAP)
c/o Mitchell Silberberg & Knupp
Attention: Carol King
Suite 900
11377 West Olympic Boulevard
Los Angeles, California 90064

C'est Music (ASCAP)
see Quackenbush Music, Ltd.

Chapin Music (ASCAP)
c/o Monte L. Morris, Esq.
130 West 57th Street
New York, New York 10019

305

List of Publishers

Chappell & Co., Inc. (ASCAP)
810 Seventh Avenue
New York, New York 10019

Chardax Music (BMI)
11337 Burbank Boulevard
North Hollywood, California 91601

Charles Family Music (BMI)
1700 Broadway
41st Floor
New York, New York 10019

Cherry Lane Music Co., Inc. (ASCAP)
110 Midland Avenue
Port Chester, New York 10573

Cheshire Music Inc. (BMI)
10 Columbus Circle
New York, New York 10019

Chess Music Inc. (ASCAP)
see Welk Music Group

Chic Music Inc. (BMI)
see WB Music Corp.

Chiplin Music Co. (ASCAP)
c/o Edward J. Penney, Jr.
1318 Hildreth Drive
Nashville, Tennessee 37215

Chrysalis Music Corp. (ASCAP)
Chrysalis Music Group
645 Madison Avenue
New York, New York 10022

Cibie Music (ASCAP)
Suite 2270
1900 Avenue of the Stars
Los Angeles, California 90067

Circle L Publishing (ASCAP)
c/o Spectrum VII Music
Attention: Otis Stokes
6th Floor
1635 North Cahuenga Boulevard
Hollywod, California 90028

Clean Sheets Music (BMI)
c/o Jess S. Morgan & Co., Inc.
6420 Wilshire Boulevard
19th Floor
Los Angeles, California 90048

Cleveland International (ASCAP)
c/o International Records
1775 Broadway
7th Floor
New York, New York 10019

Clita Music (BMI)
c/o Mietus Copyright Management
2351 Laurana Road
Post Office Box 432
Union, New Jersey 07083

Coal Miner's Music Inc. (BMI)
7 Music Circle North
Nashville, Tennessee 37203

Colgems-EMI Music Inc. (ASCAP)
see Screen Gems-EMI Music Inc.

Collins Court Music, Inc. (ASCAP)
Post Office Box 121407
Nashville, Tennessee 37212

Columbia Pictures Publications
16333 Northwest 54th Avenue
Hialeah, Florida 33014

Combine Music Corp. (BMI)
35 Music Square East
Nashville, Tennessee 37203

Comet Music Corp. (ASCAP)
c/o ATV-Kirshner Music Corp.
6255 Sunset Boulevard
Hollywood, California 90028

Commodores Entertainment Publishing Corp.
(ASCAP)
c/o Benjamin Ashburn Associates
39 West 55th Street
New York, New York 10019

Content Music, Inc. (BMI)
c/o Leo Graham, Jr.
124 Twin Oaks Drive
Oakbrook, Illinois 60521

Controversy Music (ASCAP)
c/o Manatt, Phelps, Rothenberg
Attention: Lee Phillips
11355 West Olympic Boulevard
Los Angeles, California 90064

Conus Music (ASCAP)
c/o Robert H. Flax
65 East 55th Street
Suite 604
New York, New York 10022

Roger Cook Music (BMI)
1204 16th Avenue South
Nashville, Tennessee 37212

Cookaway Music Inc. (ASCAP)
see Dick James Music Inc.

Cookhouse Music (BMI)
1204 16th Avenue S.
Nashville, Tennessee 37212

Coolwell Music (ASCAP)
c/o Granite Music Corp.
6124 Selma Avenue
Los Angeles, California 90028

Core Music Publishing (BMI)
c/o Oak Manor
Box 1000
Oak Ridges, Ontario
Canada

Cotillion Music Inc. (BMI)
75 Rockefeller Plaza
Second Floor
New York, New York 10019

Cottonpatch Music (ASCAP)
c/o Mason and Sloane
1299 Ocean Avenue
Santa Monica, California 90401

Country Road Music Inc. (BMI)
c/o Gelfand, Rennert & Feldman
Attention: Babbie Green
1880 Century Park East
Number 900
Los Angeles, California 90067

Cowbella Music (ASCAP)
No. 200
7250 Beverly Boulevard
Los Angeles, California 90036

Crazy Crow Music (BMI)
see Siquomb Publishing Corp.

Crimsco Music (ASCAP)
c/o Almo Music Corp.
1416 North La Brea
Hollywood, California 90028

Cross Keys Publishing Co., Inc. (ASCAP)
see Tree Publishing Co., Inc.

Pablo Cruise Music (BMI)
see Irving Music Inc.

Jan Crutchfield Music (BMI)
c/o Unichappell Music, Inc.
32nd Floor
810 Seventh Avenue
New York, New York 10019

D

Dad Music (BMI)
see Hancock Music Co.

Daddy Oh Music
see Lipsync Music

Dan Daley Music (BMI)
c/o Dreena Music
80 Eighth Avenue
Suite 201
New York, New York 10011

Darjen Music (BMI)
c/o Blackwood Music Inc.
49 East 52nd Street
New York, New York 10022

Dat Richfield Kat Music (BMI)
c/o Richard Fields
Post Office Box 36496
Los Angeles, California 90036

Dawnbreaker Music Co. (BMI)
c/o Manatt, Phelps, Rothenberg &
Tunney
1888 Century Park East
21st Floor
Los Angeles, California 90067

Debdave Music Inc. (BMI)
Post Office Box 140110
Donnelson, Tennessee 37214

Deco Music (BMI)
c/o Breslauer, Jacobson & Rutman
10880 Wilshire Boulevard
Los Angeles, California 90024

Freddie Dee Music (BMI)
9766 Woodale Avenue
Arleta, California 91331

Dejamus Inc. (ASCAP)
see Dick James Music Inc.

Dela Music (BMI)
see Charles Family Music

List of Publishers

Delicate Music (ASCAP)
c/o Paul Glass, CPA
Glass & Rosen
Suite 202
16530 Ventura Boulevard
Encino, California 91436

Delightful Music Ltd. (BMI)
c/o Mr. Ted Eddy
200 West 57th Street
New York, New York 10019

Desperate Music (BMI)
25671 Whittemore Drive
Calabasas, California 91302

Devo Music (BMI)
c/o Unichappel Music Inc.
810 Seventh Avenue
New York, New York 10019

Devon Music (BMI)
see TRO-Cromwell Music Inc.

Diamond Mine Music (ASCAP)
c/o Warner Brothers Music
Penthouse
9000 Sunset Boulevard
Los Angeles, California 90069

Diesel Music (BMI)
c/o J. Williams
701 Franklin Avenue
Brooklyn, New York 11238

Difficult Music (BMI)
c/o Beldock, Levine and Hoffman
565 Fifth Avenue
New York, New York 10017

Dionio Music (ASCAP)
c/o The Bug Music Group
Ninth Floor
6777 Hollywood Boulevard
Beverly Hills, California 90028

Discott Music (ASCAP)
see Rare Blue Music, Inc.

Dr. Benway Music (BMI)
c/o Phillips, Mizer, Benjamin
& Krim
Attention: Rosemary Carroll
40 West 57th Street
New York, New York 10019

Double F Music (ASCAP)
see Delightful Music Ltd.

Double Virgo Music (ASCAP)
c/o Mitchell, Silberberg, Knupp
11377 West Olympic Boulevard
Los Angeles, California 90064

Dreamette's Music (BMI)
The David Geffen Co.
9126 Sunset Boulevard
Los Angeles, California 90069

Dreamgirls Music (ASCAP)
9126 Sunset Boulevard
Los Angeles, California 90069

Dreena Music (BMI)
c/o Bradley Publications
80 Eighth Avenue
Suite 201
New York, New York 10011

Drunk Monkey Music (ASCAP)
Suite E
22458 Ventura Boulevard
Woodland Hills, California 91364

Dub Notes/WB Music Corp. (ASCAP)
c/o Levine & Thall, PC
485 Madison Avenue
New York, New York 10022

Duchess Music Corp. (BMI)
see MCA Music

Dyad Music, Ltd. (BMI)
c/o Mason & Co.
75 Rockefeller Plaza
New York, New York 10019

E

E S P Management, Inc. (ASCAP)
Attention: E. S. Prager
Evansong Ltd. Division
Crumpet Music Division
1790 Broadway
New York, New York 10019

Easy Action Music (ASCAP)
c/o Martin Cohen, Esq.
Attention: Robert Destocki
Suite 1500
6430 Sunset Boulevard
Los Angeles, California 90028

Easy Listening Music Corp. (ASCAP)
344 East 49th Street
Suite 1A/B
New York, New York 10017

Easy Money Music (ASCAP)
c/o Gelfand, Rennert & Feldman
Attention: Babbie Green
1880 Century Park East
Number 900
Los Angeles, California 90067

Edition Sunrise Publishing, Inc. (BMI)
c/o Careers Music Inc.
8370 Wilshire Boulevard
Beverly Hills, California 90211

E.G. Music, Inc. (BMI)
161 West 54th Street
New York, New York 10019

Eight/Twelve Music (BMI)
185 Pier Avenue
Santa Monica, California 90405

Eiseman Music Co., Inc. (BMI)
Post Office Box 900
Beverly Hills, California 90213

Elektra/Asylum Music Inc. (BMI)
c/o Manatt, Phelps, Rothenburg
& Tunney
1888 Century Park East
21st Floor
Los Angeles, California 90067

Elettra Music
see Braintree Music

Elliot Music Co., Inc. (ASCAP)
Post Office Box 155
Purdys, New York 10578

Ellipsis Music Corp. (ASCAP)
c/o Harold Lipsius
919 North Broad Street
Philadelphia, Pennsylvania 19123

ELMusic (ASCAP)
Post Office Box 636
Chester, New Jersey 07930

Emanuel Music (ASCAP)
c/o Breslauer, Jacobson & Rutman
Suite 2110
10880 Wilshire Boulevard
Los Angeles, California 90024

Emanuel Music/April Music, Inc. (ASCAP)
c/o Breslauer, Jacobson & Rutman
Suite 2110
10880 Wilshire Boulevard
Los Angeles, California 90024

Embassy TV
c/o Robin Rosenfeld
1901 Avenue of the Stars
Los Angeles, California 90067

Emergency Music Inc. (ASCAP)
c/o Mietus Copyright Management
2351 Laurana Road
Post Office Box 432
Union, New York 07083

Endless Frogs Music (ASCAP)
see Bug Music

Ennes Productions, Ltd. (ASCAP)
Attention: Nat Shapiro
157 West 57th Street
New York, New York 10019

Ensign Music Corp. (BMI)
c/o Sidney Herman
1 Gulf & Western Plaza
New York, New York 10023

Songs of Manhattan Island Music Co. (BMI)
see House of Cash Inc.

Entertainment Co. Music Group
40 West 57th Street
New York, New York 10019

Enz Music
c/o Grubman & Indursky
575 Madison Avenue
New York, New York 10022

Equestrian Music (ASCAP)
c/o Wayne Rooks
330 West 42nd Street
New York, New York 10036

Equinox Music (BMI)
c/o Raymond Harris
Suite 1212
7060 Hollywood Boulevard
Hollywood, California 90028

ESP Management Inc. (BMI)
Attention: E. S. Prager
1790 Broadway
New York, New York 10019

List of Publishers

Ewald Corp.
see Braintree Music

F

Face the Music (BMI)
c/o Warner Brothers Music
44 Music Square West
Nashville, Tennessee 37203

Fallwater Music (BMI)
see Hudson Bay Music Co.

Fame Publishing Co., Inc. (BMI)
603 East Avalon Avenue
Box 2527
Muscle Shoals, Alabama 35660

Famous Music Co. (ASCAP)
Gulf & Western Industries, Inc.
1 Gulf & Western Plaza
New York, New York 10023

John Farrar Music (BMI)
see Kidada Music Inc.

Fat Jack the Second Music Publishing Co.
(BMI)
c/o Paul M. Jackson, Jr.
Post Office Box 1113
Gardena, California 90249

Fate Music (ASCAP)
1046 Carol Drive
Los Angeles, California 90069

Father Music (BMI)
c/o Bobby Hart
7647 Woodrow Wilson Drive
Los Angeles, California 90046

Featherbed Music Inc. (BMI)
see Unichappell Music Inc.

Fever Music, Inc. (ASCAP)
Attention: Jules Kurz, Esq.
161 West 54th Street
New York, New York 10019

Fiddleback Music Publishing Co., Inc.
(BMI)
1270 Avenue of the Americas
New York, New York 10020

Fifth Floor Music Inc. (ASCAP)
Attention: Martin Cohen
Suite 1500
6430 Sunset Boulevard
Los Angeles, California 90028

Fifty Grand Music, Inc. (BMI)
50 Music Square West
Suite 900
Nashville, Tennessee 37203

Finchley Music Corp. (ASCAP)
c/o Arrow, Edelstein & Gross, PC
919 Third Avenue
New York, New York 10022

Fingers Music (BMI)
c/o Breslauer, Jacobson & Rutman
No. 2110
10880 Wilshire Boulevard
Los Angeles, California 90024

Fire and Water Songs (BMI)
9762 West Olympic Boulevard
Beverly Hills, California 90212

First Lady Songs, Inc. (BMI)
6 Music Circle North
Nashville, Tennessee 37203

Five of a Kind, Inc. (BMI)
156 St. James Place
Brooklyn, New York 11238

Flames Of Albion Music, Inc. (ASCAP)
Attention: Stevens H. Weiss
34 Pheasant Run
Old Westbury, New York 11568

Fleetwood Mac Music Ltd. (BMI)
315 South Beverly Drive
Suite 210
Beverly Hills, California 90212

Fleur Music (ASCAP)
see Columbia Pictures Publications

Flowering Stone Music (ASCAP)
2114 Pico Boulevard
Santa Monica, California 90405

Flying Dutchman (BMI)
c/o Copyright Management Inc.
Post Office Box 110873
Nashville, Tennessee 37211

Flyte Tyme Tunes (ASCAP)
c/o Avant Garde Music Publishing
Suite 311
9229 Sunset Boulevard
Los Angeles, California 90069

Foghorn Music (ASCAP)
10939-1/2 Camarillo
North Hollywood, California 91602

Foreverendeavor Music, Inc. (ASCAP)
Attention: Arnold E. Tencer
5 Portsmouth Towne
Southfield, Michigan 48075

Four Kids Music
276 Fifth Avenue
New York, New York 10001

Four Knights Music Co. (BMI)
8467 Beverly Boulevard
Suite 109
Los Angeles, California 90048

Fourth Floor Music Inc. (ASCAP)
Box 135
Bearsville, New York 12409

Fox Fanfare Music Inc.
see Twentieth Century-Fox Music Corp.

Franne Golde Music (BMI)
c/o Rightsong Music Inc.
810 Seventh Avenue
32nd Floor
New York, New York 10019

Frashon Music Co. (BMI)
c/o Frankie Smith
143 North Dearborn Street
Philadelphia, Pennsylvania 19139

Freejunket Music (ASCAP)
6420 Wilshire Boulevard
19th Floor
Los Angeles, California 90048

Foster Frees Music Inc. (BMI)
c/o Shankman De Blasio
185 Pier Avenue
Santa Monica, California 90405

Samuel French, Inc.
45 West 25th Street
New York, New York 10010

Front Wheel Music, Inc. (BMI)
c/o Kim Guggenheim, Esq.
6255 Sunset Boulevard
Suite 1226
Hollywood, California 90028

Frozen Butterfly Music Publishing (BMI)
c/o R. Lucas
260 Farragut Court
Teaneck, New Jersey 07666

Full Armor Publishing Co. (BMI)
2828 Azalea Place
Nashville, Tennessee 37204

Funk Groove Music Publisher Co. (ASCAP)
Post Office Box 72
South Ozone Park, New York 11420

Fust Buzza Music, Inc. (BMI)
Attention: Shari Friedman
130 West 57th Street
Suite 11B
New York, New York 10019

G

Galleon Music, Inc. (ASCAP)
Suite 1A/B
344 East 49th Street
New York, New York 10017

Al Gallico Music Corp. (BMI)
344 East 49th Street
New York, New York 10017

Garden Court Music Co. (ASCAP)
45 Holton Avenue
Montreal, Quebec H3Y 2G1
Canada

Garden Rake Music, Inc. (BMI)
c/o Shankman De Blasio
185 Pier Avenue
Main Street at Pier
Santa Monica, California 90405

Gates Music Inc. (BMI)
c/o Chuck Mangione
1845 Clinton Avenue
Rochester, New York 14621

Larry Gatlin Music (BMI)
35 Music Square East
Nashville, Tennessee 37203

List of Publishers

Gear Publishing (ASCAP)
Div. of Hideout Productions
567 Purdy
Birmingham, Michigan 48009

Geffen/Kaye Music (ASCAP)
9126 Sunset Boulevard
Los Angeles, California 90069

Gemrod Music, Inc. (BMI)
c/o Walter Hofer
221 West 57th Street
New York, New York 10019

Genevieve Music (ASCAP)
c/o Bernard Gudvi & Co., Inc.
No. 425
6420 Wilshire Boulevard
Los Angeles, California 90048

Neil Geraldo Music Co. (ASCAP)
c/o Haber & Ebrlich
No. 710
16255 Ventura Boulevard
Encino, California 91436

Gibb Brothers Music (BMI)
see Unichappell Music Inc.

Hugh & Barbara Gibb Music (BMI)
c/o Prager & Fenton
444 Madison Avenue
New York, New York 10022

Andy Gibb Music (BMI)
c/o Prager and Fenton
444 Madison Avenue
New York, New York 10022

Giorgio Moroder Pub/April Music
see April Music, Inc.

Girlsongs (ASCAP)
c/o Manatt, Phelps, Rothenberg
& Tunney
11355 West Olympic Boulevard
Los Angeles, California 90064

Gladys Music (ASCAP)
see Chappell & Co., Inc.

Glamour Music (ASCAP)
c/o Hayes & Hume
Attention: Stuart Berton, Esq.
132 South Rodeo Drive
Beverly Hills, California 90212

Glasco Music, Co. (ASCAP)
c/o CBS Songs
A Division of CBS, Inc.
49 East 52nd Street
New York, New York 10022

Beverly Glen Publishing (ASCAP)
c/o Loeb and Loeb
Attention: D. Thompson
10100 Santa Monica Boulevard
Suite 2200
Los Angeles, California 90067

Glenwood Music Corp. (ASCAP)
see Beechwood Music Corp.

Gold Hill Music, Inc. (ASCAP)
c/o Nick Ben-Meir
644 North Doheny Drive
Los Angeles, California 90069

Gold Horizon Music Corp. (BMI)
Columbia Plaza East
Suite 215
Administered by Screen Gems-EMI
Music, Inc.
Burbank, California 91505

Golden Bridge Music (BMI)
1225 16th Avenue South
Nashville, Tennessee 37212

Golden Spread Music
see WB Music Corp.

Golden Torch Music Corp. (ASCAP)
c/o Columbia Pictures
Attention: Lee Reed
Columbia Plaza
Burbank, California 91505

Goldrian Music (ASCAP)
c/o Steve Goldman
No. 221
4650 Kester
Sherman Oaks, California 91403

Bobby Goldsboro Music (ASCAP)
see House of Gold Music Inc.

Michael H. Goldsen, Inc. (ASCAP)
6124 Selma Avenue
Hollywood, California 90028

Gomace Music, Inc. (BMI)
1000 North Doheny Drive
Los Angeles, California 90069

Gone Gator Music (ASCAP)
c/o Bernard Gudvi & Co., Inc.
Suite 425
6420 Wilshire Boulevard
Los Angeles, California 90048

Grager Music (BMI)
c/o Merria Ross
8030 Via Pompeii
Burbank, California 91504

Grand Illusion Music (ASCAP)
c/o Gudvi & Co.
No. 425
6420 Wilshire Boulevard
Los Angeles, California 90048

Granite Music Corp. (ASCAP)
6124 Selma Avenue
Hollywood, California 90028

Gratitude Sky Music, Inc. (ASCAP)
c/o Gelfand
2062 Union Street
San Francisco, California 94123

Gravity Raincoat Music (ASCAP)
see WB Music Corp.

Great Pyramid Music (BMI)
10 Waterville Street
San Francisco, California 94124

Greenheart Music, Ltd. (ASCAP)
c/o Franklin, Weinrib, Rudell
Vassallo
Attention: Nicholas Gordon
950 Third Avenue
New York, New York 10022

H

Rick Hall Music (ASCAP)
603 East Avalon Avenue
Post Office Box 2527
Muscle Shoals, Alabama 35662

Hampshire House Publishing Corp.
(ASCAP)
see TRO-Cromwell Music Inc.

Hamstein Music (BMI)
c/o Bill Ham
Box 19647
Houston, Texas 77024

Hancock Music Co. (BMI)
c/o David Rubinson & Friends Inc.
827 Folsom Street
San Francisco, California 94107

Hanna Music (ASCAP)
see Brockman Enterprises Inc.

Happy Hooker Music Inc. (BMI)
c/o Alex J. Migliara
202 Adams Avenue
Memphis, Tennessee 38104

Hargreen Music (BMI)
c/o Shanks, Davis & Remer
888 Seventh Avenue
New York, New York 10106

Harrick Music Inc. (BMI)
7764 N.W. 71st Street
Miami, Florida 33166

Hat Band Music (BMI)
The Sound Seventy Suite
210 25th Avenue North
Nashville, Tennessee 37203

Edwin R. Hawkins Music Co. (ASCAP)
c/o Platoff, Heftler, Harker, Nashe
400 East 38th Street
Union City, New Jersey 07087

Haymaker Music (BMI)
c/o Dan Kavanaugh Management Inc.
6427 Sunset Boulevard
Hollywood, California 90028

Hen-Al Publishing Co. (BMI)
c/o Mr. James E. Ingram
867 South Muirfield Road
Los Angeles, California 90005

Heroic Music (ASCAP)
2037 Pine Street
Philadelphia, Pennsylvania 19103

HG Music, Inc. (ASCAP)
c/o Mr. Alvin Gladstone
Schultz & Gladstone
98 Cutter Mill Road
Great Neck, New York 10021

Hickory Grove Music (ASCAP)
see April Music, Inc.

313

Hidden Music (BMI)
c/o Machat & Machat
1501 Broadway
30th Floor
New York, New York 10036

High Wave Music, Inc. (ASCAP)
c/o Warner Brothers Music
Penthouse
9000 Sunset Boulevard
Los Angeles, California 90069

Hip-Trip Music Co. (BMI)
c/o Glen E. Davis
1635 North Cahuenga Boulevard
6th Floor
Hollywood, California 90028

Hitchings Music (ASCAP)
c/o William A. Coben, Esq.
Sklar & Coben Inc.
2029 Century Park East
Suite 260
Los Angeles, California 90067

Hobbler Music (ASCAP)
see WB Music Corp.

Holland Music
see Southern Music Publishing Co., Inc.

Hollywood Boulevard Music (ASCAP)
11800 Laughton Way
Northridge, California 91326

Holy Moley Music (BMI)
2114 Pico Boulevard
Santa Monica, California 90405

Hot Cha Music Co. (BMI)
see Six Continents Music Publishing Inc.

Hotwire Music (BMI)
c/o Atlantic Music Corp.
6124 Selma Avenue
Hollywood, California 90028

House of Bryant Publications (BMI)
Post Office Box 570
Gatlinburg, Tennessee 37738

House of Cash Inc. (BMI)
Box 508
Hendersonville, Tennessee 37075

House of Gold Music Inc.
P.O. 120967
Acklyn Station
Nashville, Tennessee 37212

Hudmar Publishing Co., Inc. (ASCAP)
c/o Edward Silver & Associates
Suite B
13418 Ventura Boulevard
Post Office Box 6008
Sherman Oaks, California 91413

Hudson Bay Music Co. (BMI)
1619 Broadway
Suite 906
New York, New York 10019

Huemar Music (BMI)
c/o Hubert Eaves
834 Jefferson Avenue
Brooklyn, New York 11221

Hulex Music (BMI)
Post Office Box 819
Mill Valley, California 94942

Hygroton
1551 Filion Street, Apt. 504
St. Lambert, Quebec J4R 1W5
Canada

Hythefield Music (BMI)
1700 York Avenue
Apartment No. 9B
New York, New York 10028

I

Ice Age Music (ASCAP)
c/o Segel & Goldman
9348 Santa Monica Boulevard
Beverly Hills, California 90210

Illegal Songs, Inc. (BMI)
c/o Beverly Martin
633 North La Brea Avenue
Hollywood, California 90036

Impulsive Music (ASCAP)
c/o Frank Management
Attention: William Joel
Suite 208
375 North Broadway
Hicksville, New York 11753

Index Music/Bleu Disque Music Co., Inc.
(ASCAP)
  c/o Radall, Nadell, Fine & Weinber
  1775 Broadway
  New York, New York 10019

Inner Sanctum (BMI)
  c/o DL Bryon
  247 Grand Street
  New York, New York 10002

Interior Music (BMI)
  Suite 211
  9229 Sunset Boulevard
  Los Angeles, California 90069

Intersong, USA Inc.
  c/o Chappell & Co, Inc.
  810 Seventh Avenue
  New York, New York 10019

Interworld Music Group
  8304 Beverly Blvd.
  Los Angeles, California 90048

Irving Music Inc. (BMI)
  1358 North La Brea
  Hollywood, California 90028

Is Hot Music, Ltd. (ASCAP)
  34 Pheasant Run
  Old Westbury, New York 11568

Island Music (BMI)
  c/o Mr. Lionel Conway
  6525 Sunset Boulevard
  Hollywood, California 90028

I've Got The Music Co. (ASCAP)
  Attention: Terry Woodford
  Post Office Box 2631
  Muscle Shoals, Alabama 35662

Izzylumoe Music
  c/o Financial Management
  International
  9200 Sunset Boulevard
  Suite 931
  Los Angeles, California 90069

J

J S H Music (ASCAP)
  c/o Nigro-Karlin & Segal
  Suite 2460
  10100 Santa Monica Boulevard
  Los Angeles, California 90067

Ja-Len Music Co./Intersong USA, Inc.
(ASCAP)
  Box 50937
  Nashville, Tennessee 37205

Jac Music Co., Inc. (ASCAP)
  5253 Lankershin Boulevard
  North Hollywood, California 91601

Jack & Bill Music Co. (ASCAP)
  see Welk Music Group

Dick James Music Inc. (BMI)
  24 Music Square East
  Nashville, Tennessee 37203

James Osterberg Music
  c/o Bug Music Group
  Ninth Floor
  6777 Hollywood Boulevard
  Hollywood, California 90028

Al Jarreau Music (BMI)
  9034 Sunset Boulevard
  Suite 250
  Los Angeles, California 90069

Jay-Boy Music Corp.
  c/o Seymour Straus Herzog & Straus
  Suite 300B
  155 East 55th Street
  New York, New York 10022

Jay's Enterprises, Inc. (ASCAP)
  c/o Chappell & Company Inc.
  810 Seventh Avenue
  New York, New York 10019

Jeffix Music Co. (ASCAP)
  c/o William Jeffery
  5143 Village Green
  Los Angeles, California 90016

Garland Jeffreys Music/April Music, Inc.
(ASCAP)
  c/o Levine & Thall, PC
  485 Madison Avenue
  New York, New York 10022

Jen-Lee Music Co. (ASCAP)
Suite B-130
5775 Peachtreet Dunwoody Road
Northeast
Atlanta, Georgia 30342

Jensong Music, Inc. (ASCAP)
Post Office Box 1273
Nashville, Tennessee 37202

Jerryco Music Co. (ASCAP)
MPL Communications, Inc.
c/o Eastman & Eastman
39 West 54th Street
New York, New York 10019

Jim-Edd Music (BMI)
Post Office Box 78681
Los Angeles, California 90016

Jiru Music (ASCAP)
201 West 77th Street
Suite 3C
New York, New York 10024

Jobete Music Co., Inc. (ASCAP)
Suite 1600
Attention: Erlinda N. Barrios
6255 Sunset Boulevard
Hollywood, California 90028

Jodaway Music (ASCAP)
c/o Cole Classic Management
Suite 38
3030 West 6th Street
Los Angeles, California 90020

Joelsongs (BMI)
see April Music, Inc.

Jolly Cheeks Music (BMI)
c/o Griesdorf, Chertkoff, Levitt. &
Associates
2200 Younge St.
Suite 502
Toronto, Ontario M4S 2O6
Canada

Jonathan Three Music Co. (BMI)
c/o Lefrak Entertainment Co., Ltd.
40 West 57th Street
Suite 1510
New York, New York 10019

Jones Music Co.
c/o Dorothy Mae Rice Jones
1916 Portman Avenue
Cincinnati, Ohio 45237

Joy U.S.A. Music Co. (BMI)
c/o Peter Shukat
111 West 57th Street
New York, New York 10019

Junior Music, Ltd.
Address unknown

Juters Publishing Co. (BMI)
c/o Funzalo Music
Attention: Mike's Management
7th Floor
445 Park Avenue
New York, New York 10022

K

Kander & Ebb Inc. (BMI)
see Unichappell Music Inc.

George Karakoglou (BMI)
see Famous Music Co.

Kashif Music (BMI)
c/o Minter & Associates Inc.
194 Lenox Road
Brooklyn, New York 11226

Kejoc Music (BMI)
c/o Shankman De Blasio
185 Pier Avenue
Santa Monica, California 90405

Kentucky Wonder Music
Address unknown

Kenwon Music (BMI)
Suite 2
5032 Lankershim Boulevard
North Hollywood, California 91601

Kid Bird Music (BMI)
c/o Ervin Cohen & Jessup
Attention: Gregg Harrison, Esq.
9th Floor
9401 Wilshire Boulevard
Beverly Hills, California 90212

Kidada Music Inc. (BMI)
7250 Beverly Boulevard
Suite 206
Los Angeles, California 90036

Kiddio Music Co. (BMI)
c/o Martin Poll
919 Third Avenue
New York, New York 10022

Kikiko Music Corp. (BMI)
see Jobete Music Co., Inc.

Kings Road Music (BMI)
Suite 1240
1901 Avenue of the Stars
Los Angeles, California 90067

Stephen A. Kipner Music (ASCAP)
Attention: Stephen A. Kipner
19646 Valley View Drive
Topanga, California 90290

Kirshner/April Music Publishing (ASCAP)
49 East 52nd Street
New York, New York 10022

Don Kirshner Music Inc. (BMI)
see Blackwood Music Inc.

Kiss
Glickman/Marks Management Corp.
Attention: Dolores Gatza
655 Madison Avenue
New York, New York 10021

Kissway Music, Inc. (BMI)
c/o Glickman Marks Management Corp.
655 Madison Avenue
New York, New York 10021

KJG Music (ASCAP)
6066 Summit Bridge Road
Townsend, Delaware 19734

Bubba Knight Enterprises Ltd. (ASCAP)
Bubs Music
Productions & Publishing
829 East Oakley Boulevard
Las Vegas, Nevada 89104

Know Music (ASCAP)
c/o Nancy Wilson
8801 Juanita Avenue
Kirkland, Washington 98034

Koppelman Family Music (ASCAP)
c/o The Entertainment Music Co.
41st Floor
1700 Broadway
New York, New York 10019

Charles Koppelman Music
see Entertainment Co. Music Group

Kortchmar Music (ASCAP)
c/o Nick M. Ben-Meir
644 North Doheny Drive
Los Angeles, California 90069

Kosher Dill Music (BMI)
162 Almonte Boulevard
Mill Valley, California 94941

Kris Publishing
Post Office Box 42218
San Francisco, California 94142

L

La Brea Music (ASCAP)
see Almo Music Corp.

Lacy Boulevard Music
see WB Music Corp.

Lake Victoria Music (ASCAP)
c/o Stephen H. Cooper, Esq.
Weil, Gotschal & Manges
767 Fifth Avenue
New York, New York 10022

Land of Dreams Music
see Arista Music, Inc.

Jay Landers Music (ASCAP)
c/o Jay Landers Music
Suite 510
9000 Sunset Boulevard
Los Angeles, California 90069

Lar-Bell Music Corp. (BMI)
Suite 140
9110 Sunset Boulevard
Los Angeles, California 90069

Lawyer's Daughter (BMI)
Homestead Road
Pottersville, New Jersey 07979

Lazy Lizard Music (BMI)
c/o Molly Giskan
2310 Ocean Parkway
Brooklyn, New York 11223

List of Publishers

Lead Sheetland Music (BMI)
c/o Jess S. Morgan & Company, Inc.
19th Floor
6420 Wilshire Boulevard
Los Angeles, California 90048

Leeds Music Corp. (ASCAP)
c/o Mr. John McKellen
445 Park Avenue
New York, New York 10022

Leggs Four Publishing (BMI)
c/o Kim Guggenheim, Esq.
Suite 1214
6255 Sunset Boulevard
Hollywood, California 90028

Legibus Music Co. (BMI)
c/o Peter Bennett, Esq.
9060 Santa Monica Boulevard
Suite 300
Los Angeles, California 90069

Jerry Leiber Music (ASCAP)
11th Floor
1619 Broadway
New York, New York 10019

Lemon Tree Music, Inc. (ASCAP)
c/o Will Holt
Apartment 8W
45 East 66th Street
New York, New York 10021

Lena Music, Inc. (BMI)
Suite 507
1619 Broadway
New York, New York 10019

Lenono Music (BMI)
The Studio
1 West 72nd Street
New York, New York 10023

Lexicon Music Inc. (ASCAP)
Box 296
Woodland Hills, California 91365

LFS III Music (ASCAP)
c/o Spectrum VII Music
Suite 200
9044 Melrose Avenue
Los Angeles, California 90069

Lido Music Inc. (BMI)
c/o Segel & Goldman Inc.
9348 Santa Monica Boulevard
Beverly Hills, California 90210

Liesse Publishing (ASCAP)
6265 Cote De Liesse
Montreal, Quebec
Canada

Lijesrika Music Pub. (BMI)
see Irving Music Inc.

Likasa Music (BMI)
260 Farragut Court
Teaneck, New Jersey 07666

Lillybilly
see Bug Music

Lincoln Pond Music (BMI)
3888 Alta Mesa Drive
Studio City, California 91604

Lionscub Music (BMI)
c/o Michael Gesas CPA
Bash Gesas & Company
9401 Wilshire
No. 700
Beverly Hills, California 90212

Lionsmate Music (ASCAP)
see Lionscub Music

Lipsync Music (ASCAP)
c/o Nick Ben-Meir, CPA
644 North Doheny Drive
Los Angeles, California 90069

Little Birdie Music (BMI)
see Bug Music

Little Dragon Music (BMI)
c/o Mustola-Jorstad
Suite 111
One Harbor Drive
Sausalito, California 94965

Lo Pressor
705 Churchill Boulevard, #202
St. Lambert, Quebec J4R 1M8
Canada

Lockhill-Selma Music (ASCAP)
c/o Trust Music Management
Suite 705
6255 Sunset Boulevard
Hollywood, California 90028

Lodge Hall Music, Inc. (ASCAP)
12 Music Circle South
Nashville, Tennessee 37203

Long Pond Music
see Revelation Music Publishing Corp.

Longdog Music (ASCAP)
c/o Ned Doheny
136 El Camino
Beverly Hills, California 90212

Los Was Cosmipolitanos
Address unknown

Lost Boys Music (BMI)
c/o Obsidian Productions, Inc.
Attention: H. Siegel
10th Floor
410 Park Avenue
New York, New York 10022

Love Wheel Music (BMI)
Post Office Box 110873
Nashville, Tennessee 37211

Lowery Music Co., Inc. (BMI)
3051 Clairmont Road North East
Atlanta, Georgia 30329

Lucky Three Music Publishing Co. (BMI)
Div. of Salsoul Record Corp.
c/o Larry Spier
401 Fifth Avenue
New York, New York 10016

Ludlow Music Inc. (BMI)
10 Columbus Circle
Suite 1406
New York, New York 10019

Lunatunes Music (BMI)
2400 Fulton Street
San Francisco, California 94118

Lyon Farm Music Ltd.
626 West Lyon Farm Road
Greenwich, Connecticut 06830

M

Mac Vac Alac Music Co. (ASCAP)
3646 Mt. Vernon Drive
Los Angeles, California 90008

Maclen Music Inc. (BMI)
see ATV Music Corp.

Magic Castle Music, Inc. (ASCAP)
Attention: Jerry Foster
Post Office Box 41147
Nashville, Tennessee 37204

Magicland Music (ASCAP)
c/o Madhouse Management
Suite 3
3101 E. Eisenhower
Ann Arbor, Michigan 48104

Make Believus Music
see Welbeck Music Corp.

Makiki Publishing Co., Ltd. (ASCAP)
Suite 323
9350 Wilshire Boulevard
Beverly Hills, California 90212

Malbiz Publishing (BMI)
see Blackwood Music Inc.

Mallven Music (ASCAP)
c/o Mason & Sloane
Post Office Box 140110
Nashville, Tennessee 37214

Mammoth Spring Music (BMI)
c/o Rose Bridge Music, Inc.
1121 South Glenstone
Springfield, Missouri 65804

Henry Mancini Enterprises (ASCAP)
see Chappell & Co., Inc.

Mann & Weil Songs Inc. (BMI)
see ATV Music Corp.

Maplehill Music (BMI)
see Welk Music Group

March 9 Music (ASCAP)
c/o Garey, Mason, Sloane
Penthouse
1299 Ocean Avenue
Santa Monica, California 90401

Markmeem Music
see Hudson Bay Music Co.

E. B. Marks Music Corp. (BMI)
1790 Broadway
New York, New York 10019

List of Publishers

Bob Marley Music, Ltd. (ASCAP)
c/o David J. Steinberg, Esq.
Rita Marley Music Division
North American Building-20th Floor
121 South Broad Street
Philadelphia, Pennsylvania 19107

Marsaint Music Inc. (BMI)
Attention: Marshall E. Sehorn
3809 Clematis Avenue
New Orleans, Louisiana 70122

Maypop Music (BMI)
Attention: Maggie Cavender
803 Eighteenth Avenue South
Nashville, Tennessee 37203

MCA, Inc. (ASCAP)
c/o Mr. John McKellen
445 Park Avenue
New York, New York 10022

MCA Music (ASCAP)
Div. of MCA Inc.
445 Park Avenue
New York, New York 10022

Earl McGrath Music (ASCAP)
c/o Jess S. Morgan & Co., Inc.
19th Floor
6420 Wilshire Boulevard
Los Angeles, California 90048

McKenzie Brothers
c/o Craig Fuller
Post Office Box 142
New Richmond, Ohio 45157

McNella Music (ASCAP)
5124 3/4 Colfax Avenue
North Hollywood, California 91601

McNoodle Music (BMI)
c/o Bernard Gudvi & Co., Inc.
Suite 425
6420 Wilshire Boulevard
Los Angeles, California 90048

Medicine Hat Music (ASCAP)
c/o Gelfand, Rennert & Feldman
Attention: Babbie Green
No. 900
1880 Century Park East
Los Angeles, California 90067

Menken Music (BMI)
c/o The Shukatt Company, Ltd.
Suite 1A
340 West 55th St.
New York, New York 10019

Mercury Shoes Music (BMI)
c/o Jesse Barish
2612 Pacific Avenue
Venice, California 90291

Merovingian Music (BMI)
c/o Chris Butler
266 West 11th Street
New York, New York 10014

Metal Machine Music
Address unknown

Metered Music, Inc. (ASCAP)
c/o Padell, Nadell, Fine
& Wienberger
1775 Broadway
New York, New York 10019

MGM Affiliated Music, Inc. (BMI)
Address unknown

MHC Music (ASCAP)
c/o Bug Music
Ninth Floor
6777 Hollywood Boulevard
Hollywood, California 90028

Michael O'Connor Music (BMI)
Post Office Box 1869
Studio City, California 91604

Midstar Music, Inc. (BMI)
6th Floor
1635 North Cahuenga Boulevard
Hollwyood, California 90028

Mighty Mathieson Music (BMI)
c/o Shankman De Blasio, Inc.
185 Pier Avenue
Santa Monica, California 90405

Mighty Three Music (BMI)
c/o Earl Shelton
309 South Broad Street
Philadelphia, Pennsylvania 19107

Mijac Music (BMI)
c/o Warner Tamerlane Pub. Corp.
Penthouse
900 Sunset Boulevard
Los Angeles, California 90069

Mike Post Productions, Inc. (ASCAP)
 Darla Music Division
 Suite 202
 11846 Ventura Boulevard
 Studio City, California 91604

Mike Stoller Music (ASCAP)
 784 Park Avenue
 New York, New York 10021

Milk Money Music (ASCAP)
 c/o Segel & Goldman Inc.
 9126 Sunset Boulevard
 Los Angeles, California 90069

Mine Music, Ltd. (ASCAP)
 c/o S. Weintraub
 271 Madison Avenue
 New York, New York 10016

Miserable Melodies (ASCAP)
 c/o Mike's Artist Management
 Suite 301
 225 West 57th Street
 New York, New York 10019

Misery Loves Co.
 c/o Bearsville Record Co.
 Wittenburg Road
 Bearsville, New York 12409

Mister Sunshine Music, Inc. (BMI)
 c/o Patrick Armstrong
 Post Office Box 7877
 College Park Station
 Orlando, Florida 32804

Monosteri Music (ASCAP)
 c/o Zachary Glickman Artist
 Management
 Suite 205
 19301 Ventura Boulevard
 Tarzana, California 91356

Moriel Music (BMI)
 c/o Robert L. Kiser
 Suite 108
 4306 Crenshaw Boulevard
 Los Angeles, California 90008

Morning Pictures Music (ASCAP)
 see Fire and Water Songs

Edwin H. Morris Co. (ASCAP)
 see MPL Communications Inc.

Dale Morris Music (BMI)
 812 19th Avenue South
 Nashville, Tennessee 37203

Bryan Morrison Music, Inc. (ASCAP)
 c/o Roemer & Nadler, Esqs.
 3rd Floor
 437 Madison Avenue
 New York, New York 10022

Mother Fortune Inc. (BMI)
 641 Lexington Avenue
 New York, New York 10022

Mother Tongue Music (ASCAP)
 see Roger Cook Music

MPL Communications Inc. (ASCAP)
 c/o Lee Eastman
 39 West 54th Street
 New York, New York 10019

MTM Enterprises Inc. (ASCAP)
 see Reno-Metz Music Inc.

Mtume Music Publishing (BMI)
 54 Main Street
 Danbury, Connecticut 06810

Mumbi Music (BMI)
 c/o Satin Tenenbaum
 Elcher Zimmerman
 Suite 3700
 2049 Century Park East
 Los Angeles, California 90067

Munchkin Music (ASCAP)
 Attention: Frank Zappa
 Post Office Box 5265
 North Hollywood, California 91616

Muscle Shoals Sound Publishing Co., Inc. (BMI)
 Post Office Box 915
 Sheffield, Alabama 35660

Muscleman Music
 c/o Super Ron Music
 Loeb & Loeb
 10100 Santa Monica Boulevard
 Suite 2200
 Los Angeles, California 90067

Music City Music Inc. (ASCAP)
 see Combine Music Corp.

Music Corp. of America (BMI)
 see MCA, Inc.

321

List of Publishers

Music Theatre International
49 East 52nd Street
New York, New York 10022

Mycenae Music Publishing Co. (ASCAP)
c/o Cohen and Steinhart
Attention: Martin Cohen
Suite 1500
6430 Sunset Boulevard
Los Angeles, California 90028

N

Narrow Dude Music (ASCAP)
c/o J. Issac Personal Management
789 Southewst Underhill
Portland, Oregon 97219

Nebraska Music (ASCAP)
8607 Sherwood Drive
Los Angeles, California 90069

Willie Nelson Music Inc. (BMI)
225 Main Street
Danbury, Connecticut 06810

Neutral Gray Music (ASCAP)
No. 4D
405 West 45th Street
New York, New York 10036

New Daddy Music (BMI)
c/o Unichappell Music, Inc.
32nd Floor
810 Seventh Avenue
New York, New York 10019

New East Music (ASCAP)
c/o The Fitzgerald Hartley Co.
Suite 200
7250 Beverly Boulevard
Los Angeles, California 90036

New Generation Music (ASCAP)
Attention: Gary D. Anderson
7046 Hollywood Boulevard
Hollywood, California 90028

New Hidden Valley Music Co. (ASCAP)
c/o Ernst & Whinney
No. 2200
1875 Century Park East
Los Angeles, California 90067

New Tandem Music Co. (ASCAP)
c/o Tandem Productions
1901 Avenue of the Stars
Los Angeles, California 90067

Randy Newman Music (ASCAP)
c/o Gelfand, Rennert & Feldman
Suite 900
1880 Century Park East
Los Angeles, California 90067

Nick-O-Val Music (ASCAP)
332 West 71st Street
New York, New York 10023

Night Garden Music (BMI)
c/o Unichappell Music, Inc.
32nd Floor
810 Seventh Avenue
New York, New York 10019

Night Kitchen Music (ASCAP)
c/o Segel, Goldman & Magnow, Inc.
9348 Santa Monica Boulevard
Beverly Hills, California 90210

Night River Publishing (ASCAP)
c/o Jack Tempchin
Apartment 1013
103 North Highway 101
Encinatas, California 92024

No Ears Music (ASCAP)
c/o Evan R. Medow, Esq.
8th Floor
8444 Wilshire Boulevard
Beverly Hills, California 90211

Nonpariel Music (ASCAP)
see Walden Music, Inc.

Norbud (BMI)
see New Tandem Music Co.

Notable Music Co., Inc. (ASCAP)
Cy Coleman Enterprises
200 West 54th Street
New York, New York 10019

Nottsongs
c/o Careers Music, Inc.
Attention: Billy Meshel
8370 Wilshire Boulevard
Beverly Hills, California 90211

List of Publishers

Now Sounds Music (BMI)
9th Floor
1880 Century Park East
Los Angeles, California 90067

Noyb Music (BMI)
c/o Gary Corbett
2164 82nd Street
Brooklyn, New York 11214

Nymph Music (BMI)
Attention: Ron Shoup
43 Perry Street
New York, New York 10014

O

Oakfield Avenue Music Ltd. (BMI)
c/o David Gotterer
Mason & Co.
Suite 1800
75 Rockefeller Plaza
New York, New York 10019

Kenny O'Dell Music (BMI)
Box 43
Nolensville, Tennessee 37135

Off Backstreet Music (BMI)
90 Universal City Plaza
Universal City, California 91608

Old Fashion Music (ASCAP)
see Brockman Enterprises Inc.

Old Friends Music (BMI)
1225 16th Avenue South
Post Office Box 121076
Nashville, Tennessee 37212

Olga Music (BMI)
c/o Delores Jabara
135 79th Street
Brooklyn, New York 11209

Ollie Brown Sugar Music, Inc. (ASCAP)
c/o Moultrie Accountancy Corp.
Post Office Box 5270
Beverly Hills, California 90210

On the Boardwalk Music (BMI)
888 7th Avenue
New York, New York 10106

One To One Music Publishing Co. (ASCAP)
c/o Robert J. Bregman
Matt-Jen Entertainments, Ltd.
Apartment 13B
15 West 81st Street
New York, New York 10024

Ono Music (BMI)
Studio One
1 West 72nd Street
New York, New York 10023

Over The Rainbow Music Co. (ASCAP)
Suite 1502
6430 Sunset Boulevard
Hollywood, California 90028

Overdue Music (ASCAP)
Attention: David Walinski
7250 Beverly Boulevard
Suite 200
Los Angeles, California 90036

P

Pal-Park Music (ASCAP)
c/o Mitchell-Silberberg-Knupp
Suite 900
11377 West Olympic Boulevard
Los Angeles, California 90064

Pants Down Music (BMI)
c/o William Richard Cuomo
19815 Big Pines Highway
Valyermo, California 93563

Paperwaite Music (BMI)
c/o Twin Management Services Ltd.
641 Lexington Avenue
New York, New York 10022

Parker Music (BMI)
10th & Parker Street
Berkeley, California 94710

Park's Music
see MCA Music

Parody Publishing (BMI)
c/o Mr. Don Bowman
1538 North Grand Oaks
Pasadena, California 91104

323

List of Publishers

Parquet Music (BMI)
Suite 1120
111 West 57th Street
New York, New York 10019

Participation Music, Inc. (ASCAP)
c/o Zomba House
1348 Lexington Avenue
New York, New York 10128

Partner Music (BMI)
1518 Chelsea Avenue
Memphis, Tennessee 38108

Patchwork Music (ASCAP)
c/o David Loggins
Post Office Box 120475
Nashville, Tennessee 37212

Peabo Bryson Enterprises, Inc. (ASCAP)
Attention: Philip F. Ransom
1290 South
Omni International
Atlanta, Georgia 30303

Peer International Corp. (BMI)
see Peer-Southern Org.

Peer-Southern Org.
1740 Broadway
New York, New York 10019

Peg Music Co. (BMI)
c/o Earl S. Shuman
111 East 88th Street
New York, New York 10028

Pentagon Music Co. (BMI)
c/o Harold B. Lipsius
919 North Broad Street
Philadelphia, Pennsylvania 19123

Perfect Pinch Music (BMI)
c/o Stephen Lunt
207 East 37th Street
No. 4K
New York, New York 10016

Perk's Music, Inc. (BMI)
c/o Duchess Music Corp.
MCA Music
445 Park Avenue
New York, New York 10022

Peso Music (BMI)
6255 Sunset Boulevard
Suite 1019
Hollywood, California 90028

Petwolf Music (ASCAP)
1506 Dorothy Avenue
Simi Valley, California 93063

Phivin International Enterprises
see Geffen/Kaye Music

Phosphene Music (BMI)
c/o Craig Krampf
4249 Rhodes Avenue
Studio City, California 91604

Pi-Gem Music Publishing Co, Inc. (BMI)
Address unknown

Pods Publishing (BMI)
c/o Law Financial
Suite E
No. 1 Gate 6 Road
Sausalito, California 94965

Buster Poindexter, Inc. (BMI)
c/o Blue Sky Records, Inc.
745 Fifth Avenue
New York, New York 10022

Anita Pointer Publishing (BMI)
c/o Manatt, Phelps, Rothenberg,
& Tunney
1888 Century Park East
21st Floor
Los Angeles, California 90067

Ruth Pointer Publishing (BMI)
c/o Manatt Phelps Rothenberg
& Tunney
1888 Century Park East
21st Floor
Los Angeles, California 90067

Poison Oak Music (ASCAP)
c/o Segel, Goldman & Macnow, Inc.
9348 Santa Monica Boulevard
Beverly Hills, California 90210

Pokazuka (ASCAP)
see Alamo Music, Inc.

Pop 'N' Roll Music (ASCAP)
114 West 7th Street
Suite 717
Austin, Texas 78701

Popular Music Co. (ASCAP)
49 West 45th Street
New York, New York 10036

Porcara Music (ASCAP)
c/o Fitzgerald Hartley Co.
Suite 200
7250 Beverly Boulevard
Los Angeles, California 90036

Portal Music (BMI)
c/o Mitchell, Silberberg & Knupp
1800 Century Park East
Los Angeles, California 90067

Posey Publishing
Attention: Deborah Allen
4306 Ester Road
Nashville, Tennessee 37215

Postvalda Music (ASCAP)
c/o Bjerre & Miller
Suite 400
9350 Wilshire Boulevard
Beverly Hills, California 90212

Pragmavision Music (ASCAP)
c/o Flying Fish Records
1304 West Schubert
Chicago, Illinois 60614

Prater Music, Inc. (ASCAP)
Attention: Jean Prater
849 Huntleigh Drive
Naperville, Illinois 60540

Prime Street Music (ASCAP)
see April Music, Inc.

Prince Street Music (ASCAP)
Attention: John Frankenheimer, Esq.
Loeb & Loeb
10100 Santa Monica Boulevard
Suite 2200
Los Angeles, California 90046

Progeny Music (BMI)
c/o David Cohen
Plant, Cohen & Company
Suite 900
10900 Wilshire Boulevard
Los Angeles, California 90024

Prophecy Publishing, Inc. (ASCAP)
Post Office Box 4945
Austin, Texas 78765

Pseudo Songs
c/o Richard Raye Publications
Suite 3
13251 Ventura Boulevard
Studio City, California 91604

Pure Prairie League Music (ASCAP)
Attention Michael P. Reilly
c/o Daniel W. Tombragel
Mellott & Mellott
105 West 4th Street, No. 1217
Cincinnati, Ohio 45202

Putzy-Putzy Music (ASCAP)
c/o Segel and Goldman, Icn.
No. 304
9348 Santa Monica Boulevard
Beverly Hills, California 90210

Q

Quackenbush Music, Ltd. (ASCAP)
c/o Gelfand, Rennert & Feldman
Attention: Babbie Green
No. 900
1880 Century Park East
Los Angeles, California 90067

Queen Music Ltd. (BMI)
see Beechwood Music Corp.

Quixotic Music Corp. (ASCAP)
Attention: Eddie Reeves
Post Office Box 120716
Nashville, Tennessee 37212

R

Rabbit Rabbit Music Co. (ASCAP)
c/o Ronald Melrose
35 West 90th Street
Suite 4G
New York, New York 10024

Chick Rains Music (BMI)
c/o Gary K. Calder, Rainsongs Ltd.
2132 Northwest 27th
Oklahoma City, Oklahoma 73107

Random Notes (ASCAP)
see April Music, Inc.

List of Publishers

Rare Blue Music, Inc. (ASCAP)
15th Floor
645 Madison Avenue
New York, New York 10022

Ratt Music (BMI)
c/o Judith C. Dornstein, Esq.
Bushkin, Gaims & Gaines
2029 Century Park
East No. 2500
Los Angeles, California 90067

Ravensong Music (ASCAP)
Post Office Box 1402
Hendersonville, Tennessee 37075

Raydiola Music (ASCAP)
Post Office Box 5270
Beverly Hills, California 90210

Receive Music (BMI)
Box 3420
Nashville, Tennessee 37219

Red Admiral Music Inc. (BMI)
see Chrysalis Music Corp.

Red Aurra Publishing (BMI)
641 Lexington Avenue
New York, New York 10022

Red Bullet Music (ASCAP)
see Chappell & Co., Inc.

Red·Cloud Music Co. (ASCAP)
c/o The Fitzgerald Hartley Co.
Suite 200
7250 Beverly Boulevard
Los Angeles, California 90036

Red Network Music (BMI)
c/o RCA Records
Attention: Dorothy Schwartz
1133 Avenue of the Americas
New York, New York 10037

Red Snapper
see Fleetwood Mac Music Ltd.

Van Ross Redding Music
see Carollon Music Co.

Redeye Music Publishing Co. (ASCAP)
c/o Michael Mainieri
Comcenter
70 Greenwich Avenue
New York, New York 10011

Reformation Publishing USA
c/o Robbins Spielman Slayton & Co.
1700 Broadway
New York, New York 10019

Refuge Music, Inc. (ASCAP)
see WB Music Corp.

Regent Music (BMI)
110 East 59th Street
New York, New York 10022

Reggatta Music, Ltd.
c/o Phillips Gold & Company
1140 Avenue of the Americas
New York, New York 10036

Rehtakul Veets Music (ASCAP)
c/o The Fitzgerald Hartley Co.
Suite 200
7250 Beverly Boulevard
Los Angeles, California 90036

Reilla Music Corp. (BMI)
c/o Joseph E. Zynczak
PC
65 West 55ths Street
No. 4G
New York, New York 10019

Renjack Music (BMI)
see Mijac Music

Reno-Metz Music Inc. (ASCAP)
9000 Sunset Boulevard
Los Angeles, California 90210

Revelation Music Publishing Corp. (ASCAP)
Tommy Valando Publishing Group Inc.
1270 Avenue of the Americas
Suite 2110
New York, New York 10020

Rewind Music, Inc. (ASCAP)
10201 West Pico Boulevard
Los Angeles, California 90035

Rich Way Music, Inc. (BMI)
1117 17th Ave, South
Nashville, Tennessee 37212

Richer Music (ASCAP)
216 Chatsworth Drive
San Fernando, California 91340

Rick's Music Inc. (BMI)
see Chappell & Co., Inc.

Rightsong Music Inc. (BMI)
see Chappell & Co., Inc.

Rilting Music Inc. (ASCAP)
see Fiddleback Music Publishing Co., Inc.

Rit of Habeas (ASCAP)
c/o Barry A. Menes
Suite 1240
1901 Avenue of the Stars
Los Angeles, California 90067

Riva Music Ltd. (ASCAP)
see Arista Music, Inc.

Roaring Fork Music
Address unknown

Rock Steady Inc. (ASCAP)
c/o Aucoin Management
Rock Steady Music Division
645 Aucoin Management
New York, New York 10022

Rocknocker Music Co. (ASCAP)
c/o Joseph F. Rascoff & Co.
666 Fifth Avenue
New York, New York 10019

Rocksmith Music (ASCAP)
c/o Trust Music Management
Suite 705
6255 Sunset Boulevard
Hollywood, California 90028

Rod Stewart (ASCAP)
c/o Armstrong Hendler & Hirsch
Attention: Barry W. Tyerman
Suite 188
1888 Century Park East
Los Angeles, California 90067

Roland Robinson Music (BMI)
see Hitchings Music

Rose Bridge Music Inc. (BMI)
1121 South Glenstone
Springfield, Missouri 65804

Fred Rose Music, Inc. (BMI)
Post Office Box 40427
Nashville, Tennessee 37204

Roseynotes Music (BMI)
c/o Martin Wolff Associates
Post Office Box 4217
North Hollywood, California 91607

Rosstown Music (ASCAP)
c/o Loeb and Loeb
Attention: John T. Frankenheimer
Suite 2200
10100 Santa Monica Boulevard
Los Angeles, California 90067

Rosy Publishing Inc. (ASCAP)
1900 Avenue of the Stars
Suite 1600
Los Angeles, California 90067

Royalhaven Music, Inc. (BMI)
Post Office Box 120249
Nashville, Tennessee 37212

Rubber Band Music, Inc. (BMI)
c/o Gelfand, Breslaver, Rennert
and Feldman
Suite 900
1800 Century Park East
Los Angeles, California 90067

Rubicon Music (BMI)
8321 Lankershim Boulevard
North Hollywood, California 91605

Rude Music (BMI)
c/o Margolis Burrill & Besser
1901 Avenue of the Stars
No. 888
Los Angeles, California 90067

Rye-Boy Music (ASCAP)
c/o Joel S. Turtle
1032 Broadway
Russian Hill
San Francisco, California 94133

S

S J C Music (ASCAP)
c/o Jess S. Morgan & Co., Inc.
Attention: John E. Rigney
19th Floor
6420 Wilshire Boulevard
Los Angeles, California 90048

Sabal Music, Inc. (ASCAP)
Attention: Maggie Ward
1520 Demonbreun Street
Nashville, Tennessee 37203

Safespace Music (BMI)
see WB Music Corp.

327

List of Publishers

Carole Bayer Sager Music (BMI)
c/o Segel, Goldman and Macnow Inc.
9348 Santa Monica Boulevard
Beverly Hills, California 90210

Saggifire Music (ASCAP)
c/o April Music, Inc.
49 East 52nd Street
New York, New York 10022

Sailmaker Music (ASCAP)
Attention: Robert M. Millsap
Post Office Box 564
Hollister, Missouri 65672

Sailor Music (ASCAP)
c/o Gregory Fischbach
2029 Century Park East
North Tower Suite 1370
Los Angeles, California 90067

Saloon Songs, Inc.
see Sergeant Music Co.

Boz Scaggs Music (ASCAP)
c/o Front Line Management
9044 Melrose Avenue
Third Floor
Los Angeles, California 90069

Screen Gems-EMI Music Inc. (BMI)
6255 Sunset Boulevard
12th Floor
Hollywood, California 90028

Second Decade Music (BMI)
c/o TWM Management
641 Lexington Avenue
New York, New York 10022

See This House Music (ASCAP)
c/o Murphy & Kress
Suite 920
1925 Century Park East
Los Angeles, California 90067

Seesquared Music (BMI)
Suite 1
1266 Stanyan Street
San Francisco, California 94117

Senor Music (ASCAP)
Suite 1019
6255 Sunset Boulevard
Hollywood, California 90028

Sergeant Music Co. (ASCAP)
c/o Sinatra Enterprises
1041 No. Formosa Avenue
Hollywood, California 90046

Terry Shaddick Music (BMI)
c/o Terry Shaddick
21219 Lopez Street
Woodland Hills, California 91364

Shade Tree Music Inc. (BMI)
c/o Merle Haggard
Box 500
Bella Vista, California 96008

Shakeji Music (ASCAP)
3221 La Mirada
Las Vegas, Nevada 89120

Shakin Baker Music, Inc. (BMI)
c/o Howard Comart CPA
Room 532
1775 Broadway
New York, New York 10019

Hal Shaper Inc. (ASCAP)
c/o Music International Inc.
Attention: Dabney Miller
235 East 31st Street
New York, New York 10016

Shapiro, Bernstein & Co., Inc. (ASCAP)
Attention: Leon Brettler
10 East 53rd Street
New York, New York 10022

Sheer Music (ASCAP)
1915 Interlaken Drive East
Seattle, Washington 98112

Shel Sounds Music (BMI)
see Irving Music Inc.

Silver Fiddle (ASCAP)
c/o Segel & Goldman Inc.
9200 Sunset Boulevard
Suite 1000
Los Angeles, California 90069

Silver Nightingale Music (ASCAP)
Attention: Ms. Joan Nemour
200 Neptune Avenue
Encinitas, California 92024

Silverline Music, Inc. (BMI)
329 Rockland Road
Hendersonville, Tennessee 37075

Simile Music, Inc. (BMI)
see Famous Music Co.

Paul Simon Music (BMI)
1619 Broadway
New York, New York 10019

Sing a Song Publishing Co. (BMI)
Route 8
Box 532
Athens, Alabama 35611

Singing Ink Music (BMI)
Post Office Drawer 1300
Trinidad, California 95570

Singletree Music Co., Inc. (BMI)
815 18th Avenue South
Nashville, Tennessee 37213

Siquomb Publishing Corp. (BMI)
c/o Segel & Goldman Inc.
9348 Santa Monica Boulevard
Beverly Hills, California 90210

Sir & Trini Music (ASCAP)
c/o Rosenfeld, Kassoy & Kraus
Third Floor
270 North Canon Drive
Beverly Hills, California 90210

Sister John Music, Inc. (BMI)
c/o Publishers Licensing Corp.
94 Grand Avenue
Englewood, New Jersey 07631

Six Continents Music Publishing Inc.
8304 Beverly Blvd.
Los Angeles, California 90048

Six Pictures Music (BMI)
c/o Gelfand, Rennert & Feldman
1880 Century Park East
Number 900
Los Angeles, California 90067

Sixty Ninth Street Music (BMI)
c/o Joey Carbone
13142 Weddington Street
Van Nuys, California 91401

Skyhill Publishing Co., Inc. (BMI)
see Island Music

Slam Dunk Music (ASCAP)
1046 Carol Drive
Los Angeles, California 90069

Slapshot Music (BMI)
c/o Shankman De Blasio
185 Pier
Santa Monica, California 90405

Sneaker Songs (BMI)
468 South Aldenville
Coving, California 91723

Snow Music
c/o Jess Morgan & Co., Inc.
6420 Wilshire Boulevard
Nineteenth Floor
Los Angeles, California 90048

Snowden Music (ASCAP)
344 West 12th Street
New York, New York 10014

Soft Music (BMI)
c/o Randall Oda
2023 Tamalpais Avenue
El Cerrito, California 94530

Solid Smash Music Publishing Co, Inc.
(ASCAP)
Post Office Box 484
Reading, Pennsylvania 01867

Some Other Music
see Lipsync Music

Somerset Songs Publishing, Inc. (ASCAP)
Attention: Michael Jones
1790 Broadway
New York, New York 10019

Song Painter Music (BMI)
see Screen Gems-EMI Music Inc.

Song Tailors Music Co. (ASCAP)
Box 2631
Muscle Shoals, Alabama 35660

Songs Can Sing (ASCAP)
Post Office Box 36496
Los Angeles, California 90046

Songs of the Knight (BMI)
136 East 57th Street
New York, New York 10001

Southern Music Publishing Co., Inc.
(ASCAP)
Attention: Ralph Peer, II
1740 Broadway
New York, New York 10019

List of Publishers

Southern Nights Music Co. (ASCAP)
  35 Music Square East
  Nashville, Tennessee 37203

Southern Soul Music (BMI)
  see Tree Publishing Co., Inc.

Spaced Hands Music (BMI)
  5233 Verdun Avenue
  Los Angeles, California 90043

Special Rider Music (ASCAP)
  Post Office Box 860
  Cooper Station
  New York, New York 10276

Spectrum VII (ASCAP)
  6th Floor
  1635 Cahuenga Boulevard
  Hollywood, California 90028

Spelling Venture Music (BMI)
  Attention: Martie Long
  1041 North Formosa Avenue
  Hollywood, California 90046

Bruce Springsteen (ASCAP)
  c/o Jon Landau Management, Inc.
  Attention: Barbara Carr
  No. 1202
  136 East 57th Street
  New York, New York 10021

Sprocket Music, Inc. (BMI)
  10201 West Pico Boulevard
  Los Angeles, California 90035

Stage & Screen Music Inc. (BMI)
  see Unichappell Music Inc.

Arthur Buster Stahr Music (ASCAP)
  see Bug Music

State of the Artless
  Address unknown

State of the Arts Music (ASCAP)
  7250 Beverly Boulevard
  Los Angeles, California 90036

Statler Brothers Music (BMI)
  14 Circle East
  Nashville, Tennessee 37203

Billy Steinberg Music (ASCAP)
  c/o Manatt, Phelps, Rothenberg,
  and Tunney
  11355 West Olympic Boulevard
  Los Angeles, California 90064

Stephen Mitchell Music (BMI)
  Portchester Music, Inc.
  121 South Rossmore Avenue
  Los Angeles, California 90004

Sterling Music Co. (ASCAP)
  Suite 202
  8150 Beverly Boulevard
  Los Angeles, California 90048

Stigwood Music Inc. (BMI)
  see Unichappell Music Inc.

Stone City Music (ASCAP)
  c/o Gross, Shuman, Brizdle
  Laub, Gilfillan PC
  2600 Main Place Tower
  Buffalo, New York 14202

Stone Diamond Music Corp. (BMI)
  6255 Sunset Boulevard
  Suite 1600-Department 4-7566
  Los Angeles, California 90028

Stonebridge Music (ASCAP)
  The Bicycle Music Co.
  8075 West Third Street, Suite 400
  Los Angeles, California 90048

Strange Euphoria Music (ASCAP)
  c/o VWC Management, Inc.
  Attention: Ann Wilson
  Suite 201
  13343 Bel-Red Road
  Bellevue, Washington 98005

Street Talk Tunes
  see April Music, Inc.

Streetwise Music (ASCAP)
  c/o Matthew Weiner
  623 North La Jolla Avenue
  Los Angeles, California 90048

Stygian Songs (ASCAP)
  see Almo Music Corp.

Sugar Hill Music Publishing, Ltd.
  96 West Street
  Englewood, New Jersey 07631

Sugar Song Publications (BMI)
  c/o Dutchess Music Corp.
  Attention: John McKellen
  445 Park Avenue
  New York, New York 10022

Sunflower County Songs (ASCAP)
Post Office Drawer No. 37
Hendersonville, Tennessee 37075

Sunset Burgundy Music, Inc. (ASCAP)
see Thriller Miller Music

SVO Music
c/o Aaron Spelling Productions
Attention: Marvin Katz-VP/BSNS AFRS
1041 North Formosa Avenue
Los Angeles, California 90046

Swallow Turn Music (ASCAP)
see WB Music Corp.

Swallowfork Music, Inc. (ASCAP)
453 Capri Road
Cocoa Beach, Florida 32931

Swanee Bravo Music (BMI)
c/o Marty Panzer
Apartment 1627
500 East 77th Street
New York, New York 10162

Sweet Jelly Roll Music, Inc. (ASCAP)
Post Office Box 9109
San Rafael, California 94912

Sweet Summer Night Music (ASCAP)
Attention: Gerald F. Rosenblatt
Wilshire Palisades Building
Penthouse
1299 Ocean Avenue
Santa Monica, California 90401

Sweet Talk Music Co. (ASCAP)
6511 Redding
Houston, Texas 77036

Swiftwater Music (ASCAP)
Attention: David L. Frishberg
6053 Burralo Avenue
Van Nuys, California 91401

Swing Tet Publishing (BMI)
c/o Dave Roberts
Box 153
2520 North Lincoln
Chicago, Illinois 60614

Sycamore Valley Music Inc. (BMI)
2 Music Circle South
Nashville, Tennessee 37203

T

Talk Dirty Music (BMI)
c/o The Bug Music Group
9th Floor
6777 Hollywood Boulevard
Hollywood, California 90028

Talk Time Music, Inc. (ASCAP)
35 Lake Shore Drive
Copake, New York 12516

Tan Division Music Publishing (ASCAP)
c/o Peter Van Brunt
1635 North Cahuenga Boulevard
Hollywood, California 90028

Tarka Music Co. (ASCAP)
see Island Music

Tauripin Tunes (ASCAP)
c/o The Doobro Corp.
Attention: Kathy Nelson
Post Office Box 359
Sonoma, California 95476

Telephone Pole Music Publishing Co. (BMI)
Post Office Box 232
Marblehead, Massachusetts 01945

Temp Co. (BMI)
Attention: Rochelle Mackabee
Suite 302A
1800 North Argyle
Hollywood, California 90028

Tempo Music (ASCAP)
c/o Alexandria House
Post Office Box 300
Alexandria, Indiana 46001

Terraform Music (ASCAP)
see Fourth Floor Music Inc.

Thames Talent Publishing, Ltd. (ASCAP)
626 Lyon Farm Road
Greenwich, Connecticut 06830

Thickouit Music (BMI)
c/o Alan Thicke
15431 Dickens Street
Sherman Oaks, California 91403

Bob Thiele Music, Ltd. (ASCAP)
1414 Avenue of the Americas
New York, New York 10019

List of Publishers

Thirty-Four Music (ASCAP)
4329 Colfax Avenue
Studio City, California 91604

Thomas Browne Publishing
Address unknown

Threesome Music
1801 Avenue of the Stars
Suite 911
Los Angeles, California 90067

Thriller Miller Music (ASCAP)
Suite 250
9034 Sunset Boulevard
Los Angeles, California 90069

Timberwolf Music (BMI)
2520 Cedar Elm Lane
Plano, Texas 75075

Time Coast Music (BMI)
No. 1128
6253 Hollywood Boulevard
Hollywood, California 90028

Tintagel Music, Inc. (ASCAP)
c/o Earle Enterprises
Attention: Linda Wortman
160 West 88th Street
New York, New York 10024

Tiny Tunes (ASCAP)
c/o Bug Music Group
9th Floor
6777 Hollywood Boulevard
Hollywood, California 90028

Tionna Music
see Controversy Music

Tom Collins Music Corp. (BMI)
Post Office Box 121407
Nashville, Tennessee 37212

Tom Eyen's Publishing Co. (BMI)
see Dreamgirls Music

Toneman Music Inc. (BMI)
6603 Lincoln Avenue
Carmichael, California 95608

Total X Publishing Co. (ASCAP)
see Tempo Music

Townsway Music (BMI)
c/o Mr. Garry Kief
Post Office Box 69180
Hollywood, California 90069

Towser Tunes Inc. (BMI)
c/o Weiss and Meibach
888 7th Avenue
New York, New York 10019

Tree Publishing Co., Inc. (BMI)
Box 1273
Nashville, Tennessee 37203

Tri-Chappell Music Inc. (ASCAP)
see Chappell & Co., Inc.

TRO-Cromwell Music Inc. (ASCAP)
10 Columbus Circle
New York, New York 10019

Troutman's Music (BMI)
c/o Larry Troutman
2010 Salem Avenue
Dayton, Ohio 45406

Trumar Music (BMI)
c/o Prelude Records
200 West 57th Street
New York, New York 10019

Trunksong Music (BMI)
c/o The Shokatt Company, Ltd.
Suite 1A
340 West 55th Street
New York, New York 10019

TSP Music, Inc.
1875 Century Park East
Suite 700
Los Angeles, California 90067

Turtle Music (BMI)
c/o Theodore Glasser
No. 17
5229 Balboa Boulevard
Encino, California 91316

Tutone-Keller Music (BMI)
see New Daddy Music

Twentieth Century-Fox Music Corp.
(ASCAP)
Attention: Herbert N. Eiseman
Post Office Box 900
Beverly Hills, California 90213

Twentieth Century Music Corp. (ASCAP)
1619 Broadway
New York, New York 10019

Twist & Shout Music (ASCAP)
2728 Union Street
San Francisco, California 94123

Two-Sons Music (ASCAP)
44 Music Square West
Nashville, Tennessee 37203

U

Ujima Music (ASCAP)
c/o Fredric W Ansis, Esq.
25th Floor
2029 Century Park East
Los Angeles, California 90067

Uncle Ronnie's Music Co., Inc. (ASCAP)
1775 Broadway
New York, New York 10019

Under Cut Music Publishing Co., Inc.
(BMI)
c/o Robert Casper
1780 Broadway
New York, New York 10019

Unforgettable Songs (BMI)
Address unknown

Unichappell Music Inc. (BMI)
810 Seventh Avenue
32nd Floor
New York, New York 10019

Unicity Music, Inc. (ASCAP)
c/o MCA Music
445 Park Avenue
New York, New York 10022

United Lion Music Inc. (BMI)
c/o United Artists Corp.
729 Seventh Avenue
New York, New York 10019

Upward Spiral Music (ASCAP)
see WB Music Corp.

Urge Music (BMI)
c/o Blackwood Music, Inc.
49 East 52nd Street
New York, New York 10022

V

Val-ie Joe Music (BMI)
c/o Shelton, Kalcheim and Cotnoir
79 West Monroe Street
Suite 1305
Chicago, Illinois 60603

Valgovino Music (BMI)
c/o Jess Morgan & Co.
Attention: John Rigney
19th Floor
6420 Wilshire Boulevard
Los Angeles, California 90048

Van Halen Music (ASCAP)
Attention: Gail Liss
6525 Sunset Boulevard
Seventh Floor
Hollywood, California 90028

Van Hoy Music (BMI)
c/o Unichappell Music, Inc.
810 Seventh Avenue
New York, New York 10019

Vandorf Songs Co. (ASCAP)
15625 Vandorf Place
Encino, California 91436

Velvet Apple Music (BMI)
Three International
8 Music Square West
Nashville, Tennessee 37212

Very Every Music, Inc. (ASCAP)
c/o Roberta Flack
One West 72nd Street
New York, New York 10023

Virgin Music, Inc. (ASCAP)
Attention: Ron Shoup
43 Perry Street
New York, New York 10014

Virgin Music Ltd. (ASCAP)
see Chappell & Co., Inc.

Visa Music (ASCAP)
c/o Happy Sack Music
Attention: Franny Parrish
5102 Vineland Avenue
North Hollywood, California 91601

333

List of Publishers

W

Walden Music, Inc. (ASCAP)
Attention: Bonnie Blumenthal
75 Rockefeller Plaza
New York, New York 10019

Walkin Music (BMI)
Ziffren Brittenham Gullent & Ingber
Suite 2350
2049 Century Park East
Los Angeles, California 90067

Wallet Music (BMI)
Suite 2270
1900 Avenue of the Stars
Los Angeles, California 90067

Warner Brothers, Inc. (ASCAP)
9000 Sunset Boulevard
Los Angeles, California 90069

Warner House of Music (BMI)
Penthouse
9000 Sunset Boulevard
Los Angeles, California 90069

Warner-Tamerlane Publishing Corp. (BMI)
see WB Music Corp.

Watch Hill Music (BMI)
c/o Unichappell Music, Inc.
32nd Floor
810 Seventh Avenue
New York, New York 10019

WB Gold Music Corp. (ASCAP)
c/o Warner Brothers Music
Penthouse
9000 Sunset Boulevard
Los Angeles, California 90069

WB Music Corp. (ASCAP)
c/o Warner Brothers, Inc.
Attention: Leslie E. Bider
Penthouse
9000 Sunset Boulevard
Los Angeles, California 90069

Web 4 Music Inc. (BMI)
2107 Faulkner Road Northeast
Atlanta, Georgia 30324

Webo Girl Music/WB Music Corp. (ASCAP)
c/o Rubin, Baum, Levin, Cowstant, Friedman
645 Fifth Avenue
New York, New York 10022

Wedot Music (ASCAP)
Attention: Joseph E. Webb
809 East 6th Street
New York, New York 10009

Weed High Nightmare Music (BMI)
c/o Screen Gems-EMI Music, Inc.
6920 Sunset Boulevard
Hollywood, California 90028

Welbeck Music
see Cherry Lane Music Co., Inc.

Welbeck Music Corp. (ASCAP)
Total Video Music
c/o ATV Music Group
Suite 723
6255 Sunset Boulevard
Hollywood, California 90028

Welk Music Group
1299 Ocean Avenue
Suite 800
Santa Monica, California 90401

Hall-Clement Publications (BMI)
see Welk Music Group

Vogue Music (BMI)
see Welk Music Group

Hall-Clement Publications (BMI)
see Welk Music Group

Vogue Music (BMI)
see Welk Music Group

Hall-Clement Publications (BMI)
see Welk Music Group

Vogue Music (BMI)
see Welk Music Group

Hall-Clement Publications (BMI)
see Welk Music Group

Vogue Music (BMI)
see Welk Music Group

Hall-Clement Publications (BMI)
see Welk Music Group

Vogue Music (BMI)
see Welk Music Group

Hall-Clement Publications (BMI)
see Welk Music Group

Well Received Music (ASCAP)
c/o Joel S. Turtle, Esq.
1032 Broadway
Russian Hill
San Francisco, California 94133

Welsh Witch Publishing (BMI)
c/o Gelfand, Breslauer, Rennert &
Feldman
1880 Century Park East
Suite 900
Los Angeles, California 90067

Wenkewa Music (ASCAP)
c/o Fitzgerald-Hartley Co.
Suite 200
7250 Beverly Boulevard
Los Angeles, California 90036

White Oak Songs (ASCAP)
see Canopy Music Inc.

Bobby Whiteside Ltd. (ASCAP)
Teapot Products Division
Attention: Bobby Whiteside
526 70th Street
Darien, Illinois 60559

Whitsett Churchill Music (BMI)
c/o Tim Whitsett
4033 Manhattan Drive
Jackson, Mississippi 39206

Wicked Stepmother Music Publishing Corp.
(ASCAP)
1790 Broadway
New York, New York 10019

Wide Music (BMI)
c/o Segel & Goldman Inc.
9348 Santa Monica, Suite 304
Los Angeles, California 90210

Wild Gator Music (ASCAP)
see Gomace Music, Inc.

Willesden Music, Inc. (BMI)
c/o Zomba House
1348 Lexington Avenue
New York, New York 10028

Wimot Music Publishing (BMI)
c/o Alan Rubens
1307 Vine Street
Philadelphia, Pennsylvania 19107

Wong Music (ASCAP)
c/o Champion Entertainment
130 West 57th Street
Suite 12B
New York, New York 10019

Wood Hall Publishing Co. (BMI)
1025 17th Avenue, South
Nashville, Tennessee 37212

Wood Street Music, Inc. (BMI)
21051 Costanso Street
Woodland Hills, California 91364

World Song Publishing, Inc. (ASCAP)
c/o Chappell & Co., Inc.
810 Seventh Avenue
New York, New York 10019

Wow and Flutter Music Publishing
(ASCAP)
c/o Jess S. Morgan & Co., Inc.
6420 Wilshire Boulevard
19th Floor
Los Angeles, California 90048

Y

Yanina Music (ASCAP)
c/o Booker
Apartment 6B
176 West 87th Street
New York, New York 10024

Yeah Inc. (ASCAP)
Mr. Melvin Van Peebles
850 7th Avenue
New York, New York 10019

Yellow Brick Road Music (ASCAP)
7250 Beverly Boulevard
Los Angeles, California 90036

Yeston Music, Ltd.
c/o Maury Yeston
21 Pine Ridge Road
Woodbridge, Connecticut 06525

Yontrop Music
see Entertainment Co. Music Group

List of Publishers

Yougoulei Music (ASCAP)
 c/o Fitzgerald-Hartley Co.
 No. 200
 7250 Beverly Boulevard
 Los Angeles, California 90036

Z

Ze'ev Music
 see Pal-Park Music

Zeitgeist Music Co. (BMI)
 c/o Gretchen Cryer
 885 West End Avenue
 New York, New York 10025

Zero Productions (BMI)
 c/o Clog Holdings
 3300 Warner Boulevard
 Burbank, California 91501

Zevon Music (BMI)
 c/o Jess Morgan & Co., Inc.
 6420 Wilshire Boulevard
 Nineteenth Floor
 Los Angeles, California 90048

Zomba Enterprises, Inc. (BMI)
 c/o Zomba House
 1348 Lexington Avenue
 New York, New York 10128

Zubaida Music (ASCAP)
 see Arista Music, Inc.